SHATTERED SILENCE

JUDITH MARSHALL

PINNACLE BOOKS
WINDSOR PUBLISHING CORP.

PINNACLE BOOKS

are published by

Windsor Publishing Corp.
475 Park Avenue South
New York, NY 10016

First Printing: April, 1993

Printed in the United States of America

One

The sound of gunfire shattered the silence of the night. Filled with sudden terror, Alison sprang from her bed and ran through the darkness to the stairway. Leaning over the balcony, she caught a glimpse of a shadowy figure dart into the foyer, open the front door, and vanish into the night. An eerie quiet enveloped the house, followed seconds later by the screech of tires on the driveway. She raced to the foot of the stairs, just as her father staggered out of his study and collapsed in a heap on the marble floor of the foyer. For one horrifying moment, she stood paralyzed, unable to comprehend.

Oh my God! No! Never before in her life had Alison known real fear, panicky fear. She tried to run, but her legs buckled; she wanted to scream, but no sound came; she struggled to breathe, but could only manage audible gasps. Forcing herself to move, she made it to his side and dropped to her knees. *The gunfire . . . oh my God, he's been shot . . . the blood . . . oh no, so much blood.* Thinking was so hard. Automatically, she felt his neck for a pulse. *Thank God . . . he's alive. Help . . . I've got to get help.* She ran to the phone and dialed 911.

When a man's voice answered, she stammered, unable to put an intelligible sentence together. "My dad . . . been shot . . . please help!"

"Ma'am, just try to settle down. Now start from the beginning." His voice was calm and reassuring. Obviously he had dealt with this kind of reaction before. "Are you located in the Dallas city limits?"

"Yes."

"And the address?"

"424 Stillmeadow, just off Inwood, and hurry!"

"Now quickly try to tell me what happened."

"Please . . . this is taking so much time . . . it's my dad—Derek Archer—he's been shot. Please, for God's sakes, get an ambulance out here!"

"Who's your doctor, ma'am?"

"Doyle Peterson. Please have him meet us at Baylor Hospital and hurry!"

"Hang in there, ma'am—we're on our way."

Alison rushed back to her father and felt for a pulse. It was weak, but his heart was still beating. Maybe, maybe he still had a chance. She took a deep breath and glanced at the clock. One fifteen. Sitting on the cold floor, she stroked Derek's hand. *Oh God, please don't let him die!* Blood had soaked through her filmy nightgown, but she barely noticed. The waiting was so hard, her breathing became heavy, as if she could force her father to cling to life while she breathed for him. *I love you, Dad, I need you . . . don't leave me.*

The police arrived just as the ambulance pulled up. Quickly the paramedics examined Derek Archer, then placed him on a stretcher. One policeman checked the study and one the downstairs rooms, while another inspected the door and walked outside shining a flashlight on the grounds and windows.

A female officer walked over to Alison and put a blanket over her shoulders. "I'll go with you to change," she said.

Reluctantly, Alison let go of her dad's hand and rose from the floor.

"Hold it a minute," one officer said. "I want to ask Miss Archer a couple of questions."

Alison drew the blanket closer around her. "Not now. I have to hurry and change, so I can go with my dad. If he comes to on the way, he'll—"

"Okay." The officer gestured his approval to the woman with Alison. "But the ambulance is going ahead without you. We'll get you to the hospital, after you explain exactly what happened here."

"Oh no . . . I'm riding in that ambulance. I'll tell you what I know, but I have to be with my father. All that can wait." Alison rushed up the stairs with the policewoman following close behind. But in the few moments it took her to throw on a pair of slacks and a sweater, she heard the scream of the siren as the ambulance raced away from the house.

"Damn! Damn you!" Alison cried as she ran down the stairs. "How dare you? What right have you to—"

"Sorry," the officer said, "but we haven't established the motive for this crime or who the perpetrator was. You could possibly be a suspect, and we can't allow—"

"What? A *suspect!* I called you, remember? All I know is that I woke up because of a noise that sounded like a shot. Someone ran out the front door, and that was when my dad came out of the study and fell on the floor right here." She pointed to the pool of blood. "I called for help immediately. I'm not staying here another second, so either you get me

7

to the hospital right now, or I'll take my own car. It's up to you."

The superior officer gave a nod and quickly Alison was ushered out the front door. The others stayed behind to continue with the investigation.

Dr. Peterson had just arrived at the hospital when Alison walked into the emergency room. His face looked solemn as he shook his head and put his arm around her. Neither spoke a word as he embraced her for a few moments, then turned to enter the trauma room, issuing swift, explicit orders to the staff. A nurse led Alison to a chair in the waiting room.

Barely aware of the throng of injured people filing through the automatic doors, Alison sat alone in utter despondency, her arms hanging loosely by her side, her face pale and drawn. Each time a white uniform rustled past her, Alison's heart gave a frenzied leap, the hope that she might glean some news rising inside her. Finally a sweet-faced nurse approached her, a paper cup in her hand.

"Would you like some coffee, Miss Archer?"

"Yes, thanks . . . any news yet?"

"No, the doctor's still working on him. Maybe it won't be much longer."

Gratefully, Alison sipped the coffee, the hot liquid slowly warming her shivering body.

"Miss Archer?"

Startled, Alison looked up and saw an officer standing over her. She nodded.

"Derek Archer is your father?" Without waiting for a reply, he went on, "Who was it that shot him?" His manner was brusk, no nonsense.

"I haven't the slightest idea." Alison's voice was curt. This man had such a cold, heartless attitude, while her dad lay in that little room fighting for his life.

"Do you own a gun?"

"No, of course not! Wait a minute . . . do you think that I—"

"If you'll just answer a few questions—"

"No, I won't. All I care about right now is my dad. I've got to know if he's going to live. Please leave me alone."

"I'm just doing my job, ma'am." The policeman looked downright bored. He'd evidently heard all this before.

Alison was on the verge of venting all her pent-up emotions when she saw a familiar figure coming toward her. Jumping to her feet, she flung herself into his arms. "Oh, John, I'm so glad you're here. How did you know?"

"Darling, are you all right?" John Carpenter was a handsome man, fair-haired, tall, and impeccably groomed. He held Alison at arm's length for a moment, looked at her face, then folded his arms around her. "Doyle had his exchange call me as soon as he got the word. He knew you'd need me."

Alison couldn't help noting that her fiancé had obviously taken the time to shower and shave before coming to her rescue. Odd, she thought, how John had held her away from himself momentarily. Maybe he was checking to see if she had on makeup. It would be so like him to guard against soiling that cashmere sports coat. What petty thoughts to be having at a time like this. She was angry with herself for being so sensitive, and held his hand as they approached the row of chairs. The policeman hadn't moved.

"John, please tell this man to leave me alone . . . I'm scared as hell. Dad's been in that room so long. I told the police at the house everything I know, and I can't answer any more questions right now. I'm afraid they even suspect me. Can you imagine anything so stupid?"

John walked over to the officer and spoke quietly. Moments later, the policeman left. Alison was grateful for the ease with which he had dismissed the man. Thank God John was with her. He sat down beside her.

"What in the world happened? What did you mean about the police suspecting you? Doyle's exchange mentioned that he'd been shot. Is that true?"

"Yes, it's true." For the next few minutes, Alison launched into the story again, reliving the nightmare. Now that she was no longer alone, she began to tremble, and the tears she'd been holding back streamed down her face.

John produced a linen handkerchief. "You poor thing. Who called the ambulance?" He held her in his arms and patted her auburn hair, as though comforting a child.

"Why, I did. No one else was in the house." Irritated, Alison wondered if he thought her incapable of knowing what to do. She glanced at the trauma room door. Oh, what was taking so long? Why didn't someone at least come out and tell her what was going on?

She looked at John and realized that she'd known him most of her life. They had grown up together, their engagement taken for granted by both of their families. They had even managed to attend college in New Orleans at the same time, Alison at Sophie Newcomb and John at Tulane. Even though the Carpenters had "old" money and were considered true Dallasites—a label hard to come by in Texas—the Archer family was also well respected, especially among bankers and those in the oil business. Having been engaged for a year, Alison and John planned to marry in June.

Derek Archer had never remarried after his wife died in an accident years ago in France, leaving him with a broken heart and a five-year-old child to raise. Instead, he threw himself into Megtex, his company that built oil and gas pipelines throughout the world. He had acquired a substantial empire for his only daughter. It would all be hers upon his death.

In order to maintain her own lifestyle and establish independence, Alison had moved out of the big house five years ago. She had been working with her father at Megtex since college, and still loved her job. Derek fondly called her his troubleshooter. Three weeks ago, she gave up her condo and moved back into the family home, the site of her upcoming wedding. Thank God she was there tonight.

"Maybe the killer thought Dad still lived alone," she said, thinking out loud. "We haven't had live-in help for years. Juanita doesn't get to work until eight, and the housecleaners only come twice a week." Her mind whirled. Who was that dark figure slinking out the front door? Who could have hated her dad enough to kill him? Alison knew these questions would haunt her for a long time to come.

"You lost me a long time ago," John said. "Just start from the beginning. I gather there was a break-in and Derek was shot. Was there a struggle? Anything stolen?"

Alison felt blank. "I really don't know. I never even looked in the study. All I could think of was getting him to a hospital. God, what a nightmare! Someone went out the door . . . and Dad's blood all over . . ." Alison hid her face in her hands.

11

"Never mind, darling, we'll talk about it later." Once again John held her close.

Moments later, Dr. Peterson emerged from the trauma room. Alison and John rose as one, anxious to hear what he had to say. Peterson looked at Alison. "The bullet went through Derek's spleen. It's lodged in his liver, and we haven't been able to stop the bleeding." He took Alison's hand. "We just can't wait any longer, so we're taking Derek up to surgery right now. It's our only hope of stopping the flow of blood . . . he's lost so much already."

"Can you remove the bullet?" John asked.

"Oh hell, we'll get it out if we can. The important thing right now is to keep him from bleeding to death." He turned to Alison again. "We'll be in the operating room on the fifth floor. A nurse will show you the waiting room up there. I'll get back to you as soon as I can."

"Please, may I just see him . . . speak to him?" Alison fought hard to control her voice.

"Sure. Tell you what, when we get him on the gurney, you can walk along with him as far as the elevator." He rushed off, leaving them looking at each other with misgivings.

Within seconds, Dr. Peterson appeared again, this time with two nurses and an intern, all handling various bottles and tubes as they pushed the gurney at a fast pace.

Alison rushed along, talking to the unconscious form that was her father. He looked so pale and shrunken that he hardly seemed like the robust man who was always there for her, the big strapping man she had joked with at dinner just a few hours ago. Tears flooded her eyes. "I'm here, Dad . . . hang tough . . . I need you . . . I love you." The elevator doors opened. That was as far as she was allowed to go.

* * *

The Archer house buzzed with activity. Lt. Nick McAllister of homicide had just arrived, and the man who had originally tried to question Alison had begun to fill him in.

McAllister was a tall, rangy man in his mid-thirties, with dark hair and a five o'clock shadow to match. It was after two in the morning, and he looked as though he'd just fallen out of bed, which was definitely the case. He paid close attention to every detail of how the investigation was going.

"Rich guy, huh? You say there's no sign of a break-in?"

"Everything's shipshape," Colby said. "No forced doors or windows. Hell, doesn't even look like an ashtray was disturbed. If there was something stolen, it sure wasn't any paintings. Just look at all this expensive stuff hanging on the walls. And you should see the jewelry upstairs. Enough to knock your eyes out. If you ask me, Zsa Zsa would kill to meet this dude."

"So how do you think this guy got in?" McAllister asked. His eyes took in every inch of the study as he listened to Colby.

"Looks like he just waltzed right through that front door. It wasn't locked when we got here. Unless, of course, the daughter did it. Claimed the sound of a shot woke her. We couldn't get much more out of her."

Nick ran his finger over Derek's desk, then held it up to the light. "Not a speck of dust, must have a good housekeeper. Sure no one else was in the house?"

"The daughter said no; she was here alone with

13

her father. Like I said, she claims she was asleep."

"Doesn't this daughter have a name?" Nick didn't try to hide the impatience in his voice.

"Yessir, Alison Archer, sir." Colby looked miffed.

"Sounds to me like you had good cause to suspect her. Why did you let her leave?"

Colby was almost twice Nick's age. He looked at him sheepishly. "She was acting like her heart was breaking. Wouldn't talk anyway, so I let Walters drive her to Baylor. Hell, she's not going anywhere. We've got Lockhart over there, keeping an eye on her."

"Yeah, I know, you're just an old softy." Nick smiled for the first time.

Colby's face flushed. "Jeez, you should have seen her, Nick, just sitting there in a white gown, on that cold floor, barefooted, with blood all over her, kinda rocking back and forth. She looked so pathetic, not a tear in sight, but what a build! Christ, you could see everything."

"So, why do you suspect her? There's a lot of compassion in your voice, buddy."

"Well, nothing's been touched, no forced entry, so it sure looks like an inside job. Who knows, maybe she let some shooter in to do the job for her. I'll tell you one thing, though, if she did it, she's already sorry. Nobody can put on an act like that."

"Okay, okay." Nick walked back into the foyer with Colby following. "Was the door latch dusted for prints? And what about the alarm system?"

"Yeah, we dusted everything. Found lots of prints, but they all look alike so far. If it was an outside job, the guy wore gloves. About the alarm—that was strange, too. We called their service, but they hadn't gotten any signal all night. I figured it could have

14

been that Archer didn't ever turn it on until he went to bed."

"Looks to me like you've done a damn thorough job. Guess I haven't been wasting my time with my daily pep talks." Nick grinned and put his arm around Colby's shoulder, then turned to the policewoman. "Did you get Miss Archer's gown? Understand it was loaded with blood."

"Sure did, right here in this plastic bag." Eve Bailey was another officer who could be counted on.

"Good, have the lab check it for powder burns, just in case." McAllister looked around to see that all the ropes of tape used to cordon off the area were in position, and walked down the wide hall to the drawing room.

When he switched on the lights, the first thing that caught his eye was the portrait of a woman hanging over the fireplace. He sucked in his breath at the sight of her. She couldn't have been over thirty years old when this portrait was painted. He noticed that glowing auburn hair, fine, even features, creamy white skin, and clear green eyes that seemed to be looking right at him. Something about her grabbed him deep inside. He wondered if she could possibly be Alison Archer. No time to dwell on that now. He checked around the room for several minutes, then stopped to stare at the portrait one more time before turning off the lights and going back to the study.

"Okay, boys, let's wrap it up and get out of here." Nick designated a patrolman who would remain on the property until the relief man showed up at eight, then he watched them board their cars and cruise down the long, winding drive that led from the Archer estate to the street. Nick stayed on another hour, carefully going through every room in the house, hoping to find some clue that the others might have missed.

The nurse coming on duty at 7:00 A.M. brought Alison a fresh cup of coffee, just as Dr. Peterson came out of the operating room. He looked haggard and tired, as though he had lost several pounds since Alison last saw him. But this time, he was smiling.

Alison held the coffee out to him. "You look like you need this more than I do." She searched his face, her eyes full of questions. John jumped up and stood beside her, holding her hand.

"No thanks, think I'll have some juice first. Derek is in intensive care. We managed to stop the bleeding and removed the bullet, too. But I have to warn you, his condition is rocky. We'll keep him in I.C.U. for the time being, and he'll be continually monitored."

"Oh thank you, thank you, Doyle." Alison touched his arm and gave him a smile of relief.

Just then, a nurse appeared with a large glass of orange juice for the doctor. Thanking her, he sat down to rest a moment, still wearing the hospital greens. Doyle Peterson had been one of Derek Archer's closest friends, as far back as Alison could remember. She knew what a strain this night had been for him, too.

"How soon can I see Dad?"

"You can go in a few minutes, but he won't be awake for several hours. Why don't you try to get some sleep? We'll fix you up in a room on this floor."

Alison looked at John. "You need some rest, too, darling. Why don't you go home? I'll be fine now that I know Dad has a fighting chance."

"Well, if you're sure you don't mind . . . I could

16

use some sleep and a shower." John gathered some of the empty styrofoam cups and napkins to discard on his way out. "I'll check with you in a couple of hours. Can I bring you anything from the house?"

"No, but do me a favor . . . call Juanita at her home." Alison rummaged in her purse, pulled out a pen, and found the back of a gasoline receipt to write on. "Here's her number . . . tell her what happened, so she won't faint when she comes to work. Poor thing, she's going to be terribly upset. I feel sure the police will still be around."

"Consider it done." John pocketed the scrap of paper, stooped to kiss Alison, and was off down the corridor.

"Here, sit next to me, Alison." Doyle Peterson moved to make room for her. "Hope you don't think I'm prying, but what the hell happened? Where did that bullet come from, and who in God's name put it there?" He looked at Alison, his eyes troubled.

"I really don't know." Alison felt distraught as she pushed her hair out of her face. For the first time, she thought of what a mess she must be, not a drop of makeup and her hair uncombed. "The sound of a shot woke me, then I saw someone go out the door. Dad staggered out of the study and collapsed, and I made the call. That's it."

"That's it?" Dr. Peterson looked at her incredulously. "How did this person get in?"

Alison put her face in her hands. "I simply don't know. It all happened so fast."

Doyle cradled her in his arms. "Don't think about it right now." He stopped a passing nurse. "Will you see that a room is prepared for Miss Archer? She's going to see her father in I.C.U., then will need to rest for a couple of hours."

"Of course." The nurse smiled at Alison. "Just come to Room 509, and I'll see that it's ready for you."

The doctor stood and stretched. "Guess I'll go on home for a little while. You should be able to see Derek now."

As Alison entered the intensive care unit, a nurse met her and led her to Derek's compartment. The sight of her father's gray color gave her a jolt. Tubes ran in so many directions that she barely recognized him. But he was alive and breathing, thank God, even though the machines gave him considerable help. He was sleeping, just as the doctor had said.

Alison leaned over to kiss his forehead. She placed her hand in his, careful not to pick it up, fearful of disturbing a needle that was taped in place in a vein. The nurse had cautioned her not to remain more than a few minutes. There was no point in staying longer.

On her way out, Alison noticed the TV setups that monitored the patients in each room. Reassured, she knew that her dad was getting the best possible care. She breathed a grateful sigh as she walked to the desk and whispered her thanks to the attending nurses. She headed for Room 509, relieved enough at last to look forward to a shower and some rest. She shuddered when she noticed a policeman rise from a chair where he had been waiting, and follow close behind her.

It was almost eleven o'clock. when Alison rose with a start, terrified that something might have happened while she slept. John was in the recliner by the window.

"Take it easy," he said, "everything's fine. Doyle

18

came by, and said Derek will probably be awake soon. I stopped by your house on my way back, and Juanita had packed some fresh clothes for you. They're in the closet. Hope they're okay."

"Oh, that's wonderful. You've no idea how I hated the thought of wearing these same, rumpled things." Alison took the case from the closet and disappeared into the bathroom.

When she emerged, she felt more like her old self, with freshly washed auburn hair that fell to her shoulders and the crisp navy slacks and white cowl-necked sweater that Juanita had sent.

"For someone who's been through so much, you look amazingly beautiful." John took her in his arms and kissed her.

Alison smiled. "I wish I could enjoy this, but I can't wait to check on Dad. Give me a couple of days, when he's out of the woods, and I won't let you go so fast."

The smile froze on Alison's face when she saw the policeman sitting outside her room. "This is preposterous! Am I really a suspect?"

The officer looked embarrassed. "Just following orders, Miss Archer. I was told to keep an eye on you."

"Well, sir, as soon as my father is able to speak, you and your whole department will feel mighty foolish." Alison stormed down the corridor with John at her side.

When they got to I.C.U., Alison showed John to a separate waiting room, while she entered the double doors leading to Derek's compartment. Dr. Peterson followed briskly behind her.

"I was just about to send for you, Alison. The internal bleeding has started again, and Derek's vital signs are very weak. Things look pretty bad."

"Oh no . . . oh God!" Alison rushed past him to Derek's bed. "Dad," she whispered, "it's Alison . . . can you hear me?"

Derek Archer opened his eyes, trying to focus on her. His lips moved, trying to speak.

"Save your strength, Dad . . . don't try to talk. I love you so much!" She knelt on the floor and put her cheek as close to her father's as possible.

"I . . . I have to . . . tell you . . ." he gasped.

"Oh, don't waste your energy. We'll find that man when you're better. He won't get away."

"No, can't wait . . . the papers . . ."

"Papers?"

Derek tried to nod. "You must get them . . . from the safe."

"Dad, are you dreaming? What papers? Why are you telling me this now?" Tears poured down Alison's cheeks. She wanted desperately to hang on to him, but he was slipping away. He couldn't die!

Derek uttered his final words: "Papers . . . important . . . be discreet."

Dr. Peterson felt for Derek's pulse, then touched Alison's shoulder. "I'm sorry, Alison, but he's gone."

She curled into a ball on the floor, devastated, because tomorrow and in all the days to come, nothing would be changed. Nothing could ever bring back her dad.

Two

Comforted by the simple dignity of the service, Alison walked solemnly to the limousine and slipped into the back seat. As the car glided out of the cemetery, she rested her head on the leather upholstery and closed her eyes. These past two days had been a blur, with nervous energy keeping her on her feet. Now she felt drained and tired. With many people following her to the house, she wondered if she could find the strength to play the role of hostess and get through the rest of this day. Relaxing for the first time in many hours, she took advantage of the half-hour ride to put her thoughts in order.

Throughout the service, she had never felt quite so alone. She had longed for a shoulder to lean on, especially John's, but he had been occupied with his ailing mother, who had insisted on coming to the funeral, despite the fact that her health had failed drastically during the past year. More than ever before, Alison needed her own mother. How she missed never having a brother or sister to share the impacts, both good and bad, that life had a way of dealing.

All too soon, her solitude ended when the driver stopped, stepped out of the car, and swung open the white, wrought iron gates. Soon the long black car wound its way down the drive lined on each side with ancient oaks, their branches laden with new spring leaves. The estate consisted of three rolling acres, landscaped to perfection and radiant in the April sunshine with fuchsia, white, and pink azaleas, yellow daffodils, and low-hanging, purple wisteria. The red brick house, where she had lived since birth, loomed before them, a mansion with six white pillars rising from the porch to the roof three floors above.

Alison thanked the driver, emerged from the car, and entered the house. On unsteady legs, she walked through the foyer, down the hallway. She had always loved this house, the magnificence of the twenty-foot ceilings, the wide expanse of rooms, all splendidly furnished in Victorian antiques. She paused to open the massive oak doors that led to the drawing room. Quickly, she surveyed the room, noting the velvet brocade and gleaming mahogany. Very soon it would be alive with people, and Alison dreaded the thought of making polite conversation and trying to keep her composure. She thought of the heavily veiled woman dressed in black, who stood away from the others at the cemetery, and wondered who she was and if she'd come to the house. How she longed for time alone, time to deal with her grief, time to figure out why someone had felt compelled to snuff out the vibrant life of the father she so dearly loved.

Heaving a sigh, Alison stepped over to a window. Already a steady stream of expensive cars had begun to line the circular drive. She smoothed away tiny wrinkles from her black silk suit and took a deep breath.

The next two hours kept Alison too busy to dwell on the sickening reality that had brought dozens of people into the house. Now and then, her eyes wandered about the room, catching glimpses of John. No longer concerned about his mother, whom he had deposited on a sofa to fend for herself, he moved about the drawing room with ease, making sure each guest was properly greeted and attended to. Dignified and dashing in his dark pinstriped suit that she knew had recently been cut and fitted by an English tailor, John was among his peers, the socially elite of Dallas, people they had both known all their lives. He spared no expense to ensure the image of one of the city's most prominent families. His white shirt was custom-made and monogrammed, his tie, a blend of black, gray and cream, subdued just enough to fit the occasion.

Alison felt as if she were operating on automatic pilot, her subconscious getting her through this whole ordeal. She walked over to the marble fireplace to collect herself, and paused to gaze at the portrait of her mother hanging above the mantel.

"You look very much like her, you know."

Alison turned, relieved to see Myra Collins, her father's faithful secretary for the past twenty-five years. In her late fifties, Myra was a small woman, wiry and alert, whose energy seemed to radiate about her. Streaks of gray had threaded their way through the short, brown pageboy that framed her face and accented her keen gray eyes.

Alison smiled. "I've always wished I did, but Mother was so petite. Seems I inherited the tall genes from my dad."

Myra gave the portrait closer scrutiny. "There's

23

still quite a resemblance . . . same auburn hair and green eyes. I wish I'd known Claudia better." She shook her head. "What a shame for someone so lovely to die so young." She reached for Alison's hand and gave it a squeeze. "How are you, dear?"

"Just getting through this, I suppose."

"Heard anything more from the police?"

Alison fought back hot tears that prickled the corners of her eyes. "Not a word in the past two days, but my mind churns all the time, trying to figure out why this happened. I actually saw the bastard who did it, but I'm no help at all. He was like a phantom, and I've no idea what he looked like."

"I've wracked my brain, too, but as far as I know, poor Derek didn't have a real enemy in the world."

"There's bound to be something we're both missing. Can you think of anything unusual . . . . anything at all?"

Myra looked thoughtful for several seconds, then a light suddenly dawned in her eyes. "Nothing I can mention right now, but something else just occurred to me. Any idea why he'd been in such close touch with Senator Lassiter lately?"

"Why no . . . why?"

"Well, you worked so closely with Derek, that I figured you'd know."

"He never mentioned Sam Lassiter at all. How strange . . ."

"It was all very hush-hush. Derek had all of the senator's calls put through on his private line. And they always talked on the phone, never any written correspondence that I know of."

"Suppose this had any connection with the

24

shooting?"

Myra shook her head. "God, I have no idea, but there's a real possibility." Her face was a mask of concern. "Are the police sure there was no sign of burglary?"

Alison nodded. "Nothing touched . . . nothing missing . . . no sign of a break-in."

"Damn, it had to be someone he knew. Can you think of anything he said that might give you a clue?"

The picture of her dad lying so white and still in that hospital bed flashed in Alison's mind. The remembrance of his weak, trembling voice brought a lump to her throat. "Just before he died, he tried to tell me something . . . about papers in his safe. He even warned me to be discreet. At the time, it didn't make much sense, but maybe he was trying to tell me why this happened."

Myra's eyes looked suddenly frightened, and Alison could sense the tension in her. "Oh, I don't think we should be talking about those papers here." She kept her voice low. "And whatever you do, don't mention them to anyone else."

Alison grabbed Myra's arm. "What is it? Oh my God, Dad was actually trying to tell me who did it!"

"Sh-h-h . . . keep your voice down. We can certainly look into it, but now's not the time to be talking about it. We can wait until you get back to work and get them out of the safe. That is, if you want my help."

Alison gave the older woman a hug. "You bet I do. Oh, Myra, you've given me some hope."

Myra patted Alison's shoulders, then broke the embrace and held her at arm's length. "One way or

25

the other, we'll get to the bottom of this."

Out of the corner of her eye, Alison caught sight of John. He walked over to them and slipped his arm around her waist.

"Doing okay?"

She nodded. "Just a little tired."

"In that case, don't you think you'd better circulate a little more? A lot of important people have come to pay their respects, and you've been neglecting all of them."

Alison felt herself bristle. Trust John to imply that other people were more noteworthy than the most loyal person in this room. "I'm sure you know Dad's secretary—Myra Collins."

"Of course, good to see you." He shook Myra's hand and quickly turned back to Alison. "Ready to make the rounds?"

"I think I've already spoken to everyone several times."

"But they'll all be leaving soon, and I think—"

"Oh, John, you'll never believe what we've been discussing. It just might be possible that we can get to the bottom of my dad's . . . of what happened to him."

"Oh, I don't think that's such a good idea. Just leave the detective work to the police . . . that's their job."

"But you don't understand. There are things we can check into at the office. We might even—"

"Maybe so, but that shouldn't concern you now. Why don't you come with me, and make sure no one feels ignored."

Myra smiled. "He's right, you know. We'll have plenty of time later to figure all this out." She gave

Alison's cheek a quick kiss. "I need to be on my way, and we'll have another talk soon," she said, and quickly turned and walked away.

When the door finally closed behind the last guest, John gave Alison a tender kiss. "I'll be back later, after Mother's settled in for the night."

All Alison could think of was her need to be alone. "If you don't mind, I'd rather go to bed early. I feel so exhausted, and besides, Warren Moore wants to go over Dad's will first thing tomorrow."

"I understand . . . talk to you later."

Odd, Alison thought, as she watched him leave, how she couldn't bear the thought of being near the man she planned to marry, tonight of all nights. She had to do some serious thinking about their engagement, but not now. She'd wait until her brain felt a little more clear.

The next morning at nine o'clock, Juanita knocked on Alison's bedroom door.

"Mr. Moore's here to see you, Miss Alison."

"Oh yes, I'm expecting him. Just have him wait in the study, and I'll be right down . . . and we'll probably need some coffee."

"Yes ma'am. There's something else, though. Mr. Moore wants to see me, too. Have I done something wrong?"

Alison smiled. "Why no, of course not. He's dad's lawyer and wants to go over the will, that's all."

27

"But why me?"

Rising from her dressing table, Alison turned to face her. "Why, you're just like a member of the family. I feel sure my dad mentioned you in his will."

Tears glistened in Juanita's brown eyes. Too emotional to utter a word, she ran to Alison and embraced her, then fled from the room.

Alison quickly brushed her hair and slipped on the white linen jacket that matched her slacks. She left her bedroom and started down the stairs, a dread gripping her deep inside. Facing the stark reality of her dad's death, and hearing his last wishes read aloud, were almost more than she could bear. These past days seemed much like a bad dream, but now she was wide-awake, about to come face to face with the cold, hard fact that he was truly gone, that the disposal of his estate was a matter of business that must be dealt with. With a knot in the pit of her stomach, she braced herself for the ordeal.

When Alison reached the last step, Juanita was showing Myra in. Myra's face lit up at the sight of Alison. Dressed in her usual office attire, she wore a conservative business suit and white blouse. "When I left yesterday, I had no idea I'd be back so soon. Warren called last night and asked me to come."

Alison kissed her cheek. "I'm glad. I didn't know what to expect, but you of all people should be here."

They walked arm in arm to the study and entered the paneled room. Juanita was already there setting up the coffee service on a small table. At the sight of Warren Moore sitting dwarfed behind

28

the mahogany desk, Alison felt a sudden pang of resentment. Never had anyone but her father occupied that chair.

His face brightened as the two women came into the room. In his late sixties, Warren was on the verge of retirement. He was a sturdy little man, short and stocky, with tufts of gray on the sides of his bald head and owl-like eyes behind horn-rimmed glasses.

"Come in," he said, smiling. "How are you feeling, my dear?"

"Better," Alison said.

"Thanks for letting me come so early. Weeks ago my wife and I made reservations for a long-planned trip to Spain. We leave from DFW late this afternoon, and we'll be gone three weeks. Unfortunately, it coincided with Derek's death."

"That's quite all right." Alison sat down beside Myra on a leather sofa and patted the extra cushion. "Here, Juanita, there's plenty of room for all three of us." With Alison in the middle, they sat in a line and looked up at the lawyer expectantly.

Warren lifted the papers from the desk and cleared his throat. "I'll try to be as brief as possible. Derek's will is very simple, just as he was—a straightforward, uncomplicated man—despite the fact that he left a very large estate. I'll read this part in its entirety, but as you'll see, the stipulations are cut and dried with no frills. This last will and testament of Derek Ryan Archer was made five years ago." He gave Alison a warm smile. "He came to me on the day he made you executive assistant in his company, my dear. He was very proud of you."

Alison fought back tears, remembering that day.

29

She had been working for her dad since graduating from college, had learned the business from the ground up. Derek had spared her no hard work, and had taught her every intricate detail of the company. She learned her lessons well, determined that no one could say that she was nothing more than an "office brat." She hoped that in the past seven years she had proven herself.

The lawyer's voice droned on, as Alison's thoughts wandered, legal terminology boggling her mind. She vaguely heard him read the bequests to her dad's favorite charities, organizations that he had generously supported for years, but her ears tuned in, alerting her, when she heard Warren read Juanita's name. She felt a tremor when the woman's hand grabbed hers.

"And to my employee, Juanita Perez, I bequeath the sum of twenty-five thousand dollars for fifteen years of faithful service. At retirement, an annuity in her name will pay a monthly sum equal to her salary for the remainder of her life."

Juanita gasped and turned to Alison. "Oh my, I never dreamed I'd be rich . . ." Overcome, her eyes filled with tears.

Warren grinned and went on, "To Myra Collins, my secretary and the glue that has held my company together for twenty-five years, I bequeath the sum of one hundred thousand dollars. At retirement, in addition to her company pension, an annuity in her name will pay a sum equal to her salary for the remainder of her life."

Myra's hands flew up to her mouth. Speechless, she stared at Warren as though she had surely misunderstood his words.

Alison took Myra's hand. Leaning toward her,

she hugged her briefly.

Again, Warren lifted the papers and pushed his glasses farther back on his nose. "The remainder of this document only concerns Alison, so maybe it would be better if we discussed it privately. If you ladies will excuse us . . ."

Myra and Juanita, their faces flushed with the news of unexpected windfalls, hastily made their exits.

Warren stepped over to the table. "Can I get you some coffee?"

"No thanks, I just had two cups at breakfast."

Warren filled his cup and sat down. "I think for the sake of time, I'll just go over this in layman's terms. As you know, Derek's company went public ten years ago, but he reserved sixty percent of the stock for himself. As his only living heir, he naturally left all of it to you, which gives you controlling interest. Since the company is under the jurisdiction of a board of directors, replacement of your dad as president and CEO is subject to the board's decision, but Derek strongly recommends that you as the major stockholder should assume these positions."

Alison felt her face turn hot. She could just imagine how Louis Bennett, the senior vice president, would react. The very idea of a twenty-eight-year-old—and a woman at that—being handed the position that he so richly deserved! To hell with nepotism! She swallowed hard. "That's probably much easier said than done."

"I realize that, and I don't envy you, but Derek put his wishes in a letter, and every stockholder will receive a copy. Still, it's a matter that's out of my hands." He took a sip of coffee and set his cup

31

on the saucer. "Now, to the rest of the document . . . in addition to the company stock, your father left you all of his other stocks, bonds, and real estate holdings, which at today's market amount to approximately thirty million dollars. Aside from that, of course, the house here in Dallas and the one on Padre Island are yours. The remaining liquid assets come to roughly five million." He finished his coffee and began to stack his papers. "That's about it. I'll send you a copy for your files, so you'll have more time to go over everything." He stood and held out his hand, admiration shining in his eyes. "You're filling some mighty big shoes, but Derek had no doubt that you could do it. Neither do I."

Alison took his hand and shook it warmly. "Thanks, Warren, you're a good friend."

"If there are any questions or anything you need, don't hesitate to call." He headed for the door with Alison following.

When they reached the foyer, Myra was waiting for Alison. "I wanted to see you before I left for the office. I can't tell you how overwhelmed I feel."

"It's no more than you deserve." Alison gave her a shrewd look and said teasingly, "Now I suppose you'll retire and leave me to fight the tigers all by myself."

"No chance of that, at least for a long time. God, I can't imagine having to take up knitting. Besides, you and I have some detective work to do. When will you get back to the office?"

"Probably tomorrow. I still have a few loose ends to clear up, and hopefully I can get some sleep now that it's all over."

"Good." Myra opened the door. "Would you believe that for the first time ever, I left my briefcase at home? Now I have to drive all the way back to Hebron to get it. Just shows how shocked I was when Warren called. Oh well, no one's expecting me at work before noon. I had no idea how long this meeting would last, so I called in to let them know."

Alison watched her leave, wondering how on earth she would get by without Myra when the day finally came. All these years, she had run the whole office with the efficiency of a Prussian general, but deep down, she was as compassionate as a nun.

After following Myra Collins all the way from Hebron, a professional killer called Piper had waited over an hour in a rented Camaro outside the gate of the Archer estate. Damn, things better get moving on this job, or Bennett would have a stroke. Hell, the old dame could be here until noon. When she left here, Myra would probably head to the office in all that traffic, and another whole day would be wasted.

Piper's ears perked up at the sound of tires rolling down the drive. Then, as if on cue, Myra Collins pulled her blue Mercury to the gate and hopped out to open it. She was a spry old bird to be so close to sixty. Not bad-looking either.

The assassin waited until the blue car had rounded the corner to start the motor of the Camaro to follow. Well, I'll be damned! Good ole Myra was headed for the north toll road, in the opposite direction of the Archer Building. Piper tried to stay two or three cars behind, but always in sight of the Mercury. Half an hour later, Myra put on her blinker. Ah, she was turning right at the 544 exit to Hebron.

Pressing on the gas pedal, the killer began to form a plan. Once on the farm to market road, the rented car whipped around the Mercury, putting distance between them, and sailed down the country road toward Myra's home about four miles ahead.

Minutes later, Piper pulled up beside the house, threw the gearshift in reverse, and backed the Camaro diagonally to block the driveway, then reached into the glove compartment, located the .22 revolver, and pulled back the hammer.

At that moment, Myra stopped at the edge of the driveway with a bewildered look on her face. "What's going on?"

Flashing a smile, Piper stepped out of the car and walked to the driver's side of the Mercury. "Are you Myra Collins?"

"I sure am. Who are you?"

"I've got something for you." Instantly Piper drew the gun and fired, point-blank, hitting Myra squarely between the eyes. This was a good, clean hit. The old dame never knew what happened. Things hadn't gone this well with the Derek Archer hit. His nosy daughter showed up and almost ruined the whole thing. Oh well, it turned out okay in the end.

Quickly Piper reached for Myra's purse, took out the wallet, then grabbed her gold watch and diamond ring. The police would call this one a robbery. What a stroke of genius to use a different gun!

Three

Alison heard the doorbell, but made no move to change her position. She was in the study, curled up in her father's armchair, thinking of all the conversations they'd had in this room. She couldn't believe he was gone, that she'd never see his face again, never hear his deep laughter. She couldn't imagine a day-to-day existence without his direction. Her eyes became misty when she realized that she'd never again see that sparkle in his eyes, the one he'd saved as a reward for her accomplishments since she was in kindergarten. Again and again, her mind cried out, *Why, oh God, why?*

Nick McAllister stood in the entry to the Archer study, a room he already knew well from his many rounds of investigation. He stared at the woman sitting in the leather chair. This couldn't be, but there she was, alive and breathing, the woman in the portrait come to life! Juanita had explained about the painting as he stared at it one day. It was of Claudia Archer, and had been painted shortly before her death. But here she was right now, alive. Deep down, Nick knew this had to be her daughter, but he allowed himself a moment to imagine that she was the young woman in the portrait, the one whose eyes had haunted him since the first time he saw her. And now she was sitting here waiting for him.

When Alison looked up, those same green eyes were bright with unshed tears. His heart did a ridiculous flip when he saw that she was even more desirable in life than in the portrait. Nick saw that he had startled her. What a lousy job this was. Here she was, not over one tragedy, when he had to bring her news of another.

"Sorry to bother you, Miss Archer, I'm Lieutenant McAllister, homicide." He took out his wallet containing his badge and identification, and handed it to her. He was standing very close, close enough to catch the scent of her fragrance. Nick had to clear his throat to go on, "I've been in and out of your house so much lately that Juanita got to know me pretty well. She told me where I'd find you. Guess she took it for granted that we'd already met."

Nick watched her uncurl herself and rise to study his credentials. She was taller than he'd imagined, slender, with enticing, soft curves. She wasn't taking any chances. Good for her, he thought, as she looked at his picture, then at him and finally handed it back to him.

"Are you here to arrest me?" Alison's voice was soft and low.

"Oh no, nothing like that." At first Nick couldn't imagine why she'd ask such a thing. Hell, he thought, why should I be surprised? The guys at the precinct had been telling him from the be-

36

ginning that she was the most likely suspect. Something was wrong with him today; his elevator seemed to be stuck between floors. He shook his head, trying to get the buttons moving. "That's one of the things I've come to tell you; no more surveillance, but if you have any reason to leave town, the chief would like to be notified."

Alison's eyes lit up. "Then you've found the murderer?"

"No, not yet, but I promise we will." He saw her eyes cloud again. This kid was really suffering. She's innocent, he determined, she couldn't have shot her father. No way.

"Isn't there something I can do to help? I want to be a part of the investigation, if you'll let me. My dad . . ." Her voice caught. She swallowed and started again, "My father was everything to me. I'd really like to help."

"We'll let you know if there's anything you can do." Nick was back to his usual self. Somehow the relatives always felt they could do a better job than the police. They watched too much TV, that's what it was. All they ever did was get in the way. He cleared his throat again. "I'm afraid I've come with more bad news."

Alison looked alarmed. "What is it?"

"Myra Collins was shot . . . killed just before noon, we figure. She must have died instantly, if that's any consolation."

"No . . . no . . . it's impossible! She was here just this morning, and left to go home and pick up her briefcase." Alison's face was chalk-white, her eyes registering utter disbelief.

"That's where it happened, right in her own

driveway. Her house is way out, kind of in the country, you know."

"Yes, but who would do such a horrible thing? My God, maybe it was the same person who shot Dad!"

"Oh no, this was a robbery. We're checking the bullet, though, just in case it came from the same gun."

"I can't believe it." Alison held onto the back of the chair to steady herself. "It's so tragic, so unfair. Just this morning, she was in this very room, so grateful . . . about the will, I mean. You see, my dad left her quite comfortable. She would never have to worry about finances again. Oh, poor Myra." Looking stricken, Alison sank into the chair near her father's desk.

"Can I get you something to drink or anything?" Nick hated that his news had made her suffer even more.

"Thank you, but I'll be all right. Tell me, Lieutenant, what's going on here? There's no way this is just a coincidence. Someone wants to hurt us, even ruin Megtex. Maybe those papers in the safe . . ."

"Papers? What papers? Is there something I should know?"

"I shouldn't have said that . . . just forget it."

"If you're holding anything back, you could hinder the investigation, and do yourself and us a great disservice." Nick's voice was testy. "Your secrets could be a killer's motive."

"Believe me, if I thought this would help, I'd tell you in a minute, but this isn't anything I actually know. It has to do with my dad's last words, and

38

since I didn't know what he meant, I repeated them to Myra. She seemed to understand, and was going to fill me in at the office. She didn't want to talk after the funeral . . . too many people around. But I gathered that she and my father were working together on something." She shook her head. "I don't want to say more, because actually, I don't know anything else." Her eyes grew suddenly wide. "Do you suppose that's why she was killed?"

Nick looked at her long and hard. She might just have something there. "Are you familiar with what goes on at the office?"

"How do you mean?"

Nick wasn't sure what he meant, other than to find out if Miss Archer did more than show up occasionally to pick up a check or remind everyone who she was. "Do you spend much time there?"

Alison smiled, and Nick felt like a light had suddenly been turned on. She wasn't beautiful in the way most people thought of beauty today, he decided. Instead, she had an inner radiance that made him want to be near her. He shook his head. Damn, he was acting like a teenager and feeling very uncomfortable. He was glad none of his men were here right now.

"Oh, just eight to ten hours a day, that's all," she said. I've worked there for the past seven years, and two years ago, I was made my father's executive assistant and vice president. Believe me, that doesn't mean I'm around to attend funerals and play golf. So, in answer to your question, I spend a lot of time there. Why?"

"Well, in that case, it seems to me that you'd

know about anything unusual your father might have been involved in."

"Not necessarily, because Megtex is an international corporation with a lot going on in various trouble spots all the time. We have a number of branch offices, so there could be many things that my dad took care of personally."

"When do you plan to go back to work? Don't misunderstand, I don't mean to rush you, it's just that—"

"Don't apologize. I hated the idea of going to the office without my father being there, but I'm not doing myself or the company any good by staying here and brooding. And now that Myra's gone . . . God, I still can't believe it." Alison stood. "I'm going to work tomorrow." Her voice was stronger than it had been since Nick arrived. "There's a lot to be done, and I might as well get started."

"In that case, Miss Archer . . ."

"Call me Alison, everyone does."

Nick grinned. "Okay, Alison." He liked the feel of her name on his tongue. "Would it be okay if I came to the office sometime tomorrow? I'd like to have a look in that safe and those papers you mentioned. I've already been there and met Bennett and most of the employees, but maybe I could get a better handle on things with you there."

"Sure. Now I won't find excuses to stay home another day . . . afraid to face reality, I mean. About three?"

"Great, I'll see you then." Nick took out a dog-eared notebook, scribbled himself a reminder, then mumbled a few words about how nice to have met her, but wished the circumstances could have been different, and took his leave.

Megtex International was located in the glass and brass Archer building on Dallas's Stemmon's Freeway. Alison's corner office was on the top floor with a northeastern view. She often stood at her floor-to-ceiling windows, watching the air traffic to and from DFW Airport in one direction and Love Field in the other. This morning, she wasn't thinking of airplanes; she was wondering how the business could function without Derek, without Myra Collins.

A buzz on the intercom interrupted her thoughts. "Yes?"

"A Mrs. Deena Perry is here to see you about Mrs. Collins's position. Angie in personnel called and didn't know if you'd want to interview so soon, but said this one looked too good to pass up. She said a lot of women had been in already today, and how lousy some of their résumés were. The agency has sent in some real duds, except this one. She's on her way upstairs."

Alison sighed. "Okay, send her in." She sat at her desk, waiting to look at the woman who could possibly replace Myra. Impossible. No one could take Myra's place.

The young woman who walked into the office could have easily been applying for a modeling job. She was a rather tall woman, blonde and curvaceous with a face like a porcelain doll and eyes the color of violets. She was wearing conservative, low-heeled shoes and a suit that did little to hide her curves. Good lord, Alison thought, she probably can't even type. What in the world made her think she could get a job at Megtex?

After asking Mrs. Perry to sit down, Alison read her résumé. Dumbfounded, she realized that the woman was probably overqualified. "What kind of position are you looking for, Mrs. Perry?"

"One that pays well and offers a challenge."

"According to this," Alison said, "you're from New Jersey. What brought you to Dallas?"

Deena frowned. "A husband who was transferred, then wanted a divorce."

"I don't see any Dallas references. Have you worked here at all?"

"No, I haven't been employed since before my marriage two years ago. My husband wouldn't hear of my working, that is, until he . . . until after he fell for someone else. I hate to bother you with these personal details, but you have a right to know why I haven't worked in so long." Deena Perry moved uncomfortably in her chair.

"And now you need employment . . . for financial reasons, or to keep yourself busy?" Alison couldn't decide whether or not she liked this young woman.

"Oh, I need a job all right. I got very little from the property settlement, and, as I'm sure you know, there's no alimony in Texas. To tell you the truth, I'd rather work day and night than to take a penny from him anyway."

"Then all these references are at least two years old?"

"Yes, but I've kept up with the latest computer technology, not wanting to lose my skills, just in case I'd ever need them. And, too, I called my last employer before leaving Fort Lee. He gave me this letter of recommendation." Deena handed the envelope to Alison. "Meanwhile, your personnel office has the list of my other references."

Alison skimmed the letter, then went back and reread it more carefully. The CEO at Tri-Delt, an oil and gas related company, spoke well of Mrs. Perry. "Well, this is certainly a glowing recommendation. It's a sad commentary on life in the business world, when even a woman judges another woman by her looks. I apologize for thinking you were just too pretty to be bright."

Deena smiled broadly and seemed to relax. "Apology accepted. You'd be surprised how hard it's always been to be taken seriously. At least you're honest, and I appreciate that."

"The position that we have open is one of the most responsible in our organization, and it will take a great deal of time to train someone new. Would you be free to put in extra time until you're acquainted with Megtex procedures?"

"Oh yes, definitely. I have lots of free time."

"Myra Collins had been here twenty-five years, and I worry about any one person being able to fill her shoes. Would you consider taking this position on a trial basis, say for a month? We'll make it worth your while, if it all works out and we both decide to continue on a permanent basis."

"That sounds fair to me."

Alison looked at the calendar. "Let's see . . . today is Friday . . . suppose you start Monday morning, nine o'clock?"

* * *

Louis Bennett, senior vice president of Megtex, sat tilted back in his leather desk chair, impatiently waiting for an important call on his private line. He had told his secretary to hold all calls until further notice. At last the phone rang.

"Well, Piper, it took you long enough to get in touch. It's already been on last night's news. By the way, congratulations on another job well done." Bennett half-whispered into the phone. He was a slender man with dyed black hair and steel gray eyes. Thinking it made him look distinguished, he usually sucked on an unlit pipe, since the taste of tobacco made him ill. His clothes were ultra conservative, all hand-tailored, the uniform fashion of the successful businessman.

"What's next?" Piper asked.

"We have to meet right away. It's two o'clock right now. Can you meet me in the usual place near the jogging track, say in thirty minutes?"

"Hey, you're sure in a hurry. More action already?"

"Keep your mouth shut, Piper, until we're together. I'll fill you in soon enough."

Once again, the killer kept Louis waiting. Sometimes he thought about hiring someone else, but Piper had been recommended highly and had worked out well so far. No sense in pressing his luck; his tongue was hanging out for the CEO position at Megtex. If Alison Archer stepped into that place, it wouldn't be long before she'd get her hands on the papers that Derek had died for. Hell, he'd go to jail for sure, and he wasn't ready for that. He had to have those papers at all costs, and that meant getting rid of the Archer girl. He noticed Piper, the one he was counting on to do it, coming toward him.

"Okay, what's the next move?" Piper never minced words.

"You've got to start working on the girl, since you didn't get anything out of Archer before you shot him."

"Don't think I didn't try to find out where your papers were. The man was ready to die rather than talk . . . so I iced him. Figured there was no point in fooling around."

"But you said Alison saw you."

"Nah, she just saw a figure moving real fast. Hell, Bennett, if she'd seen me, she'd have told the police by now. Don't worry, it was pitch-dark in that foyer."

"Okay, now for the next step. Remember, you won't have much time. The office will be closed after six, so you'll have to do it at night. Search the safe first, and if the papers aren't there, we'll go through with the alternate plan. Think you can open it, so no one will know?"

"Give me a little credit . . . there's no safe I can't open with my method. So, what if they're not there?"

"All of Myra Collins's transcripts are in the closet of her office. She had special shelves built years ago. Lucky for us, she was secretly in love with Derek Archer, and kept every word he ever dictated. It's all there on tapes."

"Do I take the tapes out of the building, or do my splicing right there?"

"Take them with you, it'll be safer. No one's going to look for those old dictaphone recordings, that's for sure. Just bring them back. Think you'll have any trouble wiring the Archer house?"

"What is it with you and your smart-assed questions? I can do it so her father's voice comes out of her toothpaste tube."

"Listen, Piper, you've got to make this believable, so don't do anything cute."

"You maybe have someone else in mind? I'd just as soon take a vacation . . . or do some work on my own. Know what I mean?"

"Damn, you're independent! Calm down. I want you to see this job through to the end. God alone knows what that end will have to be." Sweat poured from Louis Bennett's brow. He'd been warned that Piper could be volatile.

"Okay, then show some respect for my judgment. My decisions go, understand?" Piper gave Bennett a fierce look.

"Understood. You're running this part of the show. Just be careful. I intend to be CEO with a spotless record."

"A car wash couldn't get you any cleaner than *I* will when I'm through."

"Well, then, it's all yours for the time being. Just keep me informed about your progress."

Four

As soon as Deena Perry left, Alison braced herself and entered her father's office. The sight of the massive walnut desk brought a sudden lump to her throat. It was just as he left it the night he died, the pipe resting on the holder, the letters waiting for attention in neat stacks, everything the same, except for the empty chair. Alison swallowed hard. No time to dwell on sad memories now. She must steel herself against them, and get on with the business at hand—the papers that could lead to finding the monster who had murdered her dad.

She stepped over to the safe, spun the four-number combination, and opened the door. The police detective had wanted to be present for this, but she simply couldn't wait until three o'clock as she had promised. This was company business, none of his affair, unless, of course, it actually held a clue to unlock the mystery.

The safe was relatively empty except for stock certificates, property deeds, and a strong box containing a few thousand dollars, cash Derek always kept on hand in case of an emergency. Dumbfounded, Alison went through the documents one by one. Not a sign of the mysterious papers. But her dad had been so insistent about them, had struggled so hard at the end to make sure she found them! And poor Myra had known about them, and been so secretive and cautious. Someone had gotten here ahead of her. But that hardly seemed possible. Except for herself, only her dad and Myra knew the combination, and there was no sign of a break-in. Maybe in Derek's delirium, he had made a mistake. The papers could possibly be in his files, even somewhere in his desk. It was worth a try.

For the next two hours, Alison went through every scrap of paper in the files, everything in or on the desk, meticulously searching, but having no idea what she was looking for. Frustrated to the point of tears, she sank into the chair by the desk, her face in her hands. She might as well try to catch a shadow.

The buzzer on the intercom suddenly startled her. Jackie, a girl from the reception area, came on the speaker. "There's a police detective here to see you, Miss Archer."

"Send him in." Alison wondered how long Jackie had been looking for her, since she'd told no one where to find her. She glanced at her watch: 2:10. He was early. It was just as well that she'd begun her search hours ago. As it turned out, the policeman was wasting his time being here at all.

Minutes later, at the knock on the door, she looked up to see Nick McAllister. Clad in brown slacks, a camel-colored sports coat, light beige shirt and tie, he still looked nothing like her perception of a policeman.

"Come in," she said, "I've run into a dead end,

48

I'm afraid. Not a sign of those secret papers or anything at all to give us a clue."

"Nothing?"

"Nothing in the safe or the files or the desk. I'm about ready to give up."

"Maybe someone removed them."

Alison sighed. "Possible, but not very likely."

Nick's eyes wandered to the safe, its door still open, its contents still piled on a table. "Mind if I take a look?"

She threw up her hands. "Why not?"

Nick walked over to the table against the wall and began to shuffle through the various items. "Well, I'll have to admit, you're right . . . nothing here."

Alison felt a mild sense of satisfaction. This big-shot detective hadn't trusted her judgment, had to see for himself. "So now what do you suggest?"

Nick didn't answer for a few seconds, but opened the safe door wider and stretched his arm inside, all the way to the back wall. "What's this?"

Alison's hopes came alive as she hurried to his side, but dimmed when he only held up a gold key. "I have no idea . . . I've never seen it before."

Nick studied it for a few minutes. "It's a little small for a door key . . . sure you don't know what it opens?"

"No, but a thought just occurred to me. It has to be important. Why else would it be hidden in the safe? You don't suppose . . ."

"Go on."

"I know this probably sounds farfetched, but maybe Myra took the papers and locked them away somewhere else. She definitely knew how important

49

they were, and I sensed anxiety in her when I mentioned them." Alison felt her whole body shudder. "Maybe that's why she was killed."

Nick's eyes narrowed. "There was every indication of a robbery, but that could have been a setup." He turned the key over in his hand. "I've seen keys like this before, just can't put my finger on it. Mind if I take it and have the lab go over it?"

"Of course not, as long as you let me know what you find out."

"You bet." He started for the door, then hesitated. "I was just wondering . . . have you had lunch?"

"Haven't even thought of it, but now that you mention it, I suddenly feel hungry."

"Good, let's grab a bite together."

Alison considered for a moment. What could be wrong with an innocent little lunch? He seemed like a decent man, and besides, they had a common goal. Maybe they could even figure out what this key unlocked. "Sure," she said, "why not?"

"Like Mexican food?"

"One of my favorites."

Nick drove to Greenville Avenue and pulled up in the parking lot of Brazos, a restaurant noted for its Mexican cuisine. "Well, it's not the country club, but the food's good."

Alison made no comment. He obviously had preconceived ideas about her. She hated being cast in the role of a snob, and had fought against that image all her life. Longing to set him straight, she held her tongue, and together they entered the restaurant, greeted by the tantalizing aroma of rich, spicy food and the sight of colorful Mexican folk art. The crowded room buzzed with conversation from the late lunch bunch.

"Let's eat on the patio," Nick said, "perfect weather for it."

They made their way outside and seated themselves at a square table with cane-backed chairs. A dark-haired waiter soon appeared with menus, a basket of toasted tortillas, and a bowl of salsa. He jotted down their orders and quickly disappeared.

"I hope you approve of this place," Nick said.

The anxiety on his face both unnerved and surprised Alison. Nick seemed so concerned about pleasing her. "Are you kidding? I come here every chance I get."

"Really?" He grinned, and his ruggedly handsome face seemed suddenly boyish. She had never met a man quite like him, a combination of male aggressiveness and sensitivity.

"Well, now that we've gotten that out of the way, let's get back to that key you found. I've been wondering . . . could it open a strong box or something like that?"

"Probably not—too large. It looks like a locker key of some sort."

"Like in an airport?"

"Could be."

"Oh, let's go out to DFW after lunch, and check it out."

Nick laughed. "Not so fast . . . like I said, the lab can go over it first and save a lot of time. We'll send officers to every likely place."

51

"This process is so slow."

"Just have patience."

"That's easier said than done when my dad's murderer is out there somewhere, running loose. And then with Myra's death, who knows what—" She stopped, suddenly interrupted by the reappearance of the waiter bearing the taco appetizer, a wagon wheel-sized quesadilla stuffed with black beans and Texas goat cheese, then topped with guacamole and pico de gallo.

They both dug in, and Alison savored each bite. "This is probably my all-time favorite."

"I agree.

"Tell me," she said between bites, "why did the police suspect me of all people? I've never heard of anything so absurd."

"They have to be cautious at first, at least until they find some physical evidence."

"Then why did they stop following me?"

"Didn't I tell you last night?"

"No, you didn't—just said I wasn't under surveillance any longer."

"Well, we have our reasons." He looked at her intently. "Still no idea about how the killer got in?"

Alison shook her head. "I'm sure the door was locked. Dad was always so careful about that."

Minutes later, the waiter brought the main course, the house specialty, King Ranch chicken with mounds of cheese, green peppers, and tomatoes.

They ate in silence for a few moments, and then Nick surprised her with an unexpected question. "Ever been married?"

Alison couldn't be sure, but she thought she detected a faint flush in his cheeks. "No," she said.

"That's amazing." He leaned forward, his eyes holding hers with such intensity that she felt her own color rise.

"Oh really?"

"It hardly seems possible that someone so beautiful would stay unattached."

For some unexplainable reason, Alison couldn't bring herself to tell him about John, their long engagement and wedding plans. "Well, some of us take our time, I suppose."

"Guess I'm one of them."

"You're not married either?"

He grinned. "Came close a couple of times, but so far, so good."

They said nothing more for a while, both determined to let the matter rest for the time being. Alison had an uneasy feeling that she had mistakenly led him on, had given false vibes. Fine way to act just weeks away from her wedding. Nick McAllister was much too appealing for his own good. She was glad when they finally finished eating, and the waiter came with a dessert tray filled with several sumptuous offerings, among them white chocolate cheesecake topped with blueberries, a concoction she could rarely resist.

Reluctantly she shook her head. "Everything looks wonderful, but I'll have to pass this time."

"In that case, I guess I'd better get back to work," Nick said. "Time to check out that key."

"Oh yes, the key . . . let me know what happens."

* * *

53

Late that night, parked near the Archer estate, Piper sat alone in the rented Camaro, making plans. Getting into the Megtex office a few hours ago and figuring out the combination to the safe had been a snap. Too bad the papers were gone. Could be that Myra Collins had taken them. That very well could be what happened, but what the hell, the papers were probably lost forever since Myra was dead. Now came the problem of spooking the Archer house. That shouldn't be hard to do with a little know-how, and ole Piper had plenty of that. It would take all afternoon tomorrow to splice together words from the dictaphone tapes, but it could be done. Now, if the rich little bitch would just leave the house this weekend for a couple of hours, everything could be in place before she returned. Piper chuckled. This assignment could turn out to be a hell of a lot of fun.

On Sunday night, when Alison and John came back from dinner, they were still in the middle of the argument that had started before they left the restaurant. John unlocked Alison's door, deactivated the alarm, and followed her inside to the den.

"How can you even *consider* such a thing?" He sank into the sofa, exasperated.

"But I have to! My dad stated explicitly that he wanted me to head the company, and that's what I intend to do."

"What about me? I have needs, too."

"Oh, darling, you just don't understand." Alison sat down beside him and took his hand. "I've lived

54

and breathed this company for years, and I just can't turn it over right now."

John slipped his arm around her and gave her a quick kiss. "With my law practice and all our social obligations, how can we get around to it all if you're tied hand and foot to that damned company? The new house, too—who would manage it if you're never there? Think of all you have to consider . . . the servants . . . hell, the whole thing just—"

Alison laughed. "Hold it, darling. My dad did it all by himself for years and years. He even had me to worry about, and that wasn't a small job. But he managed everything, including this house, just fine." A light suddenly dawned inside. "Why, we could even live here. Juanita knows this place so well, she could run it in her sleep."

"Oh no, not here, I'd never consider it. Anyway, it's time to put this big house on the market."

Alison couldn't believe the words had come out of his mouth. Weeks ago, she'd eagerly agreed to buy the new house, but that was before Derek's tragic death. Now everything had changed. She couldn't bear the thought of selling the only home she'd ever known, much less leaving it unoccupied. Surely John loved her enough to understand how she felt. "You might as well know right now that I'll never sell this house." She gave him a pleading look and pushed a lock of auburn hair behind her ear. She knew the effect she'd always had on him, and used it now without compunction. "Living here is a wonderful idea, don't you think?"

But this time, her ploy didn't work. John's expression didn't change. "Surely you're not serious!

Why this place is almost thirty years old! We need to live in Highland Park, around people our own age." He tightened his arm around her shoulders and patted her gently. "I'm sure when you think this over, you'll see that I'm right." He gave her a light kiss. "Now that we've settled all this, I think it's time we turned in."

Alison could hardly contain her anger. "If you think this is settled, you're dead wrong."

"Well, we'll talk about it tomorrow. I'll stay here with you tonight. I'm not leaving you by yourself."

"John, if you don't mind, I'd really rather be alone. There's so much on my mind—Myra's funeral and the board meeting tomorrow. I'd like to just soak in a hot tub and fall right into bed."

"Sure you'll be okay?"

She managed a smile. "I'm sure."

As soon as John left, Alison locked the doors and set the alarm. After turning off the downstairs lights, she climbed the stairs and headed for her suite. The house had a hush about it tonight, the only sounds coming from the rustle of the wind outside and the scraping of low branches against the windowpanes.

Shrugging off faint feelings of fear, she went into the bathroom, turned on the taps of her tub, and slipped off her clothes. The half-hour soak was all it took to relax her. Regretfully, she left the soothing water, toweled herself dry, and donned her nightgown.

As she climbed into bed, the miserable conversation with John came pouring back to her. For the first time since they'd become engaged, she faced the stark reality of actually becoming his wife.

They were both too headstrong to make a marriage work. She had hoped for more sensitivity, more understanding, but his mind was set on maintaining his image by having a wife to echo his every word, to live in his shadow. She was far too independent and determined to ever fit into the mold he had set for his wife. Her thoughts wandered from John, to her dad and Myra, to missing papers, to the board meeting tomorrow, and back to John and the decision she must make very soon. Somehow, sleep finally came.

Around midnight, the ringing of the phone jarred Alison awake. She groped in the darkness for the receiver, but never had a chance to answer. The moment she picked it up, a chilling voice on the other end was already speaking, a voice that could only belong to her dead father.

Help me, why didn't you help me?

"Dad? Oh my God, Dad!"

Help me, why didn't you help me?

And then the line went dead.

Five

At one o'clock the next afternoon, Alison walked through the reception area of Megtex. It was a traditional room, bright and cheerful, decorated in rose and white with dark mahogany furniture. She spoke to Jackie, who sat behind the receptionist desk, and headed for the bank of elevators at the left rear of the foyer. As she rode to the tenth floor, Alison's head felt vacant, last night's terrifying phone call erasing any chance of sleep. Unnerved to the point of tears, she had lain awake all night. Either someone had played a heartless joke, or she had dreamed the whole thing. And then, Myra's funeral this morning had brought back the full impact of her grief.

It troubled her, too, that the woman in black had been there again, standing off to one side, away from the others at the cemetery. She had tried to speak to her after the service, but when she turned around, the woman had vanished. She had also seen her in the most unexpected places. Last night when she left the restaurant with John, the mystery woman was standing all alone in the parking lot. Oh, she had to forget this woman, get all these worries out of her mind, and clear her thinking before this critical meeting.

Moments later, she walked into the oak-paneled boardroom where members of the board of directors had already gathered. Her eyes swept across the high-ceilinged room, noting that everything was in order. On her first day at work, Deena had done her job with the efficiency of a pro. The stage was set, with everything on the long, rectangular table in place: ballots, pens, notepads, coffee cups and saucers, water glasses, ashtrays, and matches. Across the room, the sideboard was laden with French pastries and a silver coffee service. Deena, already seated off to one side with pen and notebook in hand, gave her a warm smile. Alison returned her smile with a pang of regret, still unable to believe that anyone but Myra could occupy that chair.

Louis Bennett hurried to greet her, embracing her with a fatherly hug. "This is bound to be hard for you, Alison. Just know that I'm on your side."

"I know, and thanks for being a good friend."

Tom Stockwell was next. "How are you, my dear?"

"Fine, thank you, Tom."

"If there's ever anything Alice and I can do, please let us know."

"I will." She turned and Maynard Simmons took her hand. "Good to see you," she said.

"It's still hard to believe that Derek is gone. He'll be sorely missed."

Carl Wallace and Jack Woolridge walked over together, each murmuring words of sympathy.

Louis Bennett took Alison's hand and led her to the chair at the end of the table. "Well, now that

59

we're all here, I suppose we should get started."

With her head held high, Alison took a deep breath, determined to keep her composure, and sat down. *This was Dad's chair,* she thought. *Only last week he sat in this very place and chaired a meeting.*

Maynard Simmons spoke first. "Without a chairman—" He looked at Alison, color rising in his face, and turned to Louis. "Since you're the ranking officer, why don't you chair the meeting?"

Louis looked at the others around the table, and they all nodded in agreement. "In that case, let's get on with the business at hand. This company has suffered a tragic loss. The unthinkable has happened, and all of us will miss Derek Archer terribly, but the time has come to elect a new chairman. As you all know, Derek's will stated explicitly that his wish was for his daughter to succeed him in this position." He gave Alison a sympathetic smile. "But according to the bylaws of Megtex, the election is open to all board members."

Alison's head pounded from lack of sleep. She studied the faces of those around her, their expressions unreadable.

"And so," Louis went on, "before we get into the balloting, how do you feel about this, Alison?"

Alison cleared her throat. "I've given this a great deal of thought, and I've finally decided that I want the position. My father built this company ,from the ground up, and I've worked by his side for years to learn every aspect of the business." She looked into the faces again, this time sensing shock and disbelief. "I'll need everyone's help, I admit, because there's still a lot to learn, but together we can overcome all the problems one by one."

Tom Stockwell held up his hand. "Are you sure you want this responsibility?"

Alison folded her hands on the table and looked him in the eye. "Quite sure."

Maynard Simmons gave her a patronizing smile. "I'm sure being president has a glamorous ring to it, but for someone so young and a—"

Jack Woolridge's hands flew up in annoyance. "And a woman . . . is that what you really mean? Alison is the only blood relative of Derek Archer's in this room. It's her birthright."

Stockwell broke into the murmurs around the table. "We all have to recognize Louis Bennett's thirty years with this company and his position as senior vice president."

Louis smiled gratefully. "Thank you, Tom, but I agree with Woolridge. Let's not forget that Alison is the major stockholder of Megtex. Having said that, I think the time has come to mark our ballots. In keeping with the rules, every member of the board is eligible to be chairman and president of this company. Therefore, let's dispense with any further discussion and cast our votes. You'll notice that the ballots list every name in this room. Simply draw a line under your choice. Naturally, the person with the most votes will assume the position immediately."

The room fell silent as every member hesitated, then picked up a ballot. The entire procedure took slightly over five minutes. Deena rose from her chair, silently collected the white slips of paper, and retreated to the back of the room. Minutes later, she handed the results to Louis.

"Well, Alison," he said, smiling, "congratulations are in order."

When all the others had left, Alison and Louis found themselves alone in the room. He put his arms around her and said, "It's time for the new generation to take over and give the company fresh life. This is just as it should be."

"I'm well aware of how much help I'm going to need. Thank God I can count on you."

"Always remember that," he said.

"Well, I think I'd better get to work. Stop by later and we'll have a talk." Alison gave him another hug and turned to leave.

Louis watched the door close behind her. Such a beautiful woman, he thought. What a shame she'd have to die so young.

If things had gone as he'd hoped, Alison would have been spared. When he saw the results of the election, the whole world had collapsed on his head. If he'd been named head of the company, all the killings would have come to an end. But now with Alison's hands on the reins, it was only a matter of time until she discovered his secrets.

Louis glanced at his watch. 10:40. It was about this time of day two weeks ago that Derek had walked into his office, unannounced . . .

Louis had just entered the code name Unicom on his computer to make a daily check on his bogus company when he felt a presence behind him. Filled with shock and terror, his flesh stung, every pore on his body on fire. Quickly he flipped the switch to off, causing the monitor to go blank. Somehow he mustered a semblance of control and turned around to find Derek Archer, his friend of many years, standing just a few feet away. Derek was a large man, tall and well built, whose bearing exuded the essence of wealth and power. With just a sprinkle of gray in his thick, dark hair, and blue eyes that sparkled with intelligence, he looked much younger than his fifty-nine years.

"Sorry, man," Derek said, "didn't mean to startle you."

Louis managed a grin. "No problem, just didn't hear you come in. What can I do for you?"

"I need the Linco file for a few minutes. Is it handy?"

"Sure, I'll get it."

Louis reached into the file drawer, a knot beginning to form in the pit of his stomach. He located the folder and handed it over.

"Thanks," Derek said, "I'll get it back to you sometime today."

"Take your time."

"How about lunch?"

"Sounds great."

Derek smiled. "Good, we can get together around one and go to the club."

When Derek Archer left, Louis sank into his chair, his face in his hands. Derek was onto something: he could feel it. He knew all about the late nights that his boss had spent in the office the past month, all the hours he had put in, huddled with that damned Myra searching through computer files. Until this moment, he was sure that all the probing in the world would never lead them to Unicom. No other human being knew that the code name existed. Until now.

Surely the file name meant nothing to Archer. As all-encompassing as Derek's hands-on approach to management might be, no one could possibly know every aspect of this huge conglomerate. Besides, the man had no reason to suspect him of any wrong-doing. In thirty years, he'd been Archer's right arm, the most loyal of any employee. Maybe he had panicked for nothing. He felt cold sweat pop out on his face. What in God's name would he do if the word Unicom had stuck in Archer's brain?

After a week went by, Louis started to relax. Derek hadn't uttered a word about the, Unicom file, or anything else that suggested he had picked up the trail. Since Derek's unexpected appearance, Louis had been very careful to lock his door before he entered the code on his computer. But on the tenth day, his secretary's announcement on the intercom erased his complacency.

"Mr. Archer wants to see you immediately," she said.

Louis's knees felt like jelly as he walked down the carpeted hallway and entered Derek's office. Something deep inside told him that it was all out in the open, that he could very well spend the rest of his life behind bars. When Louis walked in, Derek Archer didn't smile or offer a greeting, his eyes reflected anger and hurt. Piled in front of him on the desk were various papers and computer printouts.

"Sit down, Bennett," Derek said, "we've got a big problem."

"Oh? Maybe I can help."

"Right now all you can do is listen. For two years, I've had complaints from Linco that Megtex has supplied inferior products."

"How can that be? Why, I've—"

"Dammit, man, keep your mouth shut and listen!"

Louis slid farther down in his chair, feeling like a kid about to be carted off to the woodshed. He had to keep his cool, plead innocence. Whatever Derek had uncovered could easily be blamed on an underling, someone down the line in the chain of command. "Sorry, go on."

"With oil leaks springing up all over the world, it seems that the Environmental Protection Agency is after us now. The latest involved a national park, and now the government is up in arms. Ever hear of a company by the name of Unicom?"

Louis felt the blood drain from his face. "Can't say that I have."

"Don't lie to me, you bastard. It took a while, but Myra and I finally found a way to unlock this whole sordid mess." Derek leaned forward, his blue eyes piercing into Louis's very soul. "It seems that you weren't as damned smart as you thought—two mistakes in the Unicom file made all the difference. For one, you entered payments to a supply firm in Mexico that manufactures parts made of used, worn-out materials; the other—the numbers 1865270—a Swiss bank account with a current balance of $18,870,520—the exact difference in monies supplied to us from Linco for new materials and the amount paid to the Mexican company." He jabbed his index finger on the computer printouts. "It's all right here."

"What a terrible blow to Megtex."

"You're damned right it's a blow! If this had gone on a few months longer, we'd have to close our doors."

"Who in God's name could have done this?"

Derek looked him squarely in the eye. "Cut the conning crap, Bennett, you're wasting my time. The buck stops right in the middle of your thieving lap."

"Surely you're not serious. Hell, man, I never—"

By now Derek's face was beet red, but his voice was low and menacing. "There's no point in going on and on with this. You and I both know exactly what happened—you jeopardized the reputation of this company and fattened your bank account—so all the denials you can dream up don't amount to anymore than a pile of shit." He shook his head, his face full of anguish. "It's hard to believe that my most trusted friend and ally has sabotaged the company that we've both worked so hard to build."

Louis didn't feel like offering a rebuttal. It was no use; the whole thing was spelled out in front of him on those papers. He sat silently listening, knowing that his years of planning would come to an end unless he could stall Archer. He straightened his shoulders and looked Derek in the eye. "Who else knows about this?"

"No one but Myra."

"What about Alison?"

"I've kept her out of this."

"Then what do you propose to do?"

"I've given this a lot of thought, and have come to a possible solution. To begin with, you'll repay the stolen money. Megtex will pay the difference, and begin legitimate repairs on the pipelines throughout the world. Next, you'll sign a confession admitting to everything. You'll also sign a letter of resignation effective one week from today." Derek's face softened. "This way you can leave the company honorably, and no one will ever know the reason. I feel I owe you nothing, but I can't forget our years of friendship."

"If I sign a confession, what will you do with it?"

"Along with these printouts, I'll keep it in the safe. When I hold your certified check in my hands, I'll give the letter to you. As I said, your resignation will be dated a week from today. I expect the check by then, or I'll turn everything over to the Justice Department immediately."

"Seems fair enough. Where do I sign?"

Before the ink was dry, Louis knew that Derek Archer's time would run out even sooner than he'd planned. The bastard had been a little too benevolent for his own good.

Louis checked the time again and realized he'd stood in one spot for twenty minutes without moving. Even after years of waiting, he still couldn't grasp the fact that he'd actually had Derek Archer killed. And Myra Collins, too. All the poor woman ever did was a good job.

No time to dwell on all that. Now he had Alison Archer to worry about. She was a clever one, as astute as Derek ever was, and it was only a matter of time until she discovered his secrets. He had to be cautious, make her murder look like a suicide. Thank God he had Piper on his side, a unique individual with the brain of a computer and the conscience of a rattlesnake.

It was almost six o'clock before Alison got home from work. Now that her new position was a reality, she felt the hand of responsibility weighing heavily on her shoulders. Thousands of jobs throughout the world depended upon her, now that she was heading the company. She took a deep breath as she opened the door. No one else had such of a stake in this business; no one had grown up watching a father spend his whole life building an empire. For her dad's sake as well as her own, she'd prove to everyone that she was qualified for the job.

As soon as she walked inside, she realized how stuffy and hot the house seemed. The temperature today had risen to eighty-six degrees, above normal for April in Texas, and it felt more like a hundred in the foyer. Quickly, she went into the hallway and adjusted the thermostat, turning on the central air-conditioning. She was on her way upstairs when she became aware of a voice, low and indistinguishable at first, then gradually louder. Thinking that someone else was in the house, she felt uneasy, then a little foolish. It could be no more than a radio left on or maybe a television. Juanita always kept one of them playing, and she'd probably forgotten to turn it off before she left. But then the voice grew in volume, overwhelming the hum of the air conditioner. Alison felt dizzy. This was no radio; this was her dad, his voice clear and pleading.

I need you . . . Come to me . . . I need you . . .

Alison's heart thumped wildly against her chest. Oh no, it's happening all over again. Oh no! Terrified, she all but flew up the stairs, raced into her bedroom, and closed the door. The voice followed her.

I need you . . . come to me . . . I need you . . . come to me . . . I need you . . .

She fell on the bed and pulled the covers over her head, her whole body shaking. The voice continued, Derek pleading, begging over and over again, until she thought she'd surely go mad.

"I can't stand it," she screamed, her face wet with tears. "Stop, please stop!" Alison curled into a ball, her hands covering her ears, and sobbed.

Unrelenting, the voice went on, *I need you . . . Come to me . . . I need you.*

All at once, something stirred deep inside Alison, causing her to sit up. She had to get control of herself; there had to be a rational explanation for this. Her dad was dead, and the dead didn't call out. Someone was obviously trying to drive her insane. When did the voice begin? She wracked her brain, desperately trying to relive the moments before it started. The air conditioner! That had to be it. Somehow, turning it on had activated the voice. With her hands against her ears to ward off the sound, she made it to the upstairs hallway and flipped off the thermostat. Magically, the house fell silent. She fell back against the wall. Thank God!

She hurried back into her bedroom and dialed John's number. She wasn't expecting him to pick her up until eight and it was just a little after six. *Please be at home, John, please pick up the phone.* She breathed a sigh of relief when he finally answered.

"Oh, John, someone's been in the house and set up a recording. Please come over right now."

"My God, what's wrong?"

"Just get here as fast as you can."

"Hang on, I'm on my way."

Alison went back downstairs and waited in the foyer by the door. In less than ten minutes, she heard John's car and ran out to meet him. "Oh, I'm so glad you're here!"

"What on earth happened?" He took her in his arms and held her close.

"I heard a voice . . . Dad's voice, and I think it came through the vents."

He held her at arm's length and looked into her eyes, dumbfounded. "Wait a minute . . . you're saying—"

"I know it sounds crazy, but I'll prove it to you. Come inside."

Once in the house, she ran into the hallway. "Just listen when I turn this on." She switched on the air conditioner. "Now . . ." No sound came except the steady hum of the motor. "Damn, I just knew . . ." She turned it off and back on again. Still no voice. Tears welled up in her eyes. "But I was so sure."

John enfolded her in his arms once more. "Darling, you've been through so much . . . so much strain." He led her into the den to the sofa and sat down beside her. "It's understandable that you'd hear strange things, even see them, in the state you're in, but you've got to accept the fact that Derek is gone. I think you should see a psychiatrist, just to get yourself back on track."

"You think I'm crazy, don't you?"

He tightened his arms around her. "Of course not, but I do think your nerves are shot. Please think about it."

"I will, but you've got to believe me . . . I did hear Dad's voice."

Six

During the next few days, Alison immersed herself in her work, becoming more and more aware of the mammoth responsibility she had assumed. Thankfully there had been no further incidents at home— no voice from the vents, no heart-stopping phone calls. She gradually began to relax, finally able to accept her father's death, but even more determined to find out who murdered him, and why.

In a meticulous search through his files, she became increasingly aware of the inner workings of the company, and of an undercurrent that flowed beneath the facade of untroubled waters. During the past months, she learned, work orders from Linco had reduced to a mere trickle. Megtex had been the mainstay of every major oil company for thirty years, but Linco was the largest company it served.

Troubled, Alison had ordered a financial report. To her dismay, she found that Megtex had lost millions of dollars over a relatively short period of time. No wonder her dad had spent so many late hours at the office and at home. On the night he died, he'd been in the study working until past midnight, poring over files. He had brushed her questions aside. "Nothing to worry about," he'd said, "I'm planning a major expansion, and getting the proposal ready takes time." But now she had her doubts that any expansion had been in the works at all. Derek had desperately tried to find the source of the problem.

By Friday, her mind felt boggled with figures. Oh, how she wished that Myra were sitting at that desk outside her office. She of all people could answer some of her questions. She was thankful for Deena, though, this super secretary who had come to the rescue at such a critical time. She did the work of at least two people, never complaining, nothing too complicated or too much for her. Even today she had worked right through lunch. To top it all, she *liked* Deena, too, but there had hardly been time to get to know her very well.

Alison rubbed the back of her neck. She had sat at this desk for over four hours, her head bent over paperwork. She rose from her chair to stretch her legs, and walked over to the wide expanse of glass. Now that she occupied Derek's huge. corner office, even her view had changed. In the distance, she could see the panorama of downtown Dallas spread out before her. Across Stemmons Freeway, with its eight lanes of steady traffic, stood the complex that housed the Apparel Mart, the Market Center, and the Trade Mart, all of it sparkling in the April sunshine.

"Got a minute?" Deena had tapped on her door, then opened it a crack.

"Sure, come in."

"My, this is a beautiful office. When will you start redecorating?"

"Why should I?"

"Gosh, I'm sorry, I just noticed how masculine it looks."

"Well, now that you mention it, it does, doesn't it?" Alison realized how shaky her voice sounded. "I'm just not ready to make any changes yet."

"I've upset you . . . I'm sorry."

"That's all right. You wanted something?"

"Yes, these boxes were just hand-delivered from Neiman Marcus." Deena placed four cream-colored cartons on a console table near the door.

"Oh God, those are our wedding invitations. I totally forgot about them, and haven't even finished my guest list." She felt momentarily confused. "They shouldn't have been delivered here. The bridal consultant was supposed to have them addressed." She sighed. "Guess she gave up on getting my list."

"Then what should I do?"

"Sorry, but they'll have to go back."

"No problem." Deena turned to pick up the boxes again.

Alison looked at her watch. "Wait a minute, Deena, it's past time for lunch, and I'll bet you're starving. Why don't we have a bite together?"

"I'd love it." Deena's violet eyes sparkled. "I'll just drop these off at the mailroom and pick up my jacket." She was wearing a long, slender, plum-colored skirt with a blouse in a lighter shade. When she returned, she had on a matching jacket.

Alison admired her taste and told her so as they left the building. When they climbed into the car, she added, "I hope you like Italian food."

"It's to die for. My favorite!"

Alison smiled as she pulled away from the curb. Somehow she felt old next to Deena, even though they were about the same age. Maybe being with her dad so much made her feel older. After college, most of her friends had married and had families now.

74

She never felt the need for close friendships; her dad was her best friend, and they told each other everything. She caught her breath. Or so she thought. Now she was finding out that Derek had kept all kinds of secrets from her.

"So I tried making it, and you should have—" Deena looked at Alison and laughed. "Why, you haven't heard a word I've been saying. Your mind is always on business, isn't it?"

"Sorry, guess my thoughts were wandering. Ever been to Massimo's on Lovers Lane?"

"No, I'm so new here that I haven't been many places at all. I love the name, though, sounds good already."

Alison found that Deena's enthusiasm was contagious. She pulled up at a storefront restaurant directly across from Marie Leavell, one of her favorite places to shop for clothes. She realized how hungry she felt and could hardly wait to go inside.

A people-watching restaurant, Massimo's was jammed with customers. Its decor was simple: plain chairs and tables, no cloths, no mats, help-yourself utensils, and a buffet laden with a variety of hot vegetable or meat pizzas, cold salads, and hot or cold pastas. Alison and Deena selected different items, deciding to split with each other and sample everything. Alison piled thick slices of Italian bread and several rolls on their trays.

Deena looked at her in amazement. "Surely, we're not going to eat all this."

"Oh yes, we are, but be sure to save room for dessert, because you can't leave here without tasting the Sacher torte."

"What's that?" Deena spotted a couple leaving and

quickly dodged her way past the crowd to claim the table.

"Just the most heavenly dessert imaginable . . . a combination of chocolate on chocolate with a raspberry filling. In Vienna, it's served with whipped cream. Talk about calories!"

The conversation subsided for a few minutes as the two women downed mouthful after mouthful of the savory food, both of them groaning guiltily, especially when Deena stood to go back for more butter. The bread demanded it. Alison found herself relaxing for the first time in days, actually giggling at times, truly enjoying Deena's company.

Finally Deena got serious. "You've been working so hard, all alone. Can I help you with whatever's taking so much time?"

Alison considered for a moment. As much as she liked Deena, she hardly knew her; it didn't seem appropriate to fill her in on all the company problems just yet. "Thanks, but I think I can handle it. Believe me, if things get too tough, we'll both have work over our ears."

"Just know that I'm willing to stay late, or do anything it takes."

"I know, and don't think I haven't noticed how efficient you are."

The lunch hour stretched into an hour and a half. As they were leaving, Deena laughed and said, "I'm lucky to be out with the boss . . . now I don't have to make up an excuse for being so late."

"It's been fun," Alison said. "We'll have to have lunch again soon."

As she got out of her car in front of the office building, Alison suddenly froze. There was the woman in black again. Who was she? Everywhere she went, the woman turned up. It was time to discuss this with Nick McAllister. The thought made her blush. Maybe she was looking for an excuse to call him. Preposterous, she thought.

Nevertheless, as soon as she returned to her office, Alison fished in her purse for Nick's phone number and called him on her private line.

"Lieutenant McAllister, this is Alison Archer."

"I know."

"Now how did you know who I was?"

Nick laughed. "Very simple . . . just recognized your voice."

"I wanted to talk to you about a problem. Someone seems to be following me."

"But we've taken our man off of you. You must be imagining—"

"This time it's a woman, and she's very real."

"Maybe we'd better not talk about this on the phone. Will you be home tonight, say around eight?"

"Yes, that would be fine." She felt ashamed of her relief that John had gone out of town on legal business.

"I'll see you then."

Nick arrived on time. As he stopped on the circular drive, he thought again about how he couldn't conceive of people actually living here. He wouldn't even be able to pay the crew that kept the grounds in such perfect shape. It bothered him that Alison lived here all alone, and wondered why the Archers didn't have a staff of live-in servants, like rich people did in all those old movies. Well, that was none of his business. But she might be in danger from the same person who killed her father. He climbed out of his car and rang the doorbell. The outside lights came on immediately, as though he had activated a switch. A good safety precaution, he thought.

"Hi," he said when she opened the door. He wished he could think of something clever to say. She looked so young and beautiful with her hair loose like that. He liked the yellow jumpsuit she was wearing, too. It showed off her great figure.

"Come in," she said. "I've been looking forward to having this talk."

He followed her into the study and took a seat opposite hers. "You mentioned something about being followed."

"Oh, yes, and I'll get to that in a minute, but would you like something to drink first?"

"Yes, since I'm not on duty. Got a beer?"

"Sure do, be right back." Minutes later she returned with two beers and a bowl of pretzels. "Now, to the woman. I'll start at the beginning, because I saw her for the first time at Dad's funeral. She was standing away from the rest of the mourners . . . like she might have been visiting another gravesite, and came over to see who we were. I don't know why she was there, to tell the truth. I know it sounds ridiculous."

"What did she look like?"

"The first time, I didn't notice anything except that she was dressed in black from head to toe—hat, veil and all. But I've seen her several times since."

Nick took a swallow of his beer. "She didn't show up at the house with your friends?"

"No, but only our close friends and business associates came over . . . just fifty people or so."

"And you saw her again today?"

"Well, I took our new secretary to lunch . . . she's being trained to take Myra Collins's place . . . and when we got back, she was standing right there in front of the building."

"Good, then you got a good look at her."

"All I can tell you is that she's small, slender, always dressed in black, and always wears a wide-brimmed hat that covers her face." Alison shook her head. "She seems to appear out of nowhere, no matter where I go. I've never seen her in a car. I've no idea how she gets—"

Nick leaned forward. "What is it?"

"Nothing. Nothing I want to talk about. I just hope I'm not imagining this woman." Alison's eyes betrayed her fears.

Nick put his beer down. "We'll have her checked out for sure. Now, tell me, what are you hiding?"

"I can't . . . not yet. I'd rather deal with it alone for a while. Right now, I'm more interested in the key you found in the safe. Any word on it yet?"

"Well, it's definitely a locker key of some sort, but so far we haven't found the place."

Alison sighed. "Did they check the airports?"

"Both of them, and also the train and bus stations, but no luck. We have officers looking at every gym, fitness center, and anyplace else that seems likely."

"It might not amount to anything, but somehow I'm sure that key could hold the answer to why Dad was killed."

"Believe me, we'll do the best we can." He took a long drink of beer. "You're engaged to John Carpenter, aren't you?"

"Yes." Her voice had a dejected sound.

"And you plan to marry in June?"

79

Alison smiled. "My, you've done your homework. Yes, in June . . . that is, I think so."

Nick came alive. "You're not sure?"

"It's strange, but since my dad died, I'm seeing things in a different light. You see, John and I grew up together, and, of course, I love him. I've always loved him, but I'm wondering if I'm actually *in* love with him. There's a big difference, you know. I'm trying my best to look inside myself and make sure this is the real thing . . . just having trouble sorting all of this out in my mind." She gave him a big smile. "I'd better hurry, though. Neiman's has already had the invitations printed."

Nick suddenly felt on top of the world. There was still hope, definite hope. Not that he could ever measure up financially to the men in Alison's circle, but he could sure as hell give it a try otherwise. He wished he could think of an excuse to stay longer, but they'd already gone over everything she wanted to talk about. He'd bide his time, wait until she made her decision, and if she called off the wedding, there would be other nights. He'd make sure of that. Reluctantly, he rose to leave, hating for her to stay in this big house all alone.

The next several days at work were particularly hectic for Alison. An oil spill off the coast of New Orleans caused part of a crew to be pulled out of a trouble spot in Alaska to clean the waters. Word came in of recent damage to a Linco pipeline, but as the days wore on, no word of a work order came in.

She felt as though her desk were the eye of a huge storm. Everything piled on top of it at one time: reports from department heads, requests for meetings, equipment purchases, breakdowns. She learned all too soon that being a woman in a man's world had its drawbacks, sensing resentment at every turn.

On Friday, she had a call from John to say he couldn't make it back to Dallas before the next day. Alison realized how relieved she felt. She called Juanita at the house asking her not to prepare dinner; she'd cook for herself tonight.

On the way home, Alison had two quarters in her hand as she pulled her white Lexus convertible to a stop at the gate of the Dallas north tollway. Hitting the basket with her coins was always a challenge. Success this time; the light turned green, the gate went up, and Alison zoomed ahead, driving north on the toll road, toward Preston Royal and the supermarket where she could always count on fresh produce. She looked forward to a quiet, peaceful time alone, away from all the pressures at work. Thank God the nightmarish voices had stopped. Obviously her imagination had been playing weird tricks on her, and now she felt more like her old self. She'd enjoy fixing her own meal, relaxing, maybe watching TV, and turning in early. Nothing could spoil her mood tonight.

After cooking and consuming a dinner consisting of a tossed salad and lemon pepper chicken, Alison relaxed on the chaise in her bedroom. Inadvertently, her eyes strayed to the air-conditioning vent high on the wall. What a relief! No more voices. She leaned back and picked up the TV remote control—the flicker, she called it—and turned on the power. Something was wrong; the screen remained dark. Maybe this flicker needed new batteries. Annoyed that she was such a klutz when it came to anything mechanical, she rose and turned on the set manually. At first there was nothing, then a faint picture appeared, the image of a man. Alison pushed the button to change the channel, her heart beginning to thump irregularly. The picture cleared and stayed the same on every channel. *Oh, my God, it's Dad!* The face came closer and closer, until it covered the entire screen. The picture remained still, but a voice came over the speaker:

I need you . . . come to me . . . I need you . . .

Alison stood and walked slowly toward Derek, holding out her hand, trying to touch him, trying desperately to hold his image. She jumped when she felt only cold glass. Frightened and confused, she slowly backed away from that beckoning face and voice. Her back touched the wall and she pressed against it, wanting to run away, hide from that ghostly face, but she couldn't bring herself to turn her back on her dead father.

Slowly the picture faded, then disappeared. But the voice repeated once more, *I need you . . . come to me . . . I need you . . .* It was the last thing Alison heard. Her body slid down the wall, slowly to the floor. She couldn't move.

Moonlight filtered through the sheer draperies covering the French windows and cast a shadowy glow on the dark, quiet room. Alison hugged her knees, never so frightened in her life. She waited for an endless time, waited for a noise, anything, to break the silence.

All at once Alison heard wild laughter. She froze. The television screen came alive with the face of, not Derek, but Jay Leno — Jay Leno and his studio audience.

She sat very still, trying to be rational. Beads of perspiration formed on her forehead, threatening to run down her face. With legs of rubber, she finally managed to stand, turn off the TV, and move to her bathroom. Splashing cold water on her face and neck seemed to help.

Alison felt hot, but dreaded reaching toward the air conditioning-vent in the bathroom to feel if the cooling was still on. She couldn't bring herself to test it. Derek's voice might come through the vent again. She cringed.

She clutched her throat, a terrible fear growing inside her. Was she losing her mind? John could be right after all; maybe she needed a psychiatrist. She sat very still for a long time, unwilling to move.

Finally, with shaking hands, Alison went to the bedroom phone and dialed Louis Bennett's number. His wife, Cora Lee, answered in a sleep-filled voice.

Alison was momentarily stunned, disoriented, expecting to hear Louis's voice.

"Hello . . . hello . . . is anyone there?" Cora Lee sounded irritated, and Alison heard her speaking to Louis. "No one is saying anything, but I can hear breathing."

Then she heard another voice, Louis's this time. "Who the hell is this, and why are you calling this time of night?"

"Louis . . . I'm sorry if I disturbed Cora Lee. I thought you'd answer. I mean . . . oh, Louis, I'm so scared! Can you come right over?"

"My God, are you all right? Did someone break in again?"

"Oh no, nothing like that. But something has happened, and you said I could count on you. I need some kind of help."

"Sure, but it's after midnight. Can this wait until morning?"

"Oh, I didn't know it was so late." She couldn't believe that so much time had gone by since she first turned on the TV and saw . . . she shuddered. "Of course, it can wait, and I'm sorry I woke you."

"I can come over if you think it's necessary. Tell you what, I'm coming anyway . . . be there in half an hour."

"No, no, don't, I'll be fine. Just hearing your voice helped a lot. Please apologize to Cora Lee for me. Tell her we must have lunch one day soon. Good night, Louis."

When Louis Bennett put the phone down, he was smiling.

"What on earth did Alison want at this time of night?" Cora Lee asked. "That girl must be out of her tree! Since Derek died, everyone says she's been acting rather strangely."

"Oh really?" Glad his wife couldn't see the gloating look on his face, Louis's smile became even broader.

Seven

The sky was hazy with dawn when Alison climbed wearily out of bed. Sleep had come in short, scattered bouts, her whole night spent with her thoughts in turmoil. As hard as she tried to be rational, she felt sick with the fear that she must be losing her mind. Weeks ago, when she had heard Derek's voice on the phone, she convinced herself that some sicko had played a cruel joke. When she heard his voice coming through the vents, she wondered if someone had planted a tape in the attic. But the sight of her father's image on the TV monitor was too much for her, too outrageous to explain away. One side of her said that she had surely conjured up all of it, and that meant a series of hallucinations. The other side argued that someone had set out to drive her insane. But who? And why?

The motive had to be connected with her dad's murder. Over and over again, she played back his last words in her mind. The papers, those damned papers that had simply vanished, had to hold the key! She could still see the fear in Myra's eyes when she mentioned them to her. Myra had said something else, too, something about Derek's phone conversations with Senator Lassiter. Feeling that she was groping through heavy fog, she made up her mind to get in touch with him. She had sadly come to the conclusion that the company was in trouble, and Derek had possibly lost his life as a result. How a U.S. Senator could shed any light seemed too farfetched to imagine, but she had to start somewhere.

As soon as she reached the office, she put in a call to Washington, and paced the floor waiting to hear from him. Shortly before nine, her private phone rang. It was Senator Lassiter.

"We need to meet right away," he said. His voice sounded tense.

"I'll be on the next plane."

Deena Perry looked up in surprise when Alison came out of the office, her purse in her hand.

"You have an appointment with the comptroller at nine fifteen."

"Cancel everything for the next two days."

"Where do I say you can be reached?"

"Just say I'm not available." Alison hurried out the door. She had slightly over an hour to pack and make it to the airport before her flight.

At two o'clock eastern time, Alison arrived in Washington, checked into the hotel, and immediately called the senator.

"Where are you staying?" he asked.

"At the Willard International."

"How about meeting me for lunch in the hotel dining room, say in half an hour?"

"Sounds great . . . see you then."

A woman who had registered at the Willard International under the name of Clare Cummings sat in the lobby, hoping to catch a glimpse of Alison

Archer. This morning had been a whirlwind of activity, finding out just an hour before flight time that she had to leave for Washington, hurriedly packing, and racing to DFW to catch the plane. Until now, keeping track of Alison had been relatively simple, her routine organized and predictable with no impromptu trips to throw everything out of kilter. At first she had balked at the thought of racing off to Washington, of all places, but Louis had insisted. He felt that Senator Lassiter could possibly be tied to Derek's investigation, and somehow his daughter had found out. "Never underestimate Alison Archer," he'd said. "That girl could ruin everything for us, so don't let her out of your sight."

With her eyes trained on the elevators, Clare spotted Alison the instant one of the doors opened. Pulling the brim of her hat low on her forehead, she turned her back on the younger woman for the few seconds it took her to walk through the lobby. It soon became obvious that Alison was headed for the dining room.

Clare stood and began to follow, pausing at the door to watch. Alison was greeted by a silver-haired man in his sixties, tall and lean, with a strong face and quick, intelligent eyes. He seemed genuinely glad to see Alison, as he kissed her cheek and took her arm, leading her to a table at the side of the room.

Well, well, she's already made contact with the senator. This conversation could be very informative. Clare walked over to a table behind them and took a seat with her back to Alison.

* * *

87

"It's so good to see you, Alison," Sam Lassiter said. "How long has it been?"

"Too long . . . I think I was still in college, and that's been at least eight or nine years."

He laughed. "Don't remind me how fast the years go by." Sam took both her hands in his. "I still can't believe that Derek is gone. I'm so sorry that I was out of the country when it happened. Any idea who killed him?"

The mention of Derek's name brought back a sudden stab of loss. "Not yet, but I'm doing everything I can to find out. Just before Myra died—"

"Myra Collins? My God, what happened?"

"She was shot, too, just outside her house. The police say she was robbed, but I don't believe it." Alison shook her head sadly. "Somehow her death was connected to my dad's."

"Myra dead . . . such a loyal employee and friend to Derek. You know, I'm inclined to agree . . ." Sam didn't finish, pausing long enough for the waiter to take their soup and salad orders. As soon as he was out of earshot, Sam went on, "I never thought it would come to this."

"What do you mean?"

Sam leaned forward and lowered his voice. "Are you aware that the Environmental Protection Agency is investigating Megtex?"

Alison felt her blood run cold. "Oh no . . . why on earth?"

"It seems that the Linco officials have discovered inferior materials in the pipelines, both in structure and maintenance."

"Since when?"

"It's been going on for some time . . . for many years, but the problems are just now coming to light, and the fingers are all pointing straight at Megtex. Leaks are springing up all over the world, some of them potentially hazardous."

Alison felt the whole world crumbling all around her. "I don't understand. My dad would never allow such a thing! He built his life on integrity and the company's reputation. No wonder the financial report shows such a loss." She thought again of the missing papers that surely spelled out the reason for this whole sordid mess. "My father obviously had uncovered the person who was responsible. Now I think I know why he was killed."

"It's very important that the new CEO be informed immediately. When will he be named?"

"I'm the new CEO."

Lassiter's eyebrows flew up in surprise, and his face broke out in a broad grin. "Well, I'll be damned! Congratulations, my dear. I can't think of a better person, especially since none of the others can be trusted at this point."

"You're kidding . . ."

"No, I'm not, I'm afraid. In my last conversation with Derek, he made it very clear that one of his top men was responsible . . . obviously supplying second-rate materials and pocketing the difference. He was very closemouthed about who the culprit was, but assured me that he would take care of it confidentially, and make everything right with Linco — who, by the way, is consulting with lawyers about a lawsuit against Megtex."

"Oh my God, that would ruin us!" Alison's mind whirled with all the ramifications of a trial. It would mean the end of Megtex, public humiliation, a smear against her father's good name. "What can I do?"

Lassiter looked thoughtful. "Derek must have had

documentation. Maybe somewhere in his office . . ." He paused, giving the waiter time to serve their lunch.

Alison stared at her salad, sure that she wouldn't be able to swallow a bite. "Believe me, I've searched for days and can't find a scrap of evidence. Just before he died, my dad tried to tell me about something in his safe, but there's nothing there to give any kind of clue."

"Someone must have beat you to it."

"Oh yes, that's obvious."

Sam patted her hand, his eyes mirroring concern. "I don't mean to frighten you, but you could be in danger. Be careful about confiding in anyone."

Alison debated momentarily about mentioning the strange goings-on at her house. She finally decided that Sam Lassiter would understand. "Lately I've had reason to believe that someone is trying to scare me away, maybe even drive me to a breakdown."

Alarm flashed in Sam's eyes. "Good God—how?"

"Playing tapes of Dad's voice on the phone, things like that." Alison couldn't bring herself to say more. She couldn't bear hearing again that maybe she should see a doctor. She made an attempt to eat her lunch.

"Has anyone threatened you?"

"No, but I'm sure someone's following me—a woman who's there no matter where I go."

"Just keep your guard up all the time, and try not to go out alone."

"Tell me, Sam, how can I stall Linco and the government investigation?"

"I'm doing all I can on my end. Derek died just three days before he was due to testify at a closed committee hearing, set for the nineteenth. He knew who was responsible, and assured me that it would all be settled by then. Like I said, he felt honor-bound to protect the bastard who caused all this." He gave her a sheepish grin. "Pardon my language, my dear, it's just that I can't hold it back when it comes to this . . . this *person* who would bring Megtex down for his own profit."

"No need to apologize. I've called him much worse names in my mind during the last few minutes. How much longer do we have before this goes public and hits the press?"

"A few weeks maybe. I'll stall the committee as long as I can. Derek's untimely death will cause some kind of delay, but the people at Linco are hot, and I don't blame them."

Alison managed a weak smile. "You're a very good friend."

Sam gave her hand another fatherly pat. "Derek was more than a friend for many years — a generous supporter in every way. I'll do my best for his company . . . and you, Alison." He took the last sip of his coffee. "You haven't finished eating."

"Yes, I have . . . guess all this news took my appetite."

"How long will you be in town?"

"Until tomorrow. My flight is at noon."

"Well then, you'll be free later on. How about joining me at a cocktail party at the French Embassy? Some big government people are in town, and they're having a fancy shindig. What do you say?"

"Oh, I don't know . . . maybe I'll just stay in my room and think."

"Nonsense. A beautiful young woman needs to be seen, and besides, I hate going to these things at all, much less alone. Since Constance died, I've skipped as many as I could get by with."

Alison gave him a big smile. "You're on . . . what time?"

"I'll pick you up about five."

As soon as they parted, Alison realized that she hadn't brought anything suitable to wear to a cocktail party. Oh well, she had plenty of time, and maybe shopping would take her mind away from Sam Lassiter's devastating revelations.

She hailed a cab outside the hotel and soon found herself at Drysdale's, a little boutique tucked away on a fashionable Georgetown street. She hastily bought a black silk dress, its pencil-straight skirt a perfect fit and just the right length for a cocktail party. She dreaded the thought of a roomful of strangers, but she owed Sam Lassiter so much. She felt sure that without him, Megtex would already have come unraveled.

The embassy drawing room glowed with crystal chandeliers and polished French antiques. Alison's eyes took in the elegantly dressed people, the liveried servants, the buffets laden with exotic dishes and fine French wines. She smiled to herself, realizing that this was a typical Washington party, one that could be found somewhere in the city almost any night of the week.

When Sam became engaged in friendly debate with a fellow senator, Alison excused herself and started across the room to the bar. She stopped midway, her heart pounding. At the end of the room stood the woman who had been following her, engrossed in conversation with a group of people. Not dressed in black this time, she wore an emerald green dress with a matching turban that covered her hair. Something about her told Alison that she had to be the same woman . . . same small, petite body, same elegant bearing.

Alison hurried back to Sam Lassiter and took his hand, leading him to the center of the room. "Look . . . over by the wall . . . I think that's the woman who's been following me in Dallas. Do you know her?"

Sam gave the woman a close look. "I can't be sure, but she looks vaguely familiar."

"I'm going over there right now and confront her, find out who she is."

"Be careful."

Alison threaded her way through the milling guests, hope rising inside her that one piece of the puzzle would fall into place at last. But her spirits fell when she reached the end of the room. The woman was gone, nowhere to be seen. In desperation, she walked up to a man in the group.

"Do you remember the woman in the green dress who was here just a minute ago?"

"I think she just left the embassy."

"Do you know her name? Please, this is so important."

"Clare Cummings from London. Said she was a friend of the Ambassador's."

Alison felt defeated. How in God's name had anyone known where to find her? She was obviously dealing with someone who knew every move she made, every thought in her head. Sam was right; danger could be lurking all around her.

Eight

Alison couldn't wait to get back to tell Louis the real reason for her trip. Before boarding in Washington, she had called him from the airport to make sure he'd be in the office when she arrived. When her plane touched down at DFW, a limousine and driver were waiting to take her directly to the Archer Building. She hadn't expected this VIP treatment, even though her dad had always seen that her plane was met when she'd been off somewhere, but that was different. She didn't like this unnecessary ostentation, but realized that Louis was making every effort to be thoughtful and kind.

When she walked into her office, she found Louis waiting for her. "Thanks for sending a car," she said, "but I felt a little uncomfortable with the Las Vegas treatment."

Louis gave her a fatherly smile. "This was a special situation. Why, your life might even be in danger, and we don't know what kind of nut is running around out there."

Alison felt guilty. Here she was complaining, and Louis was just trying to protect her. "Sorry I mentioned it . . . thanks for taking such an interest. By the way, I didn't have a chance to apologize again for disturbing you and Cora Lee the other night. Guess I've been getting extra nervous lately."

She walked to the credenza against the wall, where Deena had left a silver tray containing coffee and finger sandwiches. Alison was glad she hadn't mentioned her nightmarish experiences to Louis when she called. Hopefully, seeing Derek's face and hearing his voice had been temporary hallucinations. Besides, seeing his image on TV had been so personal, so intimate. Suppose it really was her dad, managing to communicate from the great beyond? Impossible, she'd told herself a thousand times since that first phone call. Except for seeing that woman again, she had felt so much better in Washington. No voices, no visions, and she had enjoyed a full night's sleep for the first time since her dad's murder.

"I'm famished. Will you join me?" Alison poured herself a cup of coffee and picked up a sandwich. "Airline food makes me appreciate my own cooking, which leaves a lot to be desired, I'll admit. But it's ambrosia next to what was served on this afternoon's flight."

"Why, yes, I'll have some coffee."

Louis came over to pour his own, and they both moved to the conversation grouping of sofas and chairs in front of the black granite fireplace. It was too warm for a fire this time of year, but Alison could remember the days before energy conservation when Derek would turn the air-conditioning as cool as possible, so he could have fires going all spring long. So many memories, she thought. He was just too young to die. Over and over again she hoped that maybe that awful night was the real nightmare, and Derek would come walking through the door any minute. Oh, if only that could be true! Growing up without a mother had been bad enough, but he

95

had done a masterful job of being two parents in one. Losing him was more than she could bear.

"So, how long are you going to keep me in suspense?" Louis smiled. "You said on the phone that you'd learned something that might shed some light on the reasons for Derek's . . . for what happened to him."

"Oh, yes, I surely did." Alison came out of her reverie and took a bite of her sandwich. "I'll start at the beginning. Dad's last words had something to do with papers in his safe."

"Oh, really?"

Alison noticed the smile freeze on Louis's face, and realized that he, too, was suffering from the loss of a close friend.

"I mentioned the papers to Myra before she died, and she told me about the many times Dad had spoken to Senator Lassiter. So I called him, and he urged me to come to Washington. I didn't want anyone to know why I was going, because frankly, I didn't know myself." Alison walked over to the credenza, picked up another sandwich, and joined Louis again.

"And?" Louis sounded impatient.

"It turned out that he'd been consulting with Dad for a long time. It seems that Megtex is being investigated by the government for using inferior grades of materials in the Linco pipelines. Leaks and malfunctions are springing up everywhere. The Environmental Protection Agency is after us, as well as a Senate committee. And now, Linco is considering a lawsuit."

"How did this concern Derek?"

"My God, Louis, what a question! My father *was* Megtex. Linco has paid us millions to build those pipelines. You of all people know that."

"But surely Sam's not suggesting—"

"Oh brother! He's not suggesting anything . . . he *knows* that someone at Megtex is stealing Linco blind."

"That's impossible!"

"But it happened, and for all I know, it's still going on. And my dad knew who it was. He was supplying Sam Lassiter with information, everything but names. That's got to be why he was murdered, don't you think? I wanted you to be the first to know before I went to the police with this."

"Oh no, not the police! Don't rush into anything like that. Why, it would be headline news in a matter of hours. I can just see CNN sending investigators to check out every inch of Linco's pipelines. No, no, we have to be cautious. If Derek kept all this quiet, he must have had good reasons. Why, something like this could ruin us! We have to honor his memory by moving slowly, just as he did." He rubbed his forehead, his eyes filled with worry. "My God, I can't imagine who would do such a thing. Did Sam mention how they knew the materials were inferior?"

"Well, I think the troubles up and down the lines speak for themselves. You know, pilots survey the areas regularly, and they don't miss any funny stuff." She took a sip of coffee and sighed. "I suppose you're right about not alerting the police yet. I'm just so anxious to find Dad's murderer . . . and Myra's." She felt hot tears sting her eyes. "Sam believes that someone high up in the company is responsible. How could anyone be so money-hungry that he'd resort to murder? It's inconceivable, and I can't tolerate having him in the company another day . . . running around free, doing God knows what else."

Louis took her hands in his. "Don't you worry about any of this. I'll personally handle the investi-

97

gation. By God, we won't let the name of Megtex be dragged through the mud." He stood to leave, then hesitated. "You mentioned something about papers. Did you ever find them?"

"Oh, I thought I told you . . . no, nothing of significance was in the safe, and I've looked everywhere else. I wonder if Myra removed them, as soon as she heard Dad had been shot. It's possible that just the two of them knew about the papers, and where they were."

"Maybe they're somewhere in Myra's house. Have the police said anything about searching there?"

"No, but they don't tell me anything unless I ask. I do intend questioning the detective in charge the next time I see him. If they'd found the papers, surely he would have called, don't you think?" Alison didn't mention the key in the safe, because it didn't seem important enough. It could have been there for years and years. At the time Nick found it, she thought it might have a bearing, but as time went by, it seemed more likely that it opened something Derek had squirreled away years ago and forgotten about. Otherwise, why didn't he mention *it* instead of the papers?

"Well, I can't speculate on what the police might do. I've never had any occasion . . ."

"I should hope not . . . and I hope you never do. Their process seems so slow." Alison wiped her fingers and placed the napkin on the table. "You haven't eaten one bite, Louis. You usually polish off every sandwich on the tray. Do you feel all right?"

"This news you've come back with has taken my appetite."

"I know what you mean. I felt the same way in Washington when Sam dropped this bombshell."

"I can't imagine how this thieving, underhanded

business could have gone on right under my nose . . . and how Derek didn't mention it at all. It could be that Lassiter was wrong. It might be one hell of a mistake."

"Oh come on, Louis. Can you picture Derek Archer even bothering to communicate with Sam if he wasn't absolutely sure? Oh no, Dad must have had all the evidence and been sick about the dirt being heaped on Megtex's good name by some bastard. My God, someone's been stealing millions of dollars! This isn't petty larceny, it involves the U.S. government."

When Louis Bennett finally got away from Alison, his head was splitting wide open. He poured some water from a carafe on his desk and swallowed three aspirins, then sank into his leather desk chair. He held out little hope that Alison wouldn't get to the bottom of this. Now Piper would have to put more pressure on the girl. That damn trip to Washington had revived her spirits; before she went, she'd looked pretty close to falling apart. He still had to make sure her death looked like a suicide. Another murder would probably bring in the marines. It had to look like Alison couldn't face life as a basket case.

He ran his hand over his carefully combed hair. Oh hell, why worry so much? Piper would take care of the dirty work, and as long as there were no papers, who would ever suspect him?

Alison pushed the button on her intercom to answer a buzz from Jackie. She didn't feel like talking to anyone now.

"There's a call for you—"

"I'm not in. Just take a message."

"It's Lieutenant McAllister."

Alison had second thoughts. "Okay, put him on." Unconsciously, she pulled her compact out of her purse, and quickly checked her makeup before picking up the phone. This is crazy, she thought, when she realized what she'd done. Thank God no one else was in the room to see her acting like a giddy school-girl.

"Hello there, stranger," he said. "You did a disappearing act on me." Nick's voice was warm, almost intimate, but Alison bristled.

"What's that supposed to mean? I had business out of town."

"If I'm not mistaken, you'd been asked to report to the chief if you were leaving town. I'm glad you're back."

"Do you mean to say I'm still a suspect? Well, you certainly led me to believe otherwise. I can't imagine—" The warm, tingling feeling she'd felt with just the mention of his name quickly turned to anger toward this man, who had somehow wormed his way into her heart.

"Hold it, hold it . . . calm down. It's just the law, that's all. You were just asked to check in if you left town."

"Well, if you think for one moment—"

"Mind telling me where you went? I tried to call you about that matter we talked about."

"Oh, I'm sorry, I just had business to take care of. Tell you what, let me call you back on my private line, okay?" Alison wrote his number down, hung up the phone, and picked up another. "Now," she said when Nick answered.

"It's about the woman who's been following you," he said. "You were right about her. Doesn't seem to be hiding or anything."

"Well, who is she?"

"She's registered at the Fairmont under the name Clare Cummings. We checked out her home address in London."

"London, England?"

"Is there a London, Texas?"

"There's an everything in Texas. Sure, there's a New London in East Texas."

"Nice try, but this was London, England. and anyway the address was a fake—a warehouse. We couldn't arrest her because she hadn't broken any laws. Sorry, but when you left town, we lost track of her."

"That's because Clare Cummins followed me out of town!"

"Cummings."

"Whatever. It's weird, but she was in Washington at a cocktail party I decided to attend at the last minute. There's no way she could have known I'd be there."

"How did you recognize her? You said you never had a good look at her face."

"Oh, I'm positive now . . . she gave her name to a man I talked to. I tried to speak to her, but you know how those embassy parties are . . . jammed."

"Really? Frankly, I wouldn't know."

"Well, you haven't missed a thing. They're a real bore."

"Poor thing . . . how the rich have to suffer."

"Cut it out, Nick. I thought you were smarter than that."

"I am, just got whacked with a dose of jealousy."

"Oh my!" She knew he was probably teasing anyway. "*She* could be the shadowy figure who ran out the door when Dad was shot."

"Believe me, no one will be overlooked, but it happens that Clare Cummings arrived on Delta Flight

717 from New York on the morning of your dad's funeral. We haven't found out if she lives in New York, or whether she's really from Europe."

"I'm impressed. Would you be interested in a job at Megtex?"

"No thanks, I like it here. Seriously, I wanted to tell you that when my men went to search Myra Collins's house, they found it had been trashed."

"Trashed?"

"Someone had already been there and ripped the place apart."

"How awful! I spoke with some of her relatives at the funeral, and they didn't say anything about it. Must have been sparing my feelings. I wonder if whoever did it found the papers?"

"Alison, you've got to realize that your dad might not have been lucid in those last moments. It could be that there were no papers."

"Okay, then give me one good reason why he and Myra were both murdered. God, you don't have to be a Rhodes Scholar to figure there's something someone is afraid of! What about the key? Any results yet?"

"No, but we're still working on it. If we had dinner together tomorrow night, would there be anything left for us to talk about?"

"I feel sure we could think of something."

When she placed the receiver down, she was grinning from ear to ear. No need to deny it, Nick was getting to her. She'd never felt like this before. The time had come to have a long talk with John, the sooner the better. Alison picked up the phone once more, and dialed his office number.

They agreed to meet in the lobby of the Fairmont Hotel for a drink. Alison knew how John detested fighting the maze of one-way streets in downtown Dallas, but Clare Cummings was registered there, and she might get a good look at her. Well, just let her come walking in. The tables would be turned for a change. But right now, Alison had to concentrate on John.

"I've been working on the guest list for our wedding," she began.

John was visibly annoyed. "You mean you haven't finished yet? Good lord, you go rushing off to God knows where, without so much as a phone call, and now your list isn't even done?"

The drinks arrived, and they both took substantial gulps.

Alison looked him in the eye. "Maybe it's because I'm going through a trying time right now. Or maybe it's the transition at the office, I don't know."

"You shouldn't even *be* at the office. As I said the other night, you should be at Neiman's choosing china and stemware . . . a silver pattern. When are you going to realize that you're not cut out for running a large company? Why, you can't even decide what people to invite to our wedding, for God's sake. How do you expect to make multimillion-dollar decisions? I want you to be happy and rested when I need you."

Alison found it hard to keep a civil tongue. "You don't seem to understand that I don't need all that stuff. Our house is loaded with everything we could possibly use, so I don't need to register for gifts. Anyway, I think we should postpone the wedding plans until —"

"Postpone? Dammit, Alison, I'm fed up with your attitude! Ever since Derek died, you'd think the world has come to an end. He was your father, not your lover."

"Why, you bastard! Is that where your mind has been? He didn't die . . . he was murdered! I can just see your reaction if it had happened to that precious mother of yours!"

"You've never shown any feeling for my mother at all."

"You haven't shown much compassion for the woman you're supposedly in love with." Alison stood, knocking over her drink as she did so. She didn't give it a second glance. "I wanted this to be an amicable break, but I see that's not possible. You've shown me a side that makes my skin crawl, and I'm certainly glad I found out in time."

Alison felt completely exhausted, as though she had just spent a long session in the dentist's chair. Storming out of the Fairmont, she almost bumped into Clare Cummings on the way, but was too upset to care. She was in a full-blown rage, and glad she'd reduced John Carpenter to a sniveling wimp.

When she returned to the office, everyone was leaving the building, but she found Deena's light still on. She had to talk to someone—preferably a woman.

Alison stuck her head inside the door. "Hi, are you busy?"

"There's always so much to do here, I don't think I'll ever catch up." Deena was in the process of shreading papers.

"What's that all about?"

"Oh, the new computer came this morning, so I'm getting rid of the stuff I've already entered."

"Will you be much longer?" Alison couldn't keep the wistful note out of her voice.

Deena looked up. "I don't have to do all this tonight . . . it can wait until tomorrow. Why?"

"I need a sympathetic shoulder."

Deena seemed startled. "Something bad happen on your trip?"

"My trip—hell, that's a completely different story. This is personal."

"I'm a good listener and have strong shoulders."

"I'll use your shoulder, if you'll let me buy you dinner."

"Oh no, my figure can't afford the kind of meals you buy."

"Okay, we'll go to McDonald's or somewhere, and I promise not to stuff you with fries." Alison tried very hard to be flip, but couldn't quite manage it.

"Then let's go, boss." Deena stopped long enough to apply lipstick, then picked up her bag, turned off the lights, and was ready to leave.

They climbed into Alison's car in the parking garage, and began the trip through the heavy five o'clock traffic.

"I know, let's pick up Chinese . . . or better yet, have it delivered," Alison said. "Does that appeal to you?"

"Sure, and I think you could use a stiff drink when we get there. You sound pretty stressed out."

"Would you believe I've just come from cocktails with my former fiancé?"

"No wonder you're so upset—you broke your engagement?"

"I did."

Half an hour later, they had reached Inwood Road, where Alison made a right turn onto Stillmeadow. Soon they were comfortably seated in the den. Deena had fixed them each a Scotch on the rocks, then called in their order for Chinese food.

"Feel like talking about it?" Deena asked.

Alison kicked off her shoes and curled up in the oversized lounge chair, drink in hand. "What would

I do without you? Yes, I really need to talk to someone, someone I can trust not to repeat what I say. I have a feeling I can trust you."

"I appreciate that. And for what it's worth, I don't tell tales out of school."

"Well, it happened; I broke the engagement. John acted like a real prick . . . I never realized how insensitive he is. I'm actually glad to be rid of him, but you know, it's so strange. We've been planning to marry for over ten years, and that's a hell of a long time. I have to confess, I've never even dated anyone else."

"My God, I don't believe it . . . not in this day and age."

"Yes, your ultrasophisticated boss, CEO of an international corporation, has been acting like a child, and a naive jerk to boot. Everyone expected me to marry John, so I was going to oblige."

"I hope you discovered that you weren't in love with this guy, not the other way around. I don't see any tears, so that's a good sign."

"Oh, I made the choice. I walked out—no crying—and I feel good about it."

"If that's the case, why do you keep looking at the phone as if willing it to ring?"

Just at that moment, the doorbell rang. Alison almost jumped out of her chair.

Deena looked at her and laughed. "It's got to be the food. I'll get it."

When she returned, they went into the breakfast room, where they put all the cartons on the circular glass-topped table and sat down to eat.

"You didn't answer," Deena said between bites. "Why are you so uptight?"

Alison decided to trust Deena all the way—almost. She couldn't tell anyone but Louis about the trouble at Megtex, but she could talk about Derek's nocturnal messages. The thought struck her that she might hear his voice again, or even see his image, and Deena wouldn't. That was just too devastating to contemplate. "I've been this way since my father died. Before I went out of town on business, I was almost ready to check myself into a sanitarium."

"What are you saying?"

"I know it sounds melodramatic, but I was hearing Dad's voice, and once I even saw him on the TV screen. That's another reason I decided I couldn't marry John. He was a little sympathetic, but suggested I see a psychiatrist." Alison shook her head. "I'm really confused, but I know I'm not crazy. I function well at the office, but the moment I hit this house, it's as though I'm in another world." She smiled. "You know, it does help to talk things over with an outsider. Now that I'm not planning a wedding in this house, I can move to a hotel until I'm sure my head's on straight, that I'm not really driving on empty."

"Think that's a good idea? This sounds very strange, but you're no fool. If you say you heard a voice, then by God, I believe you. I think you should stay here and see this thing through, whatever it is. Suppose I spend the night with you, so I can corroborate your story? Surely you have a few extra bedrooms in this house." Deena's eyes twinkled. "I'll be your proof positive."

"Oh, that would be great, but I can't ask you to subject yourself—"

"Hold it, you didn't ask, I volunteered. It's all settled." Deena began to clear the table. "Let's throw out these cartons and . . . gosh, you hardly ate a thing. We can go to bed early and wait in the dark."

"You make it sound like a slumber party. It's been

so frightening, and I don't want you to think of this as a joke." Alison led the way to the kitchen.

Deena was silent as she rinsed out their glasses and put them in the dishwasher. "I just want to help you. All I can do is be your friend."

Alison dried her hands and smiled. "Okay then, it's a deal. I'll show you to the room next to mine. If the phone rings, pick it up in your room, too. If Dad's voice comes through the air ducts, or if he's on the TV screen, I'll come running in to alert you."

"Oh you poor thing . . . it has been frightening, hasn't it?"

Alison knew Deena wouldn't really understand unless she heard it herself. "Yes, it's been an awful nightmare." She opened her closet, pulled out a nightgown, and handed it to Deena. "This should fit, since we're about the same size."

All at once the phone rang, terrifying both women. Alison hesitated, then gingerly picked up the receiver. "Hello," she ventured in a whisper.

"Darling, are you all right?"

Alison heaved a sigh of relief, then turned to Deena. "It's only John."

Deena raised her eyebrows, then smiled and retreated to the room next door.

"Is someone in the house with you?"

Alison wished she could have told him it was another man, but he knew her too well to believe it. "Deena, the new girl from the office, is spending the night with me."

"Oh, I see. Listen, Alison, I've been puzzled about that off-the-wall outburst this afternoon. Let's just forget it ever happened."

"I'm all calmed down now, and feel exactly the same way. I hope we can still be good friends."

"You're being extremely selfish. Ever think of what you're doing to me . . . my future?"

"Let me tell you something, John, my life has been out of sync for weeks, and you certainly haven't been much help to me. Let's just worry about ourselves."

"At least have lunch with me tomorrow, and we'll talk some more."

"You haven't been listening . . . it's over. I'm going to sleep. Good night." Alison hung up, turned off the bedside light, and fell asleep.

Around midnight, the phone rang again. Alison sighed and began speaking as soon as she picked up the receiver. "Really, John, I've—"

"Come to me . . . I need you . . . come to me . . ."

Frantically, Alison dropped the receiver and screamed for Deena to pick up the phone. Holding her breath, she rushed into the next room.

Deena came awake quickly and grabbed her bedside phone, just as Alison rushed through the door. "There's just a dial tone," she said, a bewildered look on her face.

Alison grabbed the receiver away from her. Deena was right; just a dial tone. "But you did hear it ring? At least you can verify that it *did* ring?"

Deena sadly shook her head. "I'm so sorry, but I didn't hear the phone or anything, Alison."

Nine

The next day at work was a complete disaster. Everything Alison attempted seemed a waste of time. It frightened her to think of the havoc she might create in her present state of mind. She sat in her office alone, thinking about last night and the phone call that hadn't been real, all the other calls, the image of Derek on the TV, her father's death and Myra's. She felt choked, as if everything was closing in on her at one time. The burdens were too heavy, and they were piling up faster than she could bear.

She ran her fingers over the smooth top of the desk that had been her dad's for so many years. Derek had carved out Megtex with his bare hands, had started this company with little more than a dream and sheer determination. There must have been obstacles and black days in those early years, but he had come through. Somehow, she would survive, too. She was an Archer.

Alison thought about her talk with Senator Lassiter. According to him, the hearing would take place in just a few weeks, precious little time to avoid the demise of Megtex and all that Derek had stood for. So far, things were exactly the same since he died — no new evidence, no papers, no movement whatsoever toward a solution. She simply couldn't sit idly by and wait any longer. It was time to take matters into her own hands.

If she made a trip to San Diego, she could talk face to face with Kenneth Chandler at Linco, and discover for herself just how bad things looked for the company. She'd tell no one the real reason for her trip, simply explain to Louis and everyone else that she was going to La Costa for a rest and a change of scenery.

Alison picked up the receiver of her private line, dialed the number of Linco Oil, and asked to be put through to Kenneth Chandler.

"Who's calling please?"

"Alison Archer of Megtex."

Moments later, Kenneth Chandler came on the line, his greeting wary. "Miss Archer, this is a surprise. What can I do for you?"

"I think we need to meet. I've recently had news from Sam Lassiter that we've got big problems."

"You'd better believe we do. I'd have contacted you about this, but after what happened to your father, I didn't think you should be involved." His voice sounded more angry than sympathetic.

"Believe me, I am involved, but I don't want to say more over the phone. I'm planning a trip to La Costa soon, but I haven't made any reservations."

Kenneth Chandler didn't waste time on niceties. "It's almost past time for discussion. For your information, we're ready for action out here. But if you're coming anyway, you'd better make it soon. When will you get here? I can make your reservations."

"I'd like to leave on Friday, if nothing comes up here."

"Good, I'll fax everything to you by the end of the day."

"Thanks, Kenneth. Will you make that for two sepa-

111

rate rooms? I might decide to bring my secretary along. Her name is Deena Perry."

"You want the whole world in on this mess?"

From the tone of his voice, Alison thought she could use a friend when she confronted Chandler. She'd heard of his temper, his brusk manner. Originally a Texan, he was known to brook no nonsense from anyone. Almost apologetic, she said, "She doesn't know anything yet, but I believe she's trustworthy. I haven't decided whether or not to fill her in on everything, so I'll play it by ear. In any event, she could come in handy, but I'll give the idea second thoughts. I'm looking forward to seeing you."

"Thanks for calling," he said, sounding anything but grateful. "I'll see that your plane's met in San Diego."

When Alison put the receiver down, she felt apprehensive, but at least she was taking some action that might lead to her father's killer. Her adrenaline was flowing again. Feeling that she couldn't trust the police with all the details about the company's problems, she would do her own investigating. She could hardly wait. She wasn't losing her mind; someone was doing all these crazy things to her. By God, she was as sane as anyone. She pressed the button on her intercom. "Jackie, get me the chief of police."

Seconds later a voice boomed, "Anderson speaking."

"This is Alison Archer, and I was told to contact you if I had plans to leave town."

"So, since you've just gotten back, you thought you'd let me know. Well, let me tell you, Miss Archer, I don't care who you are or what connections you have in Dallas, you're legally bound to inform me of any departures from—"

"That's exactly what I'm doing. I'll be leaving for

112

San Diego on Friday, and you can contact me at the La Costa Spa if you have any news. You *are* still trying to find my father's murderer, aren't you?"

"Why certainly. Look here, you just got back from Washington yesterday. Why are you running off again so soon?"

"Oh, I see you've been speaking to Lieutenant McAllister." Alison supposed Nick had to report her whereabouts, but she wasn't sure she liked it.

"As a matter of fact, I have, and he's here right now talking in my bad ear. Just a minute, I'll get rid of him." Alison could hear a muffled argument on the other end of the line.

"Alison?" It was Nick.

She smiled into the phone. He had won that bout with the chief. "Yes, I was reporting in, just like you said, abiding by the law, like a good citizen."

"And where are you off to this time?"

"Really, Nick, do I have to report to you, too?" Alison knew she was being sarcastic, but she was flattered that he wanted to know."

"You could be in danger, and I don't want to take any chances."

"Don't worry . . . I'll be fine. No one knows where I'll be."

"Don't you understand? Two people are already dead."

"Oh yes, don't think for a minute that I don't understand. I also know that the murderer is still running around loose, and what are the police doing to make things safe for me?"

"We're working on it round the clock."

"Well, I'm leaving for California on Friday . . . unless I'm under arrest."

"I'll ignore that. Just be sure to leave your phone number and address, in case we have any news."

He hesitated. "Say, is dinner still on for tonight?"

Alison had forgotten all about their date. In fact, she had thought about checking into a hotel, but had decided against it. It entailed too much explaining to too many people. Being with Nick would make her feel safe. "Sure," she said, "what time?"

"Eight o'clock too late?"

"It's perfect; I'll be ready."

Once off the phone, Alison stepped into Deena's office. "If I decide I need you, would you be free to go out of town with me for a few days?"

"Sure, where are you going?"

"I'd rather not say, until I'm sure I'll need a secretary. But I promise to let you know as soon as possible, okay?"

"You're the boss. Just so I have time to farm out my dog."

"You never mentioned having a dog. What's its name?"

"His name is Barley, and he's been great company since Carl walked out."

Alison felt guilty. "I'm sorry, I've been so absorbed in my own problems that I forget how lost you must feel. You were so good to spend the night with me, just to help me out. How in the world could that man have left you?"

"Guess he found it easy. One morning he left for work, and never came back. The next day I heard from his lawyer."

"God, he sounds rotten." Alison couldn't understand how any man could leave Deena. She was not only beautiful, but also intelligent and compassionate.

Deena didn't seem upset. "Guess I should have seen it coming. Honestly, I don't miss him at all. Barley was always my dog, and he's about the only thing I got in the settlement besides a few pieces of furniture. I'd have fought tooth and nail for custody if I'd had to."

Alison smiled. "Okay, I'll let you know in time to make arrangements for Barley."

Alison and Nick sat across the table, drinks in hand, not saying a word, just looking at each other. A force between them gave off electric signals that seemed to bond them together like metal to magnet.

Nick spoke first, his voice low and husky. "You have the most remarkable eyes I've ever seen." He reached out and traced the lines of her hand with one finger.

Alison shivered at his touch. Something about him stirred her deep inside, a feeling she couldn't explain. "I've broken my engagement to John."

Nick's eyes lit up. "When did this happen?"

"Yesterday."

"Are you glad or sad?"

"Relieved is more like it."

"Then it calls for a toast." He poured them both more wine and raised his glass to hers. "Here's to our new beginning." Nick touched Alison's glass, and they both took a sip of wine, their eyes locked over the tops of their glasses.

"What does that mean, Nick?"

"Somehow I knew something was going to happen between us, before I even met you."

"Before you met me?"

"I know this sounds pretty soapy coming from a cop, but I fell for a portrait that I thought might be you. Juanita told me later that it was your mother. Anyway, it came to life when I saw you the first time, all curled up in that big chair. Only you were even more beautiful than the portrait."

Alison watched as his eyes focused on her, and she felt so vulnerable. She had to move cautiously, not let

115

herself fall under the spell of this tall, rangy man who oozed masculinity. The finger continued to caress her hand. "It's one thing to imagine someone in a portrait, but you don't know me at all." She looked at him, her eyes mirroring her confusion. "I like being with you, but it's too soon to think of anything more. I'm still in shock over all that's happened . . ." She stopped, unwilling to trust her voice any further.

"Sure, I know . . . don't mean to rush you. This mystery has to be cleared up first, or neither one of us will rest easy." He gave her a little smile. "Just wanted you to know how I feel before you go running off to California."

The waiter who had been hovering just out of earshot appeared with their dinner salads, and Alison was glad for the interruption. Maybe their conversation would take a new direction.

"Do you have any memory of your mother?" Nick asked.

"It's strange, but I've always felt as though I remember her very well. I grew up with that portrait and had regular conversations with it . . . sort of my lifeline with reality, even though it was pure fantasy." She laughed. "That doesn't make much sense to anyone else."

"Tell me what you remember about her." He leaned forward, not wanting to miss a word.

Nick's infatuation with the portrait of her mother fascinated Alison. She'd never known a man quite like him, so virile and sensitive. She began to relax, realizing how comfortable she felt around him. Here was a man who liked himself, nothing pretentious about him at all, even in his clothes, like the open-necked sports shirt and casual slacks he wore tonight. Alison thought about John, and immediately contrasted the two men in her mind—John so impeccably dressed

116

and precise . . . Nick so casual and unassuming. She was glad she'd worn a simple blouse and skirt.

"I might bore you." Alison felt color rise in her cheeks, feeling unexpectedly embarrassed.

"No, I'd love to hear about her."

"Her name was Claudia . . . Claudia Covainne, before she married my dad. They met in Paris and she was French."

Nick seemed surprised. "I didn't know that."

"Oh yes, she was very French, but spoke English fluently. I remember how the two of us chattered away in French all the time, but when Derek entered the room, we'd always switch to English. Strange, but I just remembered that for the first time."

"Maybe Derek didn't speak the language."

"Oh, he did, very well, now that I think of it. After my mother died, he never uttered a word of French again. I'm sure he adored her and was devastated by her death, but sometimes I get little flashes and remember angry words. Funny how little things stick in the mind of a child. I loved the smell of her hair and the feel of it . . . like silk. My grandparents took care of me when they made that last trip to Europe." She cleared her throat, then went on. "They were in an accident near Nice on a mountain road. My mother was killed, but my dad was barely scratched. He had the funeral in Paris, because of her family there, and I never saw her again."

"This is a very sad, interesting story. How did they meet?"

"They were both young, and Dad was just beginning to branch out in a big way. He was bidding for a contract to build a pipeline that a Middle Eastern country was about to start. A very rich Arab happened to be in Paris." She smiled. "I think my mother was his girlfriend."

117

"And Claudia left this man to marry your father and live in Dallas, Texas? What a comedown for her."

Alison gave him a devilish look. "Yeah, but she was in love." She sighed heavily and they both started laughing.

"That brings me to something I want to talk over with you."

"Oh?"

"I really wish you wouldn't go off by yourself at a time like this. You know, there's a killer out there, who might find it very convenient to meet up with you out of town."

"Oh, don't worry, I'll be extra careful"

"Someone was serious enough to kill your father. Who knows why crazies do what they do?"

"I'll be careful, and I may take Deena along for company."

"Who's Deena?"

"She's the woman we hired to take poor Myra's place. She's turned out to be a jewel, which goes to prove, no one is indispensable. That's sad, isn't it?"

"Well, if I were you, I wouldn't broadcast where you're going. The fewer people who know it, the better." Nick gave her a teasing look. "Sure you're not just going to a spa for a vacation?"

"Always the detective, right?" Alison turned to the waiter who was serving their steaks. "Oh, that looks marvelous. I'm starving!" Saved by the proverbial bell, she thought, as she searched for something to say that would take Nick's mind off the real reason for her trip. She didn't have to look far. Directly in the doorway of the restaurant stood the woman in black, Clare Cummings, as Alison had recently learned. "Nick . . . look! There's that Cummings woman again. Why does she follow me everywhere? What on earth does she want?" Alison started to leave the table, intending to

118

confront her, but Clare Cummings had already turned and disappeared through the front door.

"I could catch her, but I doubt if it would do any good. This is a free country, and she knows it." Nick took Alison's hand, and they both sat down again. "See what I mean? There are all kinds of kooks running around. I wish you wouldn't go."

Alison pressed his hand. She couldn't tell him yet that she had to attend to a matter on the west coast that might help to clear up everything here.

"Okay, Bennett, what's so important? Why did I have to let my dinner get cold to rush out here and meet you?"

Louis Bennett was literally shaking all over, terrified that someone might see them. He wasn't sure that meeting in the Northpark Mall parking lot was such a good idea after all, but he had to let Piper know that Alison was going to La Costa. This was the first public place he could think of on the spur of the moment. "I thought you'd want to make plans to leave town. Our new CEO already has one foot in California. Says she's going for a rest. Can you beat that? I should be the one leaving for a stay at an expensive spa, not her. Why the hell does she need a vacation? *I* do all the damned work."

"You'd better watch yourself, Lou; sounds like you're hitting the skids. If you let jealousy eat you up, you'll be no good to anyone. Just leave everything to me . . . that's what you pay me for."

"Well, I had to let you know she's leaving."

"Oh, hell, I know that, but she's not going for any back rubs. Seems she's going to meet with a guy by the name of Kenneth Chandler."

"Oh my God! Are you sure?" Bennett felt a sudden

119

pain shoot through his chest. He was sure he'd have a heart attack right in the middle of this parking lot.

"Of course, I'm sure. Hey, are you okay?"

Louis took several deep gulps of air. "Did you say Kenneth Chandler?"

"Yeah."

"How could you know that? She told me she was going to La Costa." The pain eased somewhat. He hoped he'd survive this meeting. It wouldn't do any good to get control of Megtex if he were dead, too.

"Easy. I put a tap on her private phone last week. Want to know where she is right now?" Piper didn't wait for an answer. "She's at a restaurant on Crescent Court with Lieutenant McAllister, having a good hot meal." Piper's look was ominous.

"I should have known better than to think I could tell you something you didn't already know. But I'm not sorry I ruined your dinner, so don't get smart with me. Looks like we need to speed up our plans."

Louis didn't intend giving any reasons to Piper, who was hired to do a job by any timetable prescribed. If Alison met with Chandler, she was sure to find out too much. She had to disappear soon, be out of the picture completely. This would be the perfect time to arrange a foolproof suicide. Forget trying to make her seem incompetent with those damned tapes.

"See if you can figure out a way to get rid of Alison in California. I'll leave the method up to you, as long as it looks like attempted suicide. All options are open, understand?"

Piper nodded. "In that case, you'd better send your black suit to the cleaners. Your CEO might be coming home in the proverbial pine box."

Ten

Alison decided against taking the company plane to San Diego, since she'd told everyone that this was a pleasure trip. She called Kenneth Chandler back to tell him that Deena would not be going with her and that she preferred to make her own hotel arrangements. Fortunately she was able to put in half a day at the office before her flight, giving her time to prepare for her first meeting with Kenneth Chandler in the La Costa Hotel lobby at seven. She felt nervous about this meeting; Chandler was one of the wealthiest and most knowledgeable men in the business.

Feeling that she should have as much information as she could find on every man in a key position at Megtex, she had gathered dossiers on Tom Stockwell, Maynard Simmons, Carl Wallace, and Jack Woolridge. It made her stomach turn to consider the possibility that any one of these men could be involved in theft, fraud, even murder, God forbid. Thank heavens there was no need to add Louis Bennett's name to the list; he had served the company loyally for thirty years, and been her dad's best friend.

The sun was still high in the sky when Alison arrived in San Diego. She felt relieved to see a hotel driver holding up a sign with her name on it when she stepped off the plane. After collecting her luggage, he seated her in the limousine and headed through San Diego, then took the highway leading to La Costa, a distance of about thirty miles. The cool breeze from the sea felt delightful after the muggy weather in Dallas this morning. It was hard to believe that May was already underway; weeks had gone by and still the police were no closer to solving her father's murder. Maybe this trip would uncover some clues. Oh, if only that could be true, and her life could get back to normal again. The familiar signs—La Jolla Village, Delmar, Rancho Santa Fe, Carlsbad—flew by as they traveled Highway 5, then finally, when they reached La Costa Drive, they turned right at the entry to the hotel. On hills of lush green grass were two signs, spelled out in red and white blossoms, La Costa Hotel and Spa.

The limo wound past condos on the right and hotel rooms on the left, until they arrived at the covered double entrance, where young men dressed in knickers, argyle socks, and jaunty caps busily greeted guests and parked cars.

Alison welcomed the relaxed atmosphere when she walked into her room. Even though she hadn't come for the many amenities the spa offered, she couldn't wait to get into comfortable, leisure clothes. She realized how uptight she'd been since her trip to Washington. Once again she had to question her ability to run such a complex company, and she knew Kenneth Chandler couldn't wait to vent his anger at someone from Megtex. No doubt she would be his target tonight.

If she could be confident of her emotional stability, Alison felt sure she could carry on the duties of her new title. But since these weird happenings had all but taken over her life and possibly her sanity, she worried about her ability to cope with the problems that hovered over

Megtex like a black fog. If there was ever proof of her instability, she wouldn't hesitate to pass the reins on to Louis Bennett. But first, she had to deal with this terrible scandal and financial loss. She would do her damndest to convince Chandler that Megtex would not only clean up the mess, but also make financial restitution.

Alison arrived in the lobby at precisely seven o'clock, not wanting to give Chandler any reason to be any more annoyed. Dressing carefully in white silk slacks, matching tank top, navy silk jacket, and heels for a dressier look, she had swept her hair up high on her head, trying to appear older, more sophisticated.

She didn't have to wait long. Kenneth Chandler bounded through the massive, brass doors of the entrance like a charging bull. He was in his fifties, tall and heavyset, with a head of iron gray hair that sat on a thick, short neck and gave the impression that it rested directly upon his shoulders. Dressed in gray slacks, a black sports coat, and a white open-necked shirt, his figure was so imposing that Alison almost overlooked the tall, slender young man at his side.

"So you're Alison Archer," Chandler said in a booming voice. "We've spoken on the phone so many times, that I had a preconceived idea of your looks. Seems I was all wrong . . . you're a hell of a good-looking woman."

Alison shook his hand. "And I'm glad I'm finally meeting you face to face." She gave him her most winning smile.

"This is my son, Chris. Brought him along as referee . . . also as a chaperone, since my wife doesn't trust me out of her sight." His laughter almost took over the lobby.

After shaking Alison's hand, Chris said, "We've made reservations in the Champagne Room, if that's all right . . . or we could go downstairs to the Figaro Room? Which do you prefer?" He was a good-looking young man, with dark hair and even features, and Alison could tell right away that he felt totally eclipsed by his flamboyant father.

"The Champagne Room suits me just fine." Alison was surprised that Chandler had brought his son to what she thought would be a private discussion.

On their way to the dining room, they passed groups of people seated in intimate clusters of sofas and cocktail tables, each with its own floral arrangement. Once in the Champagne Room, Chandler wasted no time in ordering drinks, then got down to the business at hand.

"Megtex has been screwing the hell out of us for years, and I hope you know that our attorneys are preparing our lawsuit." He gave her a dark look. "You're in a barrel of shit, young lady."

Alison was taken aback by the man's language, but tried her best not to look shocked. She was in a man's world and had to accept it on those terms. In her dealings with men, she couldn't expect them to make concessions that would create even more resentment toward her as a woman. "So I've been led to believe. I want you to know that this problem is news to me. I flew to Washington last Monday and met with Senator Lassiter. Believe me, I had no idea of any thefts or inferior materials until he filled me in on what my dad had been doing to trap the culprits." Alison looked him squarely in the eye, trying to keep her tone factual and honest. "I'm not trying to shirk our responsibility."

"Don't worry, you wouldn't get to first base if you tried." The dark look in his eyes made her shudder inside.

"Nor would I want to. I know that there's a criminal in a high level position at Megtex, and apparently that's why my father was killed."

"Murdered?" Chandler looked shocked. "But I thought he was shot by a burglar."

"Oh no . . . nothing was taken or even touched in the house. The only thing missing are some papers in the office safe that Dad mentioned just before he died. I think they hold the key to why he was killed. Does that sound like a robbery?"

"Well, we even heard out here that you were under suspicion for a while. We thought . . ."

"And so did the police, because it would have been very convenient." Alison looked directly into Kenneth Chandler's cold, gray eyes. "No sir, I loved my father very much, and we worked well together. I could never have harmed him in any way." She fought back tears that threatened to fill her eyes. She wouldn't let herself cry. That would ruin the image of strength she so desperately wanted him to see.

"So you think that without your knowledge, someone in your company has been stealing from us . . . and Archer . . . all these years?"

"Without question." Alison looked earnestly at both men, aware that though Chris's eyes were glued on her, he hadn't yet uttered a word. "Now . . . I'm here to ask you—beg you if I have to—for enough time to search through our files until I locate the guilty party and make restitution. In the meantime, we'll continue to search for those missing papers."

"Are you suspicious of anyone?" Chris asked, finally joining in the conversation.

"Frankly, no, and that's what makes the whole thing so unbelievable. I can't stand to think that one of the trusted men in our organization could have killed my dad."

"I've dealt directly with Derek most of the time . . . one hell of a guy," Kenneth Chandler said. "Also had a few conversations with Louis Bennett and Maynard

125

Simmons over the years . . . decent, intelligent men." His voice and manner seemed softer. Maybe the ingestion of food had something to do with his mood. He was consuming a tremendous dessert at the moment, after an enormous steak with all the trimmings.

"I know, and I can't tell you what a bad position this puts me in. I'm fond of all of them, and they do a tremendous job at Megtex. But I'll tell you for sure, I'm going to get to the bottom of this, if it's the last thing I do. And, Mr. Chandler," she added in a determined voice, "I swear to you that every faulty pipe, every leak, every break will be repaired or replaced. That's the way my father ran Megtex, and that's how it will be run in the future. You have my word on that."

"My, my, such a broad statement from a slip of a girl like you!" Chandler looked skeptical, but a smile broke out on his face.

"You'd be surprised how tough I can be."

"Well, you eat like a scrawny little bird."

Alison laughed. "You should see me when I'm relaxed."

"Well, I for one would like to see that," Chris said. "How about going cruising with me Sunday morning? I promise, no business . . . all pleasure."

"I suppose that depends on the answer I get from your father." Alison turned to the founder of one of the most successful oil companies in the world. "Will you give us time to make amends before you carry out your threats?"

Kenneth Chandler leaned back in his chair and chuckled. "Guess Derek knew what he was doing when he wanted you to head up Megtex. You're one hell of a salesman . . . er, woman." He stood and pulled out Alison's chair in a courtly manner. "You've got thirty days, young lady, no more, to see if you can keep the shit from hitting the fan." He held out his hand and shook Alison's firmly.

"So now you have your guarantee," Chris said, smiling. "Boat ride Sunday morning? I'd say tomorrow, but I have to fly to L.A. for the day."

"Sounds good to me. I'd love it." Alison felt reluctant to tell him that she'd planned to return to Dallas on Sunday, afraid to do anything that could possibly irritate Kenneth Chandler and cause him to change his mind. She could always leave Sunday night or Monday.

"Do you enjoy being on a boat?" Chris looked hopeful.

"I used to love it. We have a place on Padre Island off the southern Texas coast, and I went there often with my dad when I was a kid. We fished from the pier and did some sailing."

"Great, then I'll pick you up around eight-thirty. We'll get some juice and coffee in the Brasserie, and take them with us in thermoses. Okay with you?"

"Sounds like fun."

While Alison was saying goodbye to the Chandlers, Piper stole out of the Champagne Room. So, Miss Archer was going boating on Sunday. That presented somewhat of a problem. Bennett insisted that this icing must look like a suicide. What to do? Piper thought a minute, then took the central stairway down to the arcade floor, where the Brasserie was located. Music came from the dining room that used to be considered just a coffee shop. By walking through the kitchen like someone who was lost, it would be easy to see the back entry.

Perfect. Now locating some liquid morphine sulphate and adding about a hundred milligrams to Chandler's thermoses, would simplify the whole thing. Piper

127

laughed and crossed the driveway to the hotel side to register for a room. What the hell . . . a night or two in a beautiful room, maybe a whole free day for golf tomorrow. Everything was working out just right.

Sunday turned out to be a beautiful day for boating. Chris's cabin cruiser was an expensive model, about forty-five feet in length. Alison was glad that Chris had asked her to join him. As she came to realize, he was an amiable fellow with a lot more personality than he had displayed at dinner Friday evening when he was no doubt intimidated by his father.

"My, the weather's perfect today," Alison said.

Chris shook his head. "Don't tell me you didn't know that every Sunday is perfect here." Chris threaded his way past the many boats anchored in the marina. Soon they were speeding along in the open waters of the Pacific Ocean. "Know how to handle a cruiser?"

"You'll have to start from scratch on this one." Alison laughed, feeling wonderfully relaxed for the first time in many weeks, her hair blowing in the wind and the spray of salt hitting her face. She felt young and healthy, and best of all, free. Free of all the worries of her job, free of hallucinations, and free of the shadowy woman in black who continually stalked her.

"Want to do some fishing?" Chris seemed anxious to please, and Alison couldn't help but wonder what his life was actually like.

"Not really. I'm content right here." She was sitting in a captain's chair next to Chris. "Anytime you want to show me how to steer this cruiser, I'll be glad to take the wheel and let you fish."

"Maybe after lunch."

"Lunch? I thought you just picked up juice and coffee."

"Oh, yeah," Chris said with a smile, "it's time for breakfast now; lunch was my big surprise."

"I'll go down and get the thermoses." Alison wove her way along the outside of the cabin until she came to the steps, then descended to the tiny galley below. There were sleeping quarters for four people beyond the galley, plus a bathroom and shower. This was truly an elegant cabin cruiser. She was wearing white shorts and a yellow sweatshirt, both purchased yesterday in one of the hotel shops.

Back on the top deck, she twisted the top of the thermos and poured two glasses of orange juice, which they both downed in a hurry when the water became suddenly choppy.

"You have to be careful of the traffic out here," Chris said. "On a beautiful Sunday like this one, it seems that everyone is out on the water."

"Ah ha, I caught you! So Sundays *aren't* always sunny and bright, huh?"

"Maybe not, but please don't turn me in. I might be banned from California forever."

They both laughed and Alison poured coffee into two mugs.

"Come on," Chris said, "take the wheel. You'll see how even a child can maneuver this boat."

"Gee, thanks a lot. If I do a rotten job, will you throw me overboard?"

"You never know."

Chris gave her a few instructions, and before long, Alison had caught on. When she took the wheel alone, she felt wildly exultant, in total command of the craft and the sea. But suddenly the euphoria vanished, replaced by nausea, dizziness . . . then everything started to go black. "Chris . . . help me . . . I can't . . . oh God, that speed boat . . . we're going to . . .

129

Eleven

Kenneth Chandler burst into the emergency room at Scripps Hospital, his heart pounding hard against his chest. His only son lay somewhere in this miserable place, and no telling what they were doing to him. He spotted a man in a white coat talking to a policeman, and rushed over to the desk.

"How the hell is my son?"

"Excuse me?" the young intern said.

"My boy, Chris Chandler, how is he? I'm Kenneth Chandler."

"Looks like he's going to be fine. He's in X-ray now, and should be out shortly."

Chandler relaxed considerably as a heavy weight began to lift from his shoulders. "Thank God for that! What the hell happened anyway?"

The policeman held out his hand. "I'm Lieutenant Morgan, Mr. Chandler. Why don't we go into the waiting room, so we can talk?" He led the way and the two men sat down in facing chairs.

"Now, tell me," Chandler said. "What happened out there? Chris is an excellent sailor."

"I've just come from the marina, and it seems the girl was steering. Your son's still pretty groggy, but according to him, they both blacked out at the same time."

"Blacked out? From what, for God's sake?" Chandler stood and began pacing the floor, his large frame taking up most of the space in the waiting room.

"Is your son into drugs by any chance?"

"Hell no, never touches the stuff. And don't ask me how I know. I just do, and I still want to know how this thing happened."

"Like I said, your son said they blacked out. As a result, they ran head-on into another craft. Your son was lucky . . . seems he was thrown overboard and picked up by some guy in another boat."

Chandler could see "law suit" written all over this one. "Anyone hurt in the boat they hit?"

"Apparently not. The couple saw the cruiser coming, and they both jumped into the water just in the nick of time. Their boat was totaled, of course, but aside from a royal soaking, they're fine."

"Thank God for that. Now back to the woman . . . why the hell was she steering? Chris loves that cruiser, and wouldn't give the wheel to just anyone. Did she intend to kill them both or what?"

"Do you know this girl, uh woman? Any identification she might have had must have gone overboard, because we couldn't find any."

"Yes, I certainly do. She was visiting from Dallas, staying at La Costa. This girl, as you call her, was just made CEO of a large international corporation, by the way. She came out here on business. How is she?"

"Poor thing probably didn't know what hit her. According to the doctor, she has a pretty bad gash on her head and a few minor injuries, but other than that, she's in pretty good shape."

"Can I see her?"

"I'll ask the doc, but can you give me her name, sir?"

"Sure, Alison Archer. Seems like such a responsible young woman. I wonder what the hell came over her."

131

Morgan jotted down Alison's name in a black notebook. "That's what we're trying to find out. There's been some talk about a suicide pact. Any reason to suspect anything like that?"

"Good lord, you've got to be crazy! They just met, for God's sake! Alison came out here to see me."

"Maybe your son was jealous."

"I can see right now, you've been watching too much TV. Neither one of us had even met the woman until last Friday. Dream up another scenario, officer, and if you can't do any better than that, you'd better hand in your badge." Kenneth Chandler turned away in disgust, and plopped into another chair that didn't quite fit him.

At that moment, a nurse approached them. "Lieutenant, Dr. Cheever would like to see you. He's in the trauma room with the young woman."

Chandler jumped up. "I'm coming with you."

"Is that allowed?" Morgan asked.

"It all depends . . . is he family?"

"No, this is Kenneth Chandler, the injured man's father, and he knows her."

"Yes, I think that's all right. The doctor has finished, and we're about to move her to a private room."

Dr. Cheever greeted them when they walked into the examining room.

Chandler sucked in his breath at the sight of Alison. God, she looked so pale. "Will she be all right?"

"She's still out cold," the doctor said. "I just sewed up a nasty head wound . . . looked much worse than it turned out to be. Aside from some bruises and a couple of cracked ribs, she ought to be in pretty good shape in a couple of days. We're moving her to 610."

Alison's eyes opened slightly and focused on Morgan. "Are you a policeman?" Her voice was weak, barely audible.

132

Morgan leaned forward. "Yes, ma'am, can you tell us what happened?"

"No . . . not yet . . . oh, I feel so sleepy."

"Do you have any family, anyone we should call?"

"Yes, Lieutenant McAllister. Homicide . . . Dallas Police. Important." Alison faded away again.

Grateful for the two-hour difference in time, Nick arrived at Scripps Hospital at ten o'clock that night, just as Dr. Cheever left Alison's room and started down the hall. Fortunately he'd gotten a seat on the late flight that put him in California in time to see the doctor before he finished his evening rounds. Pulling out his badge, he stopped the man, introduced himself, and asked about Miss Archer's condition.

Dr. Cheever shook Nick's hand. "She's a lucky young woman, Lieutenant. With that head wound so close to the eye, she could have been blinded. From the way that cruiser plowed into the other boat, it's a wonder she wasn't killed. As it is, she should be up and around in a couple of days."

"Any idea how it happened?"

"Frankly no. They both seem to have suffered some kind of blackout. They looked drugged when they came in, but there was no sign of anything foreign in either of their systems. Chris's head seemed to clear sooner than Miss Archer's, and he kept wondering if there was something wrong with the drinks in the thermoses. Seems they both felt fine until they drank the juice and coffee. If that's the case, and mind you, this is pure speculation, it's possible that his head cleared faster because he'd had a full breakfast."

"Any idea who filled those thermoses?"

"Someone in the Brasserie kitchen at the La Costa Hotel, according to Chris. It's strange, though, that there was no sign of food poisoning . . . nothing like

133

that, and the police never found the jugs. Must have been lost in the crash." He looked at Nick curiously. "Tell me, officer, were you the one who asked for police protection for Miss Archer?"

"Yes, and I see they already have a man posted at the door." Nick could see room 610 from where they were standing, and could also tell that the doctor was curious.

"And you flew out here from Dallas to investigate this accident? Must be an important case."

Nick had no intention of going into an explanation. "If it's okay with you, I'd like to visit Miss Archer now, and by the way, thanks for all you've done for her. Another thing, which room is Chris Chandler in?"

"624, but I'm afraid he's asleep again, and so is Miss Archer."

Nick held out his hand. "I'll just check anyway."

After they shook hands, Nick hurried to Alison's room, showed his identification to the officer seated in front of the door, then quietly went in. Looking unusually pale, Alison lay very still on the narrow bed. Even though the doctor had assured him that she would be fine, Nick felt a stab in his heart at the sight of her bandaged head. He stood over her for some time, and finally pulled a chair close to the bed and sat down.

Alison looked so young and defenseless, too young to be out here all alone trying to do battle with a man like Kenneth Chandler. Nick had checked him out before he left Dallas, and found that he owned Linco, one of the largest oil companies in the world. What could be so important that Alison couldn't handle it on the phone? He looked forward to meeting this Kenneth Chandler. It occurred to him that maybe Alison had come all this way to do her own detective work. That sounded just like her. Her life was in constant danger, and still, she insisted on taking chances.

Alison moved her hand to the bandage on her forehead, then opened her eyes. At the sight of Nick, she smiled one of those special smiles that lit up her whole face. "I was hoping you'd come, Nick . . . you've had a haircut. I like it."

He wanted to ask a million questions, but all he could do was pick up Alison's hand and hold it to his lips. "You're going to be okay. The doctor said you could get out of here in a couple of days." He watched as her hand moved back to the bandage. "Don't pull on that. You've had a few stitches, but you'll be fine."

"You were right, Nick, someone is trying to kill me. I thought I was being so careful . . ." Her eyes filled with anxiety. "Oh God, what happened to Chris?"

When she tried to sit up, Nick eased her back down and plumped up her pillow. He could tell she was in pain, but she was trying hard to remember. "Let's wait 'til you feel better to go into all this."

"Please, I've got to know. I was steering, I remember that, but I started feeling so woozy, and everything began to fade away. The last thing I saw was another boat. Oh my God, what happened to everyone?"

"Well, if it makes you feel any better, it seems you got the worst of it. When the officer called me in Dallas, he said everyone else was in good shape, so don't worry about that."

"Then Chris is okay?"

"Sure is. In fact, the doctor said he was sleeping like a baby right down the hall."

"Oh, I wrecked his beautiful new cruiser. I feel terrible."

"Well, I don't. I'm just glad you're alive." Nick felt so awkward, trying to put his feelings into words. He had a million things he wanted to tell her, like how she'd been in his thoughts every moment since they first met, how the thought of her made him feel good all over. But he couldn't say any of these things to her now, and probably never could. They lived in two separate worlds, had different dreams, different worries. Basically, he had chosen to live a relatively simple life and had no plans to change it, while Alison's corporate lifestyle seemed almost too complex even for a John Carpenter-type. Nick was out of his class and he knew it, but that didn't stop him from longing for her.

"I'm scared, Nick. Promise you won't leave me alone."

"Of course, I won't. In fact there's a policeman stationed right outside your door."

"Funny how things change, isn't it? Remember how I resented the police surveillance in Dallas? Now I'm grateful for it. I wonder who tried to kill me."

"I don't know yet, but I'm sure going to try to find out."

Alison smiled and closed her eyes. "You'll find him. You're a good cop, Nick." She was asleep again.

Nick decided to do a little investigating on his own. When he'd rented a small compact car at the airport, he'd realized too late that it was next to impossible to twist his tall body enough to fit comfortably into the bucket seat. He was in a big hurry to get to the hospital, so he hadn't taken the time to exchange it. Now as he ducked his head and pushed his legs into place again, he cursed the automaker who must have forgotten that some Americans were oversized. He started the motor and pulled away from the curb, heading north on Highway 5 on his way to the Brasserie in the La Costa Hotel.

Piper sat in a rented Toyota outside Scripps Hospital, weighing options and trying to form a workable plan of attack on Alison Archer, while she was still in the hospital. It was one hell of a shame that the boat crash hadn't

136

killed the damned woman like it should have, but it was just as well. The hospital was a perfect place to create a bogus suicide. Here was this poor, confused young woman, suffering from injuries, giving up on life, and wanting to join her father in the great beyond. Perfect. Piper snickered. So, why shouldn't she just up and slash her own wrists? What a way to go!

Well, since Alison wasn't about to oblige Louis Bennett by turning off her own lights, she needed a little help. Piper smiled wickedly. She just might need some coaxing, have someone do it for her. There was still some liquid morphine sulphate that hadn't been added to the thermoses. Funny how the police never mentioned finding them. Must have blown up in the accident. Pity it hadn't been the Archer woman instead.

There was enough of the drug left to put her out cold again, so it would simply be a matter of slipping into her hospital room to put her out, then coming back to do a little slashing . . . maybe with a piece of broken compact mirror. Great idea.

Figuring out how to get into her room presented the biggest problem. Piper got out of the car, deciding to case the corridors right now.

Later that night, the plan was in place. Piper stole into a closet and found a white coat that fit perfectly. The next move was getting that damned cop away from Alison's door.

Stopping by room 624, Piper pushed the door open. Good, Chris Chandler was sound asleep. Piper left the room smiling, but changed expressions quickly when the policeman guarding Alison's door came into view.

"Officer, help! The patient in 624, you know the one in the accident with Miss Archer? Well, he's screaming for a policeman. Hurry! I'll stand guard here, while you see what's happened."

Joe Santos looked at Piper's white coat and the name tag, Alex Parker, then quickly rose from his post. "Okay, but don't leave this spot for a minute. No one goes in while I'm gone, okay?"

"Of course, sir . . . that's room 624 . . . hurry, because the man sounds desperate."

As soon as the cop was out of sight, Piper slipped into Alison's room, found her asleep, then crept to the closet, and pulled out the extra pillow. It took no time to place it over her face—to stifle any screams in case she woke up—then plunge the hypodermic needle containing morphine into a vein in her arm.

This was a damn good job, Piper thought. Everything went off without a hitch. Now little Miss Archer would really sleep soundly. The next challenge was figuring out how to get back into this room for the wrist-slashing bit.

When the officer returned from Chris Chandler's room, Piper was stationed outside, intently guarding the door.

"Anyone come by?" Santos asked.

"Not a soul."

"Well, I don't know if that guy was having a nightmare or what, but he was sound asleep when I got there. I found a nurse to look in on him."

"Good, then I'll be on my way. Thanks a lot."

"Hold it there a minute, are you stationed on this floor?"

"Not regularly, but sometimes I'm all over the place, like tonight when they needed me to fill in. I'm usually on Two. Why?"

"Just haven't seen you around, that's all. If something like this happens again, get a nurse instead of pulling me away from here. I'm not supposed to leave this post at all."

"Gotcha." Walking away, Piper smiled.

Once out of sight, Piper ripped off the white coat, folded it, then headed for the hospital parking lot and the rented Toyota. It wouldn't take long for the morphine to work this time. The other dose probably wasn't completely out of her system yet, so in about thirty minutes, it would be time to make another appearance. But first, a trip to an all-night drug store to purchase a compact. This one had to look like the real thing; the mirror would be broken, one piece for the dirty work, the rest of the glass placed on the bedside table. God, this gig was easy, almost too simple for a genius like Piper.

After talking to the people at the Brasserie and deciding he could learn nothing new, Nick checked into a motel near the hospital, then headed for the police station. He had heard most of what happened on the phone before he left Dallas, but wanted more details of the actual crash and a look at the pieces of debris.

Hours later, he stopped in his room long enough to freshen up and realized that food was out of the question. Right now, all that mattered was finding the person who obviously attempted to kill Alison. He had to get that bastard before anything else could happen, but damn, whoever it was always managed to cover his tracks — a professional killer, no doubt about it.

Sometime after midnight, Nick returned to the hospital and decided to stop by Chris Chandler's room before checking on Alison. Two questions gnawed at him constantly: What part did this fellow have in the accident? And what the hell was Alison doing with this kid in the first place?

When Nick knocked on the door, a burly, well-dressed bear of a man peered out demanding identification, and they introduced themselves.

"I'm spending the night right here with my son, and haven't left him at all except for the few minutes it took to get a cup of coffee," Kenneth Chandler said. "Don't trust the nurses or anyone else around Chris. Just associating with Alison Archer almost got him murdered. By God, I'm ready to take a loaded gun to the first face that looks cross-eyed at him."

"Why were the two of them together this morning?"

"Guess the boy was attracted to her—damn good-looking woman or hadn't you noticed?"

"I noticed."

"Yeah, well, we had dinner together Friday night . . . all business, you understand . . . very hush-hush, if you know what I mean."

"No, I don't know. But I do know that Derek Archer was murdered a few weeks ago, and the killer is still at large. I just can't figure out the importance of your meeting with Miss Archer. Was it a matter of life and death?" Nick studied Chander's reaction and waited.

Chandler looked thoughtful. "To her, I suppose it was, but I didn't know it at the time . . . To me it was simply a matter of money. I'm damned sorry I wasn't aware of the danger she was in. She's one brave gal, I'll tell you that."

"So you don't think your son had anything to do with this so-called accident?"

"He's a kid, for God's sake, just twenty-nine years old. A kid!"

"Then Alison must be a kid, too, because she's a year younger than that. This was no May-December couple, Mr. Chandler. They're both consenting adults. Now, tell me, was there something between them?"

"Hell no, there wasn't!" The answer came from Chris Chandler who suddenly sat up in bed. "We were out boating for the day, that's all. Alison is attractive, and I'm sorry this accident happened but it wasn't planned

140

by either one of us, I swear. She's a super person, one I'd really like to get to know better, but we only met for the first time last Friday. That's it. Period. And I resent your implications."

"Sorry, Mr. Chandler, just doing my job."

At least Nick felt he had satisfied himself that there was no failed romance between them, or any suicide pact as the local police had suggested. Now he was back to square one; someone had drugged them. He walked down the hall to room 610, and found the same officer manning his post.

Recognizing Nick immediately, Santos jumped to his feet and held out his hand as they exchanged introductions. "I saw you earlier, but we didn't have a chance to meet."

"Aren't they going to send someone to relieve you?" Nick asked.

"Not until morning, sir."

"Everything been quiet?"

"Yes, except for a kind of disturbance down the hall."

Nick's antennae went up fast. "What happened? You didn't leave this door, did you?"

"Just for a few minutes. An attendant alerted me of Chris Chandler's screams, and stood at this post until I—"

Nick was inside Alison's room before Santos could finish his sentence. Alison's face looked serene, but she wasn't breathing! With his own heart pounding so hard when he bent over, he couldn't distinguish whether the sound came from him or from her. Oh dear God, was she alive? He bent over her again and detected a slow heartbeat.

Quickly he rang for a nurse. "Get Dr. Cheever on the phone immediately, and send someone to Room 610 on the double. Miss Archer's in trouble."

141

"What should I tell Dr. Cheever, sir?" The nurse sounded like she didn't intend to be pushed around.

"Can't you put him though to this room?" Nick thought he would surely explode from frustration.

"Well, yes, I suppose so."

"Then do it! And hurry, for God's sake, this patient might be dying!"

In no time at all, the floor nurse appeared, looked at Alison, nodded to Nick, then checked her heart and blood pressure.

The phone rang and Nick grabbed it, glad to hear the doctor's voice on the line. "This is Nick McAllister of the Dallas Police. I had you called because I think someone got into Miss Archer's room. She doesn't seem to be breathing."

"Is a nurse there?"

"Yes, she's here."

"Then put her on."

Nick handed over the phone and listened to her end of the conversation.

"Yes, blood pressure is 116 over 72, pulse 92 regular, good quality. Her respirations, however, are slow but not labored. Yes, sir, yes, I do have a sheet telling what drugs they test for. Yes, I will."

"What did he say?" Nick picked up Alison's hand and it felt like lead. She wasn't just asleep; she was out cold.

"I have to call the pathologist, and you'll hear the conversation. No need to repeat it." She gave him a faint smile. "Dr. Cheever's on his way."

The nurse pushed phone buttons, then, "Dr. Harvey, this is Emma Sullivan, nursing supervisor of the sixth floor. We have a patient admitted for injury, and Dr. Cheever is in charge of the case. He asked me to call you, because her respirations are only ten per minute." She was silent momentarily, listening. "Yes sir, this is a

142

police case involving possible attempted murder or suicide. The doctor wants an emergency drug screen, including morphine, which the patient has been receiving for pain. Also test for any other substance that might produce very slow respirations. He also sent his apology for calling so late and thanks you very much."

Nick hung on to Alison's hand, hoping to God the doctor knew what he was doing.

A lab technician arrived shortly with his box of paraphernalia and proceeded to take blood samples from a vein in Alison's arm.

Dr. Cheever came in next and checked Alison carefully. "Well, there doesn't seem to be any immediate danger." He turned to Emma Sullivan. "Did Dr. Harvey say how long it would take to get the test results?"

"Yes, he should be able to report the morphine level in about an hour." She looked at her watch. "Mike left here with the samples exactly eighteen minutes ago. Would you like some coffee?"

Dr. Cheever looked at Nick, who nodded in the affirmative. "Two cups, and thanks, Emma."

Half an hour later, the lab technician handed the report to Dr. Cheever, and Nick's heart sank as he watched him read it, watched concern spread across his face.

"Well, it seems the morphine level was much higher than it should have been to relieve pain. The pathologist concluded that it was either administered by mistake or with criminal intent." He gave Nick a worried look. "Now who the hell could have done it?"

Piper watched the activity in and around room 610. Damn, there was no way to get back in there tonight. What a waste of time and money. The compact had been damned expensive, but then, a rich CEO wouldn't have carried a cheap one. With this perfect plan, Alison would be dead by now, if that bastard of a detective hadn't flown in from Dallas. Every detail but one had been carefully worked out . . . no allowance had been made for a Dallas cop with the hots for Alison Archer.

Twelve

The woman who called herself Clare Cummings sat alone in her hotel room, waiting for the phone to ring. Sick with worry and anger, she took a deep breath and shuddered. Louis had promised that Alison wouldn't be hurt, and now she lay in that hospital bed in California, the victim of an awful accident. Deep down, she wondered if Louis was somehow responsible.

If only Alison hadn't insisted on heading the company, none of this would have happened. She was like Derek in many ways, so strong-willed and stubborn. Derek had gotten no more than he deserved. How she hated him. He had ruined her life, thrown her in virtual isolation, and worst of all, kept her from Alison, her only child. Even though Derek was dead, she still had to sneak around like a criminal in black garb and answer to the name of Clare Cummings.

She picked up the old photograph album that she kept with her always, the only link to her years in Texas. Her eyes fell on an old photograph. She was sitting on the beach at Padre Island, her long auburn hair shining in the mid-summer sun. She was only twenty years old when she met Derek Archer, the dashing American who came so unexpectedly into her life. Such a long time ago . . . another lifetime . . .

The ballroom of Paris's Bristol Hotel glittered with jewels that adorned the world's most beautiful people. Claudia Covainne threaded her way through the guests, her head held high. Here she was, the daughter of a French chef, mingling with ease among great power and wealth. No one questioned her background; no one cared that less than a year ago, she had lived a hand-to-mouth existence as a dancer in the chorus of La Promenade. She was the mistress of a man worth billions of dollars. Nothing else mattered.

It was at La Promenade that Abdul Faisal, the middle son of an Arabian prince, became entranced with her, returning night after night to feast his eyes on the auburn-haired French girl, who danced in the front row and smiled just at him. One night after the last performance, a representative waited outside the dressing room and asked her to join Abdul at his hotel. Thrilled that he would choose her, she accepted without hesitation.

Throughout their first encounter, she was so nervous and Abdul so drunk that she barely remembered shedding her clothes and crawling into bed. Void of foreplay, Abdul's lovemaking amounted to nothing more than entering her with no thought to her needs, pounding her incessantly, and shuddering violently when he was satisfied. It wasn't an entirely unpleasant experience, but neither was it what she expected from one of the richest men in the world.

Abdul's infatuation grew stronger as the weeks went by, and at the end of the first month, he moved her into a large, extravagant suite at the George V Hotel, insisting only that she be available to him on his frequent trips to Paris. During the time when he was away, Claudia was free to live life as she chose, no questions asked, no fidelity required. For this, he provided her with a car and driver, unlimited use of his charge accounts, and a monthly allowance that far exceeded her wildest expectations. Abdul showered her with diamonds and luxurious furs, everything she had ever wanted or dreamed of. It was a perfect arrangement for them both, except for one important ingredient — there was never any love between them. Together they provided a classic combination of lust and greed.

She lived this life for almost a year — until Derek Archer, the handsome young man from Texas, appeared at a party at the Bristol. He was unlike any man she'd ever known — intense, strong, and totally dedicated to building an empire of his own. Intrigued by this tall, dark-haired man, Claudia decided to make inquiries. It seemed that Derek Archer had just signed a lucrative contract with Abdul to build a pipeline, thousands of miles long, that would transport oil — Saudi Arabia's black gold — from Mecca to the Persian Gulf. It was obvious to Claudia that Derek, who couldn't be much more than thirty years old, was already a very rich man. She managed an introduction, and the next thing she knew, she was in his arms on the dance floor, being whirled around the room.

"You're a wonderful dancer," he said, and she loved his soft Texas drawl.

"I've had lots of experience."

"Oh?"

"Why, yes, I was a professional dancer not long ago."

"How interesting . . . aren't you — "

She smiled. "Abdul's mistress? Is that what you were trying to say?"

"I guess I was, but forgive me . . . it's none of my business."

"It's no secret, so don't be embarrassed. We have an arrangement, nothing more. He takes care of me, but I'm free to live my own life."

Derek tightened his arm around her and pulled her close. "It's just that I'm not used to the lifestyles you Europeans seem to take for granted." He chuckled. "Guess I'm just a bumpkin from Texas."

"A bumpkin? I don't understand."

"It's a person who isn't very sophisticated, I suppose. Life in Dallas would seem dull and mundane to someone like you."

"Oh, I don't know. I've always been intrigued by all those cowboys and open ranges."

"Well again, Dallas would disappoint you. We have no open ranges and hard-riding buckaroos. Dallas is a big city and growing by leaps and bounds."

When the music stopped, they made their way to the bar and picked up two glasses of champagne.

"How long will you be in Paris?" she asked.

"A few more days. My business is finished, and I'm allowing myself a little vacation before my nose goes back to the grindstone."

She frowned. "I thought my English was good until I met you. Your nose in a grindstone? Sounds as if that would hurt."

"Oh Claudia, I forget you're French. I work very hard, and sometimes I get so tired it hurts. I suppose that's what that means."

She laughed. "Oh, I see, I shouldn't take every word so literally. Guess I need to study American expressions." She gave him a coquettish smile. "I'd like to see you again before you leave."

"That might be a little hard to arrange, with Abdul in the picture. I just made a business deal with him."

"Abdul is leaving tomorrow, and won't be back for over a month."

"In that case, where can I find you?"

They spent the next three days in Monte Carlo, most of the time in bed at the Hotel de Paris, desperate to satisfy the insatiable hunger for each other that grew more intense by the hour. By the end of the third day, they both knew that Derek couldn't leave France without her.

They flew to Dallas together and were married within a week. The first year was idyllic, filled with the magic of being in love. Derek bought the beautiful brick house on Stillmeadow Drive, and introduced his young French wife to Dallas society. A month after their first anniversary, Alison was born. To everyone who knew them, they represented the American dream: a young couple who seemed to have everything: all the money they would ever need, a mansion complete with servants and manicured grounds, expensive clothes and cars—everything, including a beautiful new daughter.

But after a while, the luster began to fade for Claudia. At the age of twenty-four, she felt hopelessly trapped, stifled in the suffocating atmosphere of Dallas. Married to a man who lived and breathed to build his empire, she found herself alone much of the time, tied hand and foot to a small child and a big house. She detested the "ooh fa fas," the name she gave the women who lived from one charity ball to the next, who sat for hours intensely playing bridge, who seemed enchanted with dinners, receptions, and meaningless chatter at lunch. Much to Derek's chagrin, she began to avoid them, making excuses and turning down invitations as often as she could.

Pleading homesickness, she began to make trips to Europe, always alone, and soon found interesting diversions, most of them men, who asked nothing of her but good, carefree sex. She even had the courage to venture out in Dallas, very discreetly, always in the afternoon, and found that men were the same the world over. Though Derek never knew it, Louis Bennett became one of her favorite playmates during the next two years. She felt reasonably happy, until one afternoon when she met the wrong man at a bar on the west side of the city.

He introduced himself as Charles Thomas, and she immediately liked his dark good looks. He reminded her of Abdul, and oh, how she missed the glamorous life in Paris. Leaving her car parked in front of the bar, she rode with Charles to his apartment, eager for the afternoon to begin.

Her eagerness turned to terror as soon as Charles closed the apartment door. He turned to her, his eyes glazed with hate, drew back his fist, and slammed her against the wall.

"You tramp! Women are all alike. You're all a bunch of whores." He hit her again, this time in the eye, and pain ripped through the center of her brain.

Oh my God! He's a maniac! He's going to kill me! Desperately she tried to scramble to her feet, but he was too fast for her. Again and again he pounded her with his fists, screaming obscenities. Claudia felt trapped between this madman and the wall, nowhere to go, no way to escape. He grabbed her by the arm and dragged her into the bedroom.

"You want to make love, baby? Is that why you're here?" He cackled, a low, menacing laugh that turned Claudia's blood to ice. "I'll give you more than you want, you goddamned whore!" He picked her up, threw her on the bed, and began tearing off his clothes.

Every inch of Claudia's body throbbed with pain, but she had to make use of the only seconds she had. Gathering every ounce of her strength, she rolled to the other side of the bed. With Charles right behind her, she made a break for the door and ran into the kitchen. Her heart thumped wildly against her chest; she had to get away from him. He would kill her this time. Charles backed her up against the kitchen counter, his face contorted in rage, his eyes blazing with hate.

As her hands frantically groped behind her on the counter, she felt the cold blade of a knife. Her fingers clutched the handle, and before she realized what had happened, she had plunged the long blade into his hairy chest. He fell backward, his hands grabbing her skirt, and collapsed on the floor.

Horrified, Claudia stood stock-still for several seconds, then forced herself to step over the lifeless body, her hands and clothes soaked in blood. She staggered into the living room and huddled against the wall, every inch of her body shaking with fear. She had to get out of here, but how? Her car was miles away, and she didn't dare call a cab. She couldn't be seen anywhere in broad daylight with all this blood. *Oh my God, what am I going to do?*

For over an hour, she sat in a stupor, with a dead man in the other room and no solution in sight. The only person in the world who could help her was Derek; she had no choice but to call him. She dragged herself up, located a telephone, and dialed his private number at Megtex. He promised to have a man move her car and agreed to pick her up himself.

His face white and drawn, Derek drove all the way home without a word. As soon as they entered the house, he rushed upstairs and began jerking Claudia's clothes from the closet and tossing them into a suitcase.

When she emerged from the shower, he glared at her with contempt. "We're leaving for Paris in half an hour. A company plane is waiting at the airport."

"For both of us?" Claudia didn't dare say more. She'd never seen Derek so angry.

"You're damned right." His eyes searched her face, taking inventory of the cuts and bruises on her battered body. "I have a feeling you got exactly what you asked for." Claudia was silent, but Derek went on, his face

151

still white with hurt and rage, "I've suspected this for a long time, but I never had any proof. Obviously I wasn't able to give you what you needed, but God knows, I tried."

"Derek, I—"

"Let me finish. I thought about this all the way home, and I know what I'm going to do. We'll go to Paris, stay in separate hotel rooms, and I'll return here a week later without you. I'll announce that you were killed in an accident. You'll never return to Dallas. Naturally, there can't be a divorce."

"Oh, Derek, you can't be serious!"

"Oh yes, I'm dead serious."

Claudia felt the sting of hot tears. "You can't keep me from my child! Oh my God, that's inhuman!"

"Would you rather explain all this to the police?"

"No, of course not, but I promise nothing will ever happen again. I won't leave the house . . . I'll always be here. Oh, Derek, I've been so lonely, but I never meant to hurt you! You've got to believe me." She couldn't bear being exiled from Alison. Derek meant forever. She couldn't let him carry this through. "Please listen to me. You can't do this to me."

"I can and I will." His voice was low, perfectly calm. "I'll deposit one million dollars in your name at a bank in Paris. That's all you'll ever get, so spend it wisely. You'll also sign a confession, admitting to killing this man, and a release from any claim to my estate. Don't ever try to contact me or Alison again. One word from you, and I'll see that you're extradited from France to face charges of murder." He snapped the suitcase shut. "Get your clothes on . . . we're leaving in half an hour."

"At least let me say goodbye to Alison. She'll be home from school very soon."

"No, you won't touch my child ever again."

152

"You can t make me go just yet. My God, she's just five years old! I'm going to see her again or die trying."

Derek reached for the phone. "Oh really?"

And so, in the end, she agreed. Derek wouldn't budge, and carried out his plan to the letter. From time to time, she ventured to Texas, like a criminal in hiding, and caught glimpses of Alison on the playground at school, sometimes in the yard at home, and once in a shopping mall.

Life went on in her beloved Paris for twenty-one years. As time went by, her hatred for Derek grew more and more intense. Someday, somehow, she'd get her revenge. The chance came unexpectedly when Louis Bennett appeared at her door. She had gotten in touch with him many years ago, confident that she could trust him, for Louis knew that she had something to hold over his head. One word to Derek about their affair, and his days at Megtex would come to an end. He made many trips to see her over the years, and he fancied himself in love with her. But this time when he came, he had a plan in mind.

"I've been skimming money off the top for years and years. It might take a while longer, but it will all be worth it. We'll have millions and can finally be married."

"But we're both already married. How will we manage that?"

"We'll take care of them both when the time comes. Just leave it all to me."

At first, Claudia had no intention of ever marrying Louis Bennett, but his plan intrigued her. As time went by, however, Claudia realized that soon she would be fifty years old, and he began to look more promising than ever. If things worked out as he said, he'd one day be a wealthy, powerful man. She could do much worse. He came back to Paris several times during the next two

153

years, more excited than ever, sure that his plan would work.

"Don't worry," he'd tell her. "It won't be long now. I'll give you a call when the time comes."

The call came just a few weeks ago.

"You can come back to Texas, my love. Derek Archer is dead."

Yes, she thought, as her eyes fell on Derek's photograph in the album, Derek Archer is finally dead, but still I have to hide like a thief in the night, away from Alison, away from anyone who might recognize me.

"Just have patience," Louis had told her time and again, "in just a few weeks, it will all be over."

Claudia jumped, startled by the sudden ring of the phone. She grabbed the receiver; it was Louis.

"I've just had word from California," he said. "Alison had only minor injuries."

Claudia felt a flood of relief, but somehow she thought she detected a note of disappointment in his voice. "You're sure?"

"She'll be fine, believe me."

"Oh, thank God!"

When Claudia hung up the phone, she wondered how all of this would end. Louis had been scheming for years, planning their future to the smallest detail. The only thing he hadn't counted on was Alison's rise to power in the company. He'd sworn to Claudia time and again that he only planned to frighten Alison into resigning her position. But something deep inside made Claudia wonder if she could trust him. She'd have to watch her daughter even more closely than ever.

Thirteen

Alison was in high spirits as she boarded the plane with Nick. In spite of her involvement in a near-fatal accident, a Band-Aid on her forehead was the only visible sign of the terrifying ordeal.

"I've had enough of California for a while," she said. "Give me good old Texas anytime." Wincing with the sharp pain in her ribs, she buckled her seat belt and settled back for the takeoff to Dallas. She smiled at Nick, gratitude for his coming to her rescue welling up inside her. "Have I thanked you for coming all this way for me? I still can't believe those cops listened to my ramblings about calling you. I was pretty zonked at the time, you know."

"Yeah, but your subconscious was crying out for me. I seem to have that effect on women."

"Oh, then you always get on your white horse and ride to the rescue?"

"Never before, as a matter of fact." Nick took Alison's hand, turning it this way, then that, studying it, as if expecting it to tell him something, or at the very least, absorb some of his embarrassment.

Alison grinned, waiting for his sense of humor to take over.

But Nick was dead serious this time. "Something in my gut told me you were in danger. I still think that so-

155

called accident was an attempt on your life, and no one can convince me otherwise. I *had* to come out here."

"Well, so far, there's been no evidence of foul play . . . all the investigations came up blank." She shuddered. "Kenneth Chandler almost took the police department apart to get us cleared of drug charges. I can't figure it out, but I've just about decided the overdose of morphine was just an error on some careless nurse's part."

"Oh sure, a little error that almost cost you your life. No, I'll never believe that." Nick searched Alison's face. "Why did you go to see Chandler instead of calling him? Seems like such a long way to go for one meeting."

Alison pulled her hand away, then began weaving her fingers together in a nervous gesture. After a long pause, she said, "I'm sorry, but I just can't tell you. It's company business, and I can only say we're in a barrel of — trouble." She couldn't help smiling as she thought of what Kenneth Chandler had said was in that barrel.

"So that's why you were so nervous before you went to Washington?"

"No, that was different. My lord, I almost forgot about those crazy nights."

"Crazy? In what way?"

Alison was sure Nick remembered Clare Cummings, and how she was always showing up at the most unexpected places. She looked directly into Nick's brown eyes. "You know all about the woman who kept following me, but I didn't tell you other things that were even more frightening. I guess I didn't know you well enough then, and was afraid you'd laugh at me or think I was nuts."

"Try me now, and trust me not to think anything but —" Nick hesitated. "Damn it, Alison, when you look at me like that, all I can think of is what it would be like to . . ." He gave her a sheepish smile.

156

She smiled back, knowing quite well what he was thinking. It had crossed her mind more than once in the last couple of days. She could feel her heart beating wildly, as a thrilling pleasure traveled right down to her toes. She put her hand back in his; it belonged to him. She had never felt so sure of anything in her life. Now she had to tell him about the hallucinations, clear the air between them, be honest and know his reaction, before she could trust herself to care for this man.

"It all started after my dad's funeral. At first I heard his voice on the phone —"

"His voice? Derek's? How do you mean?"

"I warned you this would be hard to believe. The phone would ring, I'd pick it up, and Dad's voice would cry out to me. It really was his voice . . . I'm sure of it. No one could imitate it like that."

"And then?" Nick looked at her intently.

"Well, you can imagine the state I was in . . . couldn't concentrate on anything at the office, rushed home to hear from him again, but dreaded it, because every time it happened I thought I was really losing it. This all happened over a period of two weeks, sometimes with a day or two going by with nothing. His voice came over the air vents, the TV. Then his face appeared on the TV screen, and he spoke to me! Well, you can just imagine what I thought was happening to me."

"Oh my God, you're stronger than I would have been. I'd have flipped by now for sure. Someone's doing this to you, no doubt about it. You weren't hallucinating. You're much too sane for that kind of nonsense. There has to be a rational explanation."

"John wanted me to see a psychiatrist."

"Is that why you broke your engagement?"

Alison grinned at Nick's worried look. "No, I knew it was all a mistake before that. John and I could never be happy together, and I suppose deep down I've always

157

known it, just wasn't brave enough to admit it until I saw those damned engraved wedding invitations. Somehow I just couldn't send them out."

"Think I'll make a donation to the engravers' union, if there is such a thing. They've done me a great service."

"So you really don't think I'm bonkers?"

"Let's put it this way . . . if you're unhinged, so am I, and I like it that way."

"So, what's the explanation?"

"Have you ever encountered Derek anywhere but in your home?"

"No, that's what's so strange. I had a complete recovery from my hysterical thoughts, when I spent one night in Washington. By the way, don't think I've forgotten how angry you were when I didn't check in with you." She gave him a teasing smile. "But that trip brought me back to my senses." Among other things, she thought, remembering the shocking revelations Senator Lassiter had made.

"Let me look into this for you. I'll do some checking around. Meanwhile, I don't think you should be in that house alone, especially at night."

While in California, Alison had been in touch with her office from her hospital bed, but there was nothing like being back in Dallas in the Archer Building in person. She ran her hands over the familiar leather of what used to be Derek's chair, now her own, and realized how proud she was to sit in his place and carry on his work. She was expecting Louis any minute to discuss the urgency of finding the source of the fraud and the time limit set by Kenneth Chandler. She wondered if he had made any progress at all. Linco must be reimbursed and all the pipelines repaired, a mammoth expense and undertaking, but she had made that promise to Chandler and intended to keep it.

Louis stopped outside Alison's office to make sure his smile was one of fatherly benevolence. How the hell the girl had survived that boat crash was a damned miracle. But this was no time to lose his cool. Alison suspected everyone but him; he had to keep it that way. He entered the office with outstretched arms.

"Alison! How wonderful you always manage to look, no matter what you've been through." He folded her in his arms and gave her a big bear hug. "No one would ever suspect your recent brush with . . ." Louis decided to rearrange that sentence before continuing. "Suspect that you'd been in such a terrible accident."

Alison touched the small bandage on her forehead. "As you can see, it didn't amount to much, so I'd just as soon forget about it. Gosh, it's good to be back. Everything run smoothly while I was gone?"

"Couldn't have been better."

"Oh, come on, you don't mean that. I don't want you to turn into a yes man for me, for goodness sake. I know business could hardly be any worse, so let's not kid ourselves." Alison's voice was sharper than he'd ever heard it.

"Well," he paused a moment to clear his throat, "I didn't want to upset you on your first day back."

"One of these days, I'm going to convince everyone around here to forget I'm a woman. I need to know where we stand financially. How far have you gotten in your investigation?"

"Not very, I'm afraid. There's been a ton of work to do, and—"

Alison's green eyes flashed. "You promised me that nothing would stand in your way of making an all-out investigation. My God, Louis, don't you understand

159

what's at stake here? You should have been with me when I met with Kenneth Chandler. He sure tells it like it is. Linco's attorneys were ready to go with a lawsuit against us immediately, and he only held off because of Dad's death. He didn't even know it had been murder, probably connected with Megtex."

"Neither did I exactly. Did the police ever state that as a fact?"

"No, but they don't know about the inside treachery that's been going on, and we don't want them to know. You're the one who convinced me of that."

"Yes, of course." Louis chewed his lip, realizing Alison wasn't going to buy his stalling bit. He'd have to come up with something fast. "There's no point in shielding anyone I suspect, and I know it won't go any farther than this office. I guess I was trying to spare you, but now I realize that was a mistake." He took a deep breath. "Maynard Simmons has been acting strangely lately and I—"

"Maynard? I can't believe it. Why, he's always been so honorable, so—"

Louis's feathers were ruffled. "You see, I did know better and shouldn't have mentioned it."

"You're right. Sorry. Okay, acting strangely . . . how?"

"Why don't you just leave all this to me, like you promised, until I come up with something concrete?"

"Okay, but you'd better hurry. Chandler is giving us exactly thirty days. That's one month from the date we spoke, and I've already wasted about four days of that ultimatum because of the accident. If we don't come up with the thief soon, we'll have to repair, replace, and inspect every piece of pipe we've put down in the last ten years. Any idea what that would do to our company, Louis? There wouldn't be any more Megtex."

Bennett felt his face turn hot. "How the hell could

you have made such a commitment?" You think that's how big business is run? You're out of your mind!"

"Watch yourself, Louis, you're not my father nor my keeper! You're an employee, and I trust that you'll remember that in the future. My responsibility is to the board and the stockholders. If I can't conduct a business free of corruption, I have no interest in staying in business. And believe me, if I go, this company goes with me. Now, find out who's been stealing us blind and defrauding Linco, or we'll all go down the drain in less than a month." Alison turned her back on him.

Oh, this bitch sure had to go and go fast, Louis thought, as he left Alison's office like a dismissed schoolboy. Claudia would be furious, but he'd make her understand. *Employee* indeed! He was glad he'd already given Piper the go-ahead. There was still plenty of money in Megtex. Of course, they could never follow through on Alison's ridiculous promise of full restitution. Once she was gone, he'd offer a counterplan and ward off any kind of lawsuit. It was just like a woman to make a stupid pledge like that. Women didn't belong in the business world anymore than a stuffed animal. Louis went into his office and slammed the door.

Every day brought more violence to the big cities, and Dallas was right up there in the highest bracket, Nick thought, as he headed for Las Colinas, Dallas's little Hollywood. He wanted to speak to Abel Monroe, production supervisor of a movie currently being shot at the Las Colinas studios, about a stabbing that took place on Greenville Avenue the night before.

Nick circled around until he found the set of *Stilletto*, where people in western costume were milling around and camera crews were riding high off the ground. He showed his identification to a young woman and asked for Monroe.

161

"He's out right now, but should be back in fifteen or twenty minutes." Lorry Amsterdam, a pert blond in her late twenties, looked up at Nick with big blue eyes that were clearly inviting and introduced herself. "Want to wait and watch?"

"If you're sure I won't be in the way."

"Oh, no problem, I'm just watching, too. Gives me a better perspective." She stretched both arms into the air, then ran her hands under her long blond hair, as if to cool her neck. Her curves didn't go unnoticed.

This time Nick smiled to himself. Lorry was a mighty sexy gal, but he was here on police business and had no time for a matinee. "You're just watching? Could have fooled me. Thought you were the star of the show. What do you do?"

"You've got a smooth tongue for a cop, mister." Lorry smiled her appreciation. "I'm a film editor . . . oh, oh, quiet. They're ready to shoot."

Nick sat down on a folding chair in front of a barn-like building and watched.

TAKE FIVE. ACTION!

Three men came at another man, who looked like he might be the hero. They looked as though they were ready to beat him to death. A lot of mock fighting went on with a lot of dust flying around.

CUT!

Nick turned to Lorry, who seemed mesmerized by the action taking place about thirty feet in front of them. "Was that it?" he whispered.

"No, silly, they'll pick it up again from another angle. Quiet, here they go again."

About thirty minutes later, after the men had started their fight over many times, they suddenly walked like regular people, lit cigarettes, plopped into chairs, and looked exhausted.

Nick glanced at his watch. "Monroe's been gone a

162

long time. Sure he's coming back before lunch?"

"He said he would. Hey, I have to get back to work. Glad to have met you . . . say, would you like to watch how a film editor works? You seem kind of interested in how movies are made. I do the most important part."

"As long as I'm waiting, might as well enjoy myself." Nick followed Lorry to the next building.

Lorry talked as she worked, but all business now. Nick could tell that she took a great deal of pride in what she did, and she certainly looked efficient.

"This is one reason they do so many different takes," she said, as she stretched film over a small, lighted area. "I can see in a minute which shots will work best when they're spliced together."

"Wait . . . hold it a minute!" Nick felt excitement build inside him. "You mean you splice scenes together to make them look as good as possible, right?"

"Yes, that's right. Why?"

"Can you do the same thing with voice tapes?"

"Sure, they have to match these films. What are you getting at?"

Nick bent down and gave Lorry a resounding kiss on the top of her head. "You've just helped me solve an entirely different case. You're an angel. Tell you what, when Monroe gets back, tell him I'll be here tomorrow. Something very important has just come up . . . no pun intended."

Nick drove south on Stemmons Freeway, headed for the Archer Building. He hadn't stopped long enough to call Alison at the office to tell her he was on his way. They hadn't been together at all in the three days since they'd come home, but had spoken several times. He thought of her constantly, fantasized about what it would be like to have her with him always. Sometimes those fantasies left him in a state of euphoria, but at other times, he felt a sense of impending doom. She was used to so much more than he could ever offer her. Then he'd mentally berate himself for wasting so much time on such useless dreaming. But what was a person, if not the sum total of all his dreams? Nick was glad to see the Archer Building loom up directly on his right. He was beginning to feel like a silly teenager.

"Sorry, she's not in," Deena Perry said when he walked into the office. "She had an appointment in north Dallas and I don't expect her back until after lunch."

Nick looked around, admiring the offices, the whole Megtex layout, which covered the entire floor of this building. "I just wonder if you might help me instead," Nick said.

"I'll certainly try, Lieutenant."

Nick wasted no more words. He'd noticed how attractive Deena was, glad that Alison had found an efficient secretary, one she was also fond of. "I know you haven't been working here too long, but do you know if Derek Archer used a tape machine when dictating letters?"

Deena gave Nick a strange look. "I really don't know, never gave it a thought, but I'll be glad to look in the storage room. Tons of Myra Collins's files are there. You know, Alison couldn't bring herself to part with everything when Miss Collins's office was cleared of her things."

"If you're sure it's not too much trouble." Nick's words were polite, but his manner was brusk. He was used to giving orders, and expected them to be carried out without delay.

"Not at all . . . I'll be right back. Is there something special you're looking for, in case I find a machine? Like specific correspondence that might be on a tape?"

164

"No, nothing special. Okay if I come with you?"

Deena glanced around, as if looking to get permission from someone, then shook her head. "Don't see why not. Can't imagine why anyone would object. After all, you're a policeman." She laughed. "Follow me."

Floor to ceiling files filled the storage room, all carefully marked. After searching for a short time, Deena found a whole section devoted to nothing but tapes, some of them dating back almost thirty years.

"I can't believe this," she said. "You'd expect all this to be on microfiche, if it were kept this long. It would make it easier to find a specific letter, that's for sure. Now, what approximate date are you looking for?"

"Tell you what, suppose I just pick a couple of tapes at random? Would anyone mind? I'll take good care of them."

"I'm sure that wouldn't be a problem at all. I'll just explain to Alison when she gets back, okay?"

"Frankly, I'd just as soon you didn't mention these tapes to her just yet. We're still working on the double murders, and trying to determine if there's any connection between them. I'd rather not upset her until we have something concrete to tell her."

"Sure, I understand." Deena smiled. "You can count on me."

It certainly wasn't that Nick didn't trust Deena; it was just that he wanted to surprise Alison with what he'd discovered. He hoped to God it had some merit.

Alison sat in the dining room of the Mansion on Turtle Creek, having lunch with John Carpenter. This would be the last time, she'd told him when he called yesterday, begging to see her. She had come directly from her business meeting and was glad to see that he

165

had a Kir Royale waiting for her. It was just what she needed, if she were going to make this a farewell that would finally convince him that she meant to end their relationship. If possible, she'd like to keep his friendship, but that didn't seem too likely.

"You're even more beautiful than ever," John said. His eyes never left hers as he absently twisted the stem of his wineglass. "I realize now that I never told you that before. I took a lot of things for granted in our relationship. Can you forgive me?"

"There's nothing to forgive." Alison knew he was only playing a game. "Do you think I could fall out of love with you because you didn't shower me with compliments?" She leaned forward and took his hand across the table. "We've always been great friends, we both know that, but that's not the same thing as being in love. I've really never been in love with you, and realized it in time. Please don't make this any harder for either of us than it already is."

"I just can't believe you mean that. How can you forget all those evenings when we were together in your apartment? Those wonderful times when I spent the whole night? That had to be love. Don't you —"

The waiter approached them discreetly with their food. Alison had a Cobb salad, John the fillet of sole.

Alison shook her head. "No, it wasn't. It was just good sex, John, nothing more." She noticed the shocked look on his face. "At least I think it was good, but I don't have anything to compare it with." She gave him an impish grin.

"Alison Archer, what's come over you? Why you're —"

"I'm coming out of the cocoon I've been in all my life, and you don't like me to shock you. You're much better off without me." Alison took a bite of her salad. "You'll find a lovely girl who adores golf and tennis, and who'll spend every afternoon playing bridge at the club. She'll train the servants just right, and be sweet to your mother. Don't you see, I'd be a terrible wife. I can be truthful now, and say I've never even liked your mother. Would you care for some coffee, John?"

When lunch was over and their cars were brought around to the entrance of the restaurant, Alison felt sure that it wouldn't be long before she was totally forgotten by John Carpenter.

Just as Alison was about to leave the office, her private phone rang. It was Nick and he sounded excited.

"I may have some good news for you and—"

"You're on the track of the killer! Oh Nick!"

"No, not that good, but I think you'll be happy about—"

"What is it?"

Nick laughed. "I'm trying to say something, but you keep interrupting."

"Oh, I know, I do that all the time. What is it?"

"It's kind of a show and tell. What time will you be home?"

"About six, I think."

"Are you free tonight? I mean, can I come over about six-thirty?"

"Sure, I'm free."

Alison's heart was pounding when she hung up the phone. She knew she was blushing, and couldn't deny that she might be falling in love with Nick McAllister. Maybe she'd do some exploring tonight.

Fourteen

Alison opened the front door before Nick had a chance to ring the bell. She had to control herself to keep from flying into his arms. "What kept you so long?"

Nick frowned and looked at his watch. "It's six-thirty on the dot."

"Well, you could have come early. I've been going crazy, waiting to know what you had to show me." Alison took his arm and pulled him through the marble foyer and into the den where they both sat down. "Okay, now what have you found out?"

"Well, it all started this morning at Las Colinas." For the next few minutes, he launched into his story of visiting the movie colony, meeting the film editor, and watching her splice film tapes together. "I figured if it could be done with movie films and sound, maybe the same method would work with voice tapes."

Alison felt confused, trying to absorb what he was telling her. For one thing, he was sitting much too close, close enough for her to catch the clean, fresh fragrance of Dakota, her favorite men's cologne. "I'm sure it probably would, but what does that have to do with . . . Nick! My dad's voice! Is that what you mean?"

"Yes, I went to your office this morning—"

"You came to the office? No one told me."

"I asked Deena not to give me away, because I wanted to check this out before I said anything."

For the first time, Alison noticed the tape recorder that Nick had brought with him. "What's that for?"

"Elementary, my dear, elementary. Anyway, when I didn't find you at—"

"I know, you were crushed and wanted to get out of there."

"True, but then Deena was so attractive that I—"

"Nick!"

"Well, you keep interrupting . . ."

"Sorry about that. Why did you come to the office?"

"Frankly, I was anxious to check out my theory with you, but it didn't even occur to me that you wouldn't be there. I wanted to know if Derek had dictated letters directly to his secretary all the time, or if he used a dictaphone."

Alison felt excitement bubble up inside her. "He used the dictaphone a lot. Oh Nick, are you thinking . . . you're a genius! This might even solve the case of the lunatic daughter. But how?"

"Just suppose someone wanted to drive you, well, kind of nutty. Or maybe he wanted to make you very nervous and unsure of yourself." Nick reached for Alison's hand. "What you told me wasn't a joking matter. It also didn't make sense, because you're much too smart to be taken in by all this weird stuff."

"I thought so, too, but it was all so real . . . Dad's voice coming from all directions. I really was losing it, I'm embarrassed to say, so depressed it wouldn't have taken much more to push me right over the edge. You know, in spite of the accident, going to California did a lot toward saving my sanity."

Nick stood. "Hopefully, this will do even more. As I

said, I went to your office to find out about tapes, and Deena was nice enough to let me take a couple with me. Do you know about all those tapes in the storage closet?"

"Oh yes, I know about them."

"Why in the world were they kept like that?"

"Well, it seems that Myra was in love with my dad. It's that simple. Dad respected her, but he never encouraged any kind of relationship. I guess he still loved my mother, and wouldn't even look at another woman after she died. Many times when I worked late, I'd hear Myra playing those tapes over and over, just to listen to his voice." She took a sudden intake of breath. "Oh my god, his voice!"

"Exactly."

"Oh, you don't suppose someone's been hiding here, playing spliced tapes to scare me to death . . . maybe some killer, right here in the house?"

"No, I don't think anyone had to be in the house — except the time it took to set the whole thing up! I've been talking to some electronic engineers and asking questions all afternoon . . . taking a short course in electronics. Apparently, if you know what you're doing, it's not hard at all to rig up something like this."

"But how?"

"Let's look around and see what we can find. This is a large house, darling, so let's begin in the kitchen and look in all the closets and pantries for some sort of electrical panel."

Alison's heart did a quick somersault that left her breathless. Nick didn't even realize he'd called her "darling." It had just come out naturally. Good lord, she thought, I seem to be going into a tailspin every time he opens his mouth . . . enough to give me a heart attack.

"Hey, you're holding up the search. Come on and lead the way to the kitchen."

For the next hour, Alison and Nick searched every closet in the house, from the kitchen to the attic, with no panel or box with wires in sight, other than the one in the utility room that controlled the alarm system.

Nick stopped in front of the panel one more time and looked at it carefully. "Mind if I unlock this box?"

"Of course not, but maybe I'd better call the company, in case we set off the alarm. I can say we're just testing."

"Okay, that's a good idea."

While Alison made the call, Nick unlocked the box and studied the wires. "I've seen a lot of complicated systems, but never one like this. Is there anything else connected to this box, like your TV set or telephones?"

"Not that I know of. Electronics always confused my dad, so he deliberately ordered the simplest system available, when we upgraded it several years ago. It was about the time I moved to my own apartment. He agreed that I needed my own . . . God, I hate the expression . . . space. But I didn't want to leave until he had a better system."

"This certainly looks like a TV wire to me. Let's try something. Do you have a TV in the kitchen?"

"Sure, there's one in there, but why not use the set right here? Juanita wouldn't work for us, if she couldn't watch her soaps while she did the laundry."

"Now doesn't that beat all, a TV in the utility room." Nick continued to fiddle with the wires. "Okay, turn on the set."

As soon as Alison hit the power button, Derek's face appeared.

"Oh my God . . . you've gotten Dad!" She sank onto a step stool.

"That's it all right, don't you see? Look, I'll show you how it works. Someone's been in here, and rewired this whole damned panel so it'll do all kinds of crazy things.

171

Now we know how the killer got into this house without setting off the alarm!"

Alison watched, stunned, as Nick explained how to make the picture and the voice appear, and realized how simple it was to operate. "Oh, turn that TV off! The sight of Dad's face is breaking my heart."

Nick quickly switched a wire and went over to Alison, taking her in his arms. "I'm sorry, I sure didn't mean to upset you again. You've had the last of that." He tilted her face up to his and kissed her gently on the lips. She responded as he held her closer, kissing her again, this time with passion as their lips parted and they clung together as though never wanting to be separated.

"H-how did he get in without tripping the alarm?" Alison pulled herself away from Nick, needing to breathe, but clinging to his arm as though it were her only lifeline to sanity. "Who would do this to me? Who could be so damned rotten?"

Nick bent and kissed her forehead. "Well, I think it's the same person who shot your father. You have proof now that you're not hallucinating and you're not losing it, as you put it. As for the open door, this thing can be programmed, and no doubt it is, to unman one door so someone can get in without setting off a signal at the main station. That must be how he got in the night he killed your father." Nick shook his head. "Whoever this was must be an electronic genius. Just imagine manning this box and having control of the whole house with a remote control . . . not inside, but *outside,* on the grounds or even in a car or van. Can you envision the combination of things that were rigged up to make you think you were losing your mind? Why, the possibilities are endless." Nick gathered her in his arms once more.

"But still, I have to ask why? What did I do to make

172

anyone hate me so much that they'd want me to go mad?" Alison felt angry, defiled, violated.

"Well, you're Derek Archer's daughter, and you're also CEO of a very large company. There are bound to be enemies."

"That's just it, I don't have any that I know of."

"Believe me, those are the worst kind. They sneak around in the dark, afraid to show themselves, doing their utmost to break your spirit."

Alison nestled against Nick, worried about the tapes, who masterminded the whole thing, and why. Suddenly she pulled away and glanced at the clock. "It's almost eight, and I'll bet you're starving. I know I am."

"My lord, woman, you sure bring up food at the oddest moments. Where is your sense of romance? Isn't love enough food for someone as slender as you?"

She gave him a wide-eyed, innocent look. "Love? Did I miss something?" Her heart began pounding again, and goose bumps ran up and down her limbs.

"I didn't think I'd have to spell it out for someone as savvy as you, but if you insist . . ." Nick picked her up in his arms and headed for the circular stairway leading to the bedrooms.

Alison laughed. "Put me down, you idiot! I believe, I believe! But let's have some dinner first. We can eat here. Juanita always leaves food ready, and besides, I want to be alone with you."

Nick set her feet on the floor. "Okay, tell you what, we'll eat here on the condition that I can help."

"If you think for one moment that I'll tell you no, you're the one who's crazy. I'm a pretty good cook, but I like company in the kitchen." Alison turned serious. "Do me a favor, Nick?"

"Anything."

"Make sure the voice doesn't come back on."

"It won't unless it's activated, but I'll check it out."

Alison got busy in the kitchen, leaving Nick to fiddle in the utility room. The kitchen was huge by most standards, long and wide, with a brick wall on the side that held an eight-burner cooktop, built-in barbecue pit, double ovens, warming oven, and microwave. Through the center of the room ran a long, narrow work counter with a filigreed wrought iron base and a black granite top. Aside from the brick and black granite, everything else was stainless steel, making it an efficient, yet comfortable kitchen.

Opening the refrigerator and rummaging around, Alison searched for something good to eat, something that Nick would probably like. Inside she found cold turkey breast, leftover pasta salad, fresh mushrooms, and lots of fruit. She debated about turning this into a quick, light supper by making a mushroom and turkey omelet.

"What would you rather have, dinner or supper?" Alison called out to Nick.

She jumped when her answer came from directly behind her. "Let's see what we've got to work with." He reached into the refrigerator over her bent body, molding his to hers. Alison drew in her breath and held it, not wanting to move, her whole body on fire. Nick pulled out a bottle of champagne. "Okay to open this?" His voice was low and husky.

"Perfect," she said, afraid her voice would crack if she tried to say more.

He looked in every cabinet until he came up with two stemmed, tulip glasses, then rounded the corner to the bar, and held up a corkscrew in triumph. Back in the kitchen in no time, he had a glass of champagne in each hand. When they touched glasses, Alison's heart beat a silent toast to their future together.

Soon they went to work, making dinner like two experts. Sparks flew between them as they laughed and bumped into each other in spite of the spacious kitchen. To their amazement, they ultimately had food ready that looked not only edible but also delicious.

They carried everything into the breakfast room where four chairs and a glass-topped table sat invitingly in front of a large bay window that overlooked the swimming pool and garden. Since it was almost dark, Alison flooded the area with outside lights, illuminating the grounds. She brought in placemats, napkins, and silverware, which Nick insisted on setting out himself, making a great to do of his artistry by placing everything in its proper place. His running commentary finally resulted in Alison's flicking a towel at him in mock exasperation. Again they laughed.

They ate the pasta, made huge sandwiches out of the sliced turkey, consumed a vegetable salad, and polished off the meal with more champagne and slices of the chocolate cake that Juanita had baked. With their eyes locked together through most of the meal, they licked their lips with pleasure as they devoured each other along with their food. They were in no hurry. The whole night was theirs, both knowing what was coming, both rejoicing in the excitement of prolonged anticipation.

Alison smiled provocatively over the rim of her glass, her large green eyes fixed on Nick. Finally, when he could stand the teasing no longer, he pushed his chair back, leaned over, picked her up in his arms as if she were a toy, and headed for the foyer and the stairway once more.

This time, Alison's lips eagerly sought his, no objection to being carried up the stairs. In fact, on the way up, she whispered in his ear, "Second door on the left, darling."

The next morning was like the dawn of happiness for Alison. They had gone to bed early, but to sleep quite late. With Nick's right arm thrown carelessly, yet possessively over her, she luxuriated in the power of his body next to hers, with no desire to move, feeling that to wake up each morning like this for the rest of her life was more than she could ever wish for. Now that she truly knew him, she didn't think she could live five whole minutes without him. This had to be for real, had to be forever.

Nick stirred, pulled her into his arms again, and suddenly roared, "Where's my breakfast, woman? I have to go to work."

Alison opened one eye, pretended to yawn, and stretched lazily, as though he had disturbed her sleep. "Breakfast? It's way too early."

"In that case, I'll take the next best thing." Nick grinned as he gathered her to him, then became serious. "I don't want this to end, Alison. This is the only way we're going to wake up from now on . . . with my arms around you. Every night, I want to lie down knowing you're right here beside me. I'm in love with you, especially now that I'm sure you're not out of your tree." He ducked, laughing, as a pillow came flying at him.

"You . . . you! How could you mess up that speech just when it was getting interesting?"

Nick grabbed her again, and covered her face with little kisses that sent waves of delight in every erogenous zone in her body. Alison sighed with happiness. Breakfast could wait. Who needed it anyway?

That afternoon, Alison stepped into Deena's office. "Are you free for an hour or so right after work?"

"Sure. Something important happening?"

"No fair asking questions . . . I've got something to show you." Alison gave her a teasing smile. "Meet you at my house, say about five-thirty?"

"You sure make things exciting, boss. I'll be there."

After work, Alison hurried home, and right on time, Deena rang the doorbell. When she opened the door, Alison watched Deena's face when a man's voice said, "Come in."

Deena looked all around the foyer. "Who else is here? Is a man your surprise?"

Alison could hardly contain her excitement as she led Deena to the den. "Yes, sit down and listen to what I've found out. Remember when you spent the night with me, to help me prove that I wasn't hallucinating?"

"Of course, I do, but I wasn't any help at all and felt terrible about it."

"Well, that's exactly why I asked you over. You can still verify that I'm not really out of my tree." Alison blushed, then smiled, remembering that Nick had said those very words early this morning. "Just sit right there." She rushed off, leaving Deena alone in the den.

Moments later, Deena's mouth flew open when the same man's voice said from the vents in the walls, *"Alison, come to me . . . I need you . . ."* Her head swiveled in every direction, while Alison leaned against the door frame, watching her reaction.

"For God's sake, what's going on here?" Deena asked.

"Frightening, isn't it? That's my dad's voice. Wait, I'll show you more." Alison disappeared again.

This time the television set went on, and a man's face dominated the screen, the same pleading words coming from his mouth.

"This is creepy, stop this! I don't understand . . . how did you do that?"

"Don't be scared. I just wanted you to be a witness to

177

what almost drove me mad. Nick McAllister figured it all out, and saved my sanity. Remember the tapes he borrowed from the office yesterday?"

"Yes, but he asked me not to tell you. He—"

"He wanted to be sure what he hoped was true, and sure enough, it was. It's obvious that some crazed person spliced my dad's tapes, so that bits and pieces of his voice could say just about anything. Can you imagine anyone so depraved? Besides Nick, you were the only one who believed in me, and I had to show you that I really had seen and heard my dad." She gave Deena a warm smile. "I don't know what I'd have done without your support."

Deena blushed, obviously touched. "You give me too much credit. After all, I didn't help you at all that night. I still don't understand how all this was done . . . a voice over the air vents, the TV, even the telephone. Sounds eerie to me."

"Exactly. This guy wired everything in a central panel, then controlled the entire house by remote control. Nick's determined to catch him, and when he does, he thinks he'll have my dad's killer. And probably Myra's."

"Gosh, this is all so fantastic, but it really explains a lot. You've been so brave to stay here alone. I'm sure I couldn't do it."

"Oh you would, if you had to. Well, now that that's settled, why don't you stay and have dinner with me?"

"Chinese again?" Deena grinned. "Thanks anyway, but I have a date tonight." She looked at her watch.

"Oh, you should have told me. I'm sorry if I've held you up."

"I wouldn't have missed this for anything. But he's going to call for me in less than an hour, so I'd better run. Thanks for trusting me." Deena kissed Alison's cheek and left.

Alison was sorry to see her go. Nick had called earlier to say he wouldn't be here until late, since a new murder investigation had just begun. She was getting a taste of what it would be like to be married to a policeman. No matter what, she knew for sure that Nick was the one she wanted.

Later, as she went about closing shutters and checking all the doors, a shadowy figure watching from across the swimming pool caught her attention. For a few paralyzing moments, she stood transfixed, unable to move. The person obviously saw her and suddenly darted into the shrubbery, vanishing from sight. Alison reached for the phone, then put down the receiver. No need to call the police. By the time they could get here, the intruder was sure to be gone. She sank into a chair, praying that it wouldn't be long until Nick arrived.

Fifteen

Late the next afternoon, the sky looked dark and swollen with clouds, as Louis sat on a park bench waiting for Piper. He knew he'd arrived half an hour early, but he needed time alone to think, a chance to figure out his next move. Damn, he'd counted on Piper's plan to work out in California, but it only alerted Alison to the possibility of foul play. Time was running out. He had to stop fooling around with the absurd notion of making her death look like a suicide. It wasn't his fault that the girl had to die. From the beginning, that bastard Derek Archer had caused all this.

It had all started thirty years ago, when Archer founded the company and asked him to come on board. Of course, Derek had scraped up the capital to get the business off the ground, but deep down, Louis knew why he'd been hired; he had the know-how that could make it all happen.

"Get me the Linco account, and I'll make you a full partner," Derek had promised him.

There was never any formal agreement, nothing signed by either of them, but a handshake between friends was all Louis needed. He worked his tail off for two years and finally landed the account. The day he

180

handed the good news to Derek was the proudest day of his life.

Derek beamed. "By God, Bennett, you've earned yourself a big raise and a promotion."

"And a partnership, remember?"

"Whoa, man, what the hell gave you that idea?"

"But we agreed . . . you said — "

"Don't tell me what I said. This is my business, financed by loans I risked my ass for. You're a damned good employee, and one day I'll make you a rich man, but forget about a partnership."

Right then and there, Louis learned the first commandment of big business: Thou shalt screw thy fellow man every chance you get. It might take him the rest of his life, but one way or the other, he'd bring Derek Archer down and own Megtex outright. He hit on the idea of undercutting the price of products. He'd buy used pipe, charge Linco the price of new material, and pocket the difference. He investigated used pipe in Mexico, Yugoslavia, and Greece, and finally settled on the Mexican product, the cheapest of the lot. No one would know for a long time, he figured, since inferior pipe could stay in the ground for years without being detected. Meanwhile, his stockpile of money would continue to grow, and when the company's reputation began to slide — due to leaks and other problems — the price of its stock would fall to rock bottom. That's when he'd make his move.

He felt free to invade every aspect of Derek's life, including having an affair with his beautiful French wife. The only thing he hadn't counted on was falling in love with her. As time went by, he knew he had to continue to possess Claudia, even after Derek exiled her to Paris. Archer made a mistake when he decided there would be no divorce. It was then that Louis knew that the man had to die. He would bide his time and wait for the

181

downturn of Megtex, then kill Archer, and bring Claudia back from the dead. Naturally he would become CEO of Megtex, Claudia would claim her half of the Archer stock and capital, they would be married, and he would quietly buy up the remaining stock.

It all came about even sooner than Louis had planned. It never occurred to him that Senator Lassiter would become involved, or that Derek would discover the Unicom account in the Swiss bank. All the years of scheming and biding his time would be for nothing, if the investigation actually took place. It was just as well; only his timetable had to be adjusted. Now just two people stood in his way: Alison—damn her, for insisting on heading the company—and Cora Lee, his wife, who had never been more than a nuisance. No way in hell would he let himself lose after all this time.

Except for the need to kill Alison, Claudia knew every aspect of his plan, wholeheartedly approved, and would do anything in her power to speed things along.

Louis glanced at his watch: five-thirty. It was time for Piper. He couldn't wait to be done with this meeting so he could see Claudia. They'd been very careful, never meeting anywhere they could possibly be spotted, but today he planned to go to her hotel. He looked up at the sky; it could storm any minute.

Just as Louis felt the first raindrops, he spotted Piper coming up the walk.

Piper took a seat beside him on the bench. "Been waiting long?"

"Long enough." Louis gave Piper a disgusted look. "You really fouled up in California. What happened?"

"Damned if I know. It all came about like clockwork, just as I planned, but the bitch got thrown clear. Wasn't a hell of a lot I could do about it."

Louis sighed. "Well, I'll tell you something, I'm fed

182

up with these 'suicide' attempts. You'll have to make it look like an accident."

"Why, you bastard! I was just following orders, so don't lay all this on me."

"I know, and I was wrong. Just do it."

"How?"

"How would I know? You're the professional. Just kill her."

"When?"

"Hell, when do you think? I thought this would all be over weeks ago."

Piper grinned. "An accident . . . now you're talking. I wondered why you were screwing around with her mind. Consider it done."

Suddenly the clouds cracked open and sheets of rain assaulted the park, soaking Louis's tailor-made suit. He quickly opened his umbrella and turned to make a run for his car. "Keep in touch," he said over his shoulder.

By the time Louis reached the Fairmont Hotel, the rain had slackened to a fine drizzle. He left his car a block away in a parking lot, not taking the risk of being seen in the hotel garage. He quickly made his way through the relatively empty lobby and stepped inside an elevator. When the doors opened, he made sure that no one was around before he hurried down the hallway and knocked at Room 509. The sight of Claudia made his loins ache. She looked stunning in her black hostess gown, her auburn hair framing her exquisite face, her sea green eyes wide with surprise.

"Why, Louis, what are you doing here?"

Quickly he stepped inside, took her in his arms, and kissed her. "I haven't heard from you in a while, and I just had to see you."

"I tried to call yesterday, but your secretary said you'd left early. How's Alison?"

"Doing great . . . in fact, she's back at work."

"That's good news. You know, you've never told me how it happened."

"She was driving Chris Chandler's boat and somehow crashed into another cruiser." Louis folded his umbrella, stood it in a corner by the door, and took off his wet coat.

"Come sit down and tell me more." Claudia led him to a sitting area at the end of the room. "I'll get us some drinks."

"That's really all I know. Must have been a freak accident."

Minutes later Claudia joined him on the sofa, handed him a Scotch and water, and gave him a shrewd look. "Did you have anything to do with this?"

"Darling, you've got to believe me—it was an accident, pure and simple. I wasn't anywhere near California, you know that."

"It doesn't mean you weren't responsible. You weren't anywhere near Derek's house or Myra's when they died, but—"

Louis pulled her into his arms, held her close, and gently stroked her back. "Trust me, Claudia, you know I wouldn't lie to you." Louis realized that getting rid of Alison would be much harder than he thought. Claudia must never suspect his involvement. She knew too much, and could put him behind bars for the rest of his life. But most of all he couldn't bear to lose her, lose everything he had planned and worked for all these years. It had all gone too far; everything had to be carried out to the letter. Alison had to die, but her mother must never suspect him.

"I want to trust you, darling, but I worry so about her. I've thought about this a long time, and know she's standing in your way."

Louis released her and took a long swallow of his

drink. "Megtex is on the verge of being sued, not to mention being the target of a government investigation. I have a feeling that before any of this comes down, Alison will be ready to throw in the towel, and get rid of her stock while she can. She'll be out of the picture, and that's when I'll make my move." Deep down, Louis knew that if she were allowed to live, Alison would never give up so easily. She'd see herself as the ship's captain, steadfastly holding the wheel to the very end. "I feel sure it will all work out, just as we planned." He stood and walked over to the bar to freshen his drink. "Like another one?" Claudia shook her head, and Louis went on, "We have the problem of Cora Lee to think about right now."

"Oh yes, Cora Lee. I assumed you'd take care of her. Really, Louis, I'd rather be left out of all this. She's your wife, and therefore your problem."

Louis dropped a few ice cubes in his glass. He'd already decided that Claudia must be involved in Cora Lee's death. So far, she had done nothing criminal, except of course, running away when Charles Thomas was killed. But that was so long ago, and nothing could be proved. He had to have something to hold over her head, and what would be better than accessory to murder? He loved Claudia very much, but that didn't blind him to the fact that she always put herself first. She was cold and calculating, but he'd do anything to make her his wife for two reasons: his love for her and the power she would bring him once she inherited all of Derek Archer's wealth.

He gave her a pleading look. "Oh, but I need you, darling. This has to look like an outsider killed her. Otherwise, I'd be the primary suspect."

"This is absurd. What on earth can *I* do?"

Louis returned to sit beside her again. "I've decided

185

to make it look like a kidnapping, and I need you as a decoy."

"A decoy? I don't understand. What would I have to do?"

"Simply pose as Cora Lee."

Claudia laughed. "But I don't look anything like her."

"You'd be surprised. With a little help, I think you could pull it off. You're close to the same size — Cora Lee's a little heavier, I'll admit, but not that much, and you're about the same height."

"You're forgetting that she's a blonde and I'm — "

"Wait a minute, let me tell you my plan." He reached for his wallet and pulled out a photograph of his wife. "Take a look at this hairstyle. How do you suppose it always looks the same?" He laughed. "She has a shelf full of wigs, all of them styled just alike. I wish you could see her hair without them . . . mousy brown and so thin you can see her scalp."

"Well, I'll be damned. All the time I've known her, I thought it was natural."

"I'll slip one of the wigs out of the house, and also one of her favorite outfits. I'll leave the picture here, and you'll have a few days to experiment with make-up."

Claudia looked puzzled. "But what's the purpose? What would I have to do?"

"I know you'll play an important part, but I haven't figured out the details yet."

"When will it happen?"

"Sometime during the next few days." Louis smiled at her hopefully. "Think about this . . . you want your inheritance, and I want the company. Can I count on you to cooperate?"

"Look, you're asking me to be an accomplice to murder, and I don't want any part of it."

186

"But it depends on you . . . I can't pull it off without you."

Claudia glared at him. "I simply won't do it, and that's final."

"Okay, look at it this way—what if I hire someone else to serve as a decoy? That means there'll be a witness, and before it's over, possibly another murder as a result. Do you want that on your conscience?"

"Well no, but . . ."

"Don't you see? It has to be just the two of us, so no one else will know. I simply can't do it without you."

Claudia considered for several seconds. "If my part in this is ever found out, I could be sent to prison." She shook her head. "The rewards simply aren't worth the consequences."

"There's no way anyone could ever know, I promise."

"How can you say that?"

"You won't be anywhere near Cora Lee when it happens."

"You're sure?"

"I'm positive. Please, Claudia, everything will fall apart if you won't help."

"All right, I suppose I'll do it, but something tells me I'll regret it."

Louis caressed her face and gave her a gentle kiss. "I promise you won't be in any danger, and you'll never even see Cora Lee." He decided he'd said enough for one night; more talk might cause her to change her mind. "Any plans for dinner?"

"As usual, I suppose I'll order from room service."

"Good, then we can eat together."

Claudia walked over to the phone, but Louis intercepted her before she could pick up the receiver. He approached her from behind and wrapped his arms around her waist. "Why don't we wait until later? Food's not what I'm hungry for right now." He kissed

187

the nape of her neck and pulled her closer.

She turned around and took his face in her hands, then gave him a long, lingering kiss. "What about your wife? Won't she be angry if you're late?"

Louis smiled. "A little late to worry about Cora Lee, don't you think?"

Before they reached the bed, their clothes had magically peeled away.

Late that night, Louis lay beside his sleeping wife, his mind churning. He'd have to caution Piper again about making Alison's "accident" look believable. Claudia must never suspect that it was anything more. Good lord, if she ever found out, she'd turn on him in a minute. His thoughts went to Cora Lee and what lay ahead for her. He couldn't let himself dwell on that now. He had too much planning to do.

Sixteen

On Monday, when Louis approached the park bench, he found Piper waiting for him.

"I'll need you tomorrow night at seven o'clock." Louis sat down and nervously looked around. The park was deserted, too early even for the most avid joggers.

"Just say where . . . what's up?"

Louis pulled a hand-drawn map from his pocket and began to trace Highway 80 with his finger. "Take this exit from Mesquite, and turn left on FM 205 before you reach Terrell. Go eight miles, and you'll see a gray farmhouse on the right, about fifty yards from the road. It's vacant, so there shouldn't be any problem."

Piper grinned. "Now I know where, but why?"

Louis swallowed hard. He'd planned and planned this for years, and now that it was all about to happen, he wondered if he could actually go through with it. "I'm bringing my wife out there to die . . . the rest is up to you. Just keep her alive for at least an hour after I leave. That's very important."

"Well, well . . . trouble in paradise?"

"Just business—that's all you need to know." Louis had never mentioned anything about Claudia, the company—anything. It was none of Piper's concern.

The price of a first-rate assassin came high, and he intended to squeeze every penny's worth of service.

"Okay, I follow you . . . then what?"

"Leave the body in the house and drive away, simple as that." He handed Piper a box containing Cora Lee's robe and slippers. "Before you leave, take off her clothes and dress her in the things in this box. Then take her clothes with you and burn them. I guess I don't need to tell you to keep your car out of sight."

Piper's eyes glinted with rage. "Just what do you take me for, an amateur, maybe?"

"Sorry, guess this whole thing has made me kind of jumpy. This one is different from the others."

"Anything else?"

"Just one more thing." Louis gave Piper a slip of paper. "Make a tape of this message, then call my house Wednesday night at eight o'clock sharp, and play it back on the phone."

"That's all?"

Louis nodded, realizing his palms were dripping wet.

"Consider it done."

As he watched Piper walk away, Louis wondered what he had become. What kind of man could condemn his own wife? He had stopped loving Cora Lee many years ago when he became obsessed with Claudia. Damn Derek Archer! Louis knew he would have divorced his wife back then and married Claudia, but Derek had denied him that, too, by refusing to let her go legally. Once more he realized that Derek was responsible for everything that had happened.

Many times in recent years, he had threatened to leave Cora Lee, but she had made it clear that she'd never give him a divorce. Living with her became a habit, his trips to Paris, his salvation. Cora Lee's life had been relatively good, he supposed. Many a woman would envy her big house in Highland Park, her maid who came five days a week, her expensive clothes. She seemed content with her social standing, her endless club meetings and community services. Yes, in many respects, he'd given his wife a happy life. Thank God, they'd never had any children.

Louis knew he was rationalizing, but he had to make himself feel better about what he must do. If he backed out, nothing would work out — no marriage to Claudia, no assurance that he could control the company, no ultimate revenge. He would see this through to the end; only the final step lay ahead — the demise of Alison Archer.

Louis drove to his home shortly before five o'clock the next afternoon. He found Cora Lee puttering around in the kitchen.

"Why, Louis, what are you doing here so early? I didn't expect you for another hour."

"I want you to come with me to look at a piece of land."

"Why would I do that?"

"Because if you like it, we're going to buy it."

"Buy land? What on earth for?"

"To build the dream house that you've always wanted."

Cora Lee's face broke out in a big smile. "Do you mean it — a weekend place in the country?"

"That's exactly what I mean. Come on, let's go."

"Why, I'm not even dressed to go out, and besides, I'm about to start dinner. Can't it wait?"

"It can wait long enough for you to dress and throw a few things in a suitcase. We're leaving for Houston on the eight o'clock flight."

She looked at him in amazement. "Houston . . . tonight? My God, Louis, what's gotten into you? You've never acted like this before. It isn't like you at all."

He laughed. "I know, but this came up unexpectedly. The owner lives there and he has another offer. I have to get there with the money, and we both have to sign the papers by ten o'clock tonight, or the deal's off. This is really prime property, the prettiest in the area, and I don't want to miss it." Louis gave his wife a pleading look. "Believe me, I'd have given you more notice, but I heard about the deadline just before I left the office. Please say you'll come with me."

"I don't see how I can. I have a long-standing luncheon date with Julia Childress tomorrow."

Louis felt a slow panic. Julia Childress was the epitome of Dallas society; he'd known for years that Cora Lee would all but sell her soul to be considered "in" with this woman. "Can't you postpone it?"

"Well . . . I suppose I could, but I'd really rather not."

"Please call her . . . think of all the wonderful parties you could throw at the new house. If we don't go, it might be years before we have an opportunity like this."

She sighed. "Oh all right, if it means that much to you."

"That's terrific! Now, you don't have much time—about an hour, so hurry upstairs, make your call, and pack just enough for an overnight trip." Louis felt his adrenaline rise. This was even better than he'd planned. This call to Julia Childress would make his scheme seem even more believable.

It took Cora Lee less than an hour to get herself ready to go. They headed out, following the path that he had instructed Piper to use. The five o'clock rush had subsided, but still the traffic was heavy as they wove their way out of the city through six congested lanes. It was almost seven when Louis began to slow down and came to a stop.

"That's the beginning of the land right over there." He pointed in the direction outside Cora Lee's window on the passenger-side. "Twenty-seven acres in all. What do you think?"

"It's really beautiful—all those huge oak trees and pastureland. Everything looks so green."

"Wait 'til you see the farmhouse on the property. It's been vacant for years, but it might be worth salvaging for a caretaker's house, if nothing else." He drove to the top of the hill, turned into the long driveway, and finally stopped outside the house. His heart began to thump irregularly. There wasn't a sign of Piper's car anywhere on the premises. His paid assassin was either a master of the game or a no-show. He hoped to God Piper hadn't let him down this time. Glancing at his watch, he saw that it was exactly seven o'clock.

"Let's take a look inside," he said.

"Oh, I don't know . . . it's been vacant all this time. What if it's not safe?"

"Don't worry, I've already been inside, and a little dust won't hurt us."

Louis opened his car door, stepped outside, and started up the sidewalk with Cora Lee right behind him. Opening the front door, he took a step inside and stood out of the way as Cora Lee came in behind him. The house looked dark and silent, not a hint that anyone was inside. Louis's doubts that he could count on Piper began to grow. Suddenly a hand reached out from behind the door, and jerked his wife into the house.

193

"Stop it! My God, what are you doing? Louis, help me! Louis!"

With his hands over his ears to mute the sound of Cora Lee's screams, Louis turned away and hurried back to the car. She was in Piper's hands now, and he knew he'd never set eyes on his wife again. An hour from now, she would be history. He smiled to himself as he backed out of the driveway. Not only would Cora Lee die; she would also leave him substantially richer. Five years ago, she inherited three million dollars from her mother's estate, and promptly put every penny in savings certificates, totally out of his reach. She also had a million-dollar life insurance policy that named him as beneficiary. Four million dollars—not a bad haul for a few hours' work.

Now, if Claudia turned out to be as dependable as Piper, he'd be home free. He worried, though, about how convincing she would be when posing as his wife. He had taken the wig and dress to Claudia's hotel yesterday, hadn't seen her since, and had no idea how much she could make herself look like Cora Lee. Too late to worry about that now.

As he pulled onto Highway 80 and headed back toward the city, he prayed that the traffic had subsided. He had just an hour to make it to Love Field to catch his flight.

When Claudia emerged from a cab outside the entrance of the airport, Louis's heart almost stopped beating at the sight of her. For a startling moment, he thought she *was* Cora Lee. The blond wig and makeup, along with the black and white dress his wife loved to wear, had caused a remarkable transformation. His confidence rising, he felt for the first time that his plan would actually work.

Claudia gave him an impish grin. "Well, what do you think?"

Louis wrapped his arm around her shoulders and gave her a squeeze. "Damn, I thought I might pass out when I saw you. How on earth did you manage all this?"

"Just experimented, like you said." She laughed. "I feel ridiculous, though. I know I look like a clown in this dress."

Louis snickered. "So did Cora Lee, but I never dared to tell her." He took her overnight bag from her hand. "We'd better hurry inside and pick up the tickets. Remember what we rehearsed?"

"I think so, but I'm a little scared."

"Just try to stay focused, and tell yourself this won't take long at all."

As they walked to the Southwest Airlines terminal, Claudia paused and looked him in the eye. "You haven't said a word about what happened to Cora Lee. Did everything go okay?"

"Like clockwork. She fell for the land bit, and went right along with the whole thing. It's all up to Piper now." Louis felt like a cold-blooded killer. Here he was nonchalantly talking about his wife of twenty-seven years, who could very well be dead by now. He couldn't allow himself to think about what he had done. Too much depended upon these next few minutes.

Claudia swallowed hard and nodded.

They stepped up to the counter and stood side by side, both facing the agent. "I'd like to pick up the tickets to Houston for Mr. and Mrs. Louis Bennett," Louis said.

The agent opened a drawer and began to thumb through papers. "Here they are, sir. Will this be cash or credit card?"

Louis pulled out his American Express card and turned to Claudia, who was frowning. "I wish you weren't so unhappy about this little jaunt."

"Oh, Louis, my going is so pointless, and I have so much to do here. Why do you keep insisting that I go along?"

"I think we need some time alone."

"Alone . . . what a perfect word to describe this trip. That's exactly what I'll be—alone for a whole day, while you go off to take care of business."

"But you can go shopping, do a lot of things while I'm working."

"Tell me one thing Houston has to offer that I can't do right here in Dallas. This is ridiculous."

The ticket agent eyed them impatiently. "The first boarding call has already been made, sir."

"All right, all right, Cora Lee, have it your way. Stay here and do whatever you do that makes you happy. I'll go by myself." Louis smiled apologetically at the agent. "Just make that one ticket."

"Oh, Louis, thanks for giving in. Any other time, I'd go with you, but I'm up to my ears in committee work." She gave him a peck on the cheek and picked up her overnight bag and Cora Lee's suitcase. "Enjoy your little trip, and I'll see you tomorrow night."

Louis watched her walk away, amazed at how well Claudia had pulled it off. What an actress! Her fake Texas accent would fool anyone, and she'd made herself look enough like Cora Lee that the agent would be sure to identify her if presented a photograph of the real Mrs. Bennett. By God, it was working out better than he'd ever imagined.

Outside the terminal, Claudia found a cab parked

beside the curb. She gave Louis's address in Highland Park to the driver and settled back, her nerves still jangled, every pore in her body stinging like fire. If anything went wrong with Louis's scheme, she'd be charged with accessory to murder. So much depended on how well this all played out during the next few days.

When the cab stopped in front of the Bennett driveway, she handed the driver the fare, along with a generous tip that would hopefully make him remember her. She gave him a wave and hurried up the walk to the front door. Slipping on a pair of leather gloves, she used Louis's key to unlock it.

The house seemed unusually quiet, and she shuddered as she stepped inside. She had been in this house several times, but that was many years ago when her affair with Louis first began. It was great fun back then to slip into the bed he shared with his wife and take advantage of the hours Cora Lee spent away from home. She had never really liked this house, and had no intention of living here once she and Louis were married. Cora Lee had gone overboard with her decorating, everything gauche and massive, with ornate carvings and flamboyant wall coverings everywhere. Feeling Cora Lee's ghost in every corner of the house, she rushed up the stairs, eager to do what had to be done and get out of here.

Claudia walked into the master bedroom, deposited Cora Lee's suitcase on the floor, and immediately peeled off the dead woman's dress and wig. Her skin crawled as she opened the walk-in closet door, put the wig back on its form, and hung the dress on the end of the rack. Hurrying as fast as she could, she pulled out a jogging suit and running shoes from her own overnight bag, and dropped in her hose and high-heeled black shoes. Quickly she donned the suit, then stood in the middle of the room, mentally going over all of Louis's instructions to make sure she'd remembered all the details. Satisfied that she'd done everything he said, Claudia left the room — still wearing the gloves — walked down the stairs, and made her way through the kitchen, where she unlocked the back door.

She left the house through the front entrance and locked the door behind her, relieved to be out of that house at last. Then, like any other middle-aged woman out for early evening exercise, she jogged down the sidewalk for about a block and suddenly froze in her tracks. She'd left her overnight bag in the bedroom! Damn, she'd been so careful, and still made a stupid mistake like that, one that could possibly put her in prison for life. She turned around, resigned to the fact that she had to go back inside that house.

Claudia crept through the yard to the back door, afraid that one of the neighbors might see her, now she didn't look a thing like Cora Lee. The house was totally dark, but she didn't dare turn on a light. Feeling her way through all the rooms, she finally found the stairway, and held onto the banister all the way to the second floor. Somehow she found the bedroom, retrieved her bag, and made it back outside.

She felt a little foolish jogging with an overnight case in one hand, but she had no choice. She hadn't gone far when she almost ran into a man walking his dog. She felt suddenly frightened, but consoled herself as she hurried along. Surely the man didn't get a good look at her under that dim streetlight. Parked two blocks away, her rented car was a welcome sight when she finally reached it.

Once inside the car, she lay back on the seat and sighed with relief. It was done. Louis had devised a foolproof scheme, and she couldn't imagine how either of them would ever be suspected of Cora Lee's murder. Thank God her part was finally over.

Seventeen

Louis's plane landed the next night at seven. He went directly to his house, anxious to get the next phase of his plan in motion. During his brief stay in Houston, he'd made sure that his presence was known, chatting with the desk clerk, making calls on the phone to several acquaintances in town, and ordering a late dinner from room service. This morning he'd kept an appointment with Martin Jamison, a business associate at the Megtex branch office, and the two of them had lunch at Brennan's. How well Claudia had carried out her part of the scheme remained to be seen.

He immediately checked his mail, and found the ransom note he'd sent to himself from Terrell early the previous afternoon. He chuckled as he pulled the envelope out of the mailbox. How the tongues of his friends would wag. "Poor Louis," they'd say, "he's a victim of the awful tragedies that keep happening at Megtex." He had chosen to mail the letter from Terrell to give the police a general idea of where to look for the body. No need in dragging this thing out any longer than necessary.

He looked in the master bedroom first, noting that Claudia had remembered everything, had even thought to put the black and white dress in the closet.

Downstairs, he saw that the back door was unlocked, too, everything ready to set the rest of his plan in high gear. Taking out his handkerchief, he wiped the door-knob clean.

First he called Julia Childress, inquiring if she'd seen Cora Lee, then Mavis Thompson, his wife's best friend; both women expressed concern and bewilderment. He waited a few minutes, then called the police to tell them about the ransom note.

Lieutenant McAllister was first on the scene. Although Nick was assigned to the homicide division, he decided to investigate the case personally, because it involved the wife of a Megtex official. Deep in his gut, he felt that this alleged kidnapping was somehow connected to the two murders and the quirky wiring of the Archer house. It made him even more alarmed about the danger that possibly hovered over Alison.

When Louis answered the door and ushered him inside, Nick's heart went out to the grief-stricken man. Either Bennett was a mighty good actor, Nick thought, or he had no knowledge whatsoever of the abduction.

"I found this in today's mail when I got home." Louis's voice broke as he handed Nick the envelope. "I just can't believe it."

Nick took one look and realized it was a typical ransom note, one that would be hard to trace, with the words spelled out in letters that could have been scrawled by a six-year-old:

WE HAVE YOUR WIFE AND WILL RETURN HER SAFELY IF YOU FOLLOW INSTRUCTIONS. DO NOT INVOLVE THE POLICE OR YOU'LL NEVER SEE YOUR WIFE ALIVE

"Well, Mr. Bennett," Nick said, "I guess this tells the story. Mind telling me where you were today?" He pulled out a pen and notepad.

"In Houston. In fact, my plane landed a little while ago." Louis held his face in his hands, his shoulders shaking. "Oh, if only Cora Lee hadn't changed her mind."

"What do you mean?"

"She was going with me, but decided against it after we got to the airport."

Nick continued to take notes. "Did she say why she wasn't going?"

"Oh, you know women . . . she hates these business trips and is always so bored." Louis's eyes were full of pain as he looked at Nick. "No amount of boredom could ever be as bad as this."

Nick nodded in sympathy. "Did anyone in the airport see Mrs. Bennett, maybe someone who knew her?"

"No, I don't think so, but there was the ticket agent, of course."

"When was this?"

"Last night at Love Field. We had reservations on the eight o'clock flight."

"Southwest Airlines?" Nick knew he'd asked a stupid question and felt a little embarrassed. No other commercial airline flew planes out of Love Field.

"Of course. Oh, if only she'd gone with me . . . I should have insisted."

"Don't blame yourself, Mr. Bennett. There's no way to predict something like this." He placed a hand on Louis's shoulder in an attempt to offer comfort.

"Don't panic yet. We'll do everything in our power to find her. Right now, all we can do is check out the house. Any sign of a struggle?"

"None whatsoever."

"Then maybe she never arrived home."

"Oh, she came here all right. Her suitcase is upstairs, and even the dress she was wearing. The bedroom's the first place I checked."

"Mind if I have a look?"

"Not at all." Louis led the way upstairs, pointing out the suitcase and the dress in the closet.

"Anything missing? Maybe that would tell us what she was wearing."

Louis shook his head. "I have no way of knowing."

Nick could certainly understand that. The closet was a huge walk-in, as large as a small bedroom, filled from end to end with garments of every description. He'd never seen so many clothes in his life, except in a store maybe. Damn, these rich people lived in a whole other world. Unexpectedly, he thought of Alison, and wondered if her closet compared to this. No doubt it did. He was out of his mind to think there could ever be anything really serious between them. He shook his head, chiding himself for letting his thoughts stray.

"Right now there's nothing we can do but wait," Nick said, "but for the time being, do you have a picture of your wife?"

Louis reached for his wallet and pulled out a photograph of Cora Lee. "Will this do? If not, I can find a larger one."

"It's fine for now." Nick started back downstairs with Louis following. "I hate to put you through any more questioning, but would you mind giving me the names of the people you saw in Houston?"

"Primarily Martin Jamison at the Megtex office.

203

There were others in the office, secretaries and assistants, that kind of thing, but I don't know their names."

Nick made a notation and continued, "Did you stay in a hotel?"

"Yes — the Warwick . . . checked in a little after nine."

"One more thing . . . did your wife drive herself home?"

"Why no, she took a cab. I left the car at the airport."

"Were all the doors locked when you came in?"

"Yes, I'm sure of it. Had to use my key to let myself in."

"Have you unlocked any other doors since you got home?"

"Why, no."

"Mind if I have a look?"

"Not at all."

Nick went through the house, finding every entry secure until he came to the kitchen door at the back. "Seems like this one's unlocked. Is that unusual?"

"Of course, it is. I just took for granted . . ."

"Well, this could explain how the intruders got in. We'll have it checked for fingerprints."

Nick made the last entry on his pad and turned back to Bennett. "We'll have to set up a command post here at your house, and monitor all your calls. Sorry for the inconvenience."

"Officer, I welcome anything you can do to bring my wife home safely." Louis's eyes were bright with unshed tears.

When Nick left the house, he realized something was bugging him, but he couldn't put his finger on it. Bennett's account seemed almost too pat. It wasn't often that a passenger got as far as the airport, and suddenly changed her mind about boarding the plane. He looked at Cora Lee Bennett's photograph, determined to check out personally every detail of her husband's story.

He used his car radio to order officers to the Bennett home to set up the phone system, then headed for Love Field. Perhaps he could find the agent who had handled Bennett's tickets.

Three agents were on duty at the Southwest Airlines terminal, and fortunately one of them remembered the Bennetts. Nick produced the photograph, and the young woman gave it a careful look.

"This is Mrs. Bennett all right . . . changed her mind about taking the flight at the last minute." She looked alarmed. "What's wrong? Did something happen to her?"

"We're not sure . . . just a routine check. Any idea what she was wearing?"

"Oh, I sure do. In fact I wondered where on earth she'd found such an outfit. It was a black print dress with huge white flowers all over it . . . kind of flashy, if you know what I mean, with a pencil-straight skirt and a ruffled flounce at the hem."

"Can you think of anything else?"

"Just how green her eyes were . . . the clearest green I've ever seen." She looked at the photograph again. "Funny how her eyes don't look green at all in this picture. In fact, they look kind of brown. Strange, isn't it? Must be a bad print."

Strange indeed, Nick thought. "You're sure the woman's eyes were green?"

"Positive. In fact, I even mentioned how pretty they were to one of the other girls."

"Thanks," he said, "you've been a big help."

Nick left the airport and made a mental note to check further into the color of Cora Lee Bennett's eyes. He noticed the line of cabs at curbside, and jotted in his notepad the names of the various companies represented. He'd send an officer out tonight to find out which cab and driver had taken Mrs. Bennett home. Damn, except for a possible discrepancy in the eye color, Bennett's story checked out so far. They'd have to ask for help from the Houston P.D. to verify the rest of his alibi.

When Nick got off duty, he drove straight to Alison's house, still concerned about her being alone and the danger that obviously surrounded everyone in the Megtex office. When he rang the bell, the outside light came on immediately, as it always did.

"Nick!" Alison said when she opened the door. "You're here earlier than I expected."

The sight of her, so wholesome and sexy-looking all at the same time in those jeans and white knit shirt, made him catch his breath. "My, you're beautiful."

"You amaze me, Nick. Somehow you know just how to push my buttons."

He stepped inside, immediately folded her in his arms, and kissed her. Alison was like a drug to him, a habit he couldn't kick, and he had no idea what to do about it. They might as well live on two different planets. How could he ever expect to have a future with someone like her?

"Have you had dinner?" she asked.

"Yes, I had a hamburger on the way over." Nick hadn't stopped long enough to eat a bite, but he didn't want her to know, then go to the trouble of trying to feed him. "I'm afraid I've got some more bad news."

The color suddenly drained from Alison's face. "Oh no . . . what's happened now?"

"This is strictly off the record, not to be told, but I think you should know that Cora Lee Bennett has been kidnapped."

"Kidnapped! Cora Lee? Oh, poor Louis! He must be out of his mind." She started for the door. "I have to go to him right now."

Nick stopped her. "I've told you something that hasn't been made public, because I'm worried about your safety. I don't think it's a good idea to go over there tonight. Besides, the house is full of police setting up a system to monitor his calls."

"When did this happen?"

"We don't know, because Bennett's been out of town and just got home."

"Yes, he had business in Houston."

"Seems that he discovered her missing, and found a ransom note in his mail when he got in."

Alison sank into a chair in the foyer. "Something evil is consuming Megtex, and I've got to know what it is before anything else happens."

"Let's go into the den where it's more comfortable. Your face is like chalk." He took her arm and led her to the back of the house, where they both sat down on a sofa.

"Someone in the company did this, I'm almost sure." Alison put her face in her hands.

"Why do you think that?"

"Oh, I don't know . . . it's just that — "

"You've kept something to yourself from the beginning, and I think it's time you leveled with me. What's going on?" Nick put his arm around her and pulled her close. "I can't get to the bottom of any of this, if I don't know the facts. Is Megtex in some kind of trouble?"

Alison's eyes filled with tears, and Nick felt utterly helpless. "Oh, Nick, someone high in the company has almost ruined us."

"How, for God's sake?"

"By ordering faulty material and stealing a huge sum of money, possibly millions, for many years. There's even a lawsuit pending. That's why I went to California, to try to stall Linco Oil until we found out who was responsible. They're threatening a lawsuit."

Nick's mind began to click, remembering all the details surrounding Derek Archer's murder. "Could this have anything to do with the missing papers?"

"I think so . . . that's why I've bugged you so much about that key. Has anything more been done about it?"

Nick felt terrible about almost dismissing the piece of evidence that was probably the most critical. "We have an officer checking around, but so far, he's drawn a blank. He's about to run out of places to look."

"Well, it seems to me that if the people in the lab say it opens a locker, it's bound to be somewhere in the city."

"You're right, and starting tomorrow, I'll make finding it a top priority. It's just that I had no idea of any company problems." He shook his head. "I'm making excuses, I know, and I'm—"

"No, it's my fault. I should have told you, but Louis didn't want the police involved."

"Bennett asked you not to report it? Why not?"

"Afraid of publicity, that kind of thing. If this gets out, it could ruin us."

Publicity, hell, Nick thought. He'd had a feeling that there was something phony about Louis Bennett from the beginning, and now it was starting to come together. He knew he was jumping to conclusions, something he'd been trained not to do. But he couldn't figure out how faking Cora Lee's kidnapping could have any bearing at all. It didn't make sense. "How long has he been with the company?"

"From the first day. He was dad's best friend, too. Poor thing, I wish I could go to him." She pushed her hair away from her face. "There's so much to worry about. If we don't get to the truth, we'll even be the target of a Senate investigation. I wonder if this kidnapping is some sort of a blackmail scheme. My dad told Senator Lassiter that someone high in the company was responsible, and that he'd take care of it personally." The look of pain in her eyes almost tore Nick apart. "I believe that person killed my father and Myra . . . and now look what's happened to Cora Lee."

Nick couldn't figure it out, not yet, but like Alison, he felt that it was all connected, and that she could very well be the next victim. "I don't want you to stay here by yourself."

"Oh, I'll be all right, and besides, I couldn't bear to live in a hotel very long. I have a good alarm system and plenty of telephones."

"A lot of good that did when someone rigged up a taping system right under your nose."

"Well, you do have a point."

"Then it's settled, you're getting out of here."

"Tonight? Surely you're joking . . . I'm not going anywhere right now."

"Then I'm staying with you."

She smiled for the first time. "Can't argue with that."

Nestled in the haven of Nick's arms, Alison slept the whole night through, never once sitting straight up in bed, as she had done so often lately, terrified by the replay of her dad's murder in her dreams. She awoke with the sickening reality of the news that Nick had brought her last night, and dreaded the days ahead.

Nick left for work early, and Alison was about to walk out the door when the phone rang. She was glad to hear Louis's voice.

"Just wanted to tell you that I won't be at the office today. I've had some terrible news."

"Oh no, what's happened?" Alison's heart went out to Louis; he sounded so desperate and lost.

"Cora Lee's been kidnapped."

"Louis, how awful! Are you sure?" Alison tried very hard to sound shocked, since Nick had given her this information in strict confidence. She felt relieved that Louis had made her a part of his ordeal, enabling her to go to him and offer some measure of comfort. He was the closest one to family she had left, and she knew how much he needed her.

"Yes, I'm sure. I've already received a note from the abductors."

"My God, what are you going to do? Did you call the police?"

"Yes, but that was probably a mistake. The kidnappers threatened to kill her if I did, but I felt so helpless trying to handle this alone. What if they kill —" Louis's voice broke.

"Don't feel that way. Of course, you had to tell them. When did this happen?"

"Apparently while I was in Houston. Oh, Alison, I'm really scared . . . what if they don't bring her back?"

"You've got to think positively. She'll come home to you safely, I feel sure." Alison knew how hollow her reassurance sounded. Deep down she felt that Cora

Lee, for some unexplainable reason, was yet another victim of the monster who had set out to destroy them all. "I'm coming over right now."

"Please wait until tonight. Right now, there's really nothing you can do, and besides, I'll be surrounded by police trying to figure all this out."

"But you need me."

"Just knowing that Cora Lee and I are in your thoughts is comfort enough." He hesitated, as though trying to control his voice. "There's another reason, and I think you'll agree. If we're both gone from the office, everyone will wonder why, and I don't want this to leak out until we know more."

"I understand, and trust me, no one else will know. I'll see you tonight."

Louis had braced himself for the performance of his life when Alison arrived at his house shortly before eight. She knew him better than anyone, and could spot in a minute any phony display of grief. She held onto him a long time, and before she released him, he managed to fill his eyes with tears.

"Have you heard anything more?" she asked.

"Not yet, but hopefully the kidnappers will keep their word and call tonight. I can't stand to wait much longer."

Alison locked her arm in his as he led her into the living room, where the police had set up a phone system. Three of them, including Nick, were seated on the plush chairs, prepared for a long vigil.

"I know this must have been the longest day of your life," she said. "Oh, what's happening to all of us?"

Louis shook his head. "God only knows."

As they entered the living room, he noticed the way

211

she smiled at Nick McAllister and the warm look that passed between them. Piper had informed him of their budding romance, and now he could see for himself that it was probably true. Their eyes told him they were sleeping together — Alison Archer, cozying up to a nobody cop, when she could have married John Carpenter! What a fool she was to kick Carpenter out of her life. If they had married, John would have insisted that she leave her job, and then she wouldn't have to die. Damned shame.

Louis glanced at the mantel clock. He'd given Piper instructions to call at eight o'clock. In just a minute or two, the phone should ring. So much depended on this call. Piper couldn't let him down, not now, after all that had led to this moment. He turned to Alison. "Would you like some coffee . . . maybe a sandwich? The maid left plenty of snacks."

"Just coffee, but don't bother, I'll get it." She walked over to a table against the wall and poured the hot brew into a cup. Louis watched Nick McAllister hurry across the room to join her. The two had their heads together, their voices low, and he wondered what McAllister was telling her. The bastard had grilled him for hours, trying desperately to find a hole in his story, but he had held his ground, never once flinching or contradicting himself. He worried, though, about the man's question concerning Cora Lee's eyes, and his surprised look when he learned that they were brown. It was probably his own paranoia, Louis told himself. Surely the eye color would not be important. But what if the ticket agent at the airport remembered that Claudia's were green? The possibility was so remote, that it wasn't worth a minute's worry, but he'd tried to be so careful, planning this scheme to the smallest detail. Damn, he should have thought to tell Claudia to wear dark glasses. Too late now. He had a foolproof story, one with no flaws, even if the agent happened to notice. The police would just figure she'd made a mistake.

Right now he had a more important concern. It was eight-fifteen. Why the hell hadn't Piper called? Louis looked at his hands and realized they were shaking. He knew he would fall apart, if he couldn't get this next step over with soon. At that moment, he jumped, startled when the phone suddenly rang.

McAllister rushed to his post by the extension and taping apparatus, then motioned for Louis to answer, both of them picking up the receivers simultaneously.

Louis's heart pounded as he listened to the voice on the other end:

"Listen good, because I'll only say this once. At precisely ten o'clock tomorrow morning, transfer one million dollars to the Swiss Volksbank in Bern, Switzerland, account number 1865270. If you follow these instructions to the letter, I'll let you know where to find your wife. Remember, timing is very important. I'll be waiting."

Louis hung up the phone, his hands still shaking. Piper had pulled it off, but where in hell had that voice come from? So garbled and low, it sounded like a record played at a slow speed. He had to hand it to Piper. What a genius!

He turned to Nick and noticed that he was frowning. "What do you think? Is Cora Lee still alive?"

Nick shook his head. "Guess we'll have to find out. Do you intend to pay the ransom?"

"I'm certainly going to try."

"What did the caller say?" Alison asked.

Louis took her arm, led her to the back of the room, and lowered his voice. "I'd rather the others didn't hear

213

this, but I don't know what I'm going to do. The kidnappers are demanding a million dollars by ten o'clock tomorrow morning. There's no way I can scrape up that much in such a short time." He began to wring his hands and looked at her in despair. "Maybe the bank will approve an emergency loan, or maybe I can sell—"

Alison took both his hands in hers and squeezed them reassuringly. "Money should be the least of your worries right now. I'll call the bank president at his home tonight, and make arrangements for the transfer."

"No, I can't let you do that. This is my problem, and I'll figure out how to solve it."

Alison looked him in the eye. "What do you think my dad would have done in this situation?"

"Well, he . . ."

"He would have done exactly the same thing. Why, Louis, you were his best friend." She gave him a satisfied smile. "Case closed."

Louis put his arms around her and hugged her. He conjured up a few more tears, his shoulders shaking. "I owe everything to you, Alison, dear, dear girl. How can I ever repay you? I'll be in your debt forever."

"Don't worry about it. It's the least I can do after all these years of friendship. You're just like family."

Louis blinked back his tears. "Bless you . . . you've probably saved Cora Lee's life."

Minutes later, Louis handed Alison the account number, then smiled as he watched her leave. It couldn't have worked out better in his wildest imaginings. Alison was like a lump of sugar in hot tea, just melting at his command. Now he had added another million to the pot. Cora Lee was certainly worth a hell of a lot more dead than alive.

Nick left the other two officers at their post at the Bennett house, and followed Alison to her home. There was something very puzzling about that call. For instance, the voice was indistinguishable. Could have belonged to anyone — man, woman, child, even Louis Bennett himself. And there was something else, maybe not important, but it was odd how Bennett just stood there listening, never saying a word, not even asking to speak to his wife to prove that she was still alive. Could be that the man was in shock, but even so, Nick had never seen a reaction quite like that. He'd have the lab go over it first thing tomorrow. Maybe the voice had been taped, and Bennett knew it ahead of time.

Whatever the case, he couldn't let Alison stay in that house alone. She was right; something evil hovered over Megtex, and she was the CEO, the most likely target of all.

Eighteen

Alison appeared at Louis's door shortly before ten the next morning. He quickly ushered her through the house to the breakfast room, just off the kitchen, and poured two cups of coffee. They sat down at the table, facing each other.

"We can have more privacy in here," he said. "The police are still around, manning the phones. Did everything go okay?"

"I made the call last night, and it's all taken care of."

"Thank God . . . and thank you, my dear. I don't know what I'd have done if you hadn't made this offer."

"No need for gratitude. What are friends for?" She couldn't help but notice that he seemed amazingly rested. She had expected a haggard, bleary-eyed man, but he looked as though he'd had a full night's sleep. "How are you holding up so well?"

Louis gave her a faint smile. "With a little help from a sleeping pill . . . went out like a light. Guess I needed it, since I didn't sleep a wink the night before."

Alison took a sip of coffee, then leaned forward, bracing herself for what she had to say. "I've been thinking about what happened to Cora Lee, my dad, and Myra, and I can't help but believe that all these tragedies are connected."

"You're saying that you think Cora Lee is dead?"

"Oh no, of course not . . . we have to hope for the best! I didn't mean to give that impression at all. I guess I might as well get to the point. Is there something you're not telling me?"

Louis looked shaken, his face suddenly ashen. "What do you mean?"

"Are you being blackmailed?"

"Why do you ask that?"

"You and I both know that someone in the company has almost brought Megtex down. I need to know if you've found out who's behind all this, and if Cora Lee is being held hostage to keep you quiet. You've got to know that if you told me, I'd never put her in more danger."

Louis visibly relaxed. "I wish it were that simple, but I'm no closer to the truth than when you first told me. Obviously the motive for the kidnapping was money, and I have no idea who's holding her." He patted her hand. "Now that the ransom is paid—thanks to you— I have a feeling that Cora Lee will be home today." The pained look in his eyes tore at Alison's heart. "I have to believe that."

"So do I." Alison finished her coffee and stood. "I'm going to the office for a while, but call me if you hear anything at all."

"Don't worry, I will." Louis walked her to the door and kissed her cheek. "You've been my anchor," he said.

All the way to the office, the panicky look on Louis's face kept flashing in Alison's mind. Louis was hiding something, she was almost sure, and somehow it was connected to everything else that had happened. On the other hand, except for those brief moments, he looked so calm—too calm for a man whose wife had been kidnapped, possibly even killed. Maybe he had withdrawn from reality, had lapsed into a state of denial. If Cora Lee didn't come home, it would all come crashing down on him, and he would probably fall into a million pieces. Poor Louis. She had to hope and pray that it would all turn out all right.

Nick spent the morning attempting to piece together every scrap of evidence he had gathered on the Bennett case. Clare Cummings, the mysterious lady in black, kept popping into his mind. As far as he knew, she hadn't done anything criminal, but she was always there, obviously stalking every move Alison made. She had seemed to come from nowhere, right after Derek Archer's death. He wondered if she could possibly be implicated, not only in Archer's murder, but all the other mysteries that still weren't solved. Earlier this morning, he had hung around the Fairmont Hotel lobby long enough to see her step off the elevator. He'd moved close enough to get a good look at her, especially her face. Her eyes were green, the clearest green he'd ever seen. By God, if she happened to be involved with Louis Bennett, she could have posed as his wife at the airport!

Nick's next stop had been the Bennett house, where he made an excuse to check the master bedroom closet again. This time, he observed more carefully the shelf full of blond wigs, all of them styled exactly alike. It was beginning to come together. If his theory turned out to be right, Louis Bennett had staged his own wife's kidnapping, with Clare Cummings as his accomplice. He'd bet on it, but finding proof was another matter. He sent Colby, armed with a camera equipped with a telescopic lens, to the hotel to get a close-up photo of her. How the hell he'd use it, he had no idea, but it was worth having.

Another thing nagging at him was the ransom that was paid to a numbered account in a Swiss bank, something the department couldn't touch. Sounded like it was done by someone who knew his way around in financial circles. Damned unusual, but something Louis Bennett might very well have dreamed up.

Two hours later, Officer Colby appeared at Nick's door. "Got the pictures you wanted, Lieutenant, and the lab did a rush job on them." He dropped two color photos on Nick's desk. "Anything else?"

"Yeah, go home and dress yourself in plain clothes. Then go back to the hotel and keep an eye on her. You've got a room across the hall from hers reserved for the next few days. I want to know where she goes, who knocks on her door, and anything else you can find out."

As Colby hurried out of the office, Nick noticed the grin on the older man's face. Rough duty—several days holed up at the Fairmont was hard to beat.

Nick slipped on his jacket and picked up the photographs. Time to hit the streets himself, this time Louis Bennett's neighborhood.

The houses were set far apart, many of them nestled back from the street on lush, green grounds, manicured to perfection. The likelihood that the neighbors had seen or heard anything at the Bennett home on Monday night was remote, to say the least, but Nick felt compelled to check out every possibility. The

219

people who lived on each side of the Bennetts offered no help at all, one family even out of town that night, but Nick hit pay dirt at the house directly across the street. Ronald Dirkson, the owner, answered the door, and Nick produced a badge, then introduced himself.

"What's the trouble, officer?" Dirkson asked. He was a tall man with gray hair, blue eyes, and the build of an athlete, despite the fact that he was obviously well into his sixties.

"Just wondering if you noticed anything unusual at the Bennett house on Monday night."

"No, not at all."

"Did you see a cab pull into the driveway?"

"As a matter of fact, I did, but didn't think much about it. I was just turning off the sprinkler system and was about to take my dog for his evening walk, when the cab brought Cora Lee home."

Nick knew that the cab in question had been located last night. The driver had concurred that the woman he delivered across the street matched Cora Lee Bennett's photograph. "You're sure it was Mrs. Bennett?"

"Of course . . . even waved to her, but I guess she didn't see me, since she didn't wave back."

"You say you went walking?"

"Yes, just like clockwork every night, weather permitting."

"Tell me, did you see anything unusual while you were out . . . any strangers on the street, or cars parked at odd places?"

"Now that you mention it, I almost ran head-on into a woman jogger I'd never seen in this neighborhood before."

"Oh really? Where were you?"

"Just down the street. I was on my way home, and

220

she was heading in the opposite direction."

"East?"

Ronald Dirkson nodded.

"Which side of the street?"

"On the way back every night, I always cross the street. Don't know why exactly . . . guess it keeps things from getting monotonous, but we had a near collision right down there." He pointed to his left, across the street.

Nick pulled out the photograph of Clare Cummings and handed it to Dirkson. "Could this be the woman you saw?"

Dirkson took the picture and studied it carefully. "Can't be sure . . . it was dark outside, you know, but I met her at the corner right under the streetlight." He stared at the picture again. "Her hair looks about the same color, but she had it pulled back, I remember that, so she looked a lot different. Like I said, the light wasn't all that good, so I can't be positive." He gave Nick a shrewd look. "What's going on, officer? I've noticed all kinds of activity at the Bennett house lately."

"Well, we're really not sure yet, so I'd rather not say right now, but will you be available if I need to talk to you again in the next few days?"

"Anytime."

Nick felt a surge of excitement as he climbed back into his car. He just might be onto something, but still an inner voice told him to move cautiously and keep an open mind. His training and years of experience had taught him not to yield to a predetermined theory and search for evidence to prove his suppositions. Nevertheless, nothing Ronald Dirkson told him had contradicted his scenario. With little else to go on, it was certainly worth pursuing for the time being, as long as he didn't go off half-cocked.

He had the urge to march himself over to the Fairmont Hotel and question Clare Cummings right now, but instinctively he knew better. If the woman happened to be guilty, she would only deny any involvement and be on the alert to avoid any contact with Louis Bennett. No, it was better to be patient, wait and see what turned up in Colby's surveillance.

Nick drove back to the station and had just sat down at his desk when his intercom buzzed.

"Yes?"

"Just got word from the Rockwall County Sheriff that a body matching the Bennett woman's description was found in an abandoned house on FM 205, about four miles from Terrell. The house is gray, set back on the right-hand side of the road."

A sick feeling hit the pit of Nick's stomach. Deep down, he'd had a hunch all along that Cora Lee was dead. He had little doubt that the body was hers. "I'm on my way."

Nick had no trouble locating the farmhouse. It was the only one in the vicinity on the right side, and the only gray house in sight. The front room was filled with men from the sheriff's department, who had already cordoned off the area around the house and outlined the position of the body with chalk.

The county sheriff was on the scene and introduced himself to Nick. "The body matches the description on the APB," he said, "so I thought you'd need to take a look. She's been dead a couple of days, at least."

Nick bent over the body and pulled back the plastic cover. He sucked in his breath at the sight of the blond wig that had partially slipped, revealing strands of brown hair underneath. He took the wig completely off, and knew immediately the cause of death—a single bullet wound to the head. The woman was clad in a blue satin robe and matching slippers, a closer look revealing off-white hose. Odd, he thought. Seemed as if she'd have pulled them off if she wanted to get comfortable. She was also wearing a bra and panty girdle—odd indeed.

He turned to the sheriff. "How did you find her?"

"Some boys were playing around here last night just before dark." He grinned. "Afraid to tell their parents they'd broken into the house, so they didn't mention it until this morning. One of them let it slip before he left for school. We got a call from his dad this morning . . . wanted us to check it out."

"Have you finished here?" Nick asked.

"Yes, we're ready to move the body. What do you think, is this the woman you're looking for?"

"I'm not sure, but I'd like to bring Mr. Bennett to the morgue for a positive I.D."

On the way back to Dallas, Nick thought again about how the body was dressed. It was possible that the killer had changed her into the robe and slippers after she was dead. Gruesome, he thought. Again he warned himself about a predetermined theory. Still, at this point, anything was possible.

He went straight to the Bennett home and rang the bell, dreading the hour or more that lay ahead. It was never easy to tell a man that his wife's body had been found.

Louis answered the door. "Well, hello, Lieutenant, come in. We're still waiting for a call."

Nick stepped into the foyer and forced himself to look the man in the eye. "Sorry, Mr. Bennett, but I don't think you'll be getting that call. I'm almost sure your wife's body has been found."

"My God, where?"

"In a farmhouse near Terrell."

"Why, those double-crossing bastards! I paid a cool million to get her back." Louis's eyes were dry, his voice low, completely void of emotion.

"Getting her back is still a possibility until we're sure this is your wife," Nick said. "I'd like you to come with me to make a positive I.D."

"Of course, just give me a minute to put on a tie and get my coat."

Louis was still amazingly calm when they entered the Rockwall County Morgue in Terrell. Nick was surprised that during the ride over, Bennett had asked no questions at all concerning the location of the body and the circumstances that led to finding it, almost an unconcerned attitude. Nick guarded against making any kind of judgment; each person had his own way of dealing with tragedy.

The identification took less than a minute. Louis took one look, nodded his head, and said briefly, "Yes, that's Cora Lee." With that, he turned and walked away, still no tears, no emotion.

Once back in Dallas, after delivering Bennett to his home, Nick made another stop, this time the Megtex office. The secretary took him directly to Alison's office.

"Nick! What a surprise . . . come in."

When the door closed behind him, he took her in his arms and kissed her.

"Something's wrong, isn't it?" she said.

"How can you tell?"

"By the solemn look on your face. Cora Lee's dead. I knew it the minute you walked in."

Nick nodded. "Her body was found near Terrell this morning."

Alison sank against him. "Does Louis know?"

"Yes, he knows."

"How is he?"

"Amazingly calm for a man who paid a million dollars to keep his wife alive."

"I'm afraid I'm the one who poured a million dollars down the well."

"You paid the ransom?"

"Yes, I felt it was the least I could do."

"Did he ask you for it?" Damn, he thought, Alison had been set up, duped out of a million dollars.

"No, I volunteered." She looked at Nick, her eyes brimming with tears. "They were married such a long time . . . how will he go on without her?"

Apparently quite well, Nick decided. The more he analyzed the evidence, the more convinced he became that Louis Bennett was behind his wife's death, possibly everything else. But the courts didn't convict a man on the gut feelings of a cop. The bastard hadn't left a shred of concrete evidence.

Nineteen

Alison felt weary and sad as she removed her black hat after Cora Lee's funeral. It was all just too much to bear, three funerals in the space of a few short weeks. Poor Cora Lee, she thought, she'd never deliberately harmed anyone. If the truth were to be told, she was always a self-centered woman, and probably hadn't made Louis very happy, at least in the last few years, but to have been kidnapped and murdered! She certainly didn't deserve such an awful fate.

Alison looked up at a timid knock on the door. Instinctively she knew it was Maynard Simmons. Enterprising and aggressive in business, he was one of Megtex's top officers, but when it came to confronting a woman, Maynard was a mass of Jello.

"Come in."

Maynard Simmons approached her desk. "I just wanted you to know that I—that we, Tom, Carl, Jack, and I, all want to help clear up whatever's causing all these deaths. We're all beginning to wonder if they're somehow connected to the company's recent problems." He took a deep breath before going on, "We're not blind, and we know that something's happened to slow down our business flow.

Can't you trust us enough to let us help with whatever troubles you're facing?"

Maynard was a small man, slender and slightly stooped, with thinning gray hair and dark, bushy eyebrows. Alison liked him very much, and in spite of what Louis suspected, she couldn't find it in her heart to distrust him. That was the whole trouble, she thought, she trusted all the Megtex officers. Hired and promoted by her dad, they would never betray Derek's trust, let alone steal money and even murder him. It was all too unthinkable.

"I'm sorry. It's just that I'm not ready to explain all that now. I'll tell you this though, we've got problems and they're big ones."

"Well, you're the boss now, but when Derek was alive . . ."

"Yes, I know." Though close to tears, Alison managed to keep her voice firm, determined not to be thought of as a weakling. "But he's not here, is he? I'm in charge and have to make decisions on my own. At the moment, I'd rather not reveal the reasons for the sorry state of Megtex affairs." She managed a smile. "I realize everyone must be puzzled, and when the time comes, I assure you, nothing will be left unsaid. That's all I can say about it right now, so please don't press me further." She gave him a pleading look. "Do me a favor, will you? Just hang in there, and ask the others to do the same. I'm depending on everyone more than you know."

Maynard looked confused when he left, but Alison could tell that she'd won him over. He'd pass her message along, and convince them to abide by her decision. Maynard was not the one, she decided. But who? Her head ached and she rang for her secretary.

Deena stuck her head into the office, then stopped in her tracks. "Oh my, you look like hell. What can I get you?"

"That's what I've always wanted, a secretary who was afraid to say what she thought. Got anything for a headache? Mine's about to split."

"Sure do. In fact, there are aspirins in your top, right-hand drawer." Deena poured a glass of water while Alison popped two pills into her mouth.

"What makes you so clairvoyant?" Alison leaned back in her leather chair. "Sit down a minute, and let's talk."

Deena draped herself in a comfortable chair facing Alison. "I was going to say I was psychic, but I don't have the foggiest notion what this is all about, unless, of course, you plan to offer me a raise for my excellent services."

"Well, your intuition is way off the mark. No raise today. We'll be lucky if we can pay the rent this month."

"That bad, huh?"

"Let's put it this way, I never get headaches. It's that bad."

"What on earth's going on? Where's the trouble coming from? I don't mean to pry, but everyone's been asking the same thing. You know, when the phones don't ring and the orders are going to the competitors, one begins to wonder."

"Yes, I'm sure there's been a lot of concern." Alison knew her voice had an impatient edge, but she couldn't help it. She just couldn't stand the thought of the whole building discussing and trying to guess which of the executives was guilty. No, she didn't intend to have that kind of gossip, yet things were in one hell of a mess and getting worse. For instance, Cora Lee's death could very well be connected to Megtex's troubles. Alison shuddered. "What I'd like you to do is to quietly check all outgoing and incoming phone calls on all the lines in these top floor offices. I'm trying to find out if someone inadvertently discussed Megtex business with the wrong person."

"Gosh, that's a tall order. How can I tell the difference in the innocent calls from the suspicious ones?"

Alison waved an arm in the air as if to clear away cobwebs. "I think we have to operate by that gut intuition of ours as women. If there are a number of calls to or from a particular stranger . . . God, I just don't know. But something has to be investigated, and I'm betting that we can turn it up faster than anyone else."

Deena looked skeptical. "You at least have some inkling of what we're looking for . . . I'm completely in the dark."

"I know, and I'll check with you often. Just trust me."

"Boy, I've heard that one before. But I do trust you, and I'll certainly give this thing a go."

When Deena left the office, Alison wondered if what she planned to do made any sense. She didn't want to spy on anyone or bug any phones, but it couldn't hurt to check records, even just phone bills, to see if strange numbers were repeated. It was worth a shot. Something had to be done, and now that Louis was so grief-stricken, she didn't feel right bothering him about it.

Alison was never sure that Nick would be able to

keep a date, since his first allegiance was to the police station. With all the crime in Dallas these days, he didn't have much free time, but he was determined to have dinner with her tonight. So even though it was already after nine and she hadn't heard to the contrary, she began to get ready.

After trying on several outfits, she still couldn't decide which one to wear. It was fun to feel excited about whether a blue blazer would please Nick more than a yellow one, or whether she should wear slacks or a skirt. She'd never thought about clothes like this before. John didn't seem to care what she wore. But Nick always commented, and even if his remarks couldn't be taken as direct compliments, at least he noticed. Alison blushed at such silly thoughts. Here she was, head of one of the largest pipeline companies in the world, concerned about how a policeman would like what she had on. She grinned, realizing she cared a lot.

She walked into her bathroom, a place she loved better than any room in the house. One year, while she was away in college, her dad had surprised her by combining a sitting room and her outmoded bath, creating a perfect place for bathing and relaxing. It was a glamorous room, large and luxurious, with mirrored walls, carpeted floor, fixtures of stainless steel and brass, and a shower stall walled in granite. But it was the tub that intrigued her most, a deep, steeping tub encased in the same gris carmel shade of granite.

She could still remember how she'd thrown her arms around Derek's neck and kissed him, exclaiming that a steeping tub was all the rage. "Absolutely dynamite!" was the expression she'd used back then.

A second look made her wonder how in the world the average person ever managed to get in and out of such a deep tub.

Funny, Alison thought, as she ran her bath water, how her heart began to pound at just the thought of Nick McAllister. If she didn't have so many problems at the office, she'd repeat his name with every beat. Even so, she saw his face before her constantly, and deep down she knew that if necessary she'd fight to keep him.

Lowering herself into the tub, she suddenly let out a sharp, piercing cry. The water was scalding hot! The tub was so deep that she couldn't scramble out fast enough. She reached the cold water faucet and turned the knob as far as it would go, but boiling water came pouring out. Somehow she managed to stand, and quickly pressed the button that should have released the step. Oh no, it wasn't working! Shrieking with pain, she cursed the day Derek had put this damn thing in. Finally, by sheer will, she managed to climb out.

Burning all over, Alison ran down the stairs, still naked, headed outside through the nearest sliding door, and jumped into the swimming pool. Once she hit the cold water, she felt tremendous relief. But before she could completely relax, she saw someone nearing the pool, a figure in black who reminded her of the person in the foyer the night her dad was murdered. In her frenzy to reach the pool, she hadn't turned on the outside lights. As a result, she could barely see, but she was sure the person had a long, heavy object in his hand. She screamed again, but oh God, there was no one to hear her, not even close neighbors!

The figure came closer and closer. Alison dove under the water, hoping against hope to escape a brutal attack. She held her breath until she thought her lungs would surely burst. Finally she had to surface; the figure was still there, circling the pool, stalking her. "Oh God, someone help!"

All at once, brilliant lights flooded the house, the grounds, and the pool. The black-clad figure vanished, replaced by two policeman who stood outside the pool, staring at her.

Catching her breath, Alison called, "For God's sake, don't just stand there, throw me a towel. No, no, over there in the pool house!" The younger man seemed so mesmerized at the sight of her naked body, that Alison could tell he hadn't heard a word she said.

Eventually the other man threw her a towel. Still in the water, she put it around her, then replaced it with a dry one once on firm ground. "What on earth brought you out here?" she asked, grateful, but puzzled.

The older policeman seemed in charge. "When your alarm went off, we were in the vicinity, so we got here as soon as we could. Guess it was a false alarm, huh?"

"Absolutely not. You just saved my life." Alison realized that she'd unknowingly set off the alarm when she opened the glass door.

"Pardon?"

"There was someone here about to attack me with some kind of weapon."

The two men looked at each other. "See anyone around here, Billy Bob?" the older man asked.

"No sir, I've looked all over. Haven't seen a thing."

He glanced at Alison apologetically. "I'll sure look around some more, though."

"Yeah, you do that." The officer in charge turned back to Alison. "Swim in the dark often, Miss?"

"No." Alison was furious. "I don't know if I have the strength to go into what happened before this . . . uh, swim, but I think I need to see a doctor. I've got burns on my body."

"Burns? From a pool?"

Alison felt completely exasperated. "I'll never make you understand. I'll call Dr. Peterson and Nick McAllister, but please don't leave me here alone right now." Alison walked gingerly as she entered the poolhouse.

"Lieutenant McAllister? You know him?"

"Oh yes," she called from the door.

Minutes later, one of the men said, "Well, here he comes right now."

"What happened?" Nick asked in a tight voice.

"Damned if I know," said the older officer. "This lady's house alarm went off, we answered the call, and here she was in the pool, stark naked, with all the lights off. Claims someone was about to kill her."

"Oh my God! Check every inch of this property . . . move it!" Nick started after Alison and caught up with her in the poolhouse. She winced when he threw his arms around her and held her too tight. "What the hell happened?"

Alison clung to him, tears of relief streaming down her face as she sobbed hysterically. At first no words would come, then finally she whispered, "I got burned in my tub . . . something was terribly wrong. Will you drive me to the emergency room at

Baylor? Dr. Peterson's going to meet me there. I'll explain everything on the way."

"Of course, I'll take you." Nick took a terry cloth robe off a hanger and helped her into it. "Good lord, your whole body's red!" He knew enough not to say more. After giving a few quick orders to the men, Nick picked her up and put her in his car, barefooted. One look at her feet convinced him that he shouldn't try to get her into shoes.

Once on Central Expressway, Alison finally spoke, her voice close to a whimper. "First I thought I was going to be boiled to death, but I got out of the tub and jumped in the pool. That was when I saw the figure in black."

"Clare Cummings?"

"No, not her. This time it looked like the guy who killed my dad. At least I thought it did . . . same, peculiar stealth, that black outfit from head to toe. Oh, I'm sure he was going to kill me. If I hadn't run out the door and set off the alarm, the police wouldn't have come, and I'd be dead in the pool by now. And you know what? It would have seemed like a suicide or an accident."

Less than an hour later, Alison looked considerably more comfortable as she sat in the corridor of the hospital talking to the doctor. "One of these days," she said, "I'm going to call your office for an appointment, and walk in like any ordinary patient."

"I'll look forward to that," he said. "I'm getting mighty worried about your close calls. The one in San Diego was bad enough, but this . . . try to be more careful, Alison. You were lucky this time. Apparently the water wasn't as hot as it felt to you. Believe me, if it had been boiling, you'd probably have passed out, and that would have been the end."

"Well, I guess I was lucky, wasn't I? But I felt like my skin was blistering." She pressed his arm. "Thanks a million, Doyle. I know I must have taken you away from an evening with your family, and I appreciate your rushing down here to meet me."

"Glad to do it. Just take it easy for a few days, and realize that your skin's going to feel a little sensitive for a time."

While being treated, Alison had started from the beginning and told Nick exactly what had happened. "Boy, was I glad to see those policemen. They answered that alarm in a flash."

As they were driving back to her house, Nick said, "If I'd been on time for our dinner date, none of this would have happened. As it was, I was out chasing my own shadow. Someone—the killer no doubt—called into the station about a homicide, and asked specifically for me. As it turned out, there was no body, no trouble, not even a valid address. I see now, the object was to keep me away from your house. This guy is pretty damned determined, and seems to know every move we make. I sure as hell don't like being used like that." He drew his hands into fists, ready to do battle.

"Well, how do you think I feel? I'm the target."

As Nick pulled into the circular driveway and stopped, he gave her a serious look. "Yeah, I know, and that scares the living hell out of me. That's why you need to get out of this house."

"You have to realize it was the house, the alarm, and possibly the fact that Juanita had done laundry just before she left that saved my life. I'm staying right here."

"What does doing laundry have to do with anything?"

"Well, we'd been meaning to get a new water heater for a long time, but Dad just never got around to it. This one's almost twenty years old, and is slow to warm up. So, after Juanita does a lot of washing, it takes forever to build up to its maximum temperature. I don't know much about it, so you'll have to ask our plumber. He's been trying for years to get us to replace it, but if he thinks for one moment I'll part with it after tonight, he's crazy. I firmly believe it saved my life."

Once in the house, Nick got Alison settled on the sofa in the den, then made a quick phone call to the station. He sat down beside her and held her hand. "I was planning to take you out to dinner, but I don't think you'll want to go anywhere in that robe . . . especially since you don't have a stitch on underneath and—"

Alison cut him short with a gasp. "Oh my lord, I'd forgotten. I went all the way to Baylor with wet hair, no clothes, no shoes. You stop salivating, Nick!"

He laughed. "You're in no condition for what's going on in my mind, but you do look kinda cute, like a little kid." He pulled her to him and gave her a hug.

"My lips weren't in hot water at all, thank God." Alison lifted her face and received a passionate kiss in return.

"You look so beautiful in that robe, I'm afraid to stay too close to you. Why don't you get as comfortable as possible, and I'll go pick up some take-out food. Name your poison . . . pizza? Chinese, or maybe some hamburgers?"

"Why not try the kitchen? It's faster and probably much better. Juanita made some grilled chicken because I forgot to tell her I was going out. It's great for sandwiches . . . want to play chef?"

"You bet, if you promise not to get too used to being waited on. I wouldn't want the guys at the precinct to see me in an apron."

"Male chauvinist, huh? So your true colors are finally showing."

"Call me what you will, but I like to be waited on."

"Funny, so do I, and every other woman I know. Now get in there and stop wasting time. I'm starving."

Nick became serious. "Sure you're not in a lot of pain, darling?"

"It still stings, but it's not too bad. Think you could scare up some wine while I'm waiting?"

Later, when they'd finished eating, Alison said, "I've been thinking. I'll bet the reason the police couldn't find that murdering s.o.b. on the property was that he probably ducked into the house and out another door. He certainly knows every inch of this house."

"You could be right, but then they didn't look very hard until after I got here. I guess because . . ."

"Go ahead and say it . . . they didn't believe me."

"Looks that way."

"Damn it, why do they have to see a dead body before they take a call for help seriously?"

"They searched the house and grounds — a little late, I'll admit — and I made it clear that the killer wasn't about to stand around waiting for them to move their—" Nick caught himself in time. "Well, you know what I mean. In the meantime, I just found out that when they checked the cold water faucet in your tub, it was working perfectly. Out came cold water, not hot."

"Sh—I was about to say a word I rarely use, but I'm really ticked off. That miserable creature had time to fix the faucets before he left the house. It's so infuriating!" Alison pushed her hair out of her face and attempted to stand up. "Ouch!" She sank back into the sofa. "Damn, when will all this be resolved? What's going on anyway? What about finding my dad's murderer? And Myra's? What about Cora Lee's? Was her death connected to all of this? Have you found out anything about the key in Dad's safe? Where are the answers? I'm so tired of being a target, and I want something done."

"Maybe you think you could do a better job than the police?"

"Yes, as a matter of fact, I do."

"Then why don't you get out of that big easy chair in the executive suite, and move that cute little ass of yours right over to the police station and apply for a job?" Nick knew he was getting in deeper and deeper, but he couldn't help it.

Alison glared at him. "Just who the hell do you think you're talking to? Get out of here this minute. You . . . you . . ."

"Were you trying to say 'you darling?' " Nick gathered her in his arms. "I love you, Alison. You've been through so much, and I'm a rat for making you angry. I'm sorry." He kissed her gently, then passionately. "No one could take what you've been through without blowing up. I'd have been on a rampage long before now."

Alison returned his kisses, her eyes filled with defiant, unshed tears.

Nick looked into her eyes, realizing that she probably had a month of tears stored up inside her. If she ever let go, there might be no stopping the flood. There was so much to do; there were so many unanswered questions. He felt stumped, frustrated to the point that sometimes he thought he might burst. He knew he had to get to the root of this whole thing soon, because time was running out. She might not be able to beat the odds much longer.

Louis Bennett stepped into a phone booth at a corner gas station, and called the number that Piper had specified. "What is it?" he asked when he heard Piper's voice.

"Just wanted you to know that I'm getting plenty pissed off at your boss. I'd give you part of your money back and blow this, if I didn't have a reputation to maintain."

"Hold it, hold on there. What's this all about?"

"The woman's a goddamn witch. She's got nine lives, that's what. That dame just won't die, and it's bad for my business. My whole future's at stake."

"Now calm down, I've never heard you any way but cool and collected. What happened?"

Louis could hear Piper's deep intake of breath. "Well, I decided tonight would be the night I'd really smoke her. Had it all planned, right down to the letter. Even got her boyfriend called way out to the south side on a phony homicide call, okay? You with me?"

"I'm with you." Louis couldn't believe that this

was the same calculating, professional killer who had performed so well for him three times already. "Go on."

"I rigged her fancy tub so the heat would kill her. Figured it would be so hot that she'd pass out, and that would be that. But something went wrong. Then I had the perfect chance for an accidental death because she jumped into the pool to cool off, and I was ready to clobber her. Just didn't account for that stupid alarm system. Someone's obviously fooled with the wires, because it didn't make a sound in the house. Sure alerted the cops though. They showed up and flooded the whole goddamn yard with lights, lit it up like a football field, and I had one hell of a time getting away. Had to slip back in the house to fix the faucets I'd screwed up. Good thing I know every hiding place in that damn barn, or I'd be in jail right now. She's making a fool out of me. I tell you, the bitch just won't die!"

Louis couldn't help but smile. "Get a grip, Piper. Knowing you, you'll come up with something."

"I'd feel a lot better, if I could just out and out take a gun and blast the living hell out of her. That's how I like to work."

"No, definitely not. I have my reasons, so remember, it has to look like an accident."

Twenty

Claudia unlocked the door to her room at the Fairmont, and glanced behind her. For the past few days, she'd had an uncanny feeling that a man was following her, watching every move she made. He was an older man, in his late fifties, with streaks of gray in his dark hair, and a middle-aged spread across his middle. The guilt that hung over her like an ominous cloud reinforced her paranoia, she knew, but this morning in the dining room at breakfast, she felt sure that her suspicions were true. Fear that her part in Cora Lee's death might be discovered gnawed at her constantly, and made her regret that she'd ever set eyes on Louis Bennett. Too late now. She was committed to see his plan through to the end, but damn, she had no intention of spending the rest of her life in prison.

She opened the door and went inside, determined to find out what was going on. Louis had kept her in the dark too long. For all she knew, he'd already been arrested, and was spilling the whole thing this very minute. Picking up the phone, she dialed Louis's number at home. He answered on the first ring.

"Oh, Louis, I'm going out of my mind."

"You know better than to call me. We agreed, no contact, remember?" His voice was terse and low, almost a whisper.

"I'm aware of our agreement, but I've got to see you."

"That's out of the question, forget it."

"Why, you bastard! You got me into this, and now I'm sitting here day after day wondering what's going on, with no one to talk to. Just what am I supposed to do?"

"Claudia, God knows who's listening! Don't say another word about—"

"Don't be ridiculous. Who'd listen in on your phone? No one's there but the maid. I'm more concerned about a man who keeps following me. I feel sure he's a policeman."

"Following you? Impossible."

"Oh, no it's not. I've seen him at every turn, and I've got to get out of here."

Louis was silent for several seconds, then, "That might not be a bad idea."

"Where can I go?"

"What about the Archer house on Padre Island? It's private, and no one would ever think to look there."

Relief swept over Claudia. "That's a good idea. I've saved my key all these years. Oh, I'm so glad you thought of it."

"You say you're being followed?"

"Yes, I'm sure of it."

"Then you'll have to be careful. To throw him off, make two reservations on different airlines . . . one to Houston, and the other to Brownsville from there. Be very careful, and if you see this man at the airport, you'll have to depend on your wits."

242

"I'll call you from there."

"No, don't call. It's much too risky."

"Then will you come down?"

"I'll try, but don't count on it anytime soon. Let's give things time to cool off here."

"But this waiting is so hard, and I don't like being alone so much."

"Just remember, we'll be together soon, and it will all be worth it."

"Damn, it had better be."

"I love you," he said.

Claudia hung up the phone, pretending she didn't hear his last statement. She'd never expressed love for Louis, or anyone else, if she didn't really feel it.

She left the room and punched the elevator button. If her calls from the room were traced, she had to take precautions. No one would know she'd called the airlines if she used a pay phone.

Minutes later, the elevator took Claudia to the lobby floor, where she hurried to the bank of phones and looked up the number for American Airlines. She was in the process of making a first-class reservation on the one o'clock flight to Houston out of DFW airport when she noticed her stalker standing on the other side of the lobby. The man had cop written all over him; the sight of him made her heart stop momentarily. No matter which phone she used, he was sure to be right behind her every step of the way. Her mind began to click, frantically searching for options, when an idea that just might work popped into her mind.

Thumbing through the yellow pages, she located Southwest Airlines and quickly dialed the number. It worked out much better than she'd dared to hope. A plane was scheduled to depart Love Field for

Brownsville at two o'clock. Close, but she could make it if she managed her time just right.

Claudia had only one regret about leaving Dallas right now. All during the past month, she'd counted on going to Alison, talking to her face to face, making her understand that leaving so long ago had been against her will, forced upon her by her vindictive husband. No time to dwell on that now; the time would come when she could reclaim her daughter. Right now she had to get busy. It was already ten o'clock, and she had a whole wardrobe to pack.

At twelve thirty Claudia arrived at the airport, picked up her ticket—which she paid for in cash—and walked briskly toward Gate 14 to await her flight. She had no luggage to check this time; it was safely locked away in the rented Mercedes that she'd left in the parking lot. Stealing a glance behind her, she saw her pursuer flash his badge at the ticket agent. She smiled, realizing that her plan would work out perfectly. At this moment, no doubt, he was buying a ticket on the same plane.

As soon as the speaker announced the first boarding call, Claudia went directly to the plane and took her seat in the first-class section. Trying to look nonchalant, she picked up a magazine, but kept a constant watch as the other passengers filed by. Five minutes later, there he was, the Dallas policeman who had so cleverly followed her, his eyes shifting ever so slightly in her direction. She gave him time to disappear behind the curtain that led to coach seating, then slipped out of her seat.

"I have to catch a later plane," she told the startled stewardess. "I've forgotten something very important." Not giving the young woman a chance to reply, she left the plane and hurried up the passenger tunnel to the terminal. In less than fifteen minutes, she was inside the Mercedes, headed for Love Field. Probably by now her policeman friend was airborne, on his way to a futile trip to Houston.

At two o'clock, the Southwest Airlines jet left Love Field right on time, with Claudia Archer on board. For the first time in many days, she felt relaxed and safe.

Twenty-one

When Louis came back to work the next day, Alison was shocked to see him. "Really," she said, "no one expected you so soon. There's no reason for you to rush back." She put her arm through his and led him toward the door. "What you need is rest or a complete change of scenery."

"Rest is the last thing I need." His voice had a desolate sound.

Alison brightened. "I know what, why don't you go out to La Costa for a week or so? It's so beautiful out there, and you can enjoy being pampered. I'll make all the arrangements for you and—"

"Thanks, you're very kind, my dear, but I'd rather be right here in Dallas. I'm hoping against hope that the police will find the kidnappers." He gave her a soulful look. "I'm so afraid you're not going to get your money back, and when I think how it was all for nothing . . . how Cora Lee was already dead when they called . . . I just feel sick all over. I can't thank you enough, though." He turned his head away, as if hiding tears.

"Don't give up so soon. The police probably have some leads, and maybe the money will eventually be returned. Anyway, I'm not going to worry about that.

246

It's a drop in the bucket compared with what we owe Linco. If we don't find the miserable creature who's been stealing from us, nothing much will matter."

"That's one reason I came back today. I plan to get busy on that right away."

Alison gave him a determined look. "This time, I'm helping, too, since we have so little time left. I'll check with you if anything pops up. Oh, we really need a break in this problem." Alison looked at him carefully. "Sure this is where you want to be?"

"It's the only place that feels like home right now."

Louis left Alison's office with slumped shoulders, his head bowed. Alison's eyes filled with tears at the sight of him. It would take a few minutes before she could concentrate on the day's work that lay ahead.

Around mid-morning, when Deena came into her office, Alison was on the phone. She motioned for Deena to sit down and tried to wind up her conversation. "Positively, Mr. Stoner, the job will be finished on schedule. Yes, I'll talk to you soon . . . thanks." She turned to Deena. "You've found something!"

"How did you know?"

"Wishful thinking, I guess. What have you got?"

Deena studied the stack of papers in her hand for a moment. "It doesn't necessarily condemn the man, but there have been excessive calls back and forth involving only one unlisted number, going back as far as these telephone records have been kept."

"How long is that?" Alison felt strangely uncomfortable, as if she were about to uncover something that would be better left alone.

"Eight years."

"You searched that far back? Whose records?"

"Carl Wallace's." Deena was quiet for a moment. "When you stop to think about it, he does seem to have more loose change than anyone else around here."

Alison looked at her in amazement. "Why our officers are paid a fortune, and should all be able to live well, for goodness sake. Loose change indeed!" She stood and began to pace the floor. "Any idea whose number that is?"

"Just that it's a business of some kind, and it's in . . . get this—Europe."

"Europe? No specific country?"

Deena shrugged her shoulders. "It's not much to go on, but it's in Switzerland with a Zurich area code."

Alison paused in her pacing and looked down at Deena. "Carl Wallace? Phone calls to Zurich for eight years?"

"That's what the records show." Deena swiveled her chair back and forth.

It was hard to believe. Alison began pacing again. Carl Wallace came to Megtex fifteen years ago, and next to Louis, he'd been her dad's closest friend and advisor. He was a large man, tall and broad-shouldered, quite vain about his looks, especially his shock of snow-white hair with never a strand out of place. He took care of all the legal affairs of the company, and had the reputation of being one of the finest corporate attorneys in the country. Since Megtex stretched across the United States and into Europe and the Middle East, he traveled a great deal, with frequent transatlantic calls a necessity.

But all these calls to Switzerland? Megtex had no accounts anywhere in that country, as far as Alison knew. Switzerland brought to mind secret bank accounts and hidden money, just what she was looking for. And, too, Cora Lee's murderers had instructed Louis to deposit the million dollars in just such an account. No matter how she felt about Carl Wallace, she couldn't overlook this discovery.

"Are those the phone records in your hand?"

Deena nodded. "Do you want me to leave them with you?"

"Yes." Alison took the papers from Deena, and with a sinking heart, decided she'd look them over carefully, and if her conclusion matched Deena's, she'd have to have a face-to-face meeting with Carl. She hated the idea of that kind of confrontation. This was the most difficult part of being a woman in a predominantly male business.

At two o'clock in the morning, dressed in her gown and robe, Alison sat at Derek's desk in the study going through papers in the drawers. With little free time to call his own, Nick hadn't come in, still out tracking down a suspect in a recent rash of drive-by shootings.

She felt weary, having studied all the top-floor phone records before starting on Derek's desk, something she'd been putting off for weeks. To her surprise, she'd found personal things, like records of her school grades, dating all the way back from play school to high school and college. Alison was deeply moved, never having suspected that her father had been so sentimental about her.

She opened another drawer and reached as far back as she could, her hand closing around a packet of some kind. Withdrawing it, she found herself holding several old snapshots, pictures of her mother that she never knew existed. Alison had often wondered why the portrait was the only likeness of her mother she'd ever seen, and why there were no other pictures. She spread them out under the light on the desk, and gasped at the remarkable resemblance she had to her mother. She could have been looking at pictures of herself. It was uncanny.

Funny, Alison thought, that she considered herself

attractive, never anything more, but her mother was absolutely beautiful. She wondered why her dad had never shown these to her. They were such happy family pictures: she and her mother at the beach, the three of them in a sailboat. Alison figured she must have been about four years old at the time, with a big, orange life preserver covering most of her body. These pictures were made on South Padre Island, just outside their vacation home, a place that brought back so many happy memories. She smiled at a picture of Louis Bennett with her dad. My, how young and handsome both of them were back then.

Picking up another photograph of her mother, Alison wondered if it were possible to miss someone she barely remembered. Oh, if only she were alive today, things would be so different. Her hand shook as she put everything back in the desk, keeping only the photos to take upstairs with her.

She was about to close the bottom, left-hand drawer, when she came across a small file folder with the word Unicom printed on the cover in red ink. A big circle had been drawn around the word, as if to call special attention to the name. When she opened the file, Alison caught her breath at the sight of a page filled with figures. This could have been what the killer was after when Derek was murdered.

Alison couldn't wait to get to the office that Friday morning. She went directly to the computer room, determined to find Unicom, even though she knew it wasn't a company they had ever dealt with. After working for two hours and not being able to call it up, she decided to try another approach and have a talk with Carl Wallace.

As jovial as usual, he entered her office just before

noon. "My you're looking just as beautiful as ever," he said. "You wanted to see me?"

"Yes, sit down, Carl. I'm afraid I don't have the patience for pleasantries with so much at stake, and not enough time to plug the holes." She noticed the British cut of his pin-striped suit, Italian shoes, monogrammed shirt, and expensive watch. A fastidious dresser, he always looked perfectly groomed, despite his bulk.

"Business has been bad, I know, but all of Texas has felt the crunch for some time. Things are bound to turn around before long, don't you think? The retail markets have a slight upturn, and it's going to take more time for the banks to recover, but I think Dallas will bounce back soon." He pulled his trousers up at the knees and took a seat across from Alison.

"Wait a minute, you're talking as if I were a complaining stockholder. Look at me, Carl, what international number have you been calling on a regular basis for many years?"

Carl turned beet red. "What in God's name are you talking about?"

Alison felt slow anger rising. "I'm not accusing you of anything yet. I just want to know who and where that one party is."

She watched Carl's face crumble in front of her very eyes. "Who told you? How did you find out?"

"Never mind how." Alison tried hard to keep her voice coldly professional, but felt like throwing her arms around him to ease his pain. "It's more like how much and when can we get it back?"

"What!" Carl looked genuinely confused.

"Linco Oil is about to sue us, if we don't replace all those defective pipes, and Senator Lassiter is holding off from announcing a complete investigation, only because he was a personal friend of my dad's. I can't

251

stall them much longer. My hope is that you'll return every cent you've squirreled away in the Unicom account."

"Alison! You're accusing me of stealing money from Megtex?"

She tried to remain calm. This wasn't going well at all. "Just tell me about the transatlantic calls to some office in Switzerland . . . maybe the Unicom office or a Swiss bank . . . that's all I want to know."

Carl rose to his full height, then leaned over, placing both hands flat on Alison's desk, and looked her in the eye. "I've had a mistress in Zurich for ten years. She has her own business manufacturing furniture reproductions, and I believe her income exceeds mine. I've never told this to another living soul, and I'd appreciate confidentiality. My wife and children would be devastated if they ever found out. At no time did I ever want or seek a divorce. That's all I have to say. You'll have my resignation on your desk as soon as I can get it typed." He turned abruptly toward the door with his head held high.

Alison thought she might faint. "Oh Carl, please wait." She ran after him and grabbed his arm before he reached the door. "I can't tell you how sorry I am. I acted shamefully." She fought to hold back tears. "Damn it, Carl, maybe I should stay home and knit socks or something. I've made a complete idiot of myself and humiliated you. Please don't leave. I need you. Megtex needs you. Of course, your personal life is none of my business. But you see, I'm so desperate . . ." Her voice trailed off.

"Is everything you said true?" Carl turned around to face her.

"Yes, it's true, every word. Megtex is about to go under. I know Derek had found out who was responsible, and that's why he was killed."

"Good lord, do you know what you're saying?"

She nodded. "I could fill you in on the attempts on my life, but it all sounds too implausible." She sank into a chair, and Carl joined her on a nearby sofa and took her hand.

"Several of us have discussed the possibility that the murders are connected, and now, of course, there's Cora Lee. Oh, you must be very careful. If there's anyone else you suspect in the future, don't confront him alone, for God's sake! Bring in the police first."

Alison sighed. "I was trying to avoid a scandal. Louis thought we should keep the police out of it."

Carl had a strange look on his face. "He did, did he?"

"Yes, but I've told all this to Lieutenant McAllister, because of Cora Lee and the ransom money and all the crazy things that have happened to me."

"Well, at least you told him. I don't know how you expect him to solve any of these murders without knowing all the inside facts. He and his men have questioned all of us at least three different times. If I'd known all this, I might have been more helpful."

Alison brightened. "Does that mean you have some suspicions of your own? I'm desperate to get at the truth as soon as possible. Ever heard of Unicom?" She gave him a hopeful smile.

"No, I haven't, but I'll keep my eyes and ears open." He stood and pulled Alison to her feet. "Can I count on your discretion . . . in the ah . . . European matter?"

"It's already forgotten."

As soon as Carl left, Alison rang for Deena, who stuck her head around the corner of the door as though testing the waters before entering.

Alison looked up. "Just wanted you to know that I studied the list of phone calls you worked so hard on

253

. . . spent most of the evening on it, and decided none of them shed any light on the matter I'm interested in." As nonchalantly as she could, she added, "I traced that number Carl Wallace has called so often, and sure enough, it's a company we've been dealing with off and on for years. I just wasn't personally familiar with it. Thanks a lot, Deena." She saw the curious look on her secretary's face, but her own manner left no room for further discussion.

Once Deena left, Alison went back to her desk and stared out the window, watching the traffic on Stemmons Freeway. Maybe she was just too gullible, not even thinking that Carl could have been putting on a clever act.

The desk buzzer interrupted her thoughts. "What is it?"

"Kenneth Chandler is on the line. Urgent."

The expletive on Alison's tongue was never uttered aloud. She picked up the receiver with a hearty, "Hello there, Kenneth."

"Well, it's finally happened. The biggest goddamned catastrophe in the history of Linco Oil."

"What is it? What's happened?"

"You don't have your TV on? My God, the whole coast has exploded."

"Where? What coast?"

"The west coast of Florida. A Linco pipeline blew up and killed five people, and God knows how many are injured! Chris is on a plane already, and you'd better get your ass down there with some damned good excuses and plenty of money. Whatever it costs me, it'll cost you double!"

Alison felt light-headed. "People killed? Where on the Florida coast, for God's sake?"

"Right out of Bradenton, near Sarasota and Longboat Key. Now get moving!"

Alison hung up and buzzed Deena. "Get a company plane ready to fly me to Bradenton, Florida, as soon as possible. Just give me time to go home, pack, and get to the airport. There's been a bad explosion . . . people killed. Tell all the Megtex officers that I'm leaving for Florida immediately. I'll be in touch."

Twenty-two

Before she left the office, Alison took time to call the Megtex people at the Linco facility in Bradenton. Fortunately, Guy Toler, the foreman, came on the line.

"You can't imagine the fire and smoke, all the horrors this explosion has caused. Jeez, Ms. Archer, there's so much confusion around here, that no one can be sure of anything. Houses close to the blast were blown to bits, and those in the outlying neighborhoods had the windows blown out. In a way, it was like an earthquake with cans and stuff knocked off store shelves ten or twenty miles away. I guess you heard that a man was killed, and from the looks of things, I don't see how there weren't a lot more."

"One killed? I heard there were five casualties. Sure you have the right figure?"

"Yes, ma'am, so far, and a lot of injured have already been airlifted to area hospitals."

"I'm leaving Dallas by plane in less than an hour. Can you spare someone to meet me at the airport?" She quickly added, "If that's a problem, I can rent a car."

"Oh sure, Ms. Archer, we'll be in touch with the airport to check on your plane, and I'll send Charlie Lowe to pick you up. The airport's not ten minutes from here."

At five o'clock, Alison's plane landed right outside Bradenton. Clouds of smoke hovered over the area, stinging her eyes and filling her nostrils with the smell. As promised, Charlie Lowe was there to pick her up on the private landing strip.

Full of details, he talked nonstop all the way to the Megtex office. "You wouldn't believe the noise that blast made . . . sounded like a bomb. Now that it's over, a lot of people have been saying that they'd smelled gas for a week or more, but nobody reported it. If we'd known, we would have checked it out in a flash."

Charlie sounded like he wanted to make sure he was covering his ass, Alison thought. "Where exactly did the leak come from, do you know?"

"Gosh, everything's still smoldering, and so charred that we can't get close enough to pin down the piece of pipe with the leak." He pointed to his left. "Look at those blackened trees and those houses over there . . . burned to the ground. Good thing this is a countryside . . . imagine what it would be like if this had happened in a more populated area."

Alison was no longer listening, taking in the destruction for herself, the scorched earth, dazed, frightened people searching through remnants of mobile homes for anything salvageable, black, skeletal trees; all of it much worse than she ever imagined.

When they stopped at the office, Chris Chandler came toward her and greeted her warmly. Nothing like his father, he treated Alison like an old friend. "Can you believe this? Death, injury, and destruction everywhere you look. No telling what it will look like when all this smoke clears."

257

"I can still see plenty. Any idea what triggered the blast?"

"Not yet, but there'll be a full investigation as soon as the ground cools down. It's really too early even to speculate."

"I wonder if this could have been prevented. Between us, are we responsible? I don't know if I could live with that kind of guilt."

"So often when these accidents occur, no one knows why one pipe will give way in a particular spot. There's really not much I can tell you right now." Chris brushed some ashes from his hands. "Planning to stay over?"

"Oh yes, of course."

"Have you checked into a hotel yet? Bradenton and Sarasota are already filled with media people."

"What about Longboat Key? I've stayed there at the Colony several times. Think I can get a room?"

"We can sure try."

"You don't have a room either? How long have you been here anyway?" For the first time, Alison noticed how disheveled he looked.

"Got here about two, I guess. Rented a car at the airport and been busy trying to help out since. Some of these people are pretty confused . . . but who wouldn't be with their homes burned down or blown away. My bag's still in the car."

"Can't we call the Colony from here?" Alison looked around at the eerie surroundings, everything so desolate with damaged structures and blackened grounds. A tremor ran through her body.

"Sure, I'll do it. I'll just run up to Guy's office."

Alison watched Chris rush away, such a nice young man, so handsome and well mannered. She supposed she hadn't really noticed him in San Diego, no doubt because his father dominated every situation, making

258

Chris almost like a shadow. She suddenly felt sorry for him.

Minutes later, Chris's fingers circled an okay sign as he approached Alison, who by now was helping a woman wipe off a picture she'd salvaged from the rubble.

"We've got reservations and a car, so let's get cleaned up and have something to eat. Do you know the way to Longboat Key?"

"I think so. It's kind of tricky and my sense of direction is 'inflammable,' as my dad used to say, but I know we have to go through St. Armand's Circle. That's where we'll have to watch the signs, or we'll get lost for sure. In fact, there are a lot of good restaurants, if you want to stop there first. I can get us that far, then we'll have to ask for directions the rest of the way. I remember part of it . . . we'll have to go through Sarasota, then get on a causeway to get to St. Armand's Circle, which is an island that leads to another causeway and bridge. It's pretty complicated."

Chris laughed. "You just sold me. If you can run that by me again, I think I can find it." He looked down at his rumpled clothes. "Think they'll let me in a decent restaurant looking like this?"

"Oh, you'll see all kinds. This is a vacation spot, and you'll be just fine. Wait just a minute, and I'll get my bags from Charlie's car."

"Hop in, we'll drive over there and pick them up."

They found St. Armand's Circle without any trouble, but Chris begged off stopping at any of the trendy restaurants there, opting instead to go on to the Colony and freshen up before eating.

With better directions on how to cross over to Longboat Key, they were soon in the lobby of the Colony, getting keys to their rooms. Teeming with people, the hotel seemed crowded, and Alison realized they were lucky to get reservations. They gave each other half an hour, then met again and headed north to Harry's.

When they entered the restaurant, Chris's reaction to the tea room decor amused Alison. She gave him a smug look. "Things aren't always what they seem, so just wait until you taste the food."

"Sure you've been here before?"

"Several times."

"It could have changed hands."

"Behave yourself and let's sit down. Harry's right over there behind the bar."

"You're sure that's Harry? I'm looking at an awful lot of ruffles."

"Trust me." Alison was delighted that she'd elicited a spark of personality from Chris. With so much potential, all he needed was to get away from Kenneth and meet the right girl. "Ordinarily, I drink just to be sociable, but right now I really need a cocktail."

"I'm with you, and if they don't serve a decent drink here, I'll be sure the food will be limited to watercress sandwiches." The waitress approached, and Chris turned to Alison. "What will you have?"

"JB on the rocks with a splash and a twist."

"Make that two," Chris said, and the waitress walked away, making a notation on her pad.

"Why don't we order our food when she gets back?" Alison suggested. "I haven't had a bite since breakfast."

Chris looked startled. "My God, you'll blow away if you get any thinner. What do you suggest?"

"If they still make their hot grouper salad, that's what I'll have."

"It's on the menu. Okay, I've taken your word so far, so grouper salads for each of us," he said to the waitress as she delivered their drinks. He took a sip of his cocktail and smiled his approval. "Well, you get a gold star, Alison. This is what I call a drink. I'm glad I trusted you after all."

Alison sipped slowly, her thoughts far away. "I can't help worrying about the explosion. If Megtex is to blame, I don't know how we'll ever live it down. I'll never be able to forget it."

"Now don't go blaming yourself before all the facts are in. It's possible it doesn't have anything to do with a pipe leak, so we'll just have to wait and see."

"I wish I had you to answer to at Linco, instead of your father. He can be a little intimidating, can't he?"

Chris twisted his glass around, unconsciously pushing his lemon twist down into the glass with a finger. "He's a brilliant oil man and has respect for everyone in the business, but yes, I admit, he can be difficult."

"Think he can be persuaded to postpone an action if a time limit isn't met?"

Chris grinned. "Is that a convoluted way of asking if he's going ahead with a lawsuit in a couple of weeks, if you don't come up with a bundle of cash and some commitments?"

She laughed. "Forgive me for not remembering that you were right there when your dad scared me into promising the moon. I meant every promise I made, but we still haven't been able to flush out the culprit in our company. And there's been one tragedy after another at Megtex, making it almost impossible to do much investigating."

Their salads arrived, and with the first taste, Alison realized it was as delicious as she remembered. "I never should have brought all this up, so please don't think I'm suggesting that you intercede in our behalf. I'll deal directly with your father. I'm really sorry I mentioned it."

"This fish completely vindicates you. It's everything you said it would be and more." He paused. "You

261

haven't asked me to do anything, but I do think Dad might delay any action if I speak to him."

Alison felt a surge of hope. "I'd be so grateful."

"Forget it and enjoy your dinner."

Alison's suite turned out to be a three-room cabana on the beach. With no rental car, she had no choice but to walk. She hadn't gone far when she heard someone calling her name.

"Why, Alison Archer, what are you doing here?" Wearing shorts and a T-shirt, John Carpenter was just getting out of a van. He hurried to her side.

"Because of the pipeline tragedy. I guess I could ask the same question of you."

John hesitated momentarily. "Vacationing . . . trying to get over a broken romance." He spoke loudly, and there were many other people around. "Who's that boy you were with? Are the two of you traveling together?" Alison detected the strong smell of alcohol, and felt sure he'd had too much to drink.

"Look, John, why don't we wait until morning to talk about our plans, okay?" She knew her voice was curt, but she didn't care. Putting up with John's snide remarks was the last thing she needed. He was acting like a kid, still almost shouting and causing a scene. Everyone around stopped to watch and listen. She paused outside her door and inserted the key.

"Oh, looks like you've found your room. Need a little company, or is your boyfriend planning to sleep with you?"

"Why, you—" Alison didn't want to say anymore within hearing distance of other people. "Oh, all right, come in." She could barely contain her anger. Once inside, she glared at him. "You have one hell of a nerve! What do you think you're doing?"

John looked innocent as he turned on the lights and fiddled with the air-conditioning. "I'm just surprised to see you, that's all. Never thought I'd hit it this lucky."

"As I said before, I'm not on vacation. I'm here because of the disaster, and I think your sense of humor is a little warped, when a man's been killed and some people are badly injured. If your intent was to embarrass me out there, you've succeeded. Satisfied?" John may not know it, she thought, but he had just reinforced her decision to break off their engagement. If there was an ounce of doubt before, he had just erased it.

"Is this thing going to cost Megtex a bundle?"

"I have no idea. Why would you even ask such a question? It's really in poor taste."

"Well, well, the conscientious CEO is acting mighty testy. The job too much for you already?"

"If you're deliberately trying to be obnoxious, you're succeeding. I'm tired and not looking forward to facing those families tomorrow, so why don't you leave?"

"How about dinner tomorrow night, or are you busy with the kid?"

Alison's patience had reached its limit. Physically, she tried to push him toward the door.

But John wasn't about to leave. "You always used to invite me in, don't you remember? Don't you miss all our good times together?"

"Not in the least."

John grabbed her suddenly, and pulled her to him with a force that astounded Alison. All these years, she thought she knew him so well; she realized now that he was capable of severe abuse. "Get out of here right now, John." She shoved him away from her, but he turned and would have struck her if she hadn't stared at him defiantly.

"If you so much as *touch* me, I'll see that you spend so many years behind bars, that even your mother won't recognize you when you get back."

John turned with a lurch and stormed out the door.

Never in all this time had she seen him act this way, so hateful and full of revenge. He'd shown a side that she never knew existed. "Oh no!" she said aloud. "Not John!" Could *he* have been the one trying to kill her all along?

The next morning was like reliving a nightmare. Moving from one group to another, Alison tried to give some kind of comfort and help. She spoke to various members of the media, and felt completely drained by their probing questions. Reporters and camera crews hadn't been allowed close to the disaster area the first day because of the possibility of further explosions, but now they were out in force, showing the world pictures of blackened trees totally stripped of leaves, damaged or destroyed buildings and houses, clothes and pieces of furnishings hanging from trees, not to mention dead birds, cows, and deer that littered the area.

Speaking to the mayor, the county sheriff, and the fire chief, Alison felt terrible guilt. Even though the actual cause of the blast still had not been determined, she envisioned someone in the Megtex office stuffing his pockets with wads of money, while these people suffered horrible consequences.

Late that afternoon, she stopped by the shell of a grocery store with a group of people, attempting to help the owner assess the extent of the damage to the building. Glad that she'd thought to pack jeans, she realized that wearing anything else would have been ridiculous. In just a short time, she was already covered with soot and grime.

The farther she followed the others into the back of the store, the worse the damage looked. Rafters hung precariously from a partially exposed roof as they made their way across a burned-out floor. A deputy sheriff led the way since there had already been reports of looting.

Just as Alison was about to enter what was left of the office, something made her look up in time to see a large part of the roof sag, then begin to cave in. "Watch out!" she called instinctively, then ducked, pushing those near her away from the area seconds before the crash. Debris flew in every direction, but all escaped injury. Though somewhat embarrassed by the praise for her quick thinking, Alison felt a measure of reprieve.

As the day wore on, Alison finally had a chance to talk to Guy Toler. Bombarded by members of the press, he'd been hard to find, but she caught up with him as he walked into his office.

"Guy," she called, rushing toward him. "I have to know if there's any way you can pinpoint the source of the blast."

"Just can't tell yet," he said. "So far, it looks like there was a buildup of gasses in the storage bin, but we won't know for sure for several weeks. There's no way of knowing if it was our line or someone else's." He looked exhausted.

"Is there any way faulty or inferior pipes could have caused this?"

"Oh, I doubt that very much. This was some kind of gas buildup, like I said." Guy shook his head. "Inferior pipe . . . nah."

Alison offered a silent prayer of thanks. What a relief to be freed from the guilt that had haunted her since she had first heard of the explosion. She left Toler's office and tried to find Chris, eager to tell him what she'd learned. At least it didn't seem to be related to the fraud that someone at Megtex had perpetrated.

Up ahead, she caught a glimpse of someone who looked like Chris, entering the remains of a burned-out warehouse. Hurrying toward him, she made her way through the throngs of people, still milling around either in a daze or in hopes of locating lost objects.

It was dark in the warehouse, desolate and quiet, the acrid smell of burned wood all around her. Going further seemed dangerous, especially since she was all alone and Chris was nowhere in sight. All at once, she felt sure she heard someone call her name. She stopped, stood stock-still, and listened. She heard her name again, a low, whining sound. Mesmerized, she pressed forward as the warehouse became even darker than before. There was that sound again, someone calling, beckoning her. The voice sounded vaguely familiar. John? Maybe he was in some kind of trouble. Slowly moving one foot in front of the other, she reached the center of the room. Then someone grabbed her from behind, sending terror through every pore of her body. Before she could scream, a large beam came crashing down with an ear-splitting sound, directly in her path.

"Chris! Oh Chris!" she cried when she realized he had pulled her back. "I was looking for you. Thank God you saw me in time . . . I would have been killed! Oh my God, what a close call!" She began to shake all over.

Looking stricken, Chris held her close. "That was no accident, Alison. Someone was up on that roof, waiting for you. Someone deliberately made that beam fall."

On the way back to the hotel in Chris's rented car,

Alison filled him in on her conversation with Guy To-ler.

"Then I don't see any need in your staying around here any longer," he said. "If your testimony's ever needed, you have firsthand knowledge of the damage. Besides, I'm more concerned about your safety than anything else." He reached for her hand. "I really wish you'd consider coming back to California with me, maybe check into the La Costa Hotel again . . . or even be our guest at the Jockey Club. You really need to relax. What do you say?"

"That sounds tempting, I'll admit, but I need to get back to work in Dallas."

"But it's still the weekend."

"You know, you're right, I do need a little relaxation, and I don't have to be at work until Monday. I think I'll stop off at our house on Padre Island for a day or so. It's been years since I've been there." Her mind was made up. She'd leave this very afternoon.

Piper brushed away the soot and grime. Climbing around on that shell of a roof had been downright dangerous. Damn Alison Archer! What the hell would it take to get rid of her?

Twenty-three

Chris Chandler stood on the runway of the airstrip in Bradenton, Florida, waving goodbye to the woman he'd begun to care for. She was so beautiful, yet totally unaware of the effect she had on him, regarding him only as a friend. With so much happening during the two times they'd been together, he hadn't had the chance to tell her how he felt.

She was in grave danger, he felt sure. He wished he could have gone with her to her south Texas hideaway, if for no other reason than to offer protection. Over and over again, attacks on her life had taken place, but no one seemed to care. Wanting to be independent, she had ignored his warnings to be careful; admirable, he supposed, but a killer stalked her. With a heavy heart, Chris boarded his own private plane for San Diego. The very least he could do was to persuade his father to give Alison and Megtex more time.

A rental car waited for Alison when she arrived at the Brownsville airport. As she drove the twenty-one miles to the island and crossed the long causeway, her mind went over and over the events in Florida. Aside from the disaster—which made all her own problems seem trivial — Alison began to think seriously that John Carpenter might actually be the person who had killed her father and Myra.

She shuddered. A man she'd know so intimately for such a long time? It didn't seem plausible, but still, his actions in Florida were so alien to anything he'd ever done before. It was almost as if he had a dual personality.

The familiar sight of the yellow frame house drove all other thoughts out of her head. Her eyes lit up with pleasure, realizing it looked just as she remembered it. Alison pulled up the long drive and jumped out of the car with renewed energy. Trying to think back to the last time she and her dad had been here, she decided it must have been at least five years.

Oh, it's a lovely house, she thought, as she inserted the key in the lock. She picked up her bags and walked through the large, open living room, noting how clean and orderly everything looked. Maggie and Ed Martin, the couple who looked after the place, had obviously done a fine job, but she couldn't help wondering why they kept the thermostat at such a cool temperature with no one living in the house. She made a mental note to speak to them about it. Now that the bills were her responsibility, she'd have to pay more attention to details like this.

She smiled to herself, thinking that she and Nick could come here to enjoy the sun and the sea whenever they had some free time. Walking toward the bay windows that faced the ocean, she wondered if he liked to fish. Lord, how she wished he were here with her this very minute. Why not? A thrill of happiness raced through her entire being.

Alison reached for the phone and dialed Nick's precinct. "Lieutenant McAllister, please, Homicide." She'd be calling him a lot in the future, she felt sure.

While she waited, Alison thought of all that had happened in Florida. She hadn't even had time to call Nick before she left, and could never explain everything over the phone. Also he'd never understand why she came to Padre Island. It would look like she was running away from all her responsibilities.

Nick's voice came on the line. Alison almost put the receiver down, but she couldn't bring herself to break the connection once she heard his voice. She was becoming more and more dependent on this man, she realized.

"Nick, how are you? Are you free to talk?"

"My God, Alison, why haven't you called before now? Are you okay?"

"I'm fine. Sorry I didn't call before I left Dallas, but you've probably heard all about the explosion in Florida."

"Oh sure. It was awful, all over the TV and the papers. Your office called and told me you'd rushed off as soon as you'd gotten word, so I knew where you were, but I really thought I'd hear from you before now." He hesitated a second, but Alison didn't get a chance to say a word before he added, "It doesn't matter, as long as I know you're safe." His voice had become low, almost a whisper. "Can't tell you how good it is to hear that throaty voice of yours . . . very sexy. I wish I could see you this minute. Where the hell are you?"

Alison smiled. The sparks between them could easily burn up the telephone wires. Nothing had changed in the past two days. He still sent her senses in a whirl. "Funny that I feel exactly the same way. That's why I'm calling. Can you take a day or two off?"

"To go where? Florida?" He sounded baffled.

"No," she said in her most seductive voice. "I'm in a wonderful house, very private, overlooking the bluest

270

water you've ever seen. I'm on South Padre Island. Fly down and join me, Nick. I'll meet your plane in Brownsville."

"Oh damn, I wish I could, but I'm right in the middle of this drive-by shooting thing. The kids are on a rampage . . . had another one last night. I can't leave, darling, so why don't you come home? I'll meet your plane."

"I can't say I'm not disappointed because I am, but I understand. I think I need a day or two before coming back."

"Florida was that rough, huh? I gathered that from what I heard of the blast. Take your time and just let me know when you'll arrive, so I can be at the airport. By the way, what's your phone number? I can't go that long without getting my fix. That voice of yours does it every time."

Alison gave him the number, then slowly hung up. How she wished he could have come, but she knew she'd have to get used to his odd working hours. It wouldn't be easy, she knew. All the time she'd gone with John, he'd been available at a moment's notice. Well, she thought, shrugging her shoulders, she certainly didn't want John, no matter how handy he was.

At this moment, she wanted food. She'd had breakfast at seven this morning, and now it was . . . she adjusted her watch back to Central time . . . three o'clock, but according to her stomach, it was four. Maybe eating something would keep her from feeling so depleted. She wouldn't find much at all in the kitchen, she thought, as she headed in that direction; but maybe the Martins had left some crackers or something that would tide her over until she could get to a grocery store. Too bad she didn't think to shop before she left Brownsville.

When Alison walked into the kitchen, she looked

around, dumbfounded. On the counter sat a bowl of fruit, a loaf of French bread, and a wheel of cheese under a glass dome. Then she caught the aroma of meat roasting in the oven. Good lord, someone was using this house . . . not a casual transient, that was for sure.

Just at that moment, a woman came through the doorway, carrying a bag of groceries. She was a small woman, straight and proud, with flaming red hair and the greenest eyes Alison had ever seen. Clad in jeans and a yellow cotton shirt, she stopped in her tracks, wide-eyed, and didn't move for several seconds.

Alison stared at her, spellbound, as if she were seeing herself twenty years from now. This had to be a relative, she thought; the resemblance was uncanny.

The woman moved first, putting her bag on the counter. "I'll just take a peek at my roast before we have our talk, if you don't mind." She reached for a padded glove, opened the oven door, glanced at the meat thermometer, and closed the door. "Not quite ready," she said, with a cool, collected smile.

Alison finally found her voice, her curiosity getting the best of her. "Who *are* you? And why are you living in my house?" Just as she got out the last word, she realized who this woman was. Her height, her walk, her regal bearing, everything about her was familiar. "Why, you're Clare Cummings, aren't you?"

"In a way I am. Let's sit down in the living room, where we'll be more comfortable."

Alison bristled. "How kind of you to be so hospitable in my house." She went ahead of the woman and sat down.

"Well, if the truth be known, this is every bit as much my house as yours. I simply haven't been here for many years, even though I still have my key. Care to see it?"

Alison began to tremble, sure she was seeing a ghost, some kind of apparition. "Who are you?" She must be hallucinating . . . her mother was dead.

"Well, by the look on your face, I can see that you've already guessed the truth. You're not imagining all this; I am your mother." She stood and extended her hand.

Alison cringed. "My mother is dead. She died in an accident twenty-three years ago."

"Hah, that's what Derek told you. That's what he said he'd tell everyone. But you see, I'm very much alive." Claudia began to strut around the room like a model, doing a few twists and turns. "My figure's still very good, don't you think? I haven't changed much over the years . . . can't you see how much we look alike?"

"Why . . . why are you here now? Why have you waited all this time to come back, and why did you follow me everywhere I went?" Alison ran her fingers through her hair, totally distraught. This woman, her mother? If this turned out to be true, there were twenty-three years to account for. "Did you kill my dad?" Her voice was like ice.

"Oh, don't be do melodramatic, Alison, it doesn't become you. Of course, I didn't kill Derek, but don't think I shed any tears the day I heard he was dead. I used to put myself to sleep dreaming of that day, even planning ways to kill him myself, but nothing I came up with compared to the way he tortured me all that time . . . twenty-three years of keeping me from my child." She moved toward Alison. "Now at last we can be together."

Alison shrank away from her. "You must be out of your mind! My mother wouldn't have left me, no matter what the reason. All my life Dad told me how much she loved me, what a good mother she was, that she

273

would have given up her life for me. She was nothing like you, sneaking around, spying on me at every turn, even registering at a hotel under an assumed name. If you're telling the truth, why didn't you come to the house? Maybe you just look like her, and want to use it to your advantage. There's no way I'll ever believe you."

"Oh, my dear . . . my daughter . . ."

"Don't you dare call me that!"

Claudia's face fell, and she took a deep breath. "Your father hated me."

"That's a damned lie. He adored my mother, always spoke of her so lovingly. Why he was so broken up when she died, he could never even look at another woman . . . never thought of marrying again."

"You little fool, he never married because he wouldn't give me a divorce. That's why."

"Okay, if you're my mother, what's your real name?"

Without a second's hesitation, she said, "Claudia Covainne Archer."

"I should have known you'd naturally have all the answers. How can you prove any of this?"

"Just ask Louis Bennett. He'll verify everything I've said."

"Louis knows you're here?"

"Yes, he does. I contacted him as soon as I got off the plane."

"Then why the charade . . . why this cloak-and-dagger bit? Does Louis believe you didn't murder my dad?"

"Yes, he knows I didn't arrive from Europe until after Derek was dead. I followed you because I was afraid you'd be in danger, too . . . and still feel that way. God knows how I could have protected you, but I had to try." She gave Alison an appealing look. "It was silly, I guess, but I wore black because I thought it

274

would make me less noticeable. We do look alike, you know, and I was afraid someone would recognize me, and I had to be careful." Claudia took a deep breath. "I didn't kill Derek, but many years ago I did kill someone else." She turned noticeably pale.

"What? Who, for god's sake . . . Myra?"

"No . . . no! It was a very long time ago, when I was young and such a fool." She sank into an arm chair. "It's not something I talk about."

Alison braced herself. She had been through so much lately, what more could there be to wrench her heart? Instinctively, she knew that this woman was truly her mother. She could feel the bond between them, but forgiving Claudia for letting her believe all these years that she was dead was beyond comprehension. When she thought of all the tears she'd shed growing up, there was no explanation in the world that would compensate for all those years. "If you want to tell it, I'll listen."

"I warn you, it's not very pleasant."

"Look, my father was recently murdered. That wasn't very pleasant either. I held his bloody body in my lap after he was shot. Match that if you can." Alison felt hollow inside, as if all the life had drained out of her.

Claudia rushed over to Alison and sank to the floor at her feet. "You poor child . . . please forgive me. I'll spend the rest of my life on my knees, if that will help. You're a beautiful young woman with your whole life ahead of you. Please let me be a part of it!"

"You were going to tell me your story. I'm waiting."

"Can't you just take me on faith? Don't make me tell something I've tried so hard to forget. I don't want to lose you again."

"The story." Alison knew she had to hear the worst before she could begin to understand or forgive.

275

Claudia sighed, then started from the beginning, telling about Abdul and when she first met Derek, the struggle in her early years, the luxurious lifestyle she became accustomed to. She spoke of how bored she was in Dallas after living in such lavish style at the world's most famous playgrounds . . . Monte Carlo, Paris, London . . . when she wasn't even out of her teens.

"Derek and I traveled to Europe at least once a year, but that wasn't enough . . . nothing was enough for me until you were born. For a while, my life took on new meaning, but that didn't last long. Derek was always working, and I felt neglected, needed more attention. I found it easily enough, and Derek never knew until I picked up the wrong man, a psychopath who beat me unmercifully and would have killed me if I hadn't killed him first.

"Your father got me away from there, but packed my bags and threw me out. Oh, he gave me money, but I had to sign a confession that he swore he'd use against me if I ever came back. I couldn't see you ever again . . . I'd be dead to everyone, killed in an accident." Claudia rose to her feet. "Now you have it—the story of my life. Not very pretty, is it?"

Alison curled herself into a tighter ball, her mother's words tearing at her very soul. "I find the last part hard to believe. My dad adored you until the day he died, I'm sure of it. Your portrait still hangs in the drawing room, that beautiful woman we both used to gaze at together. He'd tell me wonderful stories about you, go on about how much he missed you, how much you loved me, how you were even lovelier than the painting . . ." Her voice broke.

Claudia gave her a harsh laugh. "Derek hated me."

"There's something else that doesn't ring true. If you

276

knew he had died, why the alias, why the sneaking around? What were you afraid of?"

"I had no idea how much Derek had told you, and had to get my hands on that confession. If I could destroy it, I could claim my half of the estate and spend the rest of my life trying to make you forgive me." Claudia's eyes were bright with unshed tears.

"You expect me to believe that? If you found that paper, you'd have been around just long enough to collect your money. It seems there was more in that safe than any of us knew about."

"You never knew anything about the confession? I can't believe that Derek never told you about all this."

Alison looked at her mother in disgust. Still a beautiful woman, Claudia's face was only faintly lined with age, not marred in the least by all this ugliness. Alison wondered if she could ever accept this woman. She needed time. "How can you call yourself a mother? I'm sure my dad never told me because he didn't want to foster any hate in me. Of course, you wouldn't know about anything like that, since you never spent any time with me growing up." She glared at Claudia. "You know who killed Derek, don't you?"

Claudia suddenly turned pale, definitely caught off guard. "No . . . no, of course not."

"Oh my God, you *did* kill him, didn't you?"

"No, I swear, I didn't. I didn't! I admit, though, that I'm glad he's dead. Now that I can have you and my half of the estate, I can get that confession back and live in peace."

Alison turned away, completely repelled. "You can't have a daughter just by putting in a claim." Her words were measured and terse, her voice low and controlled. "I was ready to forgive everything . . . everything except my father's murder. If you didn't do it, you know damn well who did! You're attractive on the outside,

Claudia, but deep inside, you're nothing but a cheap, money-grabbing tramp. I feel dirty just being in the same room with you. In just these few minutes, you've managed to destroy . . . wipe out all the love I've had for the memory of my mother. I want you out of my life forever." Alison left the living room long enough to pick up her bags. Without even turning around or looking back, she walked out the front door.

It was almost five o'clock when Alison reached the Brownsville airport. While the pilot readied the plane, she called Louis, asking him to pick her up when she arrived home. Incensed that he hadn't told her that Claudia had been in Dallas for weeks, she couldn't wait to hear his explanation. She vowed never to mention Claudia's name to a living soul. As eager as she was to see Nick, she dreaded it in a way, dreaded trying to keep something like this from him. If he ever heard her mother's story, he would probably feel compelled to arrest her for that long-ago murder, and Alison didn't want that. She only wanted this woman out of her life forever, so she could finally bury the past. Alison sought no revenge, just answers to her father's murder, answers that she felt sure her mother could give. She shuddered.

Louis couldn't imagine why Alison was coming into Love Field rather than DFW. When she called, he'd asked where she was, but she didn't answer. One thing for sure, it took longer than an hour to fly from Florida.

Right on time, her private plane made its approach, then landed. When Alison came toward him, he noticed how drained she looked. Rushing toward her, he took her in his arms and gave her a fatherly hug. Quickly she pulled away. What the hell's going on? he wondered. Oh well, he'd find out soon enough. No sense in wearing himself out worrying about what she may or may not have found out.

"We've all been glued to the TV," he said. "It must have been hell for you in Florida."

"Florida?" Alison sounded vague. "Oh yes, of course, just ghastly. The only good news is that we're probably not responsible for the explosion . . . only time will tell. But all those poor people . . ." She waved her hand in the air, as if she found it impossible to describe the horrors.

Once in the car, Louis simply couldn't wait any longer to find out why she was acting so strangely. "Had you stopped somewhere to refuel when you called me?"

"No, I hadn't even left yet." Alison hesitated, then looked directly at Louis. "I called from Brownsville. In fact, I'd just come from our house on Padre Island."

Louis couldn't control a sudden intake of breath. Grateful that he was driving, he felt his face turn hot as he looked straight ahead, avoiding her gaze. "Padre? What were you doing there of all places? I thought you were in Florida."

Alison sighed. "I'd rather not go into this until we get to the house. Will you come in for a few minutes, so we can talk? It's important to me."

"Of course, my dear."

For the short time it took to reach the Archer home, they were both silent. Louis didn't need a brick wall to fall on him to know that Alison had run into Claudia. Of all the damn rotten luck, he thought. Alison hadn't been near that damn place in over five years, but the minute he stashed Claudia there, she had beaten a path to the door like a homing pigeon. God, what lousy timing.

When they reached the house, Alison led Louis to

279

the den. "Why haven't you told me that my mother was alive?" Glaring at him, her green eyes flashed like fire.

Damn, Louis thought, if only he'd known where Alison was when she called, he could have talked to Claudia and gotten the story straight. He had no idea what she'd told Alison. How should he answer? Hedging, he said, "You saw Claudia?"

"You bet I did. Can you even begin to know what a shock it was? How could you keep something like this from me?" Alison stared at him as though he had betrayed her.

"Well, she told me she read about Derek's death in an American newspaper and flew directly to Dallas wanting to see you. I guess she came to me because we had all been friends years ago and she wanted information. I told her how hard you were taking Derek's death . . . you know, you really were for a while there . . . and we were all quite worried about you." Louis hoped to God his story wasn't off the wall or completely different from Claudia's. "So I told her to wait a little longer, give you time to get over one shock before you had to face something else. Then one thing happened after the other . . . like Cora Lee . . ." He managed to squeeze out the makings of a tear.

It must have worked, because Alison was contrite for a moment. "But why the fake name? And did you know she was following me around everywhere I went?"

"Why no! Oh my dear, if I'd known . . . I thought I was doing the right thing. You have to believe me, I didn't know anything about her. As for the name, she'd already registered at the hotel as Clare Cummings before I even saw her."

"Yes, I know. Nick McAllister found that out some time ago."

Louis swallowed hard. "McAllister knows about Clare Cummings?"

"Sure he does. He's a police officer and was protecting me, so naturally he knew about her. Why, she was following me everywhere, even to Washington when I went to see Senator Lassiter. He was so worried about her that he actually thought she might have been the murderer."

"My God!" Louis thought he'd better warn Claudia that the police knew about her. Alison was bound to tell McAllister that her mother was not only alive, but in Padre. From what he could gather, she was pretty clubby with that cop.

"Don't worry, she was cleared of suspicion when Nick found that she'd arrived here after Dad's death. I remember seeing her at the funeral and wondering who she was. Now I understand. Speaking of Washington and Senator Lassiter reminds me of something I've been meaning to ask you for some time. It's totally off the subject, but have you ever heard of the word Unicom?"

Louis felt the color drain from his face. "Uni—what?" He needed time to think. Good lord, this girl would give him a heart attack before he could get rid of her.

"Unicom," she said, watching him closely.

Somehow Louis managed to look baffled. "Don't believe I have. A new company maybe?"

"No, nothing like that. I just came across the name, and it aroused my curiosity. Just forget it."

Louis intended to do just that for the time being, but he knew that Alison was getting too close to the truth. He would have to move fast. "Tell me, how did you and your mother hit it off?" It was a dicey question, he felt sure, but he had to change the direction of this conversation.

Alison visibly stiffened. "As you can see, I'm here and she's still there. Oh Louis, she's despicable! The things that woman has done. I know she's only here to get her share of the estate, so I don't want anything to do with her . . . and told her as much."

"Oh come now, aren't you being a little harsh? It's just all been too much of a shock, and I should have prepared you. I'm sure she loves you."

"I tell you the woman isn't capable of loving anyone but herself. And something else . . . I think she knows who killed my dad." Alison plopped down in a chair for the first time.

"Oh no, Alison! No!" Louis was genuinely shocked and frightened. Quickly he went to the bar and poured himself a drink. "May I?" He was sure Claudia hadn't revealed who, but she sure as hell must have talked too much.

"Sure . . . in fact, you can pour me one, too."

"What'll you have?"

"Whatever." She sounded emotionally drained.

Louis handed Alison a Scotch on the rocks, then turned his head away so that she couldn't see his face. "What in the world makes you think she knows who killed Derek?"

Alison looked straight ahead. "I don't know . . . I just feel it."

"My dear, I can't tell you how sorry I am that you had to find out about Claudia this way. It's all my fault . . . please try to forgive me." Louis knew he was practically groveling. What the hell, it wouldn't be much longer until Alison was history. Maybe now he could convince Claudia to let him go ahead with his plans. Enough of these feeble attempts to make Alison's death look like an accident.

On his way home, Louis stopped at a public phone

booth. At this stage, it wasn't wise to call Claudia from his house. He dropped in some coins and dialed the number in Padre.

"Did I wake you, darling?" he said when she answered.

"My God, Louis, where have you been? I've been calling every ten minutes."

"With your charming daughter. My, she's sure crazy about you."

"How well I know. The dust hasn't settled around here yet. How have you been able to stand her all these years? She's nothing but a clone of her dear dead father. It's uncanny, though, how much she looks like me. I felt like I was seeing myself as a young woman."

"You haven't changed at all, darling . . . more beautiful than ever."

"Oh sure, with my dyed red hair. Alison's is exactly as mine used to be . . . soft and silky. But she spoils it all with that damned self-righteous attitude. It's disgusting."

"Why did you tell her who you are? That wasn't wise at all."

"She's not blind, you know. One look at me was all it took. The wheels started turning immediately, and she knew."

"But did you have to tell her so much?"

"Listen, Louis, she's my daughter for god's sake. What I said to her is none of your business. Besides, it didn't do any good. As far as I'm concerned, I've wasted twenty-three years dreaming about that girl, and she's turned out to be a nightmare. You can go ahead with whatever plans you have. I won't stand in your way."

Louis felt elated. "You mean that?"

"Yes." There was a sob in Claudia's voice, but he could tell that she meant it.

"Okay. You keep a watch out for the police, just in case. They don't have anything on you, of course, but they know where you are."

"The hell they don't have anything on me. I made the mistake of telling Alison about Charles Thomas's death years ago."

"Then be careful."

Louis hung up the phone and smiled. Tomorrow would be a good day to put Piper's plans into motion.

Twenty-four

The following Friday, Police Chief Dwain Anderson kept his appointment with Harold Conners, the district attorney. He dreaded this meeting. Conners had hounded him for weeks to come up with a solution to the Megtex murders, and he knew he couldn't put him off much longer. Now that Cora Lee Bennett had been added to the list, the pressure to name a prime suspect had mounted tremendously.

Dwain Anderson had been on the Dallas Police Force for twenty-five years, the past ten as chief. Never in his career had he felt so stymied by a series of murders, or rendered so incapable of laying his hands on one piece of concrete evidence. He was a quiet man, mild-mannered and serious, yet others considered him a man of action and quick decision, once he had a firm hold on a case. Now he felt impotent, totally baffled by this case, unable to make a move.

Harold Conners stood and the men shared a vigorous handshake. About forty-two, he was younger than Anderson by at least ten years, with wavy brown hair and sharp, probing blue eyes. In legal circles around town, he was known as a politician willing to step on any toes, as long as he advanced his career. He'd be up for reelection in the next few months, a critical time for convicting the killer of Derek Archer, one of the city's most prominent citizens. On the other hand, dragging out this investigation for months with no arrest in sight would surely cost him his job, especially with the other two murders that were obviously connected.

"How's it going?" Conners asked as they both sat down.

"Still pretty slow, but we're working round the clock to come up with something."

"Dammit man, how long is this going to take? We should have had an indictment long before now."

Dwain Anderson felt his hackles rise, but he kept his composure intact. "How can you expect to indict without a prime suspect?"

Conners leaned forward, his eyes penetrating directly into Anderson's. "I didn't ask you over here for a sparring match. If we work together on this, maybe we can come up with something. First of all, who profited the most from Archer's death?"

"Why, his daughter, of course, no question about it, but she was his only heir."

"Nevertheless, profit can be a prime motive. Think about it from Alison Archer's viewpoint . . . she took over a large conglomerate and inherited millions of dollars . . . profit by the strongest definition."

"But she was very close to her father."

"Who told you that—Miss Archer?"

Anderson nodded his head, unable to come up with a rebuttal. He didn't like this line of interrogation. Conners seemed bent on pinning this whole thing on the Archer woman, steamrolling her straight into the defendant's chair. She was either genuinely grief-stricken over her father's death or accomplished as an actress. Whatever the case, she had convinced every investigator of the former, especially Nick McAllister. Now that was something to consider—the man was obviously smitten with the young woman, his judgment possibly clouded. Maybe he'd better listen to Conners, give him a chance to state his case.

"Another thing to consider," Conners went on. "Why did Miss Archer decide to move back with her father? My God, she'd lived out on her own for years, and came back just in time to be under his roof when he was murdered."

"Claims she went back to plan her wedding; it was set to take place at her dad's house."

Conners's smile was menacing. "How convenient. Why the hell did she have to live there to plan a wedding? Doesn't make sense." He leaned back in his chair and tapped his pencil on the desk. "Must not have been too serious about this wedding. According to my sources, she called it off and booted out the groom shortly after the murder."

"True, but you can't charge a person with murder because of a change of heart."

"Still, let me remind you, we look for three things in murder cases: motive, opportunity, and method. She definitely had two of them. Give me one more suspect that can match this one, and I'll drop the whole matter."

Anderson threw up his hands. "You know damned well that we don't have another suspect just yet, but there's nothing substantial enough to justify going after this woman."

Conners shook his head, as if to brush aside Anderson's objections. "What more do we need than motive and opportunity?"

Anderson knew that Conners had a point. Alison Archer did indeed have motive and opportunity, perhaps his own impression of her had blinded him to these facts. "I'll tell you what, we'll concentrate on this possibility and see where it leads. But until we have more, there'll be no arrest."

"If you weren't so bullheaded, you'd see that you have enough right now — just too damned stubborn to admit it."

Dwain Anderson stood, ready to take his leave. "The way I see it, you'd like to convict this girl, even if justice isn't served, so you could time it before the election."

Conners gave him a scathing look. "Just a little advice . . . you make an arrest soon, or your own job could be on the line."

Dwain Anderson left Conners's office at the Dallas County Courthouse with mixed emotions. How dare a weasel like Harold Conners threaten his job? Putting that aside, he thought the man could possibly be right about Alison Archer. He had let the investigation of her involvement drop too soon, never pursuing it because of a pretty face and very believable grief. From now on, he wouldn't let his own emotions get in the way.

As soon as the chief got back into his office, he summoned Nick McAllister.

"What's going on?" Nick asked as he sat down.

"The D.A.'s up in arms about slow progress on these Megtex murders, particularly Derek Archer's. Seems that Alison Archer is high on his list of suspects."

Nick's face turned beet red. "Good God, the man must be nuts!"

"Could be, but he's got valid reasons, and we have to pay attention to them."

"Alison didn't kill her father. That's the most absurd accusation I've ever heard. Just what's that bastard basing it on?"

"Primarily motive and opportunity."

"What motive, for God's sake?"

"Power and money . . . lots of it."

Nick suddenly stood and began to pace the room. "Do you realize there've been several attempts on her life?"

"Sure, I realize that, but can you prove that she didn't set them up herself?"

"Hell no, I can't, but I *know* she didn't do it."

Again Anderson reminded himself of McAllister's involvement with the young woman. "You have to look at this thing objectively, forget about your personal attachment, and put your feelings aside. If you hadn't cared about Alison Archer, would you have pushed for dropping her investigation? Hell no, you wouldn't, and you know it."

"You might be right, but there's something else. Remember that key in the safe?"

"Yeah, yeah, I remember the key, but she could have planted it there herself just to throw us off guard. Doesn't amount to a thing."

"It does as far as I'm concerned, and I intend to follow it through until we exhaust every possibility." Nick turned abruptly to face him. "You want to waste valuable time chasing after a woman who could very well be the next victim. I firmly believe that there's someone in the Megtex office behind all this."

"Just what do you base this on?"

"A gut feeling."

"I rest my case." Dwain Anderson knew that McAllister was his best officer, the most surefooted, levelheaded detective in the whole department. If Harold Conners's deductions turned out to be true, Nick would see that this woman had completely snowed him, then feel like an utter fool. "From now on, I want a daily report on what you've come up with."

"I don't see how I can do that."

"Then remove yourself from the case."

"I can't do that either, because I don't trust anyone to do it but myself."

"Maybe if you weren't shacking up with her, your job would be a little easier."

"I resent that. Alison Archer isn't one to shack up with anybody. In my opinion, she's in a lot of danger, and needs me there for protection."

"Well, if that's the reason, we're paying you too much for protection detail when a rookie could easily watch that house. You're a good cop, McAllister, but you're letting personal feelings get in the way. I want a full investigation of Miss Archer, and that's not a request. It's an order."

Nick gave him a resigned look. "Yes sir, you've got it, but you can be sure I'll keep following every other lead I can find."

"If you find anything at all, I'll welcome a chance to look into it, no matter where it leads. Solving these murders is top priority."

Chief Anderson watched Nick slam the door. He knew the man's heart wouldn't be in his new assignment. But Nick always did his job well, and hadn't failed him yet. Deep down, he wanted McAllister to be right. Damn, he hoped it wouldn't be long until he could put the whole matter to rest, no matter how it turned out, and dump it in the middle of Harold Conners's lap.

Nick left the chief's office with a sinking feeling in the pit of his stomach. If the D.A. lived up to his reputation, he'd convict the Pope if he thought it would win him votes. Bringing down Alison Archer, one of Dallas's elite, would shatter the idea of liberty and justice being bought off by those who could afford it, and bring the masses to the polls by the thousands to reward the courageous incumbent. He had to move fast to prove Conners wrong, before the bastard railroaded Alison straight into prison.

The only thing he had to go on right now was the possible involvement of Clare Cummings in the Bennett woman's abduction and murder. And now she'd slipped away to God knows where. The ticket agent couldn't positively identify Cora Lee's photograph as that of the woman with Bennett, so maybe he could approach it from a different angle. What good it would do, he had no idea, since Colby had lost her trail, but still it was worth pursuing.

He stopped by the crime lab where he located the blond wig found on the body. Then he paid a visit to Eric Bedford, one of the best composite artists in the country, a valuable member of the force. Pulling out the photograph of Clare Cummings, he asked, "Think you can draw a picture of this woman wearing this wig?"

"Don't see why not. When do you need it?"

"As soon as possible, and make it in color."

"No problem."

Nick left the station and drove to the law offices

of Carpenter, Spence, and Roth, housed on the seventeenth floor of a shiny glass building on Central Expressway. Might as well make some effort to follow the chief's orders, he thought, and the best place to start was with John Carpenter, the man Alison almost married.

Emerging from the elevator, Nick approached the attractive blond receptionist and produced his badge. She buzzed Carpenter, and moments later, escorted Nick down the long, imposing corridor, through a pair of glass doors, into John Carpenter's suite of offices. The rooms had a nineteenth-century Regency look, with overstuffed chairs, striped couches, dark mahogany paneling, and hand-woven carpeting.

As the man rose to greet him, Nick couldn't help but compare the opulence around him to Carpenter's perfectly tailored Versace suit. After exchanging introductions, the two sat down in rose-colored, wingbacked chairs in front of the carved wooden desk.

"Well, officer, this is an unexpected visit. What can I do for you?"

Nick felt suddenly uncomfortable, not intimidated by Carpenter's great wealth and social position, but the fact that here was a man Alison had known most of her life, the type of man who fit naturally into her world. "I won't take up much of your time . . . just need to ask a few questions." Nick pulled out a notepad and pen. "Let's see, you've known Alison Archer since college, right?"

"Oh, much longer than that. Our families belonged to the same country club, and we met when we were very young, about ten years old. Then later, we both attended Highland Park High School and started dating during our senior year."

"How did she get along with her father—any resentiment toward authority, that kind of thing?"

"No more than any other teenager. In fact, they seemed rather close, and Derek gave her everything she could possibly want."

"What about later, when they started working together?"

John shook his head. "No problems that I know of." He looked puzzled. "Say, what's this leading to? Is Alison under suspicion?"

"I wouldn't say that, we're just trying to be thorough and cover all the bases." Nick made a notation on his pad and continued, "I don't mean to pry, but would you mind telling me why the two of you suddenly cancelled your marriage plans?"

"Actually, Alison called off the wedding, not my idea at all. We had a few disagreements . . . nothing serious as far as I was concerned . . . but she was determined to be CEO of Megtex, and I wanted her to manage our home." He smiled. "Quite a difference in job prestige, I guess, and I couldn't make her come around to my way of thinking. Then there was the matter of where we'd live. She felt it was the Archer home or nowhere, and I couldn't budge her on that, even though the place is getting old and much too large for two people."

"So you're saying that she put a lot of emphasis on heading the company and keeping the house? I see." He jotted down more information. "Had she ever mentioned wanting to take over Megtex *before* Derek Archer died?"

"Not that I can think of." He gave Nick a shrewd, calculating look. "You're trying to pin this thing on her, aren't you?"

"Not at all. You can rest assured that's not my objective at all . . . just doing my job. Can you think of anything else?"

"No, not really, it's just that Alison seemed to change so much after Derek died . . . lost interest in me, the wedding, all our plans, everything. All she could think of was the company and reveling in her new authority." John was silent for a few seconds, then added, "Until lately, I never knew she could be so hostile and irritable."

Nick made a final notation and stood to leave. "Thanks for cooperating. I might need to get back to you."

"Anytime . . . wait, before you go, I'd like to add one more thing. After Derek was killed, I noticed signs of paranoia in her. She was almost irrational at times, so much so that I wondered about her mental stability."

Nick made no comment but thanked him again and left the building, feeling confused and worried. John Carpenter had certainly painted a different picture from the Alison he'd grown to love. Could be that it was nothing more than vindictiveness, but whatever the reason, a D.A. like Conners could put him on the witness stand and make Alison look like a power-hungry bitch, someone willing to do anything, even murder her own father, to take over the reins of Megtex. God help her if she were ever indicted.

As soon as Nick McAllister left, John glanced at his watch. Almost five o'clock. Maybe Alison was back from Florida and he could catch her at the office. He felt elated when he dialed her number at Megtex and heard her voice on the other end.

"Hi, glad you're back," he said. Got in last night

myself, just in time for an interesting visitor."

"Oh, why should that concern me?"

"Well, you might be interested in knowing that your new boyfriend came by for a chat . . . even took a few notes."

"Get to the point, John, you're taking up my time."

"Seems he thinks you could have murdered your dad."

"You continue to amaze me, you bastard. That's an absurd, childish trick, and I thought even you were above that kind of thing. I'm hanging up."

John laughed. "Don't be so hasty . . . you'd better hear—"

"I can't imagine what you could say to make me believe that."

"How about questions concerning how you got along with Derek? And if you'd mentioned wanting to take over Megtex before he—"

"Nick wouldn't ask anything like that. I never dreamed you could stoop so low, even after your performance in Florida."

"Believe me, I'm telling you the truth, simply because I still love you. Just thought you should be warned. Will you listen now without interrupting?"

She sighed. "All right, say what you have to say, and get it over with."

"For one thing, he seemed to think you called off the wedding because you had what you wanted and didn't need me. Even asked if you were power hungry, and insinuated you might be a little unbalanced."

"That's hard to believe."

"For your own good, you'd better believe me. When I asked if you were under suspicion, he said he was just doing his job."

"Nick said that?"

"I swear he did.

Alison was quiet on the other end of the line, and John could hear her swallowing back tears. Her voice trembled when she finally spoke again. "Thanks for telling me, John. Guess I didn't know him as well as I thought."

John heard a click and grinned to himself as he hung up the receiver. No doubt Nick McAllister was officially out of her life. He knew there wasn't a chance in hell she'd ever be arrested, but she didn't have to know that just yet. Now was the perfect time to ease back into her life. He'd give her a while to steam about this before making his next move.

Twenty-five

About seven, Nick arrived at Alison's house. For a whole week, since her return from Padre, he'd noticed something different about her. Though as sexy and beautiful as ever, Alison had seemed preoccupied, almost as if she had left part of herself on the Texas coast. He rang the bell, hoping that tonight he'd see the return of that special smile.

Instead, Alison greeted him with a hostile stare.

"Are you okay?" Nick walked inside, realizing she hadn't uttered a word.

"I'm fine."

"Oh no, you're not—what's wrong?"

"Nothing much, just wondering why you're not still out interrogating my friends."

Nick felt like she'd just dropped a bomb on top of his head. Damn John Carpenter! No doubt he had called her the second the interview ended. Nick had hoped to be the one to break the news that she was again a suspect, but now Carpenter had probably blown the whole thing out of proportion. No wonder she was so angry.

"Look, Alison, it's not what you—"

"Oh yes, it is." Tears rose to the surface of her eyes as she held out both arms and fought to steady her voice. "Go ahead, put handcuffs on me and throw me in jail! You can save yourself and my friends a lot of time."

Nick reached for her, attempting to hold her in his arms, but she squirmed away from him.

"You really had me fooled for a while, Lieutenant. I was even beginning to think I'd finally found someone I could depend on, someone who really cared about me, but it seems I was wrong." Her eyes blazed like green fire. "Why were you hanging around so much — to amuse yourself? Or maybe hoping I'd talk in my sleep and tell you my deep, dark secrets?"

"Settle down, Alison, that's nonsense, and you know it." He took a firm hold on her arm and led her through the house to the den. "We're going to sit down together and talk about this calmly."

"Oh, were you calm when you asked John if I was unbalanced?"

Nick sat on the couch and pulled her down beside him, still holding her arm. "Did it ever occur to you that he might have put his own words in my mouth?"

"Why would he do that?"

"Jealousy maybe?"

"John just called to warn me that you seem to think I killed my own father. Oh, how could you? I can't believe I trusted you, even dared to think—"

"Will you at least give me a chance to explain?"

She looked him squarely in the eye. "Go ahead. It might be interesting to watch you try to get out of this."

Nick took a deep breath. He knew he'd lose her for good if he couldn't make her understand. "The D.A. is putting pressure on the chief to make an arrest, and it seems he's chosen you as the prime target."

"Me? Why on earth . . ." Alison's face turned chalk white.

"For lack of anyone else to hang it on."

"I don't understand. Why, I'd be the last . . . how could he possibly think . . . oh my God!"

"Don't panic, I'm doing everything I can to keep this from happening."

"Then why did you go to John? That doesn't sound much like—"

"I had to make a stab at some sort of investigation."

"But you should have told the chief you didn't want any part of it." The look in her eyes hadn't softened, and Nick knew he wasn't making much headway at all.

"I tried, believe me, but he insisted."

"Then you should have turned him down. If you really loved me you wouldn't—"

"I have to go along with him . . . it's the best way I know to help you. If I refused to follow orders, I'd have to take myself off the case, and I can't do that. Somehow, some way, I'm going to solve this case, and I don't trust anyone else to do it." He took her in his arms and held onto her for dear life. "Can't I make you understand?"

"I'm trying, but it's so hard."

He held her at arm's length and looked into her eyes. "Just trust me."

"But how—why do they suspect me? I never heard of anything so outlandish."

"I know, I feel the same way, but we're fighting a politician who'd do anything to get reelected."

"Still, he has to have evidence. Where will he get it . . . out of the air? It doesn't make sense."

"He claims you had a motive."

"Motive! To kill my dad? What motive?"

299

Nick felt suddenly embarrassed, ashamed to have to tell her. "Just forget I said that."

"No, I won't forget — what was my motive?"

"Your position and inheritance."

"This is unbelievable."

Nick shook his head. "I know, but that's what we're up against. Conners is hell-bent to have a defendant and conviction before the next election. That's why I'm so determined to get to the bottom of this, but so far, I've drawn a blank . . . found lots of paths, but they all go off in different directions. There's nothing to tie it all together."

"Those papers my dad tried to tell me about have to hold all the answers."

"I agree, but where the hell are they? If I had my way, I'd search every building and house in Dallas, but I'm afraid I'd still come up short."

"I don't. Knowing Myra Collins as well as I did, I can't help but believe she moved them herself. She was probably the only one besides my dad who knew about the fraud, and she seemed so frightened when I mentioned the papers." Alison looked thoughtful for a moment. "You know, going back to the day of the funeral, I think the reason for Dad's murder dawned on her when I brought up the papers. She was such an orderly, meticulous person, and it would have been just like her to leave the key in the safe so it wouldn't get lost."

"That makes a lot of sense, but what the hell does it open?"

Alison suddenly jumped up. "There's something I've been meaning to show you. Don't know what bearing it could have, but I found it in Dad's desk in the study." She headed for the door. "Be right back." Moments later, she returned, a folder in hand. "This file is labeled Unicom, and it has several pages of strange figures in it." She sat down beside Nick and thumbed through the contents. "Look at this one . . . see the heading? Just a series of numbers. And then there's this list of dollar amounts and dates, followed by a total of $18,870,520. What do you make of it?"

Nick studied each page, realizing none of it had any meaning for him. "What does Unicom stand for?"

"I have no idea. Thought at first it was the name of a computer file, but I've searched for days and can't find it anywhere in the system."

Nick looked at the page with the list of dollar amounts. "These numbers could indicate deposits. Thought about checking bank statements?"

"No, I haven't, but that's a good idea." Her face brightened. "Wait a minute, maybe the numbers at the top are an account number totally different from the company's, even in another bank, like a foreign account maybe."

"Could be . . . possibly Switzerland or the Cayman Islands. People hide money in numbered accounts all the time." And then the obvious came to him. He couldn't believe he hadn't thought of it before. "Those numbers sound so familiar. Remember the Swiss account where Louis Bennett was told to deposit the ransom?"

"Why, of course! Are these the same?"

"I'd bet on it, but I can't be sure until I check it out."

"Oh no, if that's the case, then the kidnapping is tied directly to the Megtex murders."

Nick looked at the papers again. "Could this heading be on a separate computer file?"

"No, I've already checked that out, too, but it's bound to have been entered at one time, because these are all computer printouts and the font matches the printers at the office. Whoever entered this data has obviously deleted it."

Nick put the papers back inside the folder and shook his head in frustration. "I agree, you're onto something here, but it's just another path that takes us around in a circle. The murderer has brushed a thick layer of sand over every one of his tracks, and we can't make a move until we find him."

Later, Alison lay in Nick's arms, sleep eluding her. She knew if the murders weren't solved soon, it was only a matter of time until the district attorney would put together a case against her, all of it based on supposition and circumstantial evidence. She wanted to believe that Nick had no part in it, had to believe he didn't, but John's call still bothered her. Without Nick's faith in her innocence, they had nothing together, and she so desperately needed him.

"Nick, are you awake?"

"Un huh," he muttered in a sleep-filled voice.

"Are you sure you didn't ask John if he considered me unbalanced?"

Nick leaned forward on his elbow, his face close to hers. "I'm sure." He gave her a tender, lingering kiss. "You're about the sanest person I know."

Alison nestled against him once more, still troubled by the catastrophe the coming days might bring. Another hour passed, sleep finally overtaking the whirling thoughts in her head.

About 3:00 AM., Nick suddenly sat straight up in bed, his senses alive. There was something in the air, something he had smelled before, but he couldn't identify it. Whatever it was sent warning signals to

302

his brain, alerting him to danger. He sat perfectly still for several seconds, and then it came to him. It was a strong electrical smell, like burning wires. Any minute, the whole house could be in flames.

He reached for Alison and shook her shoulder. "Alison! Wake up!"

Abruptly she opened her eyes. "What's wrong?"

"Where's the breaker box?"

"Downstairs, in the utility room. My lord, what's that smell?" She turned the switch on the bedside lamp, but it didn't light.

"Burning wires, I think." Nick scrambled out of bed and raced through the door, down the stairs, fumbling his way in the darkness until he reached the light switch in the hall. Thank God it worked. Rushing through the kitchen, he quickly found the breaker box and opened its door. Four windows inside showed red panels, indicating they had tripped, cutting off the electricity to the sections of the house they served. Quickly he flipped the main switch to OFF, immersing the whole house in darkness.

Nick was about to feel his way back to the stairway, when he saw a beam of light eerily making its way toward him. He braced himself, ready to tackle the intruder.

"Nick? Where are you?" It was Alison. Thank God she'd found a flashlight.

"Over here, I'm coming—just stay where you are." He hurried to her, and together they found the phone in the hallway at the foot of the stairs. Hastily, Nick dialed 911.

"This is Lieutenant Nick McAllister, Dallas P.D. There's a possible fire at 424 Stillmeadow, off Inwood Road."

"We'll dispatch fire units immediately, Lieutenant."

Nick hung up the phone, going over options in his mind. He knew his imagination might be playing tricks on him, but he felt sure he detected smoke mixed with the lingering electrical smell. He debated the possibility momentarily, then made his decision.

"I think there's time, so let's hurry and get on some clothes before the fire trucks get here. I've always had a fear of getting caught out on the lawn stark naked, with gawking neighbors all around."

By the time Nick had pulled on his slacks and a shirt, Alison had dressed herself in jeans and a light sweater. Flashlight in hand, he led her back down the stairs and out the front door. Just as they stepped outside, they heard the sound of sirens in the distance; in about five minutes, two fire trucks barreled up the driveway and came to a stop.

After Nick explained what he'd found to the firemen, they rushed inside and made their way to the attic floor. Fifteen minutes later one of them approached Nick and Alison.

"Good thing you called," he said. "The whole place could have gone up if we hadn't gotten to it."

"What was the trouble?" Nick asked.

"Three main wires were stripped right down the middle—no insulation at all. Once they started to heat up, you noticed the smell. Good thing it woke you up, because they were close enough to ignite those piles of oily rags. Real fire hazard if I ever saw it."

"Oily rags?" Alison said. "How on earth did they get there?"

The fireman removed his cap and scratched the back of his head. "This is just a preliminary observation, but it looks to me like attempted arson. We'll send an investigator out tomorrow."

Nick felt a tremor in Alison's body, and she

gasped out loud. "Arson! Oh my God!"

"Tell me," Nick said, "was the insulation cut away, or were the wires just worn out?"

"Like I said, this is just a guess, but I'd say it was stripped with a knife or a razor blade. Wires don't usually wear out in one spot like that, especially three of them that close together."

"Is it safe to go back inside?" Alison asked.

"Well yes, for the moment, but I wouldn't advise you to spend the rest of the night here. I'll keep a couple of men around to make sure there's no more danger, and you'll need to get an electrician out here first thing tomorrow."

"We'll go to my apartment," Nick said.

He went inside with Alison, and waited while she gathered a few clothes and packed her makeup case. He shuddered, thinking what could have happened if he hadn't woken up in time. Thank God he was here. It bothered him though, to realize that he hadn't been much of a protector. Someone had entered the house, deactivated the alarm, and climbed the stairs all the way to the attic, moving through the house at will, and he had slept through the whole thing. It occurred to him that the perpetrator probably thought that Alison was alone. All this week, he'd parked his car in the driveway, but tonight, he'd driven to the back of the house and left it inside the garage. Alison's life was in grave peril, and he wished he could keep her with him every hour, day and night, but he knew that wasn't possible.

When Nick reported for duty the next morning, he went straight to the crime lab to double-check the Swiss account numbers on Bennett's ransom tape. Sure enough, they matched those on Alison's computer printout. The fragments of the puzzle were beginning to come together. He had no doubt now that whoever committed the fraud at Megtex was also responsible for the murders. His money was still on Louis Bennett, but proving it remained to be seen.

Next Nick went to his office, where he found the artist's composite drawing on his desk. Despite the fact that he hadn't closed his eyes since last night's scare, he felt wide-awake, keyed up with nervous energy. Pulling out Cora Lee's photograph, he compared it with the drawing. Amazing how alike they were in many respects, yet different in others, like the eye color, the shape of the face.

The day had just begun and he intended to make the most of it. He knew that the ticket agent he needed to see didn't begin her shift until one, so he headed first to visit Ronald Dirkson, Bennett's neighbor across the street. Luckily, Dirkson was in the front yard, watering his flowers.

"Well, hello there, Lieutenant. What can I do for you?"

"I'd like you to take a look at this drawing. Remember when you saw Mrs. Bennett getting out of the cab?"

"Sure do. Sad what happened to her, isn't it?"

"It certainly is, and we're trying to find out who did it." Nick handed the drawing to Dirkson. "Could you have seen *this* woman instead of Cora Lee?"

"Oh, I doubt that, seeing her from a distance like that . . . you know, across the street in the driveway." He took a closer look. "But if you ask me, she looks a lot like the woman I saw on the street that night, except of course, the hair. Hers was kind of red, I think."

"Can you think of anything else you saw?"

"Well, after you left the other day, I remembered

seeing something in her hand, a bag of some sort, like a small suitcase. Thought that was a little unusual for someone out jogging."

"Very interesting," Nick said. "Is that all you can think of?"

"That's about it. Hope I've been of some help."

"You've helped more than you know, Mr. Dirkson. Thanks for your time."

Nick's next stop was the Metro Cab Company, to try to locate the driver whose passenger had supposedly been Mrs. Bennett. To his chagrin, the driver had asked for a whole week off to visit his ailing mother somewhere in Arkansas. It was just as well. The man probably hadn't gotten a good look at her anyway.

On a hunch, he drove back to Louis Bennett's house and pulled into the driveway. The maid answered the door.

Nick flashed his badge. "Is Mr. Bennett in?"

"No sir, he's at the office."

"May I come inside and have another look around?"

"Yes sir, come in. I'm sure that's all right."

After thanking her, Nick hurried upstairs, straight to the master bedroom. He opened the closet door, turned on the light, and stepped inside the large walk-in closet. The row of wigs was still there, perched atop styrofoam heads, the sight of them bringing a knot to the pit of his stomach. One by one, Nick examined them, carefully checking inside, and found what he was looking for in the very last one—two long strands of red hair in the center of the crown. Well, well, it seemed his theory had been right after all. He decided to take the wig back to the station for safe keeping.

Nick grabbed a hamburger for lunch, checked his

messages at the station, then started out once more, this time to the Love Field airport. The ticket agent he'd spoken to before had just come on duty, and was in the process of waiting on a customer when Nick spotted her. In less than five minutes, she was free and looked up in surprise at the next person in line.

"Hello, officer, can I help you?"

"I certainly hope so." Nick pulled out the photograph of Cora Lee and the drawing. "I know it's been several days, but can you tell me which one of these looks more like the woman with Mr. Bennett?"

"You mean the one who changed her mind at the last minute? I don't know, but I'll try. Let's see . . ." She laid both pictures on the counter and leaned forward, studying them closely. "I'm pretty sure it's this one." She picked up the drawing. "You know, it's the eyes that seem like hers. This is really a good drawing."

"Then you're sure this is the woman?"

"Yes, I feel sure it is. After you left the other day, I was sorry I identified the photo, because the eyes weren't the same at all."

Nick felt excitement swell inside him. At last he'd made some headway, found a link that could possibly lead to finding the killer. Clare Cummings was involved in Cora Lee's murder, and maybe even the other two. He knew he had enough evidence to bring her in for questioning, but there was one small problem. He had no idea where to find her.

Twenty-six

Leaving Alison in his apartment hadn't been easy for Nick. He smiled to himself when he thought of how she'd puttered around in his little kitchen these past two days, making coffee and begging him to want a big breakfast, so she could show off her culinary skills. He never took the time to eat breakfast, but it seemed that she was determined to change all that. In a way, he wished they could stay in his apartment longer, but the electrician had assured Alison that the wiring in her house was safe now. He had to admit that he'd enjoyed Juanita's bacon and eggs since he'd been sleeping over. "To protect Alison," they'd told her, as if she didn't know what was going on. He grinned. One look at that rumpled bed was all it took.

He wanted to get an early start this morning. Last night he'd had a sudden thought, and couldn't wait to check it out. Last week, when Alison mentioned that she'd flown into Love Field after her flight from Brownsville, it hadn't dawned on him at the time that Colby could have lost Clare Cummings's trail at DFW because she switched airports, flying via Southwest Airlines. He hadn't even thought to check Love Field, but it was certainly worth looking into.

After tying so many ends together, he hated the idea of losing track of the Cummings woman. Somehow, he felt sure, she was involved in the kidnapping of Cora Lee Bennett.

Nick approached a ticket agent, showed his identification, and asked the young woman to check the passenger list for the fourteenth to see if a Clare Cummings had purchased a ticket to any of the Southwest destinations. While she checked, he flipped through a magazine at the bookstand. At last she looked up and beckoned him to come back to her station.

"Yes, Lieutenant, we have a Clare Cummings listed as a passenger to Brownsville on June 14."

"Brownsville? Sure it wasn't Houston?"

"No sir, Brownsville."

Strange, Nick thought. Alison had called him from Padre Island last Saturday, asking him to fly into Brownsville. Could she have asked this woman to meet her at Padre Island? It didn't make sense at all. At the time the Cummings woman left, Alison didn't even know she was going to Florida, let alone Padre. Mulling over it on his way to the station, he thought he might as well stop by the crime lab, to see if Jake had found anything significant about those red hairs in the wig.

Sure enough, Jake was full of information. "The hair belongs to a Caucasian woman," he said, looking at a form, "approximately forty to fifty years old. Seems it was dyed with a European product that's not sold in this country. She's a natural redhead, though, but her hair's faded . . .

probably why she uses the dye. Want me to go on? There's more, but it's pretty technical."

"Like maybe she's left-handed and prefers Coke to Pepsi?" Nick grinned. "You guys amaze me. Do me a favor, put it all in writing and send it up to my office. Thanks a lot."

"Yeah, and I suppose you want it yesterday."

"That's right . . . you heard me loud and clear," Nick called over his shoulder.

That evening, as Nick opened the door to Alison's house, he watched her hurry down the stairs to greet him. Looking at her made him realize that the hell she'd been through these last weeks had taken its toll. She had lost weight, and something mirrored in her eyes, something almost like death. His heart went out to her; he couldn't wait to take her in his arms.

Over and over again he had told himself that his love for this woman who had everything had to be forgotten. When she was out of his sight, it was easy to rationalize with a clear mind, but the second he set eyes on her, all his reasoning melted like snowflakes on a bed of hot coals.

He'd never known anyone quite like her. She was a delightful mixture of naivete and sophistication, bright and witty one moment, but serious and intelligent the next. Then playful and outlandish and sexy as hell seconds later. With no way to get her out of his system, he knew that Alison Archer was already a part of him. If he ever lost her, he wouldn't be able to breathe. *Hell,* he thought, *quit analyzing and be grateful to have her rushing toward him.*

311

Later, after they had gotten comfortable, Nick and Alison sat on the terrace overlooking the pool, sipped wine, and talked about the great job Juanita and the cleaning crew had done to rid the house of the burned-wire odor. It had been fun spending the night in Nick's apartment, but this was home to Alison, and as far as she was concerned, her permanent residence.

"You know, Nick," Alison said, "there's something I've been wanting to ask you all week, but never seemed to get around to it." She gave him a mischievous grin. "When I was in Florida, where did you sleep . . . your place or mine?"

"Not here, that's for sure. Imagine how spaced out your friends would have been if they'd come over without calling and found me at the door in the buff."

Alison gave him a sexy look. "You could have told them you were the butler."

"Oh, oh, better be on your guard," he said, rising. "Isn't it always the butler who winds up getting caught doing something or other to someone?" One dark eyebrow flew up and he leered, twisting a nonexistent mustache as he took Alison by the hand and led her inside to the drawing room.

"Always the detective." Alison gave a mock sigh, her pulses already racing, butterflies dancing up and down her spine. "Guess I'll never cure you of that."

"You do, and I won't have a job very long." He pulled her to him and gave her a kiss. "You know," he said, glancing around, "I've never noticed what a terrific room this is. Suppose anyone has ever made love in here before?"

At that moment, Alison looked up, her eyes resting on the portrait of her mother, and her heart almost stopped. Her mother! Her beautiful mother seemed to be sneering down at them. Pulling away from Nick, she covered her face with her hands. "No, I doubt if there was ever much real love in this whole house."

"Darling, what is it?"

Alison whispered, "Not in here, Nick . . . please, let's go to my bedroom." Their moment of mutual excitement faded like a mirage.

Knowing he didn't understand, she could see the hurt in Nick's eyes, but he put his arm through hers and headed for the stairs. Once in her room, the place that held such tender memories for both of them, he drew her close again. She pulled away, knowing Nick deserved an explanation, but how could she tell him of that bitter confrontation? She couldn't expect him to understand how Claudia had come alive, just long enough to destroy a lifetime of dreams and lost love.

Finally, Alison looked at Nick and tried to smile. "I wasn't going to tell you what happened in Padre Island . . . wasn't going to tell anyone, but now I know I have to, or you'll never understand me. Oh, it's been so awful, keeping this to myself for so long, like something horrible is gnawing inside of me." She drew both arms across her middle.

"My God, what is it?" Nick eased her down onto the love seat and sat beside her. "Can I get you something?"

It was as though she hadn't heard him. The

313

words started pouring out. "The portrait of my . . . of my mother . . . the one in the drawing room . . ." Alison's eyes burned with unshed tears, as she looked at Nick's anxious expression. "It came alive in the house on Padre Island."

"What!"

"There's no easy way to say it. My mother is alive, has been alive all these years, and I just found out."

"Darling, what are you saying?" Nick looked shocked, then Alison could see a change come over him. He understood. "Clare Cummings and your mother are one and the same, aren't they? Good lord, I should have put it all together sooner. What a lamebrain I've been." He traced the outline of Alison's face with his fingertip, then leaned forward, kissing one eye, then the other. "Those magnificent green eyes that drew me to the painting at first, then to you . . . I should have guessed it when I heard the description of the woman who was following you. Why did she follow you anyway? What was she afraid of?"

"I asked her that, and she said she was trying to protect me, that since Dad had been murdered, she was afraid my life was in danger, too. What she really wants is her half of the estate. In my opinion, she was afraid of being accused of some kind of foul play if something happened to me." Alison couldn't keep the bitterness out of her voice. "It all boils down to the fact that she was protecting her own interests, while watching me. She doesn't give a damn about me as a person."

"Why don't you start from the beginning?"

Now that it was out in the open, Alison found it

314

easier to tell him about how Claudia had walked into the room and shocked her half to death in Padre. In telling him the story of her mother's past, she omitted the part about her picking up a strange man in the middle of the afternoon and winding up killing him in self-defense. As much as she despised Claudia, she couldn't tell anyone that sordid story, ever.

"She's still very beautiful, Nick, and I can see why she's always captivated men. It's as if she has a fire in her belly, a need to be recognized and idolized ... but most of all, loved. I think Claudia's never been able to separate sex from love. To her, they're one and the same. Dad's love wasn't enough for her, or mine either, I suppose. I was just a child and hadn't learned how to give."

Alison stood, walked over to the desk, and opened the middle drawer. Miraculously, the intense pain in the pit of her stomach was gone. Talking to Nick had helped more than she realized. She pulled out the photographs that Derek had hidden away, and handled them lovingly.

"Look, see how happy we once were?" Alison smiled as she showed Nick the picture of the three of them in the sailboat. "You know, I didn't realize it, but it was actually easier when I thought my mother was dead. Derek kept my love for her alive, and I adored her memory. Strange, but now that I know she's not dead, I feel terribly lost and alone, much more so than before. She managed to destroy all my love and memories, and turned my dad's words about her into a pack of lies." She looked at Nick, her eyes brimming over. "I've never in my whole life felt so out of control."

Nick wrapped his arms around her and held her close. "You're trembling." He kissed the top of her head. "Just know that you'll never be alone as long as I'm alive." He continued to hold her as he looked at the other snapshots. The one of Louis with Claudia seemed to catch his interest. "Was Bennett married to Cora Lee when this was taken?"

"Yes, I'm sure he was. Why?"

"Just wondering . . . they look so friendly."

"Oh they were . . . I forgot about that part. Claudia told me she got in touch with Louis as soon as she landed in Dallas, because she was afraid to come to me. Believe me, I've already had all this out with Louis, and can't forgive him for not telling me she was alive. My God, I went around suspecting this strange woman in black of all kinds of things. But nothing I imagined was as bad as the truth."

"What did Bennett have to say? Had he been in touch with your mother through all those years?"

"Well, he led me to believe that he hadn't heard from her at all until after Dad's death."

"What explanation did he give for not telling you?"

"She made him promise not to, and he kept his word. To him it was cut and dried . . . very simple, and he couldn't understand why I was so angry with him." Alison picked up the photo again. "They do look happy, don't they?" She flipped through the pictures again. "As a matter of fact, we all seem happy, don't we?" Alison rose, walked over to the desk again, and made a move to tear them up and toss them into the wastebasket, but Nick stopped her.

"Don't do that, darling."

"Why not?"

"Because some day you may be very sorry. Apparently your father couldn't bring himself to destroy them, so why don't you just shove them back into the drawer for a while?"

"Seems that's just what Dad did for twenty-three years. God, imagine how he suffered . . . finding out what she was really like." She put the photos in the desk and closed the drawer.

"It looks like he must have known all that before he married her, if what she told you about living with that guy from the Middle East was true. Obviously he accepted her for what she was, because he loved her. Men sometimes do strange things for love."

Alison couldn't keep from laughing. "You sound like you're pretty familiar with some of those strange actions. Getting a little personal?"

"Maybe." Nick put his arms around her. "Nothing in your past could ever make me feel any different about you."

"Oh yeah?" Alison pulled back and looked directly into Nick's eyes. "What if I told you I went to bed with John Carpenter while I was in Florida?"

Nick's face registered such shock that she couldn't carry this any further. "Don't look at me like that! I didn't, but he was there, and I had one heck of a time getting rid of him. I was just trying to prove a point . . . see, you would have thought less of me, wouldn't you?"

Nick gave her a sheepish grin. "Guess I'm not as big a person as I thought I was. What the hell was

317

he doing in Florida anyway? And how did he wind up in your room?"

"He was already at the Colony before I arrived. Said he was on vacation, then got all sticky about our breakup and tried to act real macho. I even started wondering if he could be the killer we've been searching for. It wasn't very pleasant, but I finally managed to push him out the door." She smiled devilishly. "It made me realize how special you are, so there."

Nick made a grab for her, but Alison was too fast for him. She giggled and slipped out of his reach.

When he tried again, she evaded his grasp by climbing on the bed. Nick laughed and cried, "Gotcha!" But Alison rolled off the other side. He rolled, too, and caught a sleeve of her cotton jacket, but she wriggled out of it before he could catch her.

"Oh, if you're going to do a strip, I can play that game, too." He was triumphant as his belt came off.

"That's not fair," she cried, out of breath. "I'm not wearing a belt. Ah, I know!" She stepped out of her shoes and gave him a wicked smile. "Now top that!"

"You have just one more chance to give up, and then—watch out!" Nick lunged for her unsuccessfully, and they both wound up lying on the thick white carpet, laughing and trying to catch their breath. Nick rolled over and lay on top of her, pinning her down.

Alison felt little shivers of pleasure travel through her whole body, as Nick's lips found hers. This time she didn't pull away. She loved this man so much that her body responded with all the passion inside her, as if it had a will of its own. Her hands, locked behind his head, began a slow travel down his back, caressing, loving, toying, teasing, until, moaning with pleasure, Nick found all the hooks and buttons needed to free her of her clothes, while shedding his own at the same time, his lips never leaving hers. His fingers began an exploration of her body, so loving, so tender, that her senses were on fire. She responded in uncontrollable spasms of ecstasy.

"Now, Nick, love me now." Her mouth sought his once more, and she clung to him, half in desire, half in pure love, as Nick moved under her, guiding her to him, until he was deep inside her. And then she cried out in sweet agony.

Late that night, Nick rose on one elbow to study the sleeping figure beside him. He smiled, realizing that Alison was all any one man could handle. He was crazy about her, no need to deny it to himself any longer. Looking at her luxuriant, red brown hair spread across the pillow, he couldn't resist touching it. He watched as her breasts rose and fell with the evenness of her breathing, and thought how lucky he was that he found her, how amazing that she cared for him, too. He'd worry about their different backgrounds another time. He couldn't . . . wouldn't fight those differences any longer.

Nick was glad he was here to spend these nights with Alison for more reasons than the sensual ones. Someone was out there, someone determined to kill her, and she needed him for protection. Claudia might even be a threat, in spite of what she'd led Alison to believe. Her involvement with Louis Bennett spoke volumes. The fact that she'd worn a wig belonging to his wife and had been identified as the woman with him at the airport established her part in the murder and kidnapping of Cora Lee, and now he knew where to find her. He sighed, wondering how he could ever tell Alison that her mother was an accomplice in a murder.

Twenty-seven

Nick waited until morning to put out an all-points bulletin on Claudia Archer, then alerted the Brownsville police. It made him sick to think of how Alison would feel when she learned that her mother was a wanted fugitive, but it couldn't be helped. He had to do his job.

Nick walked into Chief Anderson's office, ready to lay all the evidence before him. Seated at his desk, Anderson looked up from his paperwork.

"I think we're getting close to solving the Bennett Case," Nick said.

"Oh? What have you got?"

Nick began relating the evidence against the suspect and pulled out the drawing, her photograph, and the one of Cora Lee Bennett. "I have two witnesses who identified this composite as the woman with Bennett at the airport. She left town, but I've learned that she's at South Padre Island. If all goes well, we'll have her back in Dallas by tonight."

"Then pick up Bennett, too, for god's sake."

"I'd rather move cautiously and make sure nothing goes wrong. When we bring in the Archer woman, it all could come together, and we'll have an airtight case."

"Archer woman? Any connection to—"

"Damn right there is . . . his estranged wife, hiding out at the Fairmont under the name of Clare Cummings. Been in Europe for twenty-three years."

"Well, I'll be damned." Anderson picked up the drawing and compared it to both photographs. "I follow your thinking, but I think we should bring Bennett down for questioning *now*. What the hell are you waiting for?"

Nick hadn't planned on telling Anderson about his suppositions just yet, nor his gut feeling that Bennett was linked to the Megtex murders as well. All he had were bits of circumstantial evidence, worth nothing without concrete proof. "If you'll give me a few days longer, and a chance to make Claudia Archer talk, I have a hunch that we can clear up the other two murders."

"My God, you think Bennett's behind all of it?"

Nick nodded. "No proof yet, but it's possible."

"Then pick him up now."

Nick stood his ground. "Dammit, if we tip our hand too early, we could blow the whole thing."

"Okay, McAllister, we'll do it your way, but once we have the woman in custody you have forty-eight hours."

Nick could understand Anderson's impatience, but damn, there wasn't much time. From what Alison had told him about her mother, he didn't think she was the type to take the whole rap by herself. He was counting on her folding under questioning, and blowing the top off. Once she realized she couldn't talk her way out of it, she was bound to crack sooner or later. But it might take longer than two days. Now it remained to be seen if the Brownsville department could even find her.

Claudia brought her coffee to the deck and stretched out on a chaise lounge. The morning sun glistened on the gulf waters; the sky was bright, blue and cloudless; the white beach was dotted with sun worshippers—everything needed to set the stage for a perfect vacation—but Claudia felt restless, bored, and lonely. Communing with nature had never been her forte; she liked people, primarily rich, influential men who could fill her life with excitement and glamour. Louis Bennett hardly fit this pattern. He was anything but exciting, even though he'd hidden away millions of dollars. Compared to the men she'd known over the years, he was quite dreary and mundane. During the past few days, she'd had time to think, time to come to the conclusion that she could never marry him and tie herself to Dallas again, especially now that her daughter had turned out to be such a bitch. She'd go along with Louis, give him a chance to clear all the obstacles, then she'd collect the fortune that was rightfully hers and quietly disappear. Oh, Louis could have the run of the company, that damned company that had been the root of all these problems, but she'd keep her part of the Megtex stock and reap all the financial rewards herself. She could hardly wait for it all to be over, so she could bid Texas goodbye forever.

Claudia stood and leaned over the deck railing,

breathing in the warm, salty air. The deck sat high above the beach, giving her a view for miles around of the ocean, the condos and houses, the flat land, and the coast road that connected the island to the mainland. In the distance, she could hear the faint wail of sirens, and wondered if there was some kind of trouble in the area. As the sound grew louder, the sight of two police cars—their red lights flashing ominously—made her heart stop momentarily. They were heading straight toward the house! She had to get away from here, couldn't take the chance that they were coming to take her away and throw her in some godforsaken jail. Damn Alison! No doubt she couldn't wait to inform the police that her own mother had killed a man many years ago and had finally come back. She would never claim Alison as her own; she was Derek's daughter through and through, as vindictive as he ever was.

The cars were less than half a mile away when she raced into the house, grabbed her purse, and dashed out the back door to her rented car. Quickly she backed out of the garage and made it to the road before the police approached the house. Slowing down to the speed limit, she tried desperately to look like any other tourist out for a leisurely morning drive, but perspiration ran down her face as she passed the two cars headed in the opposite direction. Glancing in the rearview mirror, she watched them turn into the driveway. She had missed getting caught by seconds.

Claudia's heart still pounded as she crossed the causeway connecting South Padre to the mainland and the town of Port Isabel. She tried to calm herself, knowing that she had to settle down and make an important decision: which way to go? Stopping on the other side of the bridge, she pulled a map from the glove compartment, one she had picked up for her trip to the coast. If she turned left on Highway 48, she could head straight to Matamoros, Mexico, less than thirty miles away. That would mean freedom if she made it, but she'd have to go through Brownsville . . . much too risky. Her only alternative was to turn right on FM 100, go through Harlingen, and connect with Highway 77, a four-lane road all the way to the interstate.

Claudia looked at herself as she approached Harlingen and realized her predicament. Not only was she scantly clad, she had also left all her clothes at the house. She didn't dare use her credit cards, and with less than three hundred dollars in cash, what was she to do? Where could she go, and sustain herself for any length of time? It dawned on her that the police would probably check her rental car records; any minute she might hear those damned sirens again, state troopers hot on her trail. Her eyes filled with tears of anger, fear, frustration, and most of all, hate. Hate for a daughter who could put her own mother in such peril.

She had to get rid of this car, but good lord, what would she do then? No doubt the airports would be crawling with police, and she had no idea about rail service around here. Coming to a stop at a traffic light in Harlingen, her eyes drifted to a bus station on the corner across the street. It might be worth taking a chance.

When the light changed, she pulled into an empty parking space, locked the car, and left it, now with the fear that she might be charged with stealing a rental car. That should be the least of her worries right now. Her only concern was survival.

Much to Claudia's relief, she saw no uniformed policemen when she entered the terminal. A bus would leave for Dallas in less than an hour. She had no other choice; Louis had lured her to Texas, and now he had to take care of her. Holding her breath in fear that any second someone would slap her wrists with handcuffs, she purchased a one-way ticket to Dallas, then hid in the foul-smelling restroom until time for departure.

She boarded the bus without a hitch, resigned to the fact that she'd be confined in this rolling cage for sixteen hours, stopping at every terminal between Harlingen and Dallas, for five hundred long miles. She had come a long way from the French Riviera to this . . . bumping along on a torturous ride, but she forced herself not to complain. At least for the time being, she was safe.

Her legs felt like mush when she stepped off the bus in Dallas at 4:00 A.M. The streets were quiet, practically deserted, not a policeman in sight, as she climbed into a cab parked at the curb. Wearily, she gave the driver Louis's address. She had made it this far; now if only she could get inside the house, she'd be home free. Louis would see to it.

Half an hour later, Claudia stood on his wide brick porch, ringing the doorbell. No response. She waited a minute or two, then punched the button again, this time incessantly. Still Louis didn't open the door. Claudia knew that any second, she might drop from sheer exhaustion. Damn Alison! It was all her fault, the self-righteous little bitch. She'd pay for this, just like Derek did. She rang the bell again, and instantly it opened.

Louis stood in the doorway half-asleep, still tying the sash on his dressing gown, his dark hair sticking out in all directions. "What the hell . . . Claudia? My god, is that you?"

She fell into his arms, tears streaming down her face. "Oh Louis, I'm so glad to see you."

"What on earth—"

"I barely got away . . . oh, I've had a hell of a time getting here. I've been on a bus since yesterday morning."

Cradling Claudia in his arms, Louis led her into the living room and sat her on the sofa. "Can I get you something? Some coffee maybe?"

"Oh no, I've had coffee at every pigsty between here and Harlingen. All I want is a hot bath, and days and days of sleep to block away the memory of those awful police cars."

"The police came? You mean they know about Cora Lee and everything?" Louis's face turned ashen.

"No, of course not. I'm sure Alison told them about my part in Charles Thomas's death years ago. I'm her mother, for god's sake—how could she do such a thing?"

Louis heaved a great sigh, a look of profound relief coming over him. "She talked to me about it, and that's probably what happened. How did you get away?"

"Fortunately I saw them coming, and left just in time." Tears sprang up once more. "Now I'm in even more trouble. I left the rental car in downtown Harlingen."

"Don't worry about that. You can tell me just where it is, and I'll contact them myself . . . use a pay phone so the call can't be traced, and tell them where to pick it up."

"And my clothes . . . they're all still at Padre." She ran her hands over her wrinkled shorts and halter top. "This is all I have."

"Don't worry, Cora Lee has left a whole closet full upstairs, and I'm sure—"

"Why, you bastard! How could you even think such a thing, much less suggest it? I couldn't bear to touch anything that belonged to her."

A pink flush rose from Louis's neck to the top of his head. "Forgive me, darling, I just wasn't thinking straight. This whole thing took me by surprise." He gave her a quick kiss. "Don't worry, I'll see that you have a whole new wardrobe tomorrow. I'll find a way to get it without causing a stir, if I have to drive to the next town."

"All right, I just hope your taste is better than Cora Lee's."

He smiled. "Trust me." He took her hand and helped her off the sofa. "Right now, I'm more concerned about getting you in a hot tub so you can get some rest."

On the way up the stairs, Claudia paused and looked him in the eye. "I've thought about Alison all day, and planned what I'd do if I ever saw her again. If I could, I'd kill her right now, all by myself."

"Well, you won't have to do that, because your daughter will come to her demise tomorrow, and you won't have to lift a hand."

"Really, when?"

"Late tomorrow afternoon, just before the office closes."

"Where?"

"Remember the farmhouse where they found Cora Lee? That's as good a place as any, don't you think?"

Claudia didn't flinch. "Perfect." She climbed a few more steps and stopped again. "Will Piper be there?"

"Not this time. This has gone on much too long, and too much is at stake. I'll take care of her myself."

Twenty-eight

About four-thirty, as Alison prepared to leave the office for the day, her private phone rang. She was glad to hear Louis's voice on the line. He had come in early this morning, then left, and she hadn't seen him since.

"Glad I caught you," he said. "I have some news that you'll be glad to hear."

"Good news? Oh, what is it?"

"I've found what you've been looking for."

Alison felt a lump form in her throat. "Dad's papers! You've found them?"

"Yes."

"Oh my lord, what's in them?" Tears of joy sprang up in her eyes. It was hard to believe that the nightmare could finally be over.

"We don't need to say more on the phone. Can you meet me?"

"Yes, of course. Where?"

"This is all hush-hush, so we should go where no one can possibly overhear. There's a farmhouse outside of the city, near Terrell.

Alison could hardly contain her excitement as she listened to Louis's directions and jotted them down. "So I take a left on FM 205?"

"Yes, but you'll need to go about eight miles until you come to the gray house."

"I think I've got it."

"Good, try to leave right now, or you'll get stuck in the five o'clock traffic."

"I'm on my way." Alison picked up her handbag and rushed to the outer office.

Deena stopped her typing and looked up in surprise. "From the look on your face, I'd say you just won the lottery."

"Better than that. Oh, Deena, I think Louis has finally solved my dad's and Myra's murders. I'm meeting him right now at a house near Terrell."

"Mr. Bennett? How on earth—"

"I'll tell you about it later, but I've got to hurry right now." Alison raced down the hall to the reception area, and headed for the elevators.

"Wait a minute," Jackie called from the switchboard. "Mr. Chandler from Linco is on the line, and says it's important."

"Sorry," Alison said as she punched the button. "I'm in a terrific hurry."

"Can you be reached?"

"No, I'm headed for a meeting with Mr. Bennett at a house near Terrell. I'm sure there's no phone out there. Tell him I'll call back first thing tomorrow."

At this moment, the elevator door opened, and Alison stepped inside, then leaned against the wall to catch her breath and settle down. This was the first good news she'd had since she lost her dad. Nothing could bring him back, and nothing would ever be the same, but finding his killer could solve so many problems. Louis was true blue. She'd known all along that she could count on him.

Nick's frustration level had reached an all-time high as he turned his car off the north toll road and exited on FM 544 to Hebron. He knew how futile it was to search Myra Collins's house again, but at this point, he had run out of cards. If he had to tear the place apart board by board, he'd make sure those damned papers weren't there. When Claudia Archer eluded them all, he had come to the conclusion that this case might never be solved. The woman had simply vanished without a trace. Her rental car was found in Harlingen last night, but she was obviously nowhere in the area. His men had checked every airport on the south coast, and had come up with nothing. He felt sure Claudia hadn't come to Dallas. She was too smart for that.

He drove about two miles down the country road and came to a sudden stop. a self-storage facility less than ten yards ahead arresting his attention. Well, I'll be damned! It seemed so logical that Myra Collins would have stored the papers here in a locker so convenient to her home, a place on a back road that no one would think to check. He tried not to feel too hopeful as he climbed out of the car. Too many times a sure lead had fizzled on this case.

Nick trudged up the embankment through dust-covered, dried-up weeds and entered the small office. Inside he found a short, burly man with the stub of a cigar between his teeth, and a three-day stubble on his face. Nick held out his badge, reached inside his pocket for the key, and laid it on the counter.

The man removed his cigar, put it on the edge of the scarred wooden desk, and stood. "Yes sir, what can I do for you?"

"Do your keys look anything like this?"

The man picked it up and turned it over in his hand. "Looks about the right size, but the numbers ain't on it."

"It's a copy," Nick said. "The original is still in the crime lab."

"Crime, eh? Don't see how I can help without no numbers."

"Take another look. Think you can find the duplicate?" Nick pointed to the peg board filled with keys behind the desk.

"Well, sir, won't hurt to try none, will it?"

For the next few minutes, the man held the key up to all the others on the wall, comparing the minute variations of each shape. He finally pulled one out from the middle of the fourth row. "Let's see here," he said. "Seems to me this might be the one—number 502."

Nick tried hard not to show his excitement. "Any record of who rented this space?"

"Sure is." He thumbed through a spiral notebook and ran his finger down the page. "Yes sir, this locker was rented two years ago by a Myra Collins. Moved some of her mother's things in here when she died. Don't know what the family 'tends to do with this stuff, now that Myra's gone. Real bad what happened to her, ain't it?"

"Yes, it is. Do I need a search warrant to take a look inside? It might hold a clue to who killed her."

"Well, sir, if looking at that old furniture will do any good, go right ahead. The locker's down at the far end on the left—number 502."

Nick ran out to his car, found his flashlight, and hurried down the cement walk, lined on each side with metal rooms. He stopped in front of 502, and held his breath as he inserted the key and turned it.

333

The lock sprang open immediately, and Nick couldn't believe he'd actually found the right locker. After weeks of searching, it was here in the most obvious place in the area, right under his nose, and he hadn't thought of it. Still, he reminded himself, Myra could have put the key in the safe just so it wouldn't get lost. It might have no bearing on the case at all, but damn, he intended to find out before he left.

Pitch darkness and a heavy musty smell greeted Nick when he stepped inside. With the help of the flashlight, he surveyed the contents, noting a three-cushioned sofa, a wooden chest of drawers, three chairs, a dinette set, a few odd tables, and several cardboard boxes. Nick searched every piece of furniture, picked up cushions, looked on the floor underneath, and finally moved to the boxes. Carefully going through each one, he found nothing but old dishes, cooking utensils, assorted pieces of bric-a-brac, books, pictures, and mementos, not a thing that suggested a hiding place for secret papers.

Profoundly discouraged, Nick walked over to the chest, opened the top drawer, and suddenly sucked in his breath. Inside lay a rectangular, metal strongbox. Quickly he pulled it out, realized it was locked, and reached for his pocket knife. Moments later he pried it open and felt a tremor of joy at the sight of the neat stack of white papers. His hand shook as he held the flashlight directly over the top page and read the letterhead: MEGTEX. Nick could hardly contain himself long enough to return the key to the office, get back in his car, and open the box again.

At first he thought he must be hallucinating. In neatly typed letters, the document spelled out the

334

story of massive fraud, deceit, a secret bank account, and criminal activities perpetrated against Megtex for many years. His eyes fell on the signature at the bottom of the page: Louis K. Bennett. The initials at the end indicated that Myra Collins had typed the letter. Good God, he thought, he had happened upon the motive for two murders. His skin prickled as he realized the magnitude of this discovery.

Forcing his eyes away from Bennett's confession, he leafed through the other papers, duplicates of the ones Alison had found in the folder; now they all made sense. That bastard had stashed away over eighteen million dollars, every penny stolen from Megtex and Derek Archer.

The last paper, yellow with age, had no relation to the others. He studied it with interest, then came to the conclusion that it told him something Alison hadn't mentioned—the account of Charles Thomas's death in Dallas twenty-three years before, signed by Claudia Archer. Reading between the lines, Nick surmised that Derek had written the letter in anger and Claudia had signed it under duress, her signature weak and shaky. He got a mental picture of the end of a marriage, and the heartbreak that must have preceded this confession.

Anxious to get to the station and obtain a warrant for Louis Bennett's arrest, Nick put the documents back into the box, started the motor, and pulled out on the highway. He had almost reached the toll road when it dawned on him that Alison had worked side by side with a murderer all this time, was probably with him in the office this very minute. The warrant could wait; he had to get her away from Bennett right now. In less than half an hour, he was inside an elevator in the Archer Building, headed for the top floor.

As soon as the door opened, Nick hurried over to the reception desk and pulled out his badge. "I'm here to see Alison Archer."

"I'm sorry, sir, but she's left for the day."

"Is she at home?"

"No, she's at a house somewhere near Terrell. Said she had a meeting with Mr. Bennett."

Nick felt an electric shock travel all through his body. "When did she leave?"

"About twenty minutes ago . . . you just missed her."

With a nod and a quick word of thanks, Nick boarded the elevator once more, his heart in his throat all the way down to the ground floor. He broke all records as he raced out of the building and jumped into his car. Gripping the steering wheel, his knuckles were white as he zoomed through the congested lanes of traffic, the siren blaring, the red lights flashing; he called for backup on the car radio.

He berated himself with every turn of the wheel for being so stubborn, not listening to the chief when he had wanted to pick up Bennett. Now it might be too late.

When Alison pulled into the driveway she noticed how deserted the house looked, the yard covered with weeds, the paint faded and peeling, the porch sagging from years of neglect. Louis's car was nowhere in sight. Maybe she got here ahead of him.

She poked her head inside the unlocked door. "Louis?" Her voice echoed through the rooms with no response. She called again, louder this time. "Louis, are you here?" Still no answer.

Pushing the door open wider, she went inside, tinglings of fear sweeping over her. The front room was partially furnished with a worn-looking sofa, an overstuffed chair with bits of cotton poking out from its arms, and two scarred wooden tables. Cobwebs draped the corners of the room like wisps of long, gray hairs; a thick layer of dust covered the wooden floors. Suddenly she stepped back and winced as her eyes fell on chalk marks outlining the shape of a body. Oh my lord, she thought — remembering that Cora Lee's body had been found in a country house — this is where they found her! Why in God's name would Louis want to come here?

"Louis?" she called again. When he didn't answer, she turned to leave, unwilling to stay in this awful place another second. Just as she reached the door, she jumped at the sound of his voice behind her.

"Here I am, Alison." He stood in the opening to the hallway, just inside the living room, his face unsmiling, his eyes hard and cold. "You're right on time."

Alison caught her breath. "You scared the life out of me. Where were you when I called?"

"In the next room."

"I don't understand . . . why on earth . . ."

Louis started toward her, his eyes never leaving her face, his lips beginning to curl in a sadistic smile. "No need to understand anything at this point, except that you have to die." He moved his right arm from behind his back, and pointed the barrel of a revolver straight at her heart.

For a horrifying moment, Alison thought she might faint. "Oh my God, Louis! You killed Dad and Myra. It was you all along." Her breaths came in quick, audible gasps as tears formed in her eyes and spilled down her cheeks. "Why . . ." It was more of a wail than a question, a cry of terror and utter disbelief.

Momentarily he lowered the gun and ran his left hand over the surface. "No time for explanations, my dear. Just know that you signed your death warrant when you insisted on taking over the company." He raised the revolver again and took aim.

"No! Don't shoot!" The scream came from Claudia as she burst into the room and ran headlong in front of Alison at the split second that Louis squeezed the trigger. The room was filled with the sound of the explosion.

Horrified, Alison watched her mother drop to the floor, her eyes wide open in a terror-filled stare. Oh dear God, her mother—the mother she had longed for all those years, then totally rejected—had saved her life! Now she was dead, and it was all too late. Alison felt paralyzed, numbed with grief and fear.

The gun fell from Louis's hand as he crumpled to the floor at Claudia's side, and held her lifeless body in his arms. "Darling, you'll be all right, and we'll be married soon. You'll see, everything will work out just like we planned. You'll see . . . you'll see . . ." His words became jumbled then, barely audible, as he rocked Claudia back and forth, mumbling disjointed, unintelligible pronouncements, a crazed look glistening in his eyes.

Alison forced herself to move, and knelt to feel the side of her mother's neck for a pulse. There was none. Claudia was dead. Heartsick, Alison knew she had to get away from here, find help, before Louis came back to his senses and carried out his plan. As though in a bad dream, Alison couldn't make her legs move fast enough as she slipped out the front door and headed outside.

Just as Alison touched the door handle of her car, a blue Camaro whipped into the driveway, spinning loose gravel as it ground to a stop. She turned in terror, then quickly felt relief when she recognized the driver.

"Oh, Deena, it's you!"

The woman behind the wheel winced when Alison called her "Deena." How she hated the name, Deena Perry, how sorry she was after she'd given it to the personnel director at Megtex. She had even put it on her forged letter of reference, then had to hear the name repeated day after day at the office. Since she was fourteen years old, she'd called herself Piper . . . Piper Rozelle, the name the voice whispered over and over inside her head. It would make her invincible, the voice insisted, give her incredible power. It must have been true, because she immediately noticed how easily she grasped electrical technology, anything to do with wiring or computers. The adults, including her parents, marveled at her skills; the people in Hugo, Oklahoma called her a genius. But deep down, she knew that Piper was the genius, not Deena, never Deena. The voice told her so.

At fifteen, she longed for freedom, the feel of control behind the wheel of a car. But her father was staunch in his determination to make her wait, even though she pleaded time and again.

"You're just a kid, so forget it." Her dad wouldn't budge, and neither would her mother.

One night she decided to take matters in her own hands, slipping the keys off the dresser and backing

339

the car out of the driveway. The free feeling of sailing down the open road at eighty miles an hour was even grander than she'd ever imagined, and she didn't come home until nearly dawn. Her dad stood outside in the driveway, and jerked her out of the car almost before she could turn off the motor. The beating he gave her was the worst of her life, and her mother offered no help or sympathy.

"You're just a little too smart for your britches," she said, as her only daughter lay whimpering. "A car can be a deadly weapon in the wrong hands."

That night as she lay in bed, the voice repeated her mother's words and added, YOU KNOW WHAT TO DO ABOUT IT, PIPER. LET THEM SEE HOW DEADLY THE CAR CAN BE. DO IT, PIPER, DO IT. YOU KNOW HOW.

It took a few days to gather everything she needed—dynamite that she stole from an excavation site, the wires that she found in the garage, a triggering device that she rigged herself—but she had no trouble making a small bomb, and slipping out late at night to install it under the hood of the car.

The next morning, as she calmly dressed for school, she heard both her parents call goodbye as they left for work, then listened as the door closed behind them. Seconds later, the house shook in a deafening explosion, and Piper heard the voice say, WELL DONE!

The police never thought to question her, and never solved the murders. The good people in Hugo huddled in groups, all of them brokenhearted for the young girl whose parents were so tragically killed. "Poor little thing," they said, "such a smart, pretty child, and now she's all alone."

But Piper fared well during those next few years.

As beneficiary of her parents' insurance policies, she collected twenty-five thousand dollars, a fortune to a fifteen-year-old, enough money to last forever, she thought. She bought herself a car and moved to Oklahoma City, where she lived with her aunt for two long years until her high school graduation. College was out of the question. By then the money was gone.

CALIFORNIA, PIPER, the voice whispered, THAT'S WHERE YOU NEED TO GO. YOU'LL MEET THE RIGHT PEOPLE IN LOS ANGELES.

And so she left Oklahoma, never returning again, always listening to the voice in her head. It never steered her wrong as it led her from one job to the next, each involving a murder for hire. Over the years, the victims became more and more important, her fee more and more lucrative. Piper gained the reputation as the best in the business, and word of her expertise began to spread throughout the complicated network of the underworld.

When Louis Bennett contacted her, she demanded a hundred thousand dollars up front, a sum he willingly paid, and the next thing she knew, she was high in the sky on her way to Dallas.

Now, as she sat in the car, she stared at Alison and realized that she liked her, something she rarely felt about anyone. As she turned off the motor, the voice said, BE CAUTIOUS. SHE DOESN'T KNOW WHO YOU ARE.

"What's wrong?" Deena asked. "Weren't you going to meet Mr. Bennett here?" She opened the car door and started to climb out.

"No, wait, we've got to get some help. Louis tried

to shoot me . . . oh God, I think he killed my mother!" Alison hurried around to the passenger side, her whole body shaking. "We have to get out of here. He could come out any minute and kill us both!"

Deena hopped out of the car, and stopped Alison before she could open the door. "Calm down a minute . . . you're not making any sense. Louis Bennett shot your mother? I thought she'd been dead for years." She caught Alison's arm and held her back. "We're not going anywhere until I know what's happened."

"There's no time to explain everything now. We've got to get to a phone. Oh, Deena, I've never been so scared in my life."

"Where's Bennett now?"

"Inside the house." Alison moved, attempting to get in the car, but Deena stopped her again. "He's acting so strange, like he's lost his mind!"

Deena held fast to Alison and pulled her away from the car. "We're going inside."

"Oh no, we're not! I've got to call Nick." She struggled, attempting to break away. "Let go of me! You don't understand . . . Louis killed my dad, I'm almost sure, and he's acting like a madman!"

"We'll get help in due time, but I want to see for myself, and you're going with me."

Alison stared at Deena, unable to comprehend. Here was her loyal secretary, her friend, so domineering and cold, treating her like a child with a wild imagination. "Go ahead, but I'm getting out of here."

Deena gave her an expressionless stare as she reached into her purse and pulled out a gun. "Keep your mouth shut and walk ahead of me."

Alison felt the blood drain from her face as she stared in numb disbelief. "What are you doing with—"

"Just move!"

Cold steel jabbed into Alison's back as she walked across the yard on rubbery legs, her heart pounding wildly against her chest. Somehow Deena was involved in all of this, but for the life of her, she couldn't figure out why. She had to buy some time, get Deena to talk, anything to keep from going inside that house, that awful house where her mother and Cora Lee had died, and where she would die, too, if she couldn't get away. When she reached the first step, she paused and turned to face Deena.

"Why are you doing this?"

"Just earning my fee."

"Fee? My God, you mean you—"

"Get paid for pulling a trigger?" Deena gave her a chilling smile. "Well, yes I do, if the money's right." Her eyes were void of feeling, no remorse, no sign of conscience, just a cold, heartless stare.

"Who hired you? Oh my God, not Louis!"

"You stupid bitch, it took you long enough to figure this out." She jabbed the gun harder into Alison's back. "Enough talk. Move!"

Suddenly it came together. Alison knew that she was looking into the eyes of the woman who had killed her dad, Myra, maybe even Cora Lee. And all this time, Louis Bennett, the one person she had trusted most, was responsible for everything—the murders, the attempts on her own life, and the massive fraud against the company, all in the name of greed and power.

"Move!"

As Alison climbed the steps, a rage began to build

343

inside her, a rage so powerful that all her fear vanished, replaced by sheer will and a strength she didn't know existed. As she raised her foot for the top step, she thrust it backward, sending Deena reeling, the gun flying from her hand.

Instantly Alison scrambled down the steps and reached for the gun, just as Deena pulled herself up. Shaking all over, Alison grasped the revolver with both hands. "Keep away from me, Deena. I'm not afraid to use this."

"Oh yes, you are. You wouldn't dare pull that trigger." She began to walk toward Alison her smile benign, her voice calm. "You've never shot a gun in your life."

"Stay back . . . get away . . . I'll shoot!"

Deena took a few more steps, her eyes fixed on Alison in a blank stare.

Alison's vision blurred as a slow paralysis overtook her limbs. She was dealing with a professional killer, a paid assassin, who snuffed out lives without blinking an eye, but still Alison wondered if she could actually bring herself to fire at another human being. She took a deep breath and swallowed hard, her pulse pounding in her ears. "Don't make me kill you, Deena. Stay back or I swear, I'll shoot."

"Sure you will. See how scared I am?" Deena laughed, a low, menacing laugh, and moved closer.

Alison realized that Deena was actually enjoying this. How could she ever have thought that this woman was attractive? The silky blond hair and porcelain face were still there, but the eyes—those glinting violet slits—erased all the beauty, replacing it with an ugly, evil mask.

By now, Deena stood just a foot or two away, and she held out her hand. "Give me the gun." Her eyes

344

held Alison's in a hypnotic stare, her voice low and steady. "Give me the gun."

Alison's finger curled over the trigger, but something deep inside held her back. She felt herself gasping for air, beginning to hyperventilate, helpless to prevent it. Her life depended on this gun; she had to hold onto it. "Get . . . get away from me!"

Like a snake, Deena struck out and grabbed the barrel. With all the strength in her being, Alison held on as Deena reached with her other hand and grabbed a handful of hair, jerking Alison back, then dragging her to the ground. Over and over they rolled, the gun between them. The rough dirt and weeds scraped her skin raw, but Alison wouldn't give in. She couldn't. This was her only chance to survive.

Seconds dragged by like hours as they rolled and struggled on the ground. Deena seemed so strong and Alison felt exhaustion creep over her body. Any instant, Deena would wrench the gun away, and there was nothing Alison could do to prevent it. With her last ounce of strength, Alison tightened her fingers over the gun, and suddenly it fired. Deena's hand fell away as her whole body went limp. Rolling over, Alison gasped when she looked at Deena's face. Her violet eyes were wide open, staring blankly at the blue, cloudless sky, her lips turned up at the corners in a faint smile. Alison shivered, realizing it was over.

Weak with relief, she pulled herself up and staggered to her car. Still struggling for air she laid her face against the metal, unable to believe that she was actually alive. Deena Perry—the young woman she had trusted, confided in—had come into her life for the sole purpose of killing her. And now Claudia was dead, because she stepped in front of the bullet meant for her daughter. Tears, welled up in Alison's eyes. She had to get away from here, call Nick, and bring this whole nightmare to an end. As she raised her head and opened the door, long fingers grasped her shoulders, whirled her around, and pinned her against the car.

Wave after wave of new terror swept over Alison as Louis brushed his revolver up and down the line of her jaw, his left hand resting on the roof of the car as he bent over her.

"Your mother's dead," he said, "you ruined everything . . . all my plans . . . all my hard work . . . just so *you* could take charge. You—no more than a sniveling kid!"

"You murdered my dad, didn't you?"

Louis's eyes glinted. "Derek sealed his own fate thirty years ago, but I was patient and bided my time for just the right moment."

"And Myra?"

"She knew too much . . . couldn't be helped."

Alison was desperate, frantically searching her mind for a way to distract him. It was her only hope, but what in god's name could she do? She thought of his insane reaction when he shot Claudia, the only thing that saved her from instant death just minutes ago. "*You* shot Claudia, remember, Louis?"

His eyes suddenly looked glazed as he turned his head to stare at the trees. "It'll all work out, Claudia and I will be married. Cora Lee is dead, you know, just like we planned, and we'll have all the money we'll ever need. Derek dead . . . Myra dead . . . Cora Lee . . . Claudia . . . no, no, no, not you, darling, not Claudia, no, no, no . . ."

As Louis went into oblivion and his words became

mumbles, Alison moved her head slightly out of his grasp, and saw that his thumb lay just inside the top of the open door. Gritting her teeth, she pushed back with all her strength, slamming the door with a thud, his thumb jammed inside. With the gun still dangling from his other hand, Louis's face contorted in pain as his earsplitting scream filled the country air. Alison seized her chance to get away. Pulling away from him, she ran headlong across the yard, with nowhere to go, no place to hide, but at least for the moment, she was safe. She paused at the side of the house long enough to catch her breath and scan the yard. Easing along the wall, she noticed a weather-beaten shed near the fence behind the house, the only shelter in sight.

Quickly she made her way through the waist-high weeds until she reached the small building. The door creaked open on rusted hinges, allowing in a streak of light that cut a yellow swath across the darkness inside. A damp, musty smell enveloped Alison as she strained to see through the blackness. Squeaks of protests mixed with the sound of tiny feet scurrying for safety made her jump in fright, and fight off the urge to flee. Contending with a few mice, she realized, was nothing compared to facing a madman with a loaded gun.

Boxes and cast-off farm tools filled the shed, offering little protection, but the only hope she had. If Louis discovered her in this place, it would all be over in seconds, but she had no other choice. She couldn't bring herself to enter the house again, the dreadful place that had already meant a death sentence to her mother and Cora Lee.

Spotting a stack of boxes in a back corner, she closed the door and felt her way through the darkness, then made herself as small as possible behind them. The room was hot, black, and silent, not a hint of a sound, even from the population of rodents. Time had little meaning for Alison; the minutes might well have been days as she shifted from one leg to the other to ward off cramps that persistently gripped her calves. After what seemed like an eternity, she decided that Louis might have left the car by now, even gone back inside the house. It was worth taking a look. On the verge of standing upright, she suddenly froze in terror at the swishing sound outside—footsteps that came closer with every breath she dared to take.

All at once, the door flung open, flooding the small room with sunlight. Alison crouched even lower behind the boxes—her pitiful shield—and clasped her hand over her mouth to keep from gasping out loud. Not daring to raise her head, she couldn't see Louis, but could feel his presence all around her, even smell the spicy aroma of his aftershave.

"Alison, if you're in here, you'd better come out now." His voice was low, with no emotion. He waited a full minute, then said again, "You'd better come out now. This is your last chance."

The shed suddenly grew dark as the door slammed shut, followed by loud, humorless laughter that sent chills all over her body. Alison could hear the crunch of broken weeds as footsteps circled the shed, then a crackling sound and the unmistakable smell of smoke and burning wood. Tears filled her eyes at the sight of an orange flame that began to lick like an angry tongue in and out of a crack in the wall. Louis had won after all. The monster had set fire to the shed, this tinderbox that would become an inferno in a matter of seconds. Given a choice, she knew that she'd rather die instantly from a bullet than suffer the agony of burning to death.

She stood and felt her way through the blackness and thickening smoke, knowing that the moment she stepped outside, Louis would kill her. Whispering a prayer, she took a deep breath and opened the door.

Louis stood just a few feet away, still laughing, but his eyes glinted with rage. "Well, well, there you are, Alison. I figured if you were in there, a little heat would bring you out." He raised his gun and aimed at her heart. "You realize, of course, that you brought this on yourself. You would have saved us all a lot of pain, if you weren't so damned stubborn and ambitious." He laughed again as his finger crooked around the trigger.

"Hold it right there, Bennett."

Alison's legs buckled at the sight of Nick, his pistol aimed, as he moved toward Louis from behind. Quickly whirling around, Louis countered with an aim of his own, and for a heart-stopping second, she thought he would surely shoot first. All of a sudden, the air filled with a deafening roar as a helicopter came over the treetops and swooped down into the yard. Then policemen who seemed to come from every direction surrounded Louis, and brought him whimpering to his knees.

Nick rushed to Alison and swooped her up in his arms, quickly moving her from the shed, which by now was totally engulfed in flames.

Overcome with relief, Alison could barely speak when Nick deposited her under a tree and held onto her for dear life.

"Oh, Nick, it was Louis all along."

"I know, and now I have enough proof to put him

349

away for the rest of his life. I found the papers."

"Oh thank God. Where?"

"There's plenty of time to go into all that. Right now, I need to get you to a doctor."

"Believe it or not, I came through all this without a scratch, thanks to my mother." Tears filled her eyes. "She ran in front of Louis's gun to save my life, and now she's dead."

Nick tightened his arm around her shoulders and kissed her forehead. "I'm so sorry that it had to happen, but it proved how much she loved you."

"She really did love me, didn't she?"

Nick nodded. "And so do I. Because of her, we can have a whole lifetime together."

"A lifetime." Alison breathed a grateful sigh once more, realizing he was right. The awful threats to her life were finally over. She looked into his eyes and whispered the wonderful word again. "A lifetime."

HE'S THE LAST MAN YOU'D EVER
WANT TO MEET IN A DARK ALLEY . . .

THE EXECUTIONER

By DON PENDLETON

#24: CANADIAN CRISIS	(267-X, $3.50/$4.50)
#25: COLORADO KILLZONE	(275-0, $3.50/$4.50)
#26: ACAPULCO RAMPAGE	(284-X, $3.50/$4.50)
#27: DIXIE CONVOY	(294-7, $3.50/$4.50)
#28: SAVAGE FIRE	(309-9, $3.50/$4.50)
#29: COMMAND STRIKE	(318-8, $3.50/$4.50)
#30: CLEVELAND PIPELINE	(327-7, $3.50/$4.50)
#31: ARIZONA AMBUSH	(342-0, $3.50/$4.50)
#32: TENNESSEE SMASH	(354-4, $3.50/$4.50)
#33: MONDAY'S MOB	(371-4, $3.50/$4.50)
#34: TERRIBLE TUESDAY	(382-X, $3.50/$4.50)
#35: WEDNESDAY'S WRATH	(425-7, $3.50/$4.50)
#36: THERMAL TUESDAY	(407-9, $3.50/$4.50)
#37: FRIDAY'S FEAST	(420-6, $3.50/$4.50)
#38: SATAN'S SABBATH	(444-3, $3.50/$4.50)

ALONE?

I'll stay here with you tonight," John said. "I'm not leaving you by yourself."

Alison shook her head. "No, John, I'd rather be alone." She managed a smile, but he knew she meant what she'd said.

As soon as John left, Alison locked the door, set the alarm, turned off the downstairs lights, and climbed the stairs to her room. The house had a hush about it tonight, the only sounds coming from the rustle of the wind and the scraping of low branches against the windowpanes.

Shrugging off faint feelings of fear, she went into the bathroom, turned on the taps of her bathtub, and slipped off her clothes. A half-hour soak in the tub relaxed her.

As she climbed into bed, her thoughts wandered from her argument with John, to her dad's death and Myra's, the missing papers, the board meeting tomorrow, the decisions she had to make. Somehow, sleep finally came.

Around midnight, the ringing of the phone jarred Alison awake. She groped in the darkness for the receiver, but never had a chance to answer. The moment she picked it up, a chilling voice on the other end was already speaking, a voice that could only belong to her dead father.

Help me, why didn't you help me?

"Dad? Oh, my God, Dad!"

Help me, why didn't you help me?

And then the line went dead.